Raspberry Jam

Moss Croft

Copyright © Moss Croft 2023

The moral right of Moss Croft to be identified as the author of this work has been asserted by him in accordance with the Copyright, Designs and Patents Act of 1988.

All rights reserved. No part of this publication may be reproduced, transmitted or stored in a retrieval system, in any form or by any means, without permission in writing from Moss Croft, nor be otherwise circulated in any form of binding or cover other than that in which it is published and without a similar condition being imposed on the subsequent purchaser.

ISBN: 9798386389901

The Novels of Moss Croft

Raspberry Jam

God Help the Connipians

Stickerhand

Boscombe

Crack Up or Play It Cool

Ghost in the Stables

Rucksack Jumper

The Flophouse Years

About the Author

Moss Croft is a pen name. If it's his real one too, that would be most underhand.

Contents

Chapter One:
The Actor   Page   7

Chapter Two:
A Pint of Beer   Page   85

Chapter Three:
Back On the Dancefloor   Page   133

Chapter Four:
Squash is a Game of Cunning   Page   189

Chapter Five:
Wide of Goodge Street   Page   239

Disclaimer

This is a work of fiction and any resemblance to real persons or events is the result of unforeseen coincidence.

Chapter One

The Actor

1.

Charles Quested, known as Charlie, is reviewing a new foster carer application when Roselyn walks across the open-plan office. Joins her team's cluster of desks, speaks, confirms that which he already knows. Informed by email yesterday afternoon, an email she sent, and is now reiterating. All staff must attend a meeting in the council chamber, it commences in twenty minutes time. Roselyn must be fussing because three of the team have yet to arrive. They may have ignored yesterday's directive and carried on with planned visits. She spelled out—in an email marked for the highest level of attention—that cancellation of alternative plans was a given. Attendance mandatory. Nearly half her team is absent. That will be what is bugging her—a black mark for Roselyn—failure to round up her sheep. The meeting is important, the Director of Children's Services is to address the whole department. It is about their futures. The structure of the department, most probably. How it will be configured to enable children's services to operate effectively within a restricted budget. Cuts, cuts, cuts. They are expecting loads of the damned things.

'Where are they?' she asks him.

Charlie doesn't know. He doesn't even know why he slept with Roselyn back in June. And July too. Divining where his missing team mates are is not in his orbit. Not Charlie's responsibility. 'We're all pretty busy,' he says. This was the talk amongst the team yesterday. How dare the Director summon staff at a moment's notice, make them cancel visits. Let down foster children, foster carers. Social workers plan and scheme the lives of others, glean no pleasure from being on the receiving end.

'They'll come,' says Tina. She is a colleague of Charlie's; short of stature, her dark-hair turning grey. A decade older than he is, the least talkative in the team. And they all get along.

'Perhaps,' says Roselyn.

Charlie agrees with Tina. Everyone needs to hear what Ted is going to say. He glances quickly at his manager and then back at the application pack, the completed forms and personal statements of which it is comprised. Roselyn starts picking pens off an empty desk, tidying away. There is a clear desk policy but no one follows it. Busy people, and desks are seldom shared. Roselyn has no need to do this, she simply isn't programmed to stand still.

Brenda Hardcastle—the longest serving social worker in the city, by Charlie's reckoning—asks if they want tea or coffee. He and Roselyn say the latter; Precious and Tina chip in their beverage requests. Brenda will make them all.

'I think we need to hear the plan,' Precious tells the room. Not loud but others in neighbouring teams across the large office space may hear it too. They are all in the same boat, a storm brewing for every social worker in the city. 'Find out if we're still gettin' paid tomorrow. Not much workin' while that one is hangin' there.'

Roselyn nods. Charlie knows, from his brief period of intimacy with her, that she thinks most of the team moan too much. It's not an unusual negative for a manager to ascribe to her staff. And she has a particular warmth for the youngest team members, Yasmin and Graham. She referred to them as her 'projects,' and the rest as 'hardened old lags.' Charlie thinks he is the only team member who knows this. Roselyn's pillow talk wasn't romantic for a single second. It's

The Actor

social work and not love that flows strongest in her veins. Most teams in the department comprise a majority of staff fresh out of university. In fostering it is only the two. Her projects. Newbies consume managerial time. Yasmin and Graham are smart and Roselyn hopes to mould them, nurture them into her professional image. And old hands will do what they do.

Precious has brought in chocolate fingers. It's an odd choice. A meeting about the council's penny-wise predicament—brought about by the governments relentless squeeze of the public sector—is not a cause for celebration. The team chomp on them regardless.

As they are drinking, eating, Yasmin enters the room. A little of her shiny black hair protruding from beneath a crimson headscarf, eyes looking keenly from person to person. 'Sorry I'm on the last minute,' she tells Roselyn. 'I dropped leaflets off on the way in. For the library. I got talking when I was doing the notice board. A couple of people showed interest. I had to take the chance, talk to them. Tell them wonderful things about the fostering experience.'

Roselyn looks unimpressed. Charlie knows her maxim and he expects that Yasmin has heard it more than once. Random conversations in the library—anywhere else for that matter—with people who have yet to talk fostering with their partners, are pointless. Engage the household, not just a single bleeding heart. Roselyn holds her tongue, and Charlie certainly isn't going to criticise Yasmin on her behalf. There are bigger fish skulking this morning. How the Director is to divvy up a pittance.

'Can I have a quick word,' asks Roselyn. She points at her small office. Her partitioned glass cube. She has made eye-contact with him alone.

Charlie rises from his seat, the infantryman. Precious gives him a broad smile; he cannot think why she should.

She knows nothing about the brief affair, the fling that he and Roselyn chanced upon. Got out of their system. He is sure she doesn't. She could be thinking his summons is because redundancies will target social workers with his profile. Six-foot-two-inch-tall ex-service men. That thought flitters away. She wouldn't be smiling like that if she thought he was for the push. Precious is the kindest soul. When he is inside the small enclosure—her glass box within the open-plan office—Roselyn looks him in the eye. Momentarily he thinks she is going to invite him for a game of squash.

'How are you bearing up?'

Charlie shrugs. He is unsure why she has singled him out for this pre-meeting tête-a-tête. The city council is stressed, financially stressed. His personal woes depend on the degree to which it will affect him, something which he has yet to find out. Won't match the damage their affair has riven across his marriage but Roselyn knows that already. Knows about his one-bedroomed flat.

'I'd like your help with what's about to happen,' she says.

A favour makes more sense. Charlie is unsure if he owes her one, and nor is he the type to refuse. 'Do you know what will be said?'

'God, no. It's very hush-hush. There will be redundancies, I'm certain of it. The budget's taking a massive hit.'

Charlie puts his head to one side, looks at her afresh. Roselyn is a driven woman, mid-thirties. Steeped in social work, lives it, breathes it. Talks like a textbook. Not like late-convert Charlie. He turned thirty before he finished qualifying. The army and a couple of wilderness years, trying and failing to sell for a living, preceded what he now thinks his natural vocation. Roselyn beat him on the squash court before he ever had sex with her. Mandy—his Mandy—thought that he was playing Graham, the only other male in the fostering team. Thought it until he foolishly confessed. Told his wife of his unfaithful state. The little dalliance didn't

The Actor

damage Roselyn. It could have compromised her in the team manager role, of course, but no one in the council knows it ever happened. A stone's throw from no one. For Charlie, it has cost him a place in his own home, made him a visitor to his own children. He never anticipated such an outcome; imagined Mandy might be more forgiving. 'Ros,' he states, abridging her name as he never does in front of team members, 'I need this job. I'm good at it, and I'm stacking up debt until my home life is sorted...' He pauses, Roselyn is looking squarely at him, still holding his gaze.

'I know,' she says. 'There are no certainties at times like these. I can't make any promises when I don't know what the game is yet—Ted's masterplan—I understand your situation. Sympathise.'

'...and you won't use it...' Charlie's thought tapers away, incomplete. She must know what he's getting at. Roselyn Pickford should not use this as an opportunity to get rid of him because of the embarrassing fling. A matter to which her husband, Geoff, remains oblivious. Ros was not so foolish as to blab at home, she's a little more layered than honest Charlie. She ended whatever relationship there was between them precisely because he told his wife about it. She must have feared knowledge of the affair becoming more widely known. Charlie has come to think she enjoyed the subterfuge more than she did the sex. Not that there were any complaints in his inbox.

'We're all going to have to hear what Ted says. If you prepare for the worst, you just might be pleasantly surprised. Then again, it might be more dire than we can imagine. Could you keep an eye out, please, just across our team, let me know how everyone's bearing up? We can't let performance drop because of our own worries. Not at a time like this.'

'I will.' As he turns to leave, Charlie adds, 'Are you under pressure?' It's an afterthought. Brightest young manager in the department, he doesn't expect Roselyn to lose her job. Always polite to ask.

'You know me, Charlie: I love pressure. Live and die by it.' She grins as she speaks, enlivening the seldom seen smile lines which curve around the edge of her mouth. Looking a world happier than her default setting.

He can only grin back, still the puppy dog. 'No one really likes shit.' He's sure he's right about this.

'Thanks, you're a pal.' With this phrase and the movement of her lively green eyes, Roselyn signals an end to their brief conversation. Dismissal. Charlie heads out of the tiny room, gestures that he will leave the door ajar. She gives him a quick thumbs-up. A door-open kind of manager.

Back among the team—minutes to go to the meeting in the council chamber—he sees that Graham has joined them. Roselyn's team is missing only Fiona. Getting a full complement of social workers into one room is as likely as winning the lottery. One number short, not bad at all. Worth a consolation prize in Charlie's view.

Yasmin crosses from her desk to Charlie's, a hand on her headscarf, nervously scratching where it meets her hairline. 'It won't be you, will it?' she says in a hushed voice.

'What won't be me?'

'Redundancy,' whispers Yasmin, holding his gaze in her deep brown eyes. 'Are you okay?'

'No. Yes. Nothing's clear until the great Ted speaks in five minutes.'

'Aw,' says Yasmin, 'I hope it's not you.'

He bows his head down to his work, feels embarrassed by her speculation. Members of the team joke that Charlie is thicker than the rest of them. He struggles when they talk theory and politics and psychology. They tell him he's a good social worker, it's the jargon he's thin on. He was in care himself; it might give him an insight others lack. Perhaps Yasmin Chowdhury could think of no reason but redundancy for which Roselyn would call him into her office. She might just as well have asked him if he's the only one to be saved. Savage cuts are coming: everything is in the mix.

All across the open-plan office social workers are rising up from their chairs, preparing to walk down to the chamber. No one wants to hear it; no one wants to miss it. Ted Astaire, Director of Children's Services, will tell the whole department what the future looks like. Won't be pretty, and it could be carnage. The air they breathe thrums with insecurity.

Charlie and Graham go together: mates. They have struck it off since the latter joined the team a year ago. Charlie has told Graham—and nobody else but Mandy, his wife—that he slept with Roselyn. Graham is trustworthy, a serious young man. And he was seriously unimpressed with Charlie's infidelity. Kept it to himself though, Charlie is certain of it.

Brenda and Precious are just behind them, laughing. The nervous stuff. Tina is with them but she hasn't laughed in forever. Laughter not in Tina Smith's make-up. There are a few social workers like that dotted across the department. The country.

Before this meeting had ever been called, there was already talk of cuts. Nasty blood-seeping cuts. A year of fiscal savagery. All over the country the children's services departments have taken big hits. The city is bending late to the new reality. Cameron and Osborne's sustained assault on public services. And everyone knows austerity hosts a dismal picnic. Five loaves, two fishes and no fucking saviour.

* * *

The council chamber is three-quarters full when they enter. A large domed room, with tiered seating running a three-quarter circle; Charlie points to a bench near the back. Green-padded benches, leather inlaid into walnut. The fostering team step up towards the rear, stick together. Roselyn is already in the room. She sits on the front row, engaged in a dialogue of sorts with Ted. He is their DCS—the Director of Children's Services—sits on a leather-backed upright chair. On the podium out front. He and Roselyn can't possibly hear each other. The chamber sounds like a battery-hen house; they are mouthing across the wide aisle. Gesticulating. It enters Charlie's mind, as he watches her, sees her use a familiar hand gesture, that Ted and Roselyn are close. Ted could be more than just her boss, as she was briefly more than his. He dismisses the notion. Charlie is not clairvoyant. He even thinks himself a poor reader of other people, not really a deficit a social worker should openly declare.

Precious taps his shoulder and as Charlie looks around, she glances aside at Brenda. Their colleague is silently crying. Turned away from her team, head bowed, trying to them avoid all as cannot be done in this packed hall.

Charlie leans in to her. 'It's shit, Brenda, but you're going nowhere. You are the team.'

She turns her head, clasps his upper arm, mouthing a 'thank you.' Then she whispers in Charlie's ear. 'Sixty-four. They can shunt me out for a packet of peanuts. The under-fifties get all the better deals.'

'Can but won't,' he tells her. He knows that her husband is long retired. She works to avoid turning into him. Brenda told Charlie that he marks six or eight 'unmissable' programmes a day in their TV guide. 'God help him,' she added during that morbid conversation.

Graham stands at the end of the row, brown corduroy trousers on a warm day in early September. Not enough seats to go round. And Fiona O'Shea has not shown up, the fostering team remains one short. The administrative staff have occupied the front seats. They are on lower pay, might worry more than the professionals. Charlie guesses theirs is

The Actor

a more fluid skill set, alternative work closer to hand.

A tinny sound comes through the PA system. Ted, the Director, is on his feet. Initially there is no let-up in the background gabble that fills the chamber, then his simple hand gesture, a flattened palm lowered repeatedly, calms the room. As the noise dissipates, he continues to pat his non-existent mule, does so until all sound is extinguished. The silence which has arrived is far from serene. A room full of anxious social workers. Admin too. Tomorrow is an unknown quantity, waiting this man's foretelling. The noiseless air alive with a hold-your-breath dread. 'All right here,' he drawls. He might exaggerate his American accent. 'All right,' he says again.

A thin bald man to his side—a techy whom the Director briefly looks towards—gives him the thumbs up. Ted's first utterings have been only a sound check. No one's expecting that it will be all right.

'People, people,' says the Director, 'it's great to see you all today. I do wish the circumstances were better, but take it from me, you all look beautiful.' One or two people laugh, maybe more. Not Charlie, not the fostering social workers. Ted has some explaining to do and this blather really isn't it. 'Okay, everyone, okay. This is a big deal today. I've got to tell you where we're up to, what's going to happen. What it means for each and every one of you. I think you will already have picked up a rumour or two. You may know that in some other cities, counties, north and south, axes have been swung, jobs lost...' Ted pauses, even looks solemnly up at the council chamber's ornate central chandelier before looking back at his staff, drawing his quick summary of the national picture to a conclusion. The trauma central government has passed to the cities and the shires. '...people have walked. God knows what the impact of all that has been on the children-in-need who live in those fine cities, counties. These are difficult times, my friends.' Charlie is looking directly at Ted. The man's hair is greying, he wears it short and neat. Sports a tan.

Charlie feels his hand taken in another's. Looking aside he sees that Brenda has reached across Precious, taken it to hold. An odd gesture. She is sixty-four, must have been through worse. He certainly has. Cuts aren't good but nor are they shells. A way less scary than scud missiles. 'In this city we have a plan but our circumstances are—quite frankly— no better. I'll tell you where I'm up to. That whole cut-the-cloth thing, figuring out how to make do with less money than I ever imagined having to make do with when I took this job. It's been going round and round in my head for over three weeks now. Since the Chief Executive spelled out the figures. I have to live with these numbers. I want more but I have been told quite forcibly that I won't be getting more.' Out of the blue, his rapid-fire delivery is exchanged for a slow beating pulse. Fourth gear to first. 'We... will... not... have... one... cent... more.'

Charlie has never quite worked this guy out. He's on their side all the way but with a sting in the tail. The council bent payroll rules to recruit him. Everyone knows that his pay equals that drawn by the last DCS plus three newbie social workers. Ted Astaire managed a London borough, turned it around according to the broadsheets, did the same in the city of Philadelphia before that. He's popular enough across the department. Doesn't talk like a social worker but he sounds like he cares. In two years here the changes have been only minor, gone down well enough. Nothing so outstanding as to make a cynic think he's worth the money. And Charlie hasn't heard that Philly wants him back. Ted will survive the cuts. No one has said it but Charlie is more certain about that than anything else. While these thoughts pulsate in his temple, Brenda releases his hand from her custody. He looks aside but she is no longer facing him. Precious smiles, as if on her behalf.

The Actor

'I know without question that the children of this city need our help. The forgotten, unloved and rejected of this city need our help. Your help. The downtrodden, the far-from-fulfilling-their-potential of this city—you know them, work with them every day—they cannot do without it. The helping hand we offer. We can only secure them good professional help if we invest properly in them, do everything we can to make it right.'

A scattering of social workers, most of the lowly paid admin staff too, applaud this fine sentiment. Charlie holds back. The fostering team are more circumspect, some understand the politics. They will not applaud what is not a commitment. He can see Roselyn clapping at the front. In Ted's eyeline, it might be the reason.

'How am I going to square that truth with the need for efficiencies? The austerity budget that Her Majesty's Government—through wisdom or malice—think needed to keep the whole country flip side up. Well...' Ted pauses, looks around the benches. All are hanging onto his words.

Charlie glances again at Brenda. She catches his eye, mouths a couple of words he cannot lipread with certainty. Fuck it, look the most probable. Not language she uses on a normal working day. Brenda is in a storm about this.

'...I can't do the ten percent pay cut, none of that hogwash. We don't attract the best by paying the worst.'

A nervous ripple of applause scats around the council chamber. Still Charlie does not move his hands. His thinking—the coagulation of ideas that come to him as the cogs grate together between his ears—is that those clapping hope to shame Ted Astaire into doing nothing. Charlie is too much the realist to join them: there will be cuts. Ted is pussyfooting his way to telling them the truth. Cuts hurt, they cost jobs. Somebody is going to feel them; someone here in this room. A large number would be Charlie's guess.

'I value my staff—without you guys, I am nothing—this

year needs an inflation adjusted pay rise at the very least. We cannot move backwards.' Ted is sticking to his theme; not yet making financial sense, as Charlie sees it. 'The only thing I can in all good conscience consider, is the efficiency of our working practice. Can we ratchet it up a few notches?' Ted Astaire eyes the room, as though his staff have, in this very second, become an adversary. 'Eleven per cent. That, my friends, is the figure I have to find. The drop in available expenditure that I have to comply with. Quite frankly, I feel it like a punch in the gut. Didn't know numbers could hurt so much until a month ago.' He pauses for a moment, mouths eleven per cent so quietly no one in the room can possibly hear it. Then he whispers it up close to the microphone, 'Eleven per cent.' Leaves the silent room in no doubt about the numbers. 'Eleven per cent...' He has dropped the frown now, scanning the rows before him with benign purpose. '...could a number sound more sickening?'

Charlie is not surprised by the figure. Union members—of whom there are many—will have already read about eleven per cent. A hastily photocopied flier made the rounds of the offices late yesterday. The numbers mean little without saying where the knife will be slid in.

'Shattering, isn't it?' says Ted, back in his measured, drawling delivery. 'By my calculation, we need to lose one in eight, and still do the work...'

He can barely make himself heard. The room calls back, no clear voice, just angry noise.

'I don't want the children of this city, the children who require our services—kids off track—to fall further from their rightful destinies,' says Ted above the din. The tech guy must have turned the amps up, his point comes through. 'Not just because a bunch of bankers screwed up three or four years ago,' Ted shouts, and again a smattering of applause approves the sentiment. 'We can do better than them. Hold up our end of the bargain. We have to do it with

The Actor

an eleven percent budget reduction. Can and will. That is the scale of our task.'

Charlie sees Brenda, to his right, flashing a V-sign at Ted. He tugs it down. She's behaving like a teenager. 'One in eight,' Charlie tells her. Precious nods vigorously from her seat between the pair of them. 'There are only seven in our team.'

Brenda grimaces at his comment.

'You'll be home and dry. You are the team.' He doesn't know if it's true—longest serving member, so it sounds plausible—he has never seen Brenda so upset or angry before.

In the aisle, Yasmin who stands next to Graham, dips her head to Charlie's. 'What did Roselyn tell you, Mr Q?'

Charlie wants to be straight with his colleague. He puts a hand on the back of her head, touching the headscarf she wears. Draws her close to whisper in her ear. 'She cares about us, wants to know if we're bearing up,' he says. Yasmin shrugs. He guesses that she wants names. Wants to learn the parameters of the coming cull.

'My solution to our conundrum,' says Ted, having given the room brief pause to digest the horrific one-in-eight reduction in the workforce which he has planned, 'is to begin again. I am not a leader who asks team managers to bring me heads on plates. Teams are not a thing I toy with lightly. They have each evolved into the sweetly formed entities which your endeavours have made them. You know this, they are your teams. I do not believe random acts of butchery aid them. And so, we begin again. What I propose is that we all apply for our jobs. There will be...' Ted plants his left foot a distance aside from the right, sets himself in a gun-duel pose before making his next point. '...no external competition whatsoever. It's us applying for our own jobs. We have an external assessor, a recruitment company, lined up to assist us in this. To take the pressure off your hard-working managers. It will be one in eight. That is, I am sorry to say, the proportion of posts I must lose. Delete, as the boys in the ministry call it. One in eight. Not anybody's job, everybody's job. We all have an equal chance. It will be painful but please, please, please, do not forget how much we have achieved through cooperation. Teamwork and cooperation are the before and after of this sorry mess. Those sweet qualities have brought us this far and will see us out the other side. Competition for the reduced number of positions is inevitable. It's got to be done, folks. Voluntary redundancies cannot really be considered, or rather...' Ted glances down, possibly at Roselyn, discharges a conspiratorial wink. '...you can ask but don't forget what I said about efficiencies. If you are good at your job, we cannot let you leave. The city needs you that badly. I want good social workers. And I really don't want to lose the one in eight. Cameron is to blame for the whole shooting match. I have to do something. Can't let the money run out altogether.' Those gathered in the hall begin talking again, the sound quickly ratcheting up. Once more, Ted Astaire makes his flat-palmed gesture, dampening the hall back down to silence. 'No one will have a job; everyone will have an equal shot at a job. Have you got that?' There seems to be a murmur of agreement. A noise which is more resigned than angry, Brenda Hardcastle aside. 'The aim of the assessment centres—a process you will all undertake over a one- or two-week period—is for this department to work out which of you really has what it takes. It will be most of you, that's how you got the department purring along so nicely first time around. Do the math, one in eight. Those who are unsuccessful, we wish you well; nothing personal, we must get ourselves within budget or the whole service is in jeopardy. As Alan, Alan Harding our Chief Executive, said to me, "The bankers buggered up the books. Now it is for us with real jobs to rescue the fantasy that is capitalism." He said that, not me. I'm not political at all. Really, I'm not. You guys know it already, I imagine.' He looks all around the room, a steady gaze, lingering momentarily at every section of seating. 'Time to wrap up. You all have team meetings in the afternoon when your manager will give you details of the process. They each know the time for their teams, will tell you in the next few minutes. Over this lunch hour, I will be briefing all the team managers. They know no more than you at this moment. They will be able to tell you all about it—what it means for you—when you meet in just a couple of hours or thereabouts. Be strong, trust in God, trust in your own endeavours. You are a wonderful group of staff. Truly. We can do this. Thank you.'

Ted turns his back and walks out of a small side door. No questions, no sense of what the assessment centres to which he has consigned them will be like. No one knows how he will identify the weak links in his chain. One in eight, it could mean each team loses one, a bitter pill. Charlie doesn't expect it to be him but all is fluid. Roselyn will tell the team what the next steps are this afternoon, that's what the Director said. For the next hour they have only anxiety—that and its twin sister turmoil—with which to wrestle.

* * *

Over lunch hour, Charlie and Graham walk out for a sandwich. Children's Services are city-centre based, occupy the first floor of the Town Hall. Every imaginable shop is close at hand. The pair sit in an upmarket coffee bar. Pay more to eat than they allow themselves on a regular lunchtime.

'Can I join you?' asks Yasmin. She and Graham are the only members of the fostering team under thirty.

'Her or me, isn't it?' says Graham, while Yasmin queues at the serving counter,

Charlie knows what he is referring to. 'We're being put through an assessment centre. All applying for our own jobs.

I think all the usual calculations—how long have you worked here, that stuff—have gone by the board.' He looks across at the serving counter, Yasmin paying as he speaks. 'I don't mind if it's Roselyn who goes.'

'Not now you don't,' says Graham.

'Eight pounds fifty,' grumbles Yasmin as she sits beside Graham. 'For soup, coffee and a cereal bar.' She picks at a strand of hair that has made its way out from under her headscarf, turns it nervously within her fingers.

'You're splashing out,' says Charlie.

'It's our death row meal, in't it.'

Charlie likes her voice. A rich Yorkshire brogue but not entirely. Something of the old country in it. 'Maybe we've all been given a reprieve,' he suggests. Both Graham and Yasmin look to him, interested. Charlie has been in the work many more years than either of them. Might be an authority in their eyes. 'Ted's generally very good, a better DCS than the last one. He backed me when I turned down that couple who went on to complain about me. When they alleged that I was just being anti-Christian, which I really wasn't.' His younger colleagues nod their heads. They know the story, potential foster carers not up to the mark, blaming the messenger. 'This slashing the budget is one big gladiatorial fight to the death, I haven't worked out if his plan is brilliant or madness.' Charlie has already thought that sending all the staff to an assessment centre, to see if they are up to keeping their jobs, keeping mortgage payments going through without interruption, will drive the entire workforce crazy. Out of their minds for a few weeks, and he has felt close to the edge ever since he did more than just play squash with Roselyn. Got himself thrown out of the family home. Insights which he keeps from these anxious colleagues. 'What is the secret to job interviews?' he asks them.

'Preparation,' Yasmin fires back. She's a bright spark. Finger always hovering over the buzzer.

'The same with this assessment centre. Don't rely on what you know already. Read the departmental plan, know all the department's objectives for the year inside out. Make sure you can recite them off-pat. Master all that shit. We can pass assessments, that's how we got these jobs in the first place.'

Both look back keenly at Charlie Quested. They want more but must wait. The real briefing is to come later. Learn the content: exactly what the assessment centre will demand of them. And Graham has seen a flaw. 'The bar has to be higher,' he states. 'Ted knows that we all got in at our last interview. He will make it much trickier. He has to send one in eight to the knacker-man this time around.'

* * *

The team has the use of Buxton Room for precisely one hour. Roselyn asked them to arrive on the dot, ensure they use their available time well. All six social workers have seated themselves, left the chair at the head of the table unoccupied. 'Hi all,' says Roselyn on entering, taking up the vacant seat. 'Any word yet as to why Fiona couldn't make it in for the meeting?'

The team minus Fiona O'Shea look blankly back. Roselyn stares them down until Charlie says, 'An out-of-county visit. She didn't want to cancel, not letting the kid down.'

Roselyn nods her head at this, does not thank him for the belated intelligence. Letting kids down was the instruction yesterday. Charlie is unsure if Fiona has won or lost. She's always been headstrong. Does it her way. When the silence has lasted long enough, Roselyn speaks. 'Don't all look so worried. You heard what Ted had to say. His plan is a good one...'

Charlie doubts if this blanket reassurance is the best approach, and before Roselyn has got further than imploring staff to put on a brave face, Brenda interrupts. 'One in eight, Roselyn. That's a lot. Ted won't be cutting those closest to him. I think we should be worried.' Charlie's pleased to hear her speak so levelly. She didn't shout or cry.

'Don't be. I've spent the lunch hour going over the plans with Ted and all the team managers. Service managers too. We must ensure that our clients—the service we give to the public—is unaffected. That's our priority. We have budget trimming to do. We've been through it before; we're just doing it again. Between you and I, Brenda...' Roselyn points her index finger back and forth to suggest this exchange is only for the two of them, excludes the other team members although they hear it perfectly clearly. '...there are quite a few social workers who will fall below the mark you set. It's an assessment centre. Checking out your skills. Just be yourself.'

'What will happen at this assessment centre?' asks Graham. 'Ted said that it will be run by a recruitment company.'

'Good question. You need to know this. Need to be ready for it.' Roselyn is getting into her stride. The positive face. 'No application forms; however, before you get there, you will each hand in a two-part personal statement. You need to tell us what you give to your role—that's part one—and to the children's services as a whole.' She wrinkles her nose, puts a finger to it as if to sneeze, then doesn't. 'That's part two.'

Tina Smith, sitting next to Charlie, whispers to him, 'We're social workers, we don't brag. The young ones will clean up at this.'

'Do you want to share it more widely, Tina?' asks Roselyn.

'Yeah...' Tina looks quickly around the table before speaking. '...some of us haven't done an interview for years. We're out of the habit. Writing down all your good points is a pretty cheesy way to go about it.'

'Tina,' says Roselyn, 'I hope you've still got last April's appraisal. I can recall that you wrote a decent self-appraisal. I wrote something similarly positive about you, wrote it sincerely. That has got to be your starting point. You write reports on prospective foster carers every week. You take them to panel, convince the great and the good of the merits of your decisions. That's the process here, give or take. You guys are all staying in my book; you do your jobs well. Make sure you prepare for the assessment centre just like you do for fostering panel.'

'Will you be submitting something on our behalf?' asks Brenda. 'Saying how much you want to keep us.'

Roselyn gives a short laugh, not that the question was funny in Charlie's mind. 'Thanks, Bren. I can see why you ask but the answer is no. I think you can all guess why if you think on it. Deepika asked Ted the same at lunchtime. He pointed out that it wouldn't add to the process. None of us are going to write negatively. Not about the staff we've nurtured, hope to keep. And that is all of you, or it is in my case. There is another matter I need to raise here. Reluctantly raise. Voluntary redundancies. They are sort-of available; however, that's only if you and your manager make the case for saying that you're dead wood. Someone the department would be wisest to offload while they can.'

'What!' Graham has never before barked in a team meeting. Roselyn's wording can be brutal. Not always: Charlie has, in a sports club changing room and once in a hotel bedroom, found a less combative side to her. That post-coital slowing of the blood.

'Graham, Graham, don't even think about it. How could I possibly support the voluntary redundancy of my new young star. The point is, we—me, Ted, all the other managers—we want you to take on the process. Fight for your jobs. If you think it is time to go, that you should leave before the assessment centre then I suppose you're welcome to ask. If you are good at your job—and I think you all are—we want to keep you. Comprendez? And that's all of you guys, it really is. I want you fighting for your jobs, not giving up. Someone will come a cropper, quite a few across the council. No reason at all why any of you should. You're the best team in the department. An asset.'

'It isn't one per team he wants shot of?' says Charlie.

'Not at all.' Roselyn shakes her head. 'This brings me to a really important point. Those personal statements—think broadly—get your head outside your day-to-day role. Think social work in the round. It might be that in the new structure there are slightly fewer roles in fostering. That doesn't mean any of you guys have to lose your jobs. The council will be keeping the best and the brightest. That's you, in my very unbiased opinion. Let them know you can do Care Proceedings, Youth Justice, the whole bloody caboodle.'

'I've been doing fostering for yonks,' says Brenda. 'I'll walk before they put me in Child Protection.'

'Brenda, Bren, fitting staff into roles comes later. First, let's get over the hurdle of these applications. The assessment centre...'

'Do you know what the new structure will be?' says Yasmin. Charlie thinks the way she says it sounds accusatory. Puffing her chest out. Not really her usual self. She's very calm on a regular day, far more so than nervous Graham, her similarly young colleague.

'Not entirely,' says Roselyn, 'but—I don't think this is going to surprise you—fostering will go back in with adoption. What goes around comes around.'

'You or Tariq? Who will the manager be?' Yasmin still looks cross, her frowning face framed by her crimson headscarf. Charlie thinks her follow up question a harsh one. Tariq Ali currently manages the adoption team; they're all coming to terms with the forthcoming assessment centre; Roselyn's only passing on what Ted has decided, and the team she calls the best in the department behaves like a remedial class.

'Me or Tariq? Maybe somebody else if we both get the boot. We're all applying for our jobs, Yaz. Me, you, Tariq: we're all in exactly the same boat.'

Yasmin's face drops. Charlie guesses she genuinely expected Roselyn to know. 'Everybody except dancing Fred Astaire,' she says. 'Good luck, Roselyn, we need you here, you know.' He's pleased to finally hear something conciliatory.

'Shh, shh,' Roselyn hisses back. Council staff are not supposed to make this joke about Ted. He is sensitive on the matter. She has stressed this point to the team over the months. Not that such a plea can stop the banter. As a big-picture man he should count himself lucky to have obtained so inoffensive a nickname. 'In answer to your question, a fuller answer than I've yet had chance to give, I'd heard nothing of the new structure until lunchtime today. Our guru, Ted, does seem to have a pretty clear vision. He said he was sure that a certain structure would enable us to maintain performance despite the cuts. Cuts to staff before the autumn is out. A structure that guides us to optimum performance.'

'Do you believe that, Roselyn?' asks Graham. 'Cut out the fat without nicking a blood vessel...'

'Yes, I do...'

'We all believe it, Graham.' Charlie hopes to be helpful to her cause. 'You, me, every last one of us. We've an assessment centre to get through. Don't entertain doubts about the process. A waste of mental energy, and being off-message will hardly endear us to the bigwigs choosing who can board the ark.'

'Thanks, Charlie,' says Roselyn, 'but I really think Ted is on to something worthwhile. A good way forward. His vision is specialist teams—something like now—with enhanced cooperation. We can use the skills we've gleaned to support Child Protection, Care Proceedings, the Intake team. We're all to be specialists while retaining a generalist outlook. Help each other more than we ever seem to do in the current structure.'

Brenda shrugs while making eye contact with Charlie. She has become a specialist within the confines of fostering, spends the bulk of her time fulfilling only a narrow range of the team's many functions. Recruiter and trainer of foster carers. She avoids meeting children for the most part but not in a way that shows. Handles herself okay when the need arises.

'The assessment centre,' Roselyn continues, 'will be run by a company called Right On Track. Have any of you come across them?'

'Are they social workers?' asks Precious.

Roselyn shakes her head, shrugs slightly. They are not.

'That's a bit weird, innit?' Precious sounds incredulous.

'They're recruiters. They have loads of experience partnering in public service projects across the country. Ted has a small working party drawing up a specification. They'll tell them what we need and then Right On Track will crack on with it. They know how to sift the wheat from the chaff: that's their thing. The company will design the assessment day—no bias if they do it—but the department will have made it inordinately clear what we are looking for. They work to our spec.'

'Day!' Charlie is astonished. 'It isn't an hour's interview? Are we going to be grilled for a whole day?'

'Important decisions, Mr Quested. We can't get this wrong. Ted was most clear about that. Trimming what isn't needed, to leave the department running along as a sleek and well-oiled machine. Only cutting those who don't have what it takes to hack it in the new...'

'How much is it costing?' interrupts Yasmin. They might all have thought it. Charlie certainly did.

'It's turnaround money, systems change. The government

has a different pot. No money is being siphoned from any child-focussed budget. Truly, it isn't.'

'Money is money,' says Yasmin, and Charlie agrees with her logic. Secret pots of money to sack the social workers who don't fit in. It stinks a bit, could even get personal. Fiona always says that a good social worker is meant to rock the boat. It's got to be a part of their make-up. He's not so sure, long been a conformist. Wonders which side the casualties will come from. Can't believe senior managers require day-long assessments to make their minds up. It's staff they manage week in and week out. Madness. Give the money to the kids.

* * *

The team vacate Buxton Room at three o'clock, as required. An adult services team coming in as they depart. These are social workers, not ones who were in the eleven o'clock meeting, the one that Ted Astaire called. Gloomy-looking adult services social workers. The fostering team glance at each other; the scale of the cuts made clear to all. Misery is in vogue council-wide.

Back in the open plan, team members turn on their screens, start to look busy. They are wiser for the talk, more clued in. To be wise is not, of itself, to be happy. Roselyn was encouraging, made sense most of the time, but an upbeat leader alone doesn't quell the pervasive anxiety. Ted Astaire plans a more harmonious structure, peace and cooperation between social workers. Before that can happen, they must first square off. A bun fight to determine who is to depart the department. And they moan about Right On Track, the hitherto unknown company, coming in to orchestrate the proceedings. Not even social workers and they're going to push them all through a day-long assessment. It sounds gruelling. Charlie's known nothing like it in a decade with the city. It could create a savage undercurrent that doesn't belong. Recruiting foster carers, placing children with them;

sorting it all out for those in need of a decent home. Social workers like to help, and this dust up goes against the grain. Charlie's ex-army, he might be able to draw on that.

While they are checking their emails, or just staring blankly at computer screens—the energy for further work eluding many—Fiona bounces into the office like she's come into money. They all look at her—so much to tell—she's the one bursting to talk. 'I saw Russell, out in Derbyshire.'

Charlie nods, knows the boy well, co-works the case. 'Of course. How is he?' A tricky lad who's doing better than they could have imagined in the fostering placement only they recommended. Fiona and Charlie stuck their necks out to have Russell Chope placed with the Goodings. Roselyn favoured a specialist children's home, would have passed poor Russell to a different social work team altogether, recommend the council spend more on him than any five foster children cost. Only Fiona and Charlie thought he could crack reality, live in a family home. Russell is a disturbed boy—victim of the most horrific parental abuse—his carers were new to fostering when they took him in, have since proven themselves a dedicated couple. They put up gamely with a lot more crap than many a foster carer has to.

'Mary and Colin are loving it, going to take him on a half-term getaway to that woodland adventure park outside Nottingham. Poor Russell is bewildered by the idea. Changes his mind every two hours. He doesn't really know how to be loved.'

As she is telling this to Charlie, others listening in, Roselyn has emerged from her glass box to join them. Have words with the absentee.

'You need to hear what you've missed, Fi,' says Charlie.

Fiona's face drops while Charlie just smiles at her. Marvellous really, just carrying on with her visit when Ted and Roselyn were rounding them up like sheep. It must be the secret to keeping as buoyant as Fiona first sounded. The

The Actor

assessment centre might catch her like flypaper. She needs to know what's coming.

'Fiona,' says Roselyn, 'did you see my email yesterday afternoon?' She clears her throat. 'Well, I know you saw it because I set it to read-receipt. You really should have cancelled today's visit.'

'Roselyn, we've talked about Russell in supervision. He's paranoid enough. I can't let him down when he's expecting to see me. Can't and won't.'

'You could have but I'll let that go. Listen, I have a team managers' meeting starting now, so I'll let our Charlie tell you what the restructure is all about. What's going to be happening to you all. Any questions, please come to me. And you will have questions.' She turns to the rest of the team, the small swathe of desks which the fostering social workers occupy. 'My door is open, nothing has changed. Love you and leave you for today. Onwards and upwards tomorrow. It's the only way for an all-star team like ours.' With pad and pen in hand, Roselyn leaves the room.

'Tell me the crap,' says Fiona, staring at the door through which Roselyn has gone, head held high. Their manager breathes confidence in and out. Thirty puffs of the stuff every minute of the day.

Yasmin comes across and she and Charlie bring Fiona up to speed. Rehash what Ted said earlier, all that Roselyn told them in the meeting room.

'I'm hopeless at that stuff,' says Fiona. Her inflexion and the hint of Irish in her voice seem to make light of it whether she intends it or not. Hearing it makes Charlie think the whole plan sounds implausible. Everyone in the Children's Service Department must apply for their current jobs—nobody is certain of their future—a day-long assessment centre to wheedle out one in eight. Mud wrestling.

'Roselyn said it will involve actors,' Yasmin explains. 'We'll be expected to handle a difficult client. Roleplay it. A complainant probably. Roselyn wouldn't confirm that part—what role the actor will play—it's really got to be something like that. If he was just going to be nice to us there wouldn't be any point. This Right On Track crowd who are leading the day, putting us through all the tests, they aren't even social workers. We don't know what they are. Smart arses probably. We have to give a presentation, and we won't learn what the topic is until the day. And there'll be a written exercise but I didn't understand what that was about. Then an interview.' She reaches a hand to her head, index finger scratching at the hairline beneath her headscarf. 'One of the team managers will be on the panel, not Roselyn for us. She said it can't be her because it has to be someone impartial. I don't think anyone really is anymore.'

'Not doing it,' says Fiona. 'Just give me my P.45 now.'

Charlie laughs, Yasmin doesn't. It must be a joke. Fiona will take it all seriously in time, he's sure of it. Serious is not a face she ever shares. The whole assessment day, playing at being a social worker with an actor for a client, could be a funny game if their livelihoods—and their self-esteem—were not so bound up in it. Nice to see Fiona isn't bothered.

* * *

Charlie is alone in his flat, looking at the council's website—the internal one, staff information—when his mobile buzzes. It's all up there: the process; the time frame. Ted must have been planning this for some time. The talk, the lunchtime briefing of the managers. Long ago lined up Right On Track, whoever they are. The DCS has had the whole shooting match up his sleeve for weeks.

Graham, on the other end of the phone, is worried. Fears becoming jobless just as social work departments are voiding all their usual vacancies. No work in the city, no work up north. Not for Charlie and Graham, those not cut out to be baristas or burger flippers. Not that Charlie is above all that, just thought he'd left it behind. A squaddie no more.

Graham's worries make a lot of sense, but Charlie wants him to put his mind to better use. Think about the assessment centre, how he will present himself. They talk for several minutes and when Charlie says, 'Just pass the fucking thing,' Graham finally laughs. That's good to hear and brings an idea to his mind. Charlie checks with Graham that he is still living on Duke Street. 'I am,' he replies.

They've never met outside work, although they've been living only a mile apart since Mandy threw Charlie out of his marital home. Banished him from the suburbs. 'Should we meet up for a drink? The Crown looks all right. Do you know it? On Maple Street.' Graham agrees. It is nine-forty, never too late for a beer in Charlie's experience. The boy's nerves need calming. Charlie's too, and he's not the one phoning colleagues at all hours.

* * *

Graham is waiting outside the door as Charlie approaches the pub. The same corduroy trousers he wore at work, with a T-shirt this evening, not the blue-check of earlier. He holds a sweater in his hands, it might be needed for the walk home. They go inside together. A Wednesday night, and the place is heaving. Tough times, everybody has a lot to drink about. Graham insists on buying first. The pair find seats on high stools, perch themselves beside a tall round table. There are three women sitting at it already but room enough for all the drinks. Charlie can't help himself from looking over the girls. A quick glance between sups. On another night, he could be interested to talk to the dark one. She looks about a decade younger than he is. Maybe two decades, any reciprocation would be a long shot. Charlie thinks that Graham has a girl back in his flat, doesn't know it for a fact. The lad is here for the pep talk not chasing skirt. Charlie likes to look into girls' faces, get a smile back. Engagement. He is still the soldier; a pretty rum social worker. He knows it too, pretty good at the job, just wired differently than most. Tonight, he determines, he must devote himself to reassuring his colleague, give the lad hope that his career will stay afloat. Come up with a strategy for assessment day. When he looks at him, Graham seems oblivious to the pretty ladies so close to hand. All right for him if he already has one at home, as Charlie no longer does. He is actually quite uncertain who Graham lives with. They—Charlie and Graham—talk to each other every week day, talk work. The younger has asked a few questions about his military past. Graham is curious but shy with it. They have never raised homelife beyond the odd passing comment. A TV programme both enjoy. Graham seems to step lightly around home and relationships. Charlie can't think of his girlfriend's name or even be sure he has one. In the office, everyone knows Charlie has buggered up his private life. Living in a flat three miles from wife and family. Only Graham knows why.

'I'm bricking it,' says Graham.

Charlie points out that the assessment centre will only differ in the deployment of an actor—the role-play component—from the ordeal he went through some twelve months ago. The interview for his current job was pretty similar. 'You gave a presentation, did a desk-top exercise.'

'No pressure back then,' says Graham. 'I had a lot of irons in the fire. I wanted it, didn't expect to get it. Pleasantly surprised when it happened, when the city took me on. Applying for your own job: that's a nightmare. The best of all possible outcomes is the status quo. Which is the worst in proper job applications. I'm not good with pressure, Charlie.'

Graham is talking good pessimistic sense, and Charlie thinks the reassurance with which he tries to counter it sounds like new-age bollocks. He can't stop himself, hates to see Graham so unnerved. In their work, they both cope with a lot of crap. Placement breakdowns, foster kids getting into

The Actor

trouble. A cool head for the day job won't necessarily keep nerves under wraps in the ordeal to come. 'You're twelve months wiser,' says Charlie. 'You convince me you should be in the role whenever we talk shop. And I'm probably a harsher judge than these clowns from Right On Track. You'll convince them easily. The only true professional on the interview panel will be one of ours. It might be Tariq and he's okay. They'll be impressed by all that you've done in so little time.'

'I'm shitting it.'

'What's your home support, Graham?' asks Charlie. 'You don't live alone?'

'I do.'

His reply is a surprise to Charlie. Can't recall if his contrary impression came from Graham, or an aside by Yasmin. 'Girlfriend?' Charlie tries. 'Family close by?'

'You know my family are in London, mate. You do hear my accent, right?' He has a point about this; there is nothing northern in Graham's diphthongs.

'Girlfriend?' Charlie tries again.

'Not quite.' Graham is evasive on the personal front.

It's his business, and Charlie decides not to pry. 'Ring me anytime, Graham. I'm happy to help.'

They talk a little. Graham is unexpectedly vitriolic about Roselyn. Her afternoon pep talk was 'cagey' and 'she is holding something back.' That is how he sees it, and he never seemed the suspicious type before.

Charlie disagrees, guesses Graham just needs a person to blame for the feelings of fear the imminent reorganisation has prompted. Charlie has no bitterness towards their manager. Smart enough to take responsibility for their brief affair—him and Roselyn—it was pretty good apart from cleaving apart his marriage. Not worth it but the allure was too good to pass over untested. Charlie has thought since that he was foolish to even tell Graham about it. He did that on the same day he later told Mandy. Graham kept the knowledge of it to himself. Told neither Yasmin nor Precious, he is as certain as he can be about that. Mandy— his wife on paper if no longer in any practising sense—was less circumspect with the information. Threw him out of the house within the hour. That was personal stuff: the fling; the sex; the decision to kill it stone dead. As a manager Charlie has always found Roselyn decent enough; nothing for this ex-army boy to disobey.

'Do you not think she should be the one to go,' Graham asks. 'For taking advantage of you?'

Charlie laughs out loud. 'Roselyn didn't really have to groom me. I guess the squash and the sweat did it, and I thought it mutual at the time. Still do. Don't be prissy about it, Graham. I wish I'd never told you.'

'She's as married as you, and seems to have got away with it,' says Graham. It doesn't add to Charlie's insight.

They talk a little about Graham's family. He grew up in Lewisham. Charlie doesn't know where that is. Saw only Buckingham Palace, Tower Bridge and a West-End show on his visit to the capital, family in tow, a few months before Mikey was born. Always a northerner; his army regiment was Yorkshire based.

Graham seems glad to be away from the place. 'I don't know why my parents still stay. Dad took a health retirement while I was studying, and Mum's bakery job could as easily be anywhere.'

'Do you think they'll move up north, nearer to you?' asks Charlie.

'God, I hope not. My sister, Caroline, is in Croydon; she has kids. They don't help or anything but I guess they'll stay where they are. Near their grandkids.'

Charlie asks Graham about his sister. They've never really compared personal notes before. His own background, the kid in care, can make others avoid the topic. Graham likes

The Actor

the kids, two nieces and a nephew, but doesn't see them often. Charlie keeps thinking they need to go over the assessment centre rubbish, that's why Graham phoned him. Or perhaps it is because they both live alone. Stewing solo on the coming brouhaha makes for a miserable evening.

'Will you have kids? You've a girlfriend, I recall.'

Graham waves a dismissive hand, shrugs. Maybe Charlie doesn't recall so well, it wouldn't be the first time. 'You're confident, I take it?' says Graham.

Charlie thinks about this. He is not confident, could be out of a job in a month. Telling Graham that will not make him feel better. It's simply that army training exceeds social worker training in the not-revealing-your-true-feelings stakes. Never show it when you're bricking it. Even being in care gave Charlie a head-start on that one. Military training covers it comprehensively. No one goes into battle not bricking it, but it is for the greater good of the regiment that no signs are evident. Bottle it up, keep the cork up your arse. Social workers focus on feelings relentlessly. Charlie likes his colleagues, still finds their constant self-analysis makes for painful listening. Feelings mostly impede; he is a doer. He thinks himself an emotion-free-zone much of the time. It's his secret weapon which no other social worker can fathom.

'I think we should all be okay. Really hope so. Just don't forget, recruitment processes—which is what we are going through, we're all out of a job on the morning of the assessment, and either back in or shut out for good by the end—they can be brutal. Think about why and how you do your job. Think about it until you can describe it in your sleep. Our brains all go a bit wobbly in interviews. The autopilot needs decent instructions.'

'Jesus, Charlie, you're scaring me. I've never flown a plane before.'

Charlie laughs, goes to the bar to buy another round of drinks before the bell goes. Last orders.

'Are you a walker?' asks Charlie on his return. Setting two new pints before them.

Before Graham can answer, the dark girl—Afro-Caribbean, he guesses—nudges him. 'Be careful,' she says. A bit of beer sloshed on to her purse as he placed them on the high table.

'Sorry,' says Charlie. 'It looks waterproof.'

'Do I know you?' says the girl.

Charlie shakes his head. He would have remembered her pretty face by now. Would have if he'd seen her before.

'Quested,' she announces.

Charlie feels disoriented by her recognition.

The girl dips her head to talk conspiratorially to Charlie. To her man, Quested. 'I'm Tawni Walsh,' she says. 'God, I was a kid, I recognise...'

'Tawni!' Now, he smiles broadly, quietens his voice when he realises that her two friends are staring at them. She seemed not to wish to involve them. He understands why. 'How are you doing?' he says quietly.

'Not so bad. Not so bad at all.'

They gaze at each other, and for Charlie, there is no reading what Tawni is thinking about him. 'I'm so pleased to hear that,' he says.

'Yeah.'

The other girls have climbed down from their high stools. One is looking intently at Tawni. Could be gauging if her friend needs rescuing or leaving to the luck of the night.

Tawni slides off her stool, stands as her friends do, then she leans in to speak exclusively to Charlie. 'You were a bit shit and I expect I was no better,' she pronounces.

Charlie tries to speak, can't catch her eye. Tawni has her purse in her hand, pulls a green fur-lined jacket from the back of a chair to the table's side. Walks out of The Crown, head held high and he surmises there is deliberation in it.

'Who was that?' asks Graham.

The Actor

'A dozen years ago, when I was still a student social worker, I wrote the social report for a court case which prevented poor Tawni from living back home in her teenage years. I didn't recognise her at all, not until she said. You'd think I would, right? I don't remember her being half as good-looking when she was a kid. Just a poor little misery back then. Something must have gone right. And she didn't thump me which I'll take as positive feedback about my professional skills.' Charlie puts a hand to his mouth, makes it into a bugle, calls out to the now closed door. 'Reference for the assessment-day palaver, please Miss?'

'Shush,' says Graham, laughing. 'Kid in care? She was dressed like she works at a good job.'

'Or for a night out. It's hard to tell. I should have asked.'

'What's with the walking, Charlie?'

'I think they were all three for going home,' he says. 'She might have stayed to chat but you can bet her friends never knew she had a social worker. We seldom volunteer it, you know. Us former care kids. What's done is done.'

'No, not her. You asked me about walking before she interrupted.'

'Oh, that. I remember. I do a bit, hiking. Up in the hills. We should go one weekend when all this hang-on-to-your-job nonsense is over. Are you up for it?'

'I like walking, not so keen if it's wet. Muddy footpaths and drizzle.'

'Wet is best. I love it when the hills are empty. Let's do it, Graham. The girls in the team will just down gin, none of them are very outdoorsy. A cross-country hike, you and me?'

'Yeah,' agrees the younger. 'Job or dole, whatever the weather, a walk over the hills would be good. I'll have to buy a waterproof if we're to go up Snowdon in November, but we'll do it. Good shout, mate.'

2.

'I saw a kid I used to work with.'

Charlie listens to the interjection, waits politely.

'No, a child I had put in care. Not from the army. I don't really see any of them.'

Again, the lady on the other end of the phone asks for more detail, seeks clarification. She is hard of hearing. the telephone a challenge for her in the last year or two.

'She seemed to be doing all right, Mum,' he continues. 'We didn't talk long, just nice to see it's not all gone belly up.'

Charlie hears her laughing, agreeing. Putting him in the same category. Charlie's foster mother is in her eighties now. On this call, he has explained that his social work position is in jeopardy. That he must impress on assessment day if he is to continue in the job he loves. The job which she said—when he first secured it—made her 'feel it has all been worthwhile.' He loved hearing that; she deserves to get something back.

Charlie knows that he is one of several former children in care who keep contact with Grace Bell. Kept up with Mr Bell too—Norman—until he passed away. She lives in a small flat now, he has not gone to Wakefield in five years and it is ten since he was at the family home. Mandy—still his wife whatever he has done to confuse that state—called it 'strange but lovely' that he thought of her house that way. He was there barely three years, left at sixteen. Care kids usually did back then. She turned him around: a good for nothing who became a staff sergeant in the British Army; became a qualified social worker; became a caring father of three. She doesn't need to know that the living arrangement and marriage that produced the kids are up shit creek. That's his current take on it. Perhaps the tide will turn. He once confided everything in his foster mother but she is the more vulnerable these days. Charlie would hate to disappoint her. Can't do that to her at the age she is now, and after all the good she has done him. Shepherded teenaged Charlie onto the straight and narrow.

3.

Yasmin and Graham went through theirs two days ago, Brenda yesterday. They have told their colleagues how the assessment centre works. Brenda told them through tears. Mostly just said she hated it. Charlie, Precious and Fiona are to go through it today. And Roselyn too, although she has told them that her assessment is quite different. She's a manager after all. Tina's will take place tomorrow and then it will be over. From Monday through Friday, all the staff of the Children's Services Department are being done alphabetically. Through the mill from A to Z.

Charlie sees Fiona across the car park, raises a hand meaning for her to wait. They will walk in together. The assessments are taking place in a suite of rooms at The Kirkaldy, a spectacularly large hotel, four miles out from the city centre. Not a convenient location, is the consensus. Faiza from the Care Proceedings team disagrees, lives a stone's throw away. Precious is in the hotel lobby when the pair walk in. They are early. A coffee before showtime.

'Been here long?' Fiona asks.

Precious could be attending a party. Her hair beaded in an array of bright colours, skirt a rainbow. 'An age,' she answers. 'Don't think I slept for a minute last night.'

A girl with a London accent introduces herself. She is from Right On Track, the company running the assessment day. A streak of pink in her black hair. The rest of her could be a secretary in a nineteen-fifties comedy film. Black and white. It is the colour of her skirt-suit; she sports black-rimmed glasses. Fiona chats to her, Charlie overhears that the firm are London-based. Eight of them are staying in this hotel all week. The girl says she likes it. 'I've never been up north before. It's a lot nicer than I thought it would be.'

Social workers keep arriving. Nervous looking social workers wearing tightly knotted ties, or dark skirts and white blouses. One or two ask if they are in the right place when the answer is self-evident. Roselyn walks through the door at five minutes to nine. She has a short fawn-coloured skirt on, no tights, a light blue blouse with prominent toggle-shaped buttons. A couple open down the front when one might be enough. Charlie wonders if she's banking on a horny male assessor. A wild play but it could work. Something similar snagged him last summer. 'Freezing cold,' she says by way of greeting.

Fiona turns to Charlie so that her face is not in Roselyn's field of vision, gives him a cross-eyed look.

'Have I got a coffee?' says their boss, and Charlie points to the jugs on a table up the corridor.

They haven't seen their manager all week. She's been involved in delivering the assessments. Observing the role play. Colleagues whose surnames are closer to the start of the alphabet said so. Today she must undergo the managers' bespoke process. 'Is it fun or hell?' asks Fiona.

'Roll with it. You guys will be okay but it's demanding. You have to think on your feet.'

Precious asks what the questions are.

'You know I can't tell you that.'

Yasmin and Graham have told them already. Colleagues not managers, they felt no compulsion to keep it secret. Both wanted to offload, debrief. Excrete out the whole experience. There were one or two discrepancies in what they each recalled. 'It's full on,' Graham told Charlie. 'Messes with your mind a bit. Just full on.'

Precious bows her head at Roselyn's answer. A little sulk. Charlie thinks about this: a team of mates before the week began. If they all come through it, the camaraderie will be intact, sulks and groans forgiven. How it will feel if there are casualties is a worry. Their tight little team could be on the verge of unravelling.

* * *

The evening before this daunting day, Charlie went to Mandy's.

He still thinks of it as home while sleeping in a one-bedroom flat. His city pad, he calls it, not central but close enough. She had agreed to the visit in advance. He saw his children. Adores them, feels clumsy trying to express it. Played and talked with them. Michelle was great, she's always great. Ten years old, nothing too complicated. Paul was out, came in before he left. Little Mikey worries Charlie. Not that he didn't play nicely with him. The lad loves to play with his daddy, likes nothing better. He's a little boy of three. Charlie worries that if Mandy doesn't relent, he will lose his place in his son's life.

When Mandy told him of her new boyfriend, Barry—and he wasn't even aware that she was looking for one—it destabilised him. 'Now!' he said, thinking her insensitive to spring this on him the day before the assessment. Survival games for social workers.

'Is it tomorrow?' asked Mandy after he had explained his point. It cannot be looming so large in her life.

The visit was okay—he loves his children—went to The Crown late on. A gnawing feeling in his stomach. Mandy taking up with a boyfriend: he never expected that one to come out of the shadows. Drinking before the big day was a bad idea; he knew it and ignored the knowing. Couldn't help himself after the Barry-bombshell.

Tawni wasn't there, and he is pretty sure that her absence was a good thing. He would like to meet her again, learn more. Last night might have been too much. He recalls how much he liked the look of her before he even realised who she was. A glance across the high table; her brown eyes alert and shining. She wore a single braid in her hair. When he found out that she had been his client a dozen years before, when she was twelve or thirteen, he tried to shake all that from his mind. He wonders if he would have told her about his breakup with Mandy. Would he have been embarrassed, or somehow cool about it? Told it like a busted marriage is a needed life lesson. Nothing lasts. He's thankful she wasn't there precisely because he was in the mood to look for her. To learn that he is old and of little interest—none whatsoever, most probably—to a girl in her twenties. And chasing skirt is not the behaviour of a man who hopes his marriage can recover from the sickness he has inflicted upon it. It's a long way off course right now—Mandy's started seeing a man called Barry—still, he can hope. It doesn't cost and it's a sight better than misery. Charlie and Mandy were a proper couple for a long, long time. She might just be getting her own back with the new guy, not serious about him. Just levelling the score.

Tawni Walsh wasn't there, and Charlie talked football and played darts with a bunch of men he has no need to see again. No real wish to. He is a little bit hungover this morning, not so much that anyone will notice. His stomach is fine but sleep was a bit of a stranger. Precious was not the only one to struggle into that other realm. It came to him only for a short disturbing visitation. Army dreams are never gratifying.

* * *

As it reaches nine o'clock, Roselyn signals to Charlie that she'd like a quiet word. He concurs, and they walk a short way down the corridor. Step into an alcove.

'It should be starting now,' says Charlie.

'They're never on time,' says Roselyn, and as soon as they have rounded the corner, she takes a hold of his arm. 'I'm worried about this.' Her face has lost its buoyancy, a rigidity in her expression that he finds unusual. 'I think I might be too maverick for this lot. For Right On Track.'

'You'll nail it,' says Charlie. He speaks the phrase without an attached thought. Would rather hear encouraging words than have to dredge them up.

Roselyn's face lights up. Her first smile of the morning. 'Thanks. You're just what they're looking for, you know?' She leans into him, pecks him quickly on the lips. 'Let's do this.' Then she turns to walk back to the foyer where the rest of their colleagues are waiting.

Charlie thinks it extraordinary. She lays no claim to him, or him to her. Whatever it was that they had was also an error—enjoyable, unsustainable—and still she uses him for whatever fillip that kiss was.

'What did she want?' asks Precious when he is back with his team mates, a man in a three-piece suit ushering them all into a nearby room for the initial briefing. Roselyn has left them. The assessment of managers taking place elsewhere in The Kirkaldy.

'Keen to hear how everyone's bearing up,' says Charlie.

'Why doesn't she ask me?'

Charlie cannot answer this or, more precisely, he will not. He wonders if Precious has a suspicion, if she is pressing him for salacious gossip. Surely not. Graham is always good to his word. Roselyn gives nothing away. The depth of the alcove hid the unasked-for kiss from those whose business it isn't.

* * *

Eight social workers sit in the briefing: today's cohort. The man in the suit puts them into pairs. Charlie and Fiona form one. Each grouping will do the four-part centre in a different order. Half the time spent waiting while their paired applicant is in action. The actor is to be busy all day.

First up for Charlie and Fiona will be the interview. He feels strangely cheated. In his mind, this event should come last; it is where he hoped to explain away any cock-ups made in the less predictable segments. This unexpected ordering has snatched away that opportunity. Graham had his interview last. Told them all four events are on the go at once for some poor sod. Foolish of Charlie to think he'd experience it just as his friend had.

Outside the interview room, Fiona suggests that they toss a coin to decide who goes first. As she is saying it, a head pops around the door, the man in the three-piece suit. 'Miss O'Shea?' he asks. Right On Track know their alphabet.

'Ms,' replies Fiona, rising.

Charlie is alone only a moment before the young girl, the employee of Right On Track introduces herself—'I'm Cheryl'—and gives him a paper, saying, 'This is your topic for the presentation.' Charlie looks at the streak of pink in her hair. Wonders if this is the sum total of rebellion that her company allows its employees. She looks strait-laced and only that single splotch of dye suggests otherwise. Then he reverses the thought. She could be as square as Princess Anne, and her image-conscious organisation insists on the pink. Wish to mask their reliance on the dull clerical staff who keep the show on the road. A London company would be that flash. She has taken her black jacket off. Her blouse is a plain light blue, short-sleeved. Skin the same pallor as every bookworm. 'You will need to prepare it now, you're first up after the interview. Your colleague will be preparing while you're in there.'

Charlie did not anticipate such a demand. He wants to think about answers to interview questions, probable and even definite ones. Yasmin and Graham were very specific about the topics. There will be a safeguarding question; showing a good understanding of child-protection procedures is a must. He asks Cheryl if it will wait.

'The instructions are clear on my screen,' she tells him. Cheryl gives Charlie a pen and paper, a briefing note about the ten-minute presentation. He must outline an improvement plan for any area of the city's children's services he thinks ripe for betterment.

Graham told him this was coming, and he's had some ideas but wanted to prepare today. Not look overprepared in case that gets marked down. He writes, crosses out, writes some more. Last night's beer was a big mistake, Mandy's new boyfriend a bigger one. She's getting back at him, that's the explanation. He had sex when he shouldn't have, and so she's doing the same. Two wrongs are hardly going to put Humpty Dumpty back together. He could be out of a job by the day's end although no one will know it that quickly. They will each fear it. Nagging doubts in their reflection on today's performance. The outcomes—stay or go—will not be handed down until the end of next week. The doomed will walk amongst them like ghosts, yet to know that they have passed over to the other side. He glances down, left-hand ring finger. His whole life is epitomised in the wedding band he still wears. Wishes and pretence.

* * *

When Fiona re-joins him in the waiting area, she smiles and gives him the executioner's cut-throat signal. Index finger running horizontally across her own neck. He decides that he likes Fiona; it is his opinion of her most of the time. A bright and breezy Irish girl when she's not talking intensely about foster children, and he's on her side all the way when she does that. She can be a bit abrasive, needs to have everything her own way. His liking her fluctuates quite a lot. The hand signal might be funny or it might be portentous. There is no reading Fiona, whether he likes her or not.

The interview room door opens again. The cut of a summer dress, the tanned knees of a well-groomed woman, catches his eye. 'Charles Quested, please?' she says. He wonders what happened to the guy in the three-piece. Fiona might have slain him, no fan of the overdressed. Fiona's husband—partner, whatever their relationship is—lectures at the university, and wears his hair in dreadlocks. White guy, probably not a Rastafarian at all; Charlie doesn't think he is. Spends more time protesting about the environment than he does any proper work as far as Charlie has gathered.

He follows the woman into the room. Two interviewers sit at the table. The man in the three-piece suit still lives. Karen Foley, manager of the care proceedings team, is in here too. The good-looking woman and Charlie join the table.

'Good morning, Mr Quested. I'm Adam Johnstone of Right On Track,' says the suit. 'I will be leading this interview, aided by Rachel Barrington...' Johnstone indicates the lady who came to the door. Charlie looks directly into her face and sees eyes of the deepest blue, smile lines around them. She's his best bet, her face is kind. '...and Ms Foley, whom you already know. Would you like a glass of water? Any questions before we start?'

Charlie shrugs, says, 'Begin,' while feeling bombarded by information. Two new names. Mustn't forget them, it would give the wrong impression entirely. Adam and Rachel. The stiff and the pretty one.

'In your role in the...' Johnstone of the three-piece suit glances down at his notes. '...fostering team, can you tell us...'

'Water would be good,' interrupts Charlie. Head a bit thick from last night's beer. He should have taken it first time.

Karen Foley smiles at him as she pours from jug to glass, looks friendlier than he expected. She's not a team manager he has ever warmed to. The two Right On Track interviewers are not social workers at all apparently; they are likely to be impressed if he just emphasises how high the stakes are. That they make a difference to kids' lives; keep a good few out of trouble altogether.

'...tell us what you believe to be the most important skills for an effective social worker? Please address more than the areas of knowledge required. Describe the attributes and behaviours which you consider essential in performing your duties to the benefit of clients and society.'

Charlie sips his water. At his request, Adam Johnstone reads the question back in full, and then he begins to answer. 'I need to emphasise that our judgement is what is most important. When you look at foster care, it's the carers, the good folk who open their homes up to these really vulnerable kids, who do all the day-to-day stuff. It's our call if they are the right people for the task. The same with matching children to placements. Vital that we get those decisions spot on. We support children in placements through the advice we give foster carers. We have to be spot on, give them something to really work with. People ask me, is it a science or an art? I say, it's all science. Say it because it is. All science. We must build on what we know, cannot take risks with unsubstantiated hunches. We have bags of experience in our team...'

'Learn from your mistakes, is that what you're saying?' Adam Johnstone sounds a rum interviewer to Charlie's thinking. Cut him off in full flow.

'Yes and no. We can't really afford to make mistakes. We need to be cautious with new foster carers, not give them really difficult children until we've got their true measure. Of course, things sometimes go a bit belly-up, these are human beings we're talking about. Unpredictable, but that's more because there are no miracles; substantial mistakes just can't be made.'

'Can you tell me about that, about what might go wrong?'

The questions the suit asks confirm Charlie's view that those who are not social workers don't really have a clue. Cannot visualise his job. He makes reference to his own upbringing, being in foster care—both the Right On Track interviewers instantly write on their pads—he is more than a career social worker. They may see something in it which sets him apart.

Karen repeats the question about what might go wrong. It's true that he hasn't answered it, he thinks the other two didn't notice. Got excited because he was in care. Could be that they have never met one before, a kid in care or a grown-up out of it. Karen's question seems churlish. If he has satisfied two out of three, she should shut up.

'Offences, says Charlie. 'A kid who was getting into trouble with the law, taken into care to stop it, moved into foster care in the local community, carries on offending. Breaking the law. Shoplifting, vandalism, whatever it is they do. It would be a minor miracle if it stopped overnight. He still has the same contacts, same peer pressure. If we move him thirty miles away it might stop the behaviour more quickly in the short term, but cutting him off from friends, changing schools, that can play with a child's head. Sending kids into the unknown can go far more pear-shaped than simply managing all the known concerns.' He thinks he is getting into his stride. Not said anything special but it sounds okay. 'We have to work alongside the child, get them to value the right things. They often start to listen to the foster carers—and us—as their home lives begin to stabilise. This, quite simply, will not be the case on day one. We all need patience.'

As he rabbits on, Charlie feels he is just talking twaddle for the unconverted. Karen Foley knows the facts: taking hardened offenders into care—it's often done—is a mug's game. There is little shifting them by this point. Early intervention, spotting the signs before the behaviour becomes ingrained, that is the real skill. Charlie doesn't want to talk about that. He left the intake team, moved to fostering, because he didn't really have it. Maybe that's the art to his science, or maybe the lot of it is chance, and they are just spreading fairy dust on goblins. He doesn't like thinking on his feet, not when so much is riding on it. His mouth is dry. Hangovers do that.

The Actor

* * *

As he arrives back in the waiting area, Fiona rises from the table at which she is writing, and gives him an unexpected hug. 'How did you get on,' she asks. And before he can answer, she adds, 'I'm sure you did fine. Really sure you did.'

Charlie grimaces. 'Could have gone better.'

'Tell me about it. Wasn't that Rachel girl a bitch.'

Charlie can't answer this. He liked her more than he did Karen Foley in the context of what has just gone on. Couldn't stand the sight of pin-striped Johnstone, then again, interviews muddle with regular thinking. They'd all be okay over a pint, most likely. Rachel especially, although she looked more of a white wine drinker. 'Did you get the safeguarding scenario?' he asks.

'We'll all get it. There's no leaving that one out.'

'No, but did you understand it? I thought it was a trick question.'

'I get you,' says Fiona. 'Yeah, you had to think about the family situation and the safety of the professionals. There were flaws in their protection practice that needed pointing out.'

'Shit,' says Charlie. 'I got a bit stuck on the wider family members. Said something about the procedures, I think. I can't really remember what I said in there.'

'Ah, you'll have sailed through, Charlie Quested. You've memorised the handbook. Everyone in the office comes to you for that stuff. Roselyn and the lot of us.'

'It doesn't matter what you know if you didn't say it in front of that overdressed panel.'

Fiona laughs at his put-down. 'Two out of three,' she says, and Charlie sees accuracy in her clarification. Three-piece Johnstone and Rachel in a blue-and-cream summer dress could dine at the Ritz in the clothes they wear today. Karen Foley, meanwhile, sports black dungarees with a bit of a stain on the bib. Spilled tea or the cream off a cream cake.

Her hair knows neither comb or brush. She always looks like this. Colleagues say she's good at her job; she wouldn't be the best dressed in a homeless shelter.

'Are you ready, Mr Quested?' asks Cheryl who has just walked back into the break-out area.

He must go to his presentation. 'Not really,' he says. 'I've only just come from the interview.'

'It's a tight turnaround, we understand that this reflects how children's services tends to be these days,' she says.

'Always. Always was, not just these days.' He is finding a previously hidden dislike for this young upstart. 'Can I take five, please? Review what I wrote before I went into the interview.'

Cheryl looks intently at her watch. 'The schedule is tight. I'll take you across in two minutes-thirty.'

'Bloody hell,' he mutters, an aside to Fiona, not directed at pink hair. 'I'll go now.' Charlie rises from his seat. Towers above the girl with the streak.

* * *

'Statutory visits,' Charlie tells the panel, 'they're resource hungry but we have to do them. We also make a lot of visits to children in foster placements over and above that minimum. These are always reactive. Not good. We need to see ourselves coming. Contingency plan at the statutory visit stage. Being legally obliged to conduct them is not enough. We've got to use them better. We plan really well in the most difficult of cases. I think we need to put the same application in across the board. It can prevent the everyday from drifting into the category of difficult.'

As he speaks, Charlie can see that Tariq, team leader of adoption, who may become his manager if both are still standing when their teams merge, is nodding sagely. He doesn't know if he has convinced the freaks from Right On Track. Not sure if they have a clue what he's talking about. They probably measure the confidence of his manner, his eye contact. Evaluate what his dress sense tells them. These things matter in the twenty-first century; an understanding of needy children is old hat.

When he gets to the end of the presentation—having made the case for efficiency and good child-care practice—he asks the panel if they have questions for him.

'Have you costed this?' asks Marcia. She is a grey-haired panel member who introduced herself by telling him that she is a partner in Right On Track. Good for her. She tried explaining that her organisation is a limited liability partnership. Mistakenly thought the workings of her money-making scam might be of interest to a dedicated public servant. Missing the mark there; Charlie is not actively against entrepreneurism, but this lot just dress up and talk down. Whatever money they make, it doesn't arise from putting anything visible into the world. Sacking a few social workers this week, although Ted will come up with fancier words for it.

He decides it would be poor form to make his opinions known, to shout back, 'What a stupid question that is.' He is a social work practitioner, not a financial analyst; he prepared this guff in the waiting area in the last hour. 'The ideas stack up,' he says. 'I couldn't access the data while waiting, can't exactly quantify the number of additional visits we make. It's a hell of a lot. My plan would reduce the additional visits, and it would not require more planning time. Just more focussed use of what we have.' He thinks this blandness to be a wise choice. Wiser than going bananas, that is.

Tariq asks Charlie if he already plans his visits as meticulously as he is suggesting should become common practice. Another trick question, he thinks. To say yes would be a lie that Roselyn could verify; going with no would suggest he is a more dilatory worker than he wishes to present himself as. Or even thinks to be true. 'I'm starting to,' he says. 'Fiona and I work a very difficult case in Derbyshire. Set goals, review them each visit. It works. Fewer extra visits needed, certainly.'

Tariq nods, smiles, maybe he was just giving Charlie a chance to show his practical worth. The man is not a game player, he is straightforward.

* * *

When he comes out of the room, giving a nod to Fiona who is about to go in, the girl with the pink streak in her hair—Cheryl—tells Charlie that he can take an extended lunch hour. It is the upside of going in first.

'I'd like to wait for Fiona.' He obeys orders but not from a girl with braces on her teeth.

'The waiting area is available,' says Cheryl. 'And others will be coming out soon.'

Charlie sits. Looks upon the coffee table by the breakout sofas. He picks up a magazine, it's a holiday brochure aimed exclusively at the over fifty-fives. The hotel's usual custom, he supposes. Thumbing the pages, it comes to him that he has only a dozen years to go. He spent half of yesterday evening contemplating the beautiful black girl—Tawni—a care leaver like himself. He needs to face facts, get real: tedious river cruises await him.

Precious walks across the lobby, shares a joke with Cheryl. Charlie gets to his feet, thinking of the hug Fiona gave when he came into this waiting space after his first task.

'You know each other?' asks Cheryl.

'We all know each other,' says Precious.

'Lovely,' says the girl, drifting back to her desk in an alcove.

'What have you just had?' says Charlie.

'Flippin' interview.'

They have this in common, talk it over. Like Fiona before her, Precious didn't like Rachel. Charlie suspects he fell for her looks. The insight came to him months ago that he is superficial: when his brain idles, the cock thinks. Why do

The Actor

the girls not hate Johnstone? The smarmiest by a mile.

Charlie tells her about the presentation, suggests Tariq is a decent guy in there.

Precious moans about the written exercise. Fifteen emails to prioritise and answer. 'And you know I never answer mine in real life, right?'

As they are talking, two social workers from Child Protection join them, Simon and Ahmed. These two immediately start talking about the role play, the actor. His silly little beard. Both thought the exercise to have been utterly stupid.

'It wasn't realistic,' says Ahmed.

'It wasn't likely,' says Simon.

'It wasn't fair,' they agree upon.

Precious and Charlie have been on the nursery slopes, it seems.

Just four social workers can babble as loudly as a shed full of geese. Cheryl in her alcove places her hands over her ears while looking at her laptop screen. When the other candidates for their own jobs finally come from their assessment exercises, four become eight. They all drift down the corridor and out into the autumn sun. Coffee shops proliferate even this far from the city's hub.

* * *

'I can't keep her any longer,' the actor tells Charlie.

He was prepared for this. At least, he understood that this was the nature of the scenario, the actor seems to have changed it, gone off script. Got it wrong, maybe. The colleagues he spoke to earlier in the week, who undertook the assessment before him, all said that the actor pretended to be a foster carer whose wife had left him and he felt he could no longer offer the foster boy a home. The imaginary boy has just turned into a girl. He thinks to ask if it is a foster child or a budgerigar, restrains himself. Flippancy not a quality sought today. He tries thinking how to proceed now the goalposts have become a netball hoop, worries that his pause will mentally dislodge him from the role he is playing. 'Have you any support?' asks Charlie.

'You,' says the actor. 'I thought you were my support.'

At lunchtime, more than one social worker spoke of wanting to thump the actor. Charlie empathises with them. The interplay continues; Charlie is holding up his end, giving positive strokes. This is a widely used ploy, telling the foster carer how much he values his work with the girl. At the back of his mind, he thinks only safeguarding. They said the girl was eleven but age isn't the issue. He knows that. Foster carers are always vetted but, if this were a real case, he would want to re-evaluate the safety of the placement in the light of the guy's wife leaving him. Placement stability is not the only consideration, however important it is generally. He could go for it, ask the actor if he has sexual feelings toward the girl. If that is why he wants her out. Feeling overly tempted, the murky mucky stuff. Not an accusation, not as such. The actor might thump him, of course, and that too will decide the outcome. He's a forthright social worker, might as well be himself in this make-believe role-play assessment garbage.

'John,' he asks—it is the name that the actor has adopted for the role, could even be his real one for all Charlie knows—'you seem very apprehensive about keeping little Judy here with you, in your home. Do you find you have sexual feelings towards her? Is that what's worrying you?'

As soon as he has said it, he can see Deepika—the team manager who observes him—scribbling furiously on her notepad. He has gone through the gears quickly, made a mark for the observer to comment upon. Worth a note one way or another.

'I don't know what to say,' answers the actor. It comes to Charlie's mind that the guy is finally speaking the truth. He's not as in-role as he thought he was. Never visualised this turn to Charlie's questioning. 'She looks cute,' he says, 'but no. Not sexual feelings.'

Charlie calculates his next steps as though imaginary little Judy's wellbeing depends upon him and only him. Mentally, he has already lifted her from the placement. She sounded no trouble in the briefing, he can get her another placement away from this creep who thinks she looks cute. She's a child in need of a home, not eye-candy for the guy whose partner has buggered off. It was surely an error to place an eleven-year-old girl with a man sporting a goatee even when the wife was home. The actor isn't really acting, to Charlie's best guess. Looks cute, was the rum fucker's first thought on picturing an eleven-year-old girl. Find the guy's real name and prohibit him from fostering as a precaution. Whoa, his thoughts are running amok.

'But is this your area of doubt?' he asks. 'The feelings you find yourself harbouring towards little Judy.'

The actor changes, he snaps. 'Take her away.' He's good at role-play, hand him that. Found out as a pervert and embraced the role.

'Mr Peabody,' says Charlie, trying to look into his eyes, not exclusively at his chin, 'I came here in the hope of salvaging the placement. It is now my assessment that it is for the best that Judy should come with me, as you request. We will find her a temporary place this evening, and a new long-term foster home in no time. I must advise, also, that you remain on our list of approved foster carers; however, I shall be recommending to my manager that a thorough reassessment is conducted before any further children are placed with you.'

That's it. Meeting concluded, nothing more to say. He shakes the actor's hand. What idiot came up with the name John Peabody?

* * *

At four-thirty it is over. Fiona pulls Precious and Charlie into a quick group hug. They all wish to talk before driving back to their respective homes. Fiona suggests a pub, in the end, the three plus Faiza Pitafi and Sian Redmond from the care proceedings team—two more survivors of this assessment day—go across to the same coffee shop they had lunch in.

The mood is surprisingly ebullient. None boast that they have passed but all kept going, performed with some residual functioning brain even in the fourth test of the day. The two who saw the actor in the morning confirm that the foster child was a boy, only flipped gender in the afternoon. They all laugh when Charlie tells them that he outed John Peabody as a paedophile; Fiona says she asked questions about his feelings towards the girl but the actor was straight as an arrow. 'He got his story in order for you,' says Charlie.

Precious worries that she didn't test this angle, missed an important point. Then she says, 'The presentation was my strongest.' Tells them that the Director will use her ideas even if he sacks her. 'That's a win-win for the council, isn't it? Pinch your ideas and then save all your salary.'

Faiza, a well-liked young social worker, but not one Charlie has the measure of yet, says she's heard the whole assessment centre is a sham. 'They have to pretend there's some logic in it,' she explains. 'They can't really compare the value of different social workers. Not meaningfully. No one knows what's going to happen, who'll be most needed for whatever comes next.'

'What will they do then?' asks Fiona. 'How will they decide who goes?'

'Draw names out of a hat. Ted will do it alone in his office, or maybe with the head of Right On Track. The stuck-up one, Marcia. Everyone will believe it's been fair so long as they keep quiet about their little lottery.'

As Charlie grins around he notices his colleagues seem to be taking this bull seriously.

'Names out of hats will do me,' says Fiona.

4.

They are all in the office by nine. Even Fiona could find no reason to do otherwise. They are nail-bitingly nervous. Brenda frequents the toilet like a tic. Roselyn is to tell each their fate. Pass fail, stay or go.

She informs them, at the start of the day, that HR has yet to pass their assessment day outcomes to her. As soon as that happens, she will call them in. Fiona and Yasmin query this. She was part of the assessments on the first two days, must have a pretty good inkling. 'Only what I saw. I've not seen any total scores, and I was never observing you guys, remember.' She looks at her shoes for a few seconds. 'You'll all be okay.'

'We're all keeping our jobs?' asks Precious.

'I didn't say that. I don't know anything. I hope you are. You're good. I won't know until...'

'You must have talked to the other managers,' interrupts Tina.

Others nod at this, it's a fair comment.

'We've tried not to. No point playing detective and getting it wrong. Ted and Right On Track are the ones calling the shots today. We just threw in a bit of feedback, observations.'

Precious gives Fiona and Charlie a questioning look. He guesses she is thinking of young Faiza's conjecture. The hat of fate.

'Nothing said at all?' asks Charlie.

'Only about you telling the actor he was a perv. Deepika couldn't keep that one to herself. Far too funny, Charlie. How Ted and the rest of them have evaluated it is not in my in-tray. Not yet.'

'When will we know?' asks Yasmin. She has been as anxious as any in the team. Any except Brenda.

'I'll be emailed by HR at nine-thirty. Then I've to tell you all within the hour. At ten-thirty, I have to go down to Ted's office for my own feedback. This is one mental day, don't you think?'

* * *

Soon after nine-thirty, Roselyn summons Yasmin Chowdhury into her small office. The alphabet again dictates the order of play.

She comes out wearing a broad smile. Then she says quietly to Graham, her friend, and in Charlie's hearing, 'It doesn't look good to me; Roselyn is in one foul mood. Not over me this time.'

Charlie is pleased for her, Yasmin's a good social worker who has worried too much. Her assessment of their manager is depressing. He knows that Roselyn has consistently told the team they will be safe. She'll hate it if Ted and the Right On Track crowd have sent one or two packing.

Graham Ford leaves the bunker of his desk next. He is duly and unceremoniously caught by a sniper's bullet.

'I fucked up the presentation and the actor shit,' he tells Charlie bitterly, on returning to his desk. 'She says that I can take the day off. Come in when my head's right. It's bollocks. I'll work while I'm here, who knows if I'll be in this stinking place on Monday.'

Charlie has never before heard such anger from young Graham. The drink in the pub, a couple of lunchtime pep talks, none of it worked. He is worried he might have done no better himself.

Brenda Hardcastle goes into Roselyn's small glass office, and the team can see her standing in front of their manager. The words are inaudible and they are few. Brenda never sits; she waves a dismissive arm at one point. When she comes out, she walks past their desks without making eye contact. Charlie is unsure exactly what the words are which she mutters. 'Fucking useless,' or something proximate to it. He thinks he sees tears in her eyes. Feels no surprise at that, only sympathy. She gathers together a few bits and bobs from her desk—a plastic box of uneaten sandwiches—prepares to leave the office. Fiona and Tina both manage to hug her before she goes but there is anger in Brenda's every breath. Her face a different person—a mask of fury—even as her colleagues apply their attempted kindness.

A few minutes later and Fiona, who managed about a five-minute chat with Roselyn, comes out with a shrug and a smile for her colleagues. 'My name was left in the hat,' she tells them.

Charlie laughs, an achievement on this particular day. If Fiona takes anything in life seriously, she keeps it well hidden.

Precious rises to hear her feedback while those in the room are still enjoying Fiona's feigned indifference to the whole charade. Only then does Charlie see that she already has tears in her eyes.

'You're good,' he tells her as she is leaving her desk. 'Good at your job.'

She blinks away her tears, returns his smile.

'Two gone,' he adds unnecessarily, 'that must be the last of it.'

Precious spends a long time inside the glass cabin, talking to Roselyn. They are a pair to gossip together, not that there is time for it today. When she finally comes out, she goes straight to Charlie. 'Good luck,' she says. He is up next.

'You?' says Charlie.

'It was fine. I worry too much, that's all.'

Roselyn stands at the door while Charlie approaches. 'Come on in,' she says. He hears no obvious indicators in her voice. Tells himself that this is a good sign.

She waits for him to pass, closes the door. 'Charlie, Charlie, Charles, a really big thank you for helping me with the team these past weeks.' He nods. He has kept her appraised of the worries of Precious, Yasmin, Brenda. Even

61

Graham. He would have done so without the private pep talk. Charlie is ex-military, respects authority more than any proper social worker should. Ted Astaire has pushed his luck with this whole assessment-day stunt. As of this morning, Charlie hates Ted regardless of his own fate. Who doesn't despise a World War One general? 'Firstly, boyo,' she says, 'you're still in a job. So really well done on that front.'

'Thank Christ,' says Charlie. 'The team can't afford to lose two. Certainly not three.' As he speaks, he sees Roselyn lower her eyes. Guesses what it means. 'You've still to talk to Tina. Is her news bad?'

'That's for me and Tina,' she says. 'I need to give you your full feedback.'

Her evasion has answered the question. This is some hit the team is taking. Graham's departure is the big one for Charlie, even though Brenda's absence will affect the team more. How will he manage as the lone man? An unusual situation for him. The army was nonsense looking back. The other squaddies teased Charlie for having pin-ups in swimsuits on the wall above his bed, where most of the men displayed pornography. In the department, the girls laugh if they catch him watching a woman's behind. Fiona has mimicked his tongue hanging out, which it never does. Graham is young, he must look at girls, he's just not as obvious in the doing of it. It's a generational thing. Charlie is barely listening to Roselyn's feedback. He is still on his feet, although she long slipped onto her swivel chair. Standing to attention, keeping to ritual. His thoughts are all about the decimation of the fostering team. Then he tunes in when she says that all involved graded his safeguarding practice as excellent.

'I think the actor wasn't prepared for you to be so direct. You put the principles into practice: great stuff.'

He learns that his presentation was pretty mediocre. The marks given would not have got him through, but his scores

The Actor

elsewhere were so high it all turned out fine.

'Thanks,' says Charlie. He wonders if it really was just names pulled out of a hat. Aside from his turning the tables on the actor, his feedback doesn't register much at all. Could apply to anyone. Maybe he has blanked out the whole assessment day, forgotten what he said, what he wrote. Even the topics covered. That's how trauma works he long ago learnt. Childhood trauma, the Gulf War. This is less intense but not dissimilar. Brenda and Graham have been blown out of the water. Poor Tina is still to learn what's coming.

'Charlie,' she says, taking his eye for the first time since the opening moments of this talk, 'we're good, aren't we?'

'Of course.'

'I'm dreading my feedback later. Will you come and see me at home this evening?'

He feels astonished by her request. They never met in her marital home when they enjoyed the illicit fling. Months have passed. 'What about Geoff?'

'Gone.'

They stare at each other in silence for over thirty seconds.

'Can I phone you?' he says.

'Oh shit, there's someone else, isn't there? I'm sorry. I should have thought. Asked about that first.'

'I'll phone you,' he says again, rising to leave. There is no one else. Mandy, who has started seeing Barry, is someone else. The question of Charlie's availability doesn't have a fixed answer. He let Mandy down and she will not give him a moment to repair it. He is not entirely averse to Roselyn's proposal. Something sleeping in his trousers has yawned itself awake. Wants to take a look at this evening's menu.

* * *

Tina comes out of Roselyn's office without tears. Just a face of stone. The fostering team has been demolished.

'What will you do?' asks Precious.

'Drink heavily. I was fifty in March. I've had it. Graham

will pick up a job long before I will.'

Charlie doesn't like hearing this envy of a similarly upended colleague. 'You'll both get work. There will be vacancies soon enough; social workers are always needed. You have a hell of a track record, Tina.'

'The liquor cabinet is well stocked,' she says.

Charlie doesn't know if Graham heard the comment about him; Tina's desk is four along from his. He might understand that it's just self-pity, a normal enough reaction. Tina isn't down on Graham. Not as Charlie has ever known. It's been a bad day for both, they must see that. Graham goes across and talks to her. Mutual commiseration. There is relief in the room that neither cry. Precious manages more tears, on behalf of those less fortunate than herself. She acknowledges that it is for them, that she has nothing rational to cry over. Simply feels she must.

Roselyn emerges from her glass box. 'Wish me luck,' she says, as she ventures in the direction of Ted's office. Goes to find out what fate has in store for her. Charlie, Precious, Yasmin all nod in her direction. No such luck wished by the two she could show no mercy. Or Fiona who is busily sorting paperclips.

5.

In the early evening, Charlie calls Mandy and tells her his job is safe. She sounds disinterested, says that Barry is coming around later; she seeks reassurance that he won't do the same. 'The children don't need to see us quarrel.'

'They don't. We don't. I was a jerk. You know I'm sorry about it. Regret.' He doesn't say a thing about the Barry guy. Has no angle on him yet. Hopes his inevitable dislike is not too obvious. He's never met Barry Brice, knows better than to appear narrow minded. It is the thought of a man muscling in on Mandy which he dislikes. Doing so when the

The Actor

poor girl is vulnerable—trying to cope with his adultery—on the basis of that alone he has decided the man is a creep. Hasn't tried to judge, it's simply obvious. And it might contradict her current thinking; he has figured that out too.

When the call is complete, one comes in from Graham. Charlie is unsure what to say, how to console him. It proves straightforward. Graham seeks only reassurance that they will still undertake the walking weekend they spoke of. Agreed to it back in the pub on the day Ted first told them how the department would divvy up its reduced budget. A goal they set—get themselves out in the countryside for a hiking weekend—long before the whole assessment blather really caught fire.

'Yes, looking forward to it,' says Charlie. Graham is a nice chap; it will be good to spend time with him. Perhaps they'll keep up with each other over the months and years. Charlie should hold on to his friends, hasn't tended to so far in this life. He might need them now that family is sliding away.

Next up, he phones his foster-mum, tells her that he was able to retain his job. She congratulates him but it is not fulsome.

'They couldn't really let *you* go, could they?' she says. 'Not being as you understand it all more than any of them. What it's really like being in care.'

Charlie appreciates her certainty that it was a shoe-in while wondering if she thinks his past gets him special treatment. His experience doesn't bear that out. He tells her that a lot of good people lost their jobs. Victims of austerity, government cuts. The diminution of the welfare state.

'Good people, yes,' she tells him. 'It doesn't make them good social workers, like you. Not with the feel for it that you have.'

He thanks her for the comments, thinks she might have lost touch with the reality she once handled brilliantly. She, of all people, must know that more former kids-in-care are in prison than in all the white-collar professions combined. He is the aberration, and Grace Bell is the one who made the difference. Being in care is a good grounding for nothing in particular. Spending three years in her home another matter altogether. She inspired Charlie. Kickstarted him to better than once seemed possible.

It is eight o'clock before he finally resolves that he will phone his manager. As he'd earlier told her he would. 'Hi, only me,' he begins.

'Charlie, are you coming over?'

Her tone is soft, his friend and not his manager this evening. He regrets that he has not resolved the answer to the question before phoning. The two of them have been only in misstep since he told Mandy of their affair. It was a course of action—confessing all—which he never ran past his manager. It surprised her, annoyed her, he surmised. She wanted the fun of it, and no part in the marriage-ruining guilt.

'Ros,' says Charlie tentatively, 'what happened to Geoff? I didn't know...'

'Does it matter, Charlie? He's gone. This has been some day and I'd like your company...' He hears a husky warmth in her voice that he recalls from the summer past. '...I need to feel your arms around me, Charlie. I've missed that, you know?'

'Shall I bring a red. We can talk.'

'Talking?' she says sharply, as though it is a dirty word. 'Hurry. I've got red here.'

'About thirty minutes,' he says.

'Stay over, Charlie,' she purrs.

* * *

Why is he doing this? The thought runs round and round in his head as he drives out of the city to her suburban house. The big old semi-detached he has dropped her off at only once, and that following a work event, long before their

The Actor

affair had even started. Happened. He's driven past it more than he lets himself think about. Did it a few times after the fling was over. Deliberating which relationship to try to revive, and there really was no contest. He has never entered Roselyn's property before. Mandy won in his mental wrestling match those few short months ago. Mandy and the kids. Not that his wife let him explain his thinking. No route back into Bramley Road, and now here he is again.

He has parked four or five houses down the street from her door. Guesses it is the custom in these circumstances. Leave no trail for neighbours' gossip to accumulate around. As he walks from car to front door, he realises that he never asked Roselyn if she secured her post. Perhaps she has gone the way of Graham and this is motivating her need to have him in her bed tonight. Then he remembers how she suggested he join her before she knew her fate—he is not just a consolation prize—not a clue what mood he is walking into. Jubilation, anger. Either might make for good sex, and with the thought, Charlie spots himself becoming superficial again. Roselyn is less predictable than Mandy, to his way of thinking. And he never anticipated his wife summarily dismissing him when he chose honesty over subterfuge. Her assertive ejection of him from the house, from her life. She has Barry tonight. Cannot castigate him for being here this time. When he rings the bell, the door opens in two seconds. Roselyn wears a maroon sweatshirt, grey tracksuit bottoms. She looks as she had in the summer when they went to play squash. Before the tracksuit came off, before the sight of her flesh and the scent of her sweat guided him up the sugar trail. To where he never should have gone.

'Have you come from playing?' he asks.

'I've showered, that's all. I've fuck all on underneath.' She murmurs the second point quietly. Mouth not quite around the final word; he wonders if she is upset, or it could be she's knocked back a little alcohol in advance of his arrival.

He walks into her lounge; its high ceiling gives it a cavernous feel. There is a large open fireplace, unlit, a corner sofa and separate armchair and one large coffee table awash with papers. Work stuff to Charlie's eye. An otherwise a spartan room.

'Where's Geoff?' he asks. He is apprehensive, not a natural stealer of another man's woman.

'He's fucked off. I'm all yours, Charlie. Can you handle that?' He can smell it on her breath now. Some wine or other. Can't be sure either way about the upset. 'Seriously. All yours.' Roselyn thrusts her chest out, pushes it into him with an unasked-for embrace. It feels true—the softness of her breasts against his chest—she has nothing on beneath the sweatshirt. He wants to laugh about it but there is an undercurrent he doesn't understand. Charlie has made love to no one since he last lay with Roselyn. It's been months.

'Ros,' he says, 'what did Ted say? This afternoon. Are you okay?'

'That,' she says, pushing herself away from him, a hand inside the waistband of her tracksuit bottom. Running it around to her hip. She seems distracted. 'It's a complicated story. Not too good really. I won't be managing you, Tariq will. I'll be working on the care proceedings team.'

'Managing care proceedings?'

'Working on the team. It's a fucking demotion really, didn't quite handle the assessment as well as I'd hoped. I live to fight another day.'

'Oh God, Ros. You must be gutted?'

'Filleted, Charlie. Filleted by an arrogant American, I'm sorry to say.'

Charlie sees that her face is crumpling as she says this, an unprecedented thing. Tears flowing from steely Roselyn Pickford. He lowers her down onto the sofa, puts an arm around her. Roselyn half pushes him away but he is strong, holds her and she nestles into him, lets her sweatshirt ride up. He is trying only to comfort her; she is pulling at his clothing. Hers is a confused need, a flight from sympathy. She clamps her mouth upon his. He tastes the red wine that only she has drunk, may have started on long before he phoned her. Pretty slurry of words now he is getting the measure of her. It feels wrong to him, she has quickly found her way inside his clothing. Without understanding the rules of this new incarnation of their relationship, his own hands are within her tracksuit bottoms, touching her most private place. Roselyn is speaking of the pleasure he is giving her, asking him to take her, to put himself inside her. On the drive over, he had a list of questions in his head. He feels dissatisfied with her answer to the Geoff question, can't recall the rest of the quiz he planned. He is removing his socks. She has asserted her authority over him before her demotion diminishes it. In a moment he is upon her, within her, feels enlarged by her. He relishes the physical intimacy, the missing dimension of his recent life. She has an inner strength, tells him how great it is to feel him inside her once more. She takes and pulls him as though they are sharing a task, achieving something together. She gasps, 'Brilliant,' as his performance quickly culminates. He suspects it was less than that, it has been too long. He kisses her mouth, whispers a grateful, thank you, in her ear. There will be more. They are rediscovering the shared pulse they once found. On and off the squash court.

* * *

There was wine and then sleep. Now, at three in the morning and after further mutually enjoyed intercourse, they are talking. He senses a change in her. It is in her nature to assert herself, although the impending removal of a stripe from her sleeve has shaken her confidence. Not completely, she is still who she is, but a regrouping is underway. Charlie likes this less arrogant Roselyn. She seems less expectant, more appreciative. And now she wants to talk about his rounding upon the actor in the role play. She has only heard Deepika's re-enactment. It sounds to be the team managers' highlight. The funniest story in a week of watching social workers squirm in front of their assessors. The tables momentarily turned. Even the managers hated Right On Track, Roselyn's made that very clear. Charlie is not a natural boaster, tells the story diffidently. It was a risk that paid off, not even funny at the time. Everyone has talked of the goateed actor as though he were a jerk, an idiot. Charlie has done his share of it, this time he aims for objectivity.

'He was good at his job. No one liked him because they didn't really want to be there. Stuck under the spotlight, being observed while making up next steps with a tricky customer.'

'He just reacted to the candidate—the social worker—gave back what was given. Passive if unstirred, aggressive if confronted.' Like Deepika, Roselyn had observed the actor sparring with social workers; did it for a couple of sessions when none from her own team were on display. The manager's assessment of the candidate was the point. The thespian antics just the canvas on which it was painted.

'A goatee doesn't look so stupid to another goat.'

'I've missed you, Charlie,' Ros tells him, once more pulling him closer. Her hands upon his naked hips beneath the covers.

He is a muddle of thoughts, of fears. The animal passion is strong within him. Geoff, a team manager across the Pennines—until very recently the sharer of this bed, with this woman—has gone. Charlie seems to be only a short dance sequence from leaving his paltry one bed, moving into this smart residence, and bringing reliability to their opportunistic sex. He has no idea what the moves might be. Nor if she wishes him to attempt such a sequence.

He has been hoping to win his own wife around, not

someone else's. No fix on it yet, no clear view of this Barry bloke. His rival for Mandy has yet to appear in Charlie's crosshairs. It could be a walkover—a bye—will be if he chooses to make a play for Ros. He fears becoming a distant father to his children, avoids thinking about it as much as he is able. Knows it doesn't necessarily follow marital breakdown; he has a past with few constructs from which to form a better expectation. Charlie is many things. A fostering social worker; ex-army; adulterer only with this particular woman; a confused and loving father; a child of a very broken home; a man who speaks regularly to his ageing foster mother. The lucky guy whose name never emerged from Ted Astaire's hat of humiliation.

And now Mandy has a boyfriend. Charlie has mostly been thinking how to prove to her that he is the better man. Imagined that, after however long it takes her to drop Barry—as he thought he had Roselyn—Mandy would allow him back. Give him another chance. Forgiven and wiser for their pointless dalliance. Geoff's departure changes the shape of the drawing, the possibilities; makes this naked athlete in the bed beside him both a hope and a threat. Mandy cannot compete in the energy she has for lovemaking, but Roselyn is the more abrasive and she has mothered him no children. His stupid cock always points in the wrong direction.

6.

On the Monday morning after the cull, Graham tells Charlie the simple truth. There is no appeals process. They all resigned; all previous posts across children's services were deleted. The survivors are, effectively, new appointments made after the assessments were complete. It was in the small print which they signed when agreeing to attend The Kirkaldy. To let Right On Track put them through the mincer. They signed it with a loaded gun to their heads; the alternative was a more ignoble sacking. The giving up of the ghost of a chance.

Roselyn comes over and says a few inappropriate words. 'Thanks, Graham, glad to see you were man enough to come in today.'

He doesn't reply, doesn't even look up. A cough covers whatever he might have said. Tina and Brenda have not shown their faces and her comment feels like an untimely dig. Team members have spoken to them over the weekend, telephoned. Tina has made good on her resolve to drink harder. Brenda said little. 'Let's see what happens next.' It meant nothing then or now. She is not in, not sick and not on leave. Nothing like it has happened in twenty years.

The office is still awash with talk of who has gone and who has stayed. Roselyn is not the only demoted team manager. Deepika Deshpande has suffered the same fate; she will be joining the depleted and reformed fostering and adoption team. No longer the manager of anything, and a salary reduction to go with it. Some social workers are cross about these outcomes; Graham says as much to Charlie. They all thought there was no outside competition, a fair fight for a reduced number of positions, only to find two team managers suffering only the mildly humiliating lowering of their status, and as a consequence two social workers who would otherwise have made the cut must walk austerity's plank. 'We'll never know which of us it was,' he concedes, 'but Roselyn and Deepika didn't even have the same questions or tasks as us. It's not right.'

It becomes more awkward when the two men realise Roselyn is only a desk away, ostensibly talking to Fiona. On overhearing, she comes straight across to kill the innuendo in its tracks. 'Graham, love...' She has never used this term of endearment towards him before. Not in Charlie's hearing, and Graham has never played her at squash. '...team

The Actor

managers did a much harder assessment than you guys. And then the Right On Track jobsworths scored them as like for like.

'Funny that no managers were offloaded,' says Graham, looking away.

'Look,' snaps Roselyn, 'we're bloody good at our jobs. You too—very unlucky—don't blame it on me and Deepika. That's not right.'

Charlie thinks that he hears his colleague mumble, 'Fucking Ted,' but it is barely audible. Roselyn ignores it, maybe shares the sentiment, has possibly done the activity. And to no avail if she has. That thought, his speculative inference from watching the pair of them in the council chamber at the beginning of this whole debacle, he chose not to raise on Friday night.

'We'll have another heart to heart, Graham,' she says. 'I'll be giving you a bloody good reference. You already know that. Don't worry about the day job. Scour job adverts, we're with you.' Then she turns to Charlie and says, 'A word.' Roselyn walks off into her glass box.

He gives Graham a puzzled look and then follows his manager. His boss until the month's end when the slide from her perch is complete.

As he steps inside, closes the door, she says, 'Geoff phoned Sunday. We're going to give it another go.'

He looks into her face, can see no emotion at all. A steeliness that was absent when Graham implied that she and Deepika are the beneficiaries of bias. 'Is that what you want?'

'I said we're giving it another go, didn't I?'

'Sorry, Ros. I'm not trying to argue. I'll just go.'

'Stop,' she says, 'I need to say something about work.'

He does as she asks, stays standing before her desk. She's a different girl from Friday night. The disappointment which made her vulnerable has frozen over, hardened. He waits, she has yet to say what for, then he looks over his shoulder. Charlie looks around too, sees what has caught Roselyn's attention. Through the glass frontage of the little capsule, both see that Tariq has entered the main room. He is speaking with Yasmin and Precious, social workers he is soon to manage.

'Yeah, all I need right now,' says Roselyn.

'It's tough,' says Charlie, 'I can see that. I'm just not sure what the other night was.'

She shrugs. 'It was great, fella. You were great. Just what I needed. Now please keep it between us, eh?' She gestures for him to sit. Charlie falls in. 'Tariq will be managing the team from the start of the month, and you know fostering far better than he ever will. For the first three months, I've fixed you a senior practitioner bonus. It's worth an extra three hundred a month. I hope you're up for it, Charlie. I told Tariq and Ted that you were the right man.'

This is unexpected—left field—not quite kosher. No application, no contest. Fiona might hate him for it. She's the more maverick of the pair; probably understands the textbooks better than he does. 'Is it a done deal?'

'That or Tariq manages alone, and you're so bloody loyal you'd do it all for him anyway. Take the bonus, Charlie.'

He agrees, murmurs that he could use the money right now. House and flat. Then he says, 'Sorry,' as the thought of Roselyn's impending pay cut ambles into his brain.

'You take it, Charlie. I've got to speak to Tariq now. Plan the handover.' With a gesture she beckons her fellow team manager into the glass capsule.

Charlie goes back to his desk. Ponders whether it is hush money that she has lined up for him. He'll tell Mandy about the senior-practitioner thing, the extra money for a short time. Not about Friday night's link. Wouldn't want her thinking that he's the gigolo he isn't. He feels only confused about Roselyn. She can be very distant, doesn't relate to people in the normal way. Lives for work which is a very boring trait. Looks good naked. He decides to concentrate on the first two points. Mandy takes the bout by a majority decision.

* * *

Graham goes out on a late morning visit. Meeting a foster child at Rosebank, at the special school not four hundred yards from The Kirkaldy. The four survivors of the assessment centre take their lunchtime break together. Fiona, Precious, Yasmin and their senior practitioner who is keeping quiet about his new and temporary appointment for the time being. They find a booth in a bar, order sandwiches and soft drinks. No one drinks alcohol at work, every-one after it. Everyone except Yasmin.

'What makes me really sad,' Precious tells them, 'is that none of them will get decent leaving presents. Fourteen social workers goin' to the job centre. If we all put in twenty for each—like they deserve—we'll end up with our electric bein' cut off. That's how thoughtless Ted Astaire really is.'

'Can we give them a joint send-off?' says Charlie. 'Make it a night to remember.'

'Why our team lost three I'll never know,' says Fiona. 'We're good at our stuff. And now we're going to become so over worked.'

'Allocate the work of those three to Deepika,' says Yasmin, a finger to her headscarf. Pointing at her raised eyebrow.

As they talk about the weekend, Charlie learns they all did something special on Friday. Celebrated their success. It is not a conversation they could have had with Graham, or even Roselyn, in the room.

Fiona saw girlfriends, drank more than her usual too much.

Yasmin's husband took her to a Turkish restaurant, 'The full works,' she says. Charlie grins at her apt phrase, the elegant Pakistani northerner. She sees his grin. 'We really pushed the boat out. Sea food. Dead pricey, and I didn't give a monkey's bum about that. Still in work, worth pushing the boat out for, innit?'

Precious says that she and Brantly—her partner—had wine, opened a second bottle. 'And you know I never do that.'

When all have spoken, they look at Charlie. 'I couldn't really do anything,' he says. 'I was having the kids in the morning. Got to keep a level head.'

No one questions this, no one guesses that anything contrary took place. Precious asks about the children. Her eldest is the same age as his middle child, his Michelle.

'Paul wouldn't come,' he says. 'Fourteen now, seeing mates. 'Shelley and Mikey made my day though. Mostly round at my flat, out in the park too. I really...' He lets his voice taper away. He was starting to say he misses them, a mantra he speaks aloud in his flat. He sees no need to burden his colleagues with it. '...it's all good,' he adjusts. 'For us at least. Still in work, still solvent.'

7.

Charlie goes, hopes everyone goes. A farewell get-together for the fostering team as was. All three are coming—at least they have said they will—the team members no more. The shafted.

Fiona is hosting. Her flat in the city is a terrific venue for it. A loft on the top floor of one of the old mill buildings. The lounge could fit a dozen seated. He and Mandy spent New Year's Eve there two years ago. Taxied home.

Tonight, it will be the complete seven, provided Brenda shows up. Danny—Fiona's long-haired partner—is present. Forty with ginger dreadlocks. She's picked an original. He has cooked the food, a task at which—according to Fiona—he is highly accomplished. Precious has brought her

The Actor

husband, Brantly, he's IT, nothing to do with social work. Yasmin has a partner at home. Charlie thinks Tina and Graham both live alone; if they have a romantic interest this is hardly the party to bring them to. It could be a tearful send-off, and the one-dimensional intimacy of working relationships seldom presents a person's best side. Not the place to bring a date.

Tina and Graham have both elected to dress for Halloween. Stupid, in Charlie's view: there are no kids here. The thirty-first of October is the end of their employment with the city, its other designation coincidental. Graham's effort is modest, a T-shirt with skeleton ribs upon it, a mask held in the hand and only fleetingly pulled to his face. Tina looks witchy, made more of an effort.

When Brenda arrives, she is dressed up to the nines. Looks as the team have never seen her before. Hair in a bun, professionally coiffed, elaborate. She was all leggings and sweatshirts at work, poorly chosen clothing for one so overweight. Perhaps retirement will prove a more glamorous vocation. She hands out cards to the other guests, her former team members. They display pretty, arty photographs of the North Wales coastline. 'Lovely working with you,' written inside. Precious bubbles up. She's a fountain at the best of times. They all chat, drink flows. A few nibbles are on the table, the proper food is yet a promise, a smell carried from the kitchen. Danny jumps up and down from his bean bag. Ensuring there will be a feast down the line.

Tina has a carrier bag and brings out a dart board, Ted Astaire's photograph secured beneath the metal grid. They laugh but do not play. Elect not to pierce his smug facsimile.

Fiona, the host, relates an episode from when she was a student social worker, Brenda Hardcastle, her mentor at the time, leading the way with a particular child. A girl who had been in multiple foster placements before Brenda worked her magic. Stability and success came after many, many hiccoughs. Brenda smiles as Fiona tells the story. Must remember it all fondly. 'Little Tara isn't little anymore, this was in nineteen-ninety-nine, now, so many years later she works in television. Her name on the credits of TV shows every night.' They all nod approvingly at this. When Danny asks what programme she is in, Brenda explains that Tara works in wardrobe. Tara became a fashion student when she left her foster carers.

Charlie senses that Danny is disappointed by the payoff: the former foster child picks out clothes. He tells the non-social worker that it is a fantastic outcome, not to be sniffed at. He infers that the academic-cum-environmental-protestor had a secure childhood, doesn't recognise the great achievement that settling down truly is. Securing a steady job. Not falling off the cliff edge. Charlie has managed it too, teetering a bit now. The family breakdown is getting to him.

The talk turns to Roselyn. Brenda says she is the worst manager in her seventeen years in the team. Charlie disagrees, he doesn't think his particular experience causes any bias in his judgement of her managerial skill. Will not be voicing the possibility that it might. On a personal level he finds her slippery; she treats her own marriage like an old umbrella. 'I've learned from her,' he ventures.

'Teacher's pet,' replies Fiona. She smiles as she says it. Never wanted the senior practitioner fuss, she has told him.

Graham says that Roselyn seemed okay to him, although he had no one to compare her to. This was his first job after qualifying. Charlie senses a coming to terms in his young friend. An attempt at reconciling his muddled feelings.

Yasmin gets analytical about it all. 'Short skirts, nice legs and the two fellas in the team think she's good at her job.'

Graham tries to protest; says he doesn't look at her legs. The room laughs at him.

'She looks okay,' says Charlie, 'but that's a different point, isn't it?'

'No,' says Fiona. It's not an evening for fine debate.

Danny brings out some cooked food. Little tartlets with tofu and pine nuts, ingredients that Charlie seldom eats. They taste terrific, and he tells Danny this. Quickly the others begin praising the vegan food. It is alternative, it is what social workers should be eating. Charlie thinks Fiona is the only true vegetarian in the team. And Danny the more hardcore in this household.

Graham has an interview next week for a job in a private company which operates residential children's homes. A role managing the admission process. Assessing and matching children to placements. 'Profit makers, Graham,' warns Brenda. 'It always compromises professional standards.' Precious points out that their team sometimes places children with independent fostering agencies, get a good service from them for the most part. 'Not in my view,' says Brenda, more politically certain in retirement than she seemed just a few days ago.

'The Chope boy—the lad Fiona and I work, who lives up in the Derbyshire hills—the foster carers work through an independent agency. They're not ours,' says Charlie, hopes to show he sides with Graham. He is pleased the boy is sticking to social work. It's a rotten time for it with all the cutbacks. The room quietens. Everyone in the team knows about Russell Chope, the badly damaged boy who was the subject of a presentation at a team meeting three months back. At this moment in time, it is a success story; however, his mental health might always be touch and go.

'The Goodings are brilliant,' confirms Fiona. 'Not the cleverest foster carers, just the most brilliant. On my first visit after he started the placement he was shouting at Colin, Colin Gooding, "I hate you, I'm going to kill you," all the stuff that usually ends placements and Colin just replied, "I hope you don't, mate, because we'll never hurt you. Never ever." It floored him. The kid was apologising to Colin before I'd even left.'

'Kids don't need psychoanalysing,' says Charlie. 'TLC and don't ball them out just because they fuck up once in a while. Forgiveness. The bible's full of it, then no one wants to give it to the most troubled souls in society.' Charlie notices that Danny—not a social worker at all—is scrutinising him closely. He cannot guess what it means, whether he is on his side in this debate, if such it is.

'I reckon you're preaching to the converted,' says Precious. She and Brantly are the only practicing Christians in the room.

'Forgive but learn,' says Fiona.

'It troubles philosophers,' says Danny. He rubs his hand behind his head, a nervous gesture, feeling the frayed hair of his odd dreadlocks. 'The actions people make under duress: who is responsible? The obvious culprits have ready-made excuses. The terrified were terrified, the abused were abused. Repercussions are funny things too, the beating of a butterfly's wings that cause a storm. If I tap my cigarette ash off the balcony out there, it looks an innocent act, not a murderous one. What if it drifts down the three flights into a passing cyclist's eyes, momentarily blinds him and he veers in front of traffic. The car behind him brakes. Too hard. The one behind that tries to swerve around. Bang. Hits the one coming from the other direction. Bang again. The body count goes mental. Is it caused by the drivers? The cyclist? By me, careless with my cigarette ash?'

Fiona looks levelly at her partner. He seems less on edge than anyone else in the room, unperturbed by the discomfort of their three departing colleagues. Charlie has answers to his conundrum queuing up in his head, knows that Danny is the academic. May be the superior maker of a case, whatever claptrap he is cleverly spouting.

'A kid whose arsehole was irreparably damaged with a

broom handle before he hit school age,' says Fiona, continuing to hold Danny's gaze, 'by his dad, the man entrusted to raise him, his own DNA, that kid is not to be blamed if he fucks up every now and then.'

Charlie senses that this disagreement between the couple is not the intellectual one it seems; it might mean much more than the words spoken. He has no idea in which direction they each push and pull the other, cannot tell who is championing what.

Danny nods at Fiona, gives her a curt little smile. 'It's a philosophical view. His trauma gives him a free pass. It won't though. Society will blame him. Everybody but you fine guys in this room feel nothing but fear if they think about that poor kid at all. They'd lock him up just for giving them the heebie-jeebies. You guys are about a million times more liberally minded than Joe Public. It's a good quality but it puts you out there. On the edge with that wee laddie.'

Fiona makes a point of going around the room with red and white wine. Charlie continues to give the gauntlet of their dispute a wide berth. Danny's the philosopher, not him. The gradations of human responsibility, our relative influence upon a situation, are not subjects that this practical man ever dwells upon. There are kids who need help, Charlie is glad if he can give it.

Yasmin and Tina are talking while others are quiet. They all overhear Tina confirm that she expects to receive thirteen months pay in the coming days, it's not a bad sign off. Charlie notices Brenda's head go down. He is not sure if she gets three months or six. It will be no more than that. Close to retirement, the redundancy rules are stacked against her. A fraction of what she deserves.

'I might go and work on a check-out till,' says Tina.

'No,' Yasmin shakes her head, 'you'd hate it.'

'I'm sick of responsibility. I'll not go back into social work unless kids come with barcodes. Decisions about them made by the central computer. Do you know, I hated being given the push, and now it's like a weight off my shoulders?'

Charlie glances at Graham, his eyes go up. Not buying it. His choice of jumping straight back in was roundly rubbished because he won't be working for the council; Charlie disagrees, knows that the government have stymied the local authorities. There are no jobs up for grabs where social workers belong. He would have done the same as Graham, set to work in the private sector if it was the only option. The supermarket check-out must be mind-numbing.

Tina must have seen them exchange glances. 'It's a lottery, Charlie,' she says. 'You praise Ted because he supported you on the complaint case, the foster carers you turned down, but he wouldn't support you if the tables were turned. He smells the shit and runs from it. You turned them down for good reason; their complaint would never resonate with Ted. Having rubbish carers on the books is the bigger risk. He only backed you because you took the cautious option. Kids sometimes need social workers to take risks on their behalf, kickstarting them towards something better than care can provide. But it's a mugs' game. You're always on your own when taking the risk is the right thing to do.'

'What do you suggest?' asks Charlie.

'Work down the supermarket. Safety first.'

* * *

Later, after taking to the dining table to consume mushroom risotto and vegan trifle, they are once more strewn around the lounge, interior lights dimmed, no blinds drawn and city lights shimmering from a few high buildings in their site line. Precious and Graham have only beanbags. Three to a sofa and Brenda in the easy chair.

'The fun will be gone,' says Charlie. 'Deepika is unlikely to provide any. Demoted and what have you. You guys were always the life and soul.'

The Actor

Graham, Tina and Brenda are being eulogised. Their facial expressions are all fixed smiles as they listen to how much they will be missed. It is poor compensation for being dead.

Yasmin picks up Charlie's theme. 'I learned a lot more from you, Brenda, than I ever did from that cow, Roselyn.'

Charlie exchanges a glance with Graham. Bad language from demur Yasmin is a rare thing. And Roselyn more bull than cow.

'Thanks, Yaz,' says the complimented recipient. 'I know I'll miss it—working with all of you—hate how it was done. That ruddy actor. But maybe it was just my time. Donkey's years in the job, a change might be good for me.'

Charlie and Fiona exchange a glance. For him, there is relief in it. Brenda's ire has subsided.

'So, what will you do?' asks Fiona.

'I won't be watching stupid property programmes with Graham. My Graham that is, not you, young lad.'

Everyone giggles, Brenda and Graham are strangely opposite. He and Yasmin once the bright young things in the office and Brenda the dinosaur, the technophobe. Craver of all things pertaining to yesterday.

'And instead?' asks Yasmin.

'I think I should write crime novels,' she says. 'I've read enough shockers. I can do better.'

'Good on you,' says Tina, 'I reckon you could.'

'Not crime,' says Yasmin. 'All dead bodies and brooding detectives. Why not write something cheerful?'

'There's no market for happiness,' says the philosophical Danny. 'Not unless you're telling people how to achieve it. Diet, stress relief, those old chestnuts. And they only sell because none of them work. If one did—bingo—we'd all buy it and be happy or thin or whatever the hell we were chasing. And no one could sell another book on the subject. They wouldn't publish it in the first place. Only bogus panaceas

83

are allowed down the bookshop.'

'Write your life story,' says Charlie. 'Not the personal stuff, not unless you really want to. The trials and tribulations of a fostering social worker. There's a lot in there.'

'Crime novels, they're my bag,' says Brenda. 'I was chronic at writing my self-appraisals. I'm not writing about myself when I don't have to.' Fiona pours more wine. Brenda tries to explain a storyline she has thought up. A break-in while the home owners are on holiday; nothing taken, the intruders leave a dead body under the bed. The pads of all ten finger ends have been disfigured by an electric sander leaving no fingerprints. Half the book will be the search to identify who has died. Where and how. The second half will get to the criminals, the murderers. Those who disposed of the body in this unlikely location. Charlie tells her it sounds great while thinking it terribly farfetched.

Graham makes a move. Soon after him, Brenda and Tina follow. All three carry their small presents, keepsakes to remember their colleagues by. Gift tokens too. Nothing that really raises a pulse but it's a nice gesture. Charlie thinks both ladies had tears in their eyes. The remaining four plus the two partners talk for only a few minutes. Charlie usually finds Fiona easy company but Danny's presence is a strain. An argumentative bugger. Yasmin calls a taxi and Precious and Brantly agree to share it. Charlie has a twenty-minute walk, twenty-five if he saunters. It is over, not even eleven o'clock.

Tomorrow morning Deepika Deshpande will join the newly reconstituted fostering and adoption team. Tariq their team leader.

Chapter Two

A Pint of Beer

1.

Dusk is approaching and they have only passed Bristol, skimming up Gloucestershire now, still a long way from home. Graham is telling Charlie about gay websites, telling him why he never uses them. Charlie keeps glancing at the petrol gauge, realises he'll need to fill up somewhere before they get back. He hates paying motorway prices.

'The guys on those things are mostly just horny for it, not looking for any kind of relationship at all. Some sites claim to be different; I reckon the punters are the same right across the net.'

Out of the corner of his eye Charlie catches sight of a speeding car in the rear-view mirror. Some nutter really going for it. He hears the high-pitched growl of its overworked engine. The guy is gunning it. Not a new car or a decent car. Just gunning it. He glances in the mirror again before changing lanes. Decides to move from middle to inside. The speeder is crazy; he could be involved in a chase, going that fast. Stupid-fast. Charlie can't see it now but it was in the wingmirror a moment ago. The one on Charlie's passenger side is not at the best angle, needs to check that one before swinging across to the inside lane. He strains his neck, starts to manoeuvre. Shit! It's undertaking. The crazy speeding guy is in the inside lane, making a sudden appearance in Charlie's left-side wingmirror. Charlie swings the wheel back; he must get his car out of the way. Really must. A split second too late. The metallic punch pushes up his pulse—the speeding car has clipped his and he was pretty much back in his own lane—the noise is an ugly one. Charlie's car goes into a spin, motion he cannot control. He was clipped at a hundred-and-too-many miles an hour. The nutter was flying. Charlie grips the steering wheel like a rodeo rider does his reins, tries to wrestle the car from its manic fairground ride. He bashes into another car—one hell of a bang, the sickeningly deep cymbal of metal on metal—his bumper into the side of some other poor sod's car. It was the first speeder that caused this, not him. And it's not this other car's fault either. Just plain unlucky. He loses all speed with this second impact, then the car—Charlie and Graham inside—goes into a slow roll, over onto the roof, and then it carries on back up the right way, his magic tin once more standing on its wheels. They have come to a halt facing south on the northbound M5. It all feels like a red-wine headache to Charlie. Unpleasant but he's known worse. He's worried that his car is one of many. He only heard the two knocks, bangs, one into him by the lunatic. Who in their right mind drives tonne-up in the slow lane? He lost control, hit the second car. If there are others, he never heard them. He looks out from where his car has come to rest. Facing the oncoming traffic, but nothing is moving; three lanes have stopped like time itself. All the guys staring back at him must have done some serious braking while he was spinning like a top, him and Graham, and whatever other vehicles caught the worst of it. Traffic noise persists and this puzzles Charlie for a moment, then he glances across to the far side of the motorway, the north-to-south is unaffected. He looks across at Graham while letting out a deep exhalation, following it with a smile: they are okay. The boy doesn't return the look. They are not okay. Charlie stares. His friend is sitting at an awkward angle, head slumped forward.

'Mate!'

A Pint of Beer

Graham says nothing in reply.

Charlie reaches a hand—tentatively, strangely scared to touch—it is not an affliction he's known himself to suffer from. He got through a war without a hint of it. Long time ago. 'Graham, mate.' Now Charlie leans across. He feels the bruising on his own body as he tries to do it, across his chest where the seatbelt gripped him, pinned him to his carousel seat. He unclasps the buckle, leans into Graham. He is out of it, not quite here; Charlie's training kicks in. Feels neck and wrist for vital signs.

'Graham. I'm right with you. Come on, boy. I'm with you.'

He gives the man's right hand a squeeze with his own left, opening the driver's door with his other hand as he does so. 'I'm not going anywhere,' he tells his friend, his former colleague.

Why did he try to change lanes? The fucking speed merchant wasn't in the left-side mirror at first glance, not left, not right, it was like trying to pick up a ruddy aircraft coming in. Christ knows what speed the idiot was doing, it caught him as he was swerving back, trying to get himself out of its line. No accident in twenty years, not on British roads, not driving a private car. And tanks are allowed to knock stuff over. It must have been the other guy's fault. He's the one who's done this to Graham. The lad needs help. Quickly, quickly.

Stepping into the still life of the arrested motorway, the freeze-frame of the northbound carriageway, Charlie sees the growing tailback of traffic. Bumper to bumper, no movement in the near ground, the tailback starting to snake up a Gloucestershire hillside. It looks like a line of beads: the road, still visible in the gloom of the late afternoon, has swallowed the shapes of individual cars, only their lights show after the first fifty yards. Away to Charlie's right—quite close—there is one car upturned on its roof. He thinks he did that, inadvertently. The second car he hit. Charlie and

Graham managed the full three-sixty. Way up the road he sees a red car buckled up into the crash barrier, entwined with it, off the hard shoulder. It has come to rest in the act of humping the metal barrier. That'll be the speeder, going nowhere right now.

A young man comes towards him. 'Are you okay?'

'Ambulance?' asks Charlie.

'My girlfriend's phoning them. I'm a first aider.'

Charlie has that—can't think straight right now—signals for the young man to come to the passenger side.

They both look at Graham; he breathes. Charlie thinks that his head looks all wrong, it's like he has become someone else, the facial expression really isn't Graham's.

'Keep a hold of him, talk to him,' instructs the young man. 'I'd better look inside the other vehicle.'

Charlie nods, he must wait for the ambulance. He doesn't mention the car up ahead to this good Samaritan, a first aider on his game. Anything he can do for the upside-downers is a blessing. The guy in the red car should be last in the queue. Cause and effect. 'We'll get you out of here, Graham,' he says. The inside lane, thinks Charlie, what kind of nutter even thinks of doing that sort of speed up the inside lane.

2.

Charlie had driven down to Seaton on Friday morning, Graham his passenger. A crack of dawn start, dawn coming around pretty late this time of year. They did the coastal walk—it was to be the first of three—Seaton to Sidmouth, in the afternoon. The original plan was to go to the Lake District, only for Graham to chicken out.

'Won't it be rainy and muddy?' he had asked Charlie.

'Torrential, we'll be walking on goo.' Charlie gave this reply with great enthusiasm. Enjoys a battle with the

A Pint of Beer

elements; an adversary as a camping companion.

'No tent,' was Graham's first stipulation, and 'Go south,' his second. It was a surprise to Charlie that Graham was so keen to go, despite also saying his survival skills were poor. 'If I was a caveman, Charlie, I expect I'd be a dead caveman.' That made the older man laugh. He knows that he's closer to the primitive than any normal social worker; trundling up and down the Rocky Mountains of Alberta, a fifty-pound pack on his back, were the best of times. He is not simply a more experienced walker than Graham, it's men and boys.

Doing a stretch of the southwest coastal path was new to him; Charlie knows the Pennines better than he does his own garden or, more accurately, Mandy's garden. Down in Devon, he said, they would need to make use of their map-reading skills. He tried to delegate the task to Graham but the lad was not great at folding and unfolding it. Locating oneself and interpreting its many symbols was out of the question.

The weather didn't look good on Friday. They had a bed and breakfast booked; Charlie accepted that late-November camping is an acquired taste. Graham ribbed him about the size of his tentless pack. Suggested he might have a spare wheel in it. Charlie thought it was on the light side, although there were a couple of sleeping bags in there; not that they would be getting lost but Charlie is a just-in-case sort of hiker. They had decent boots, anoraks. Walked companionably through the drizzle on Friday afternoon. There were some breaks in it, some good clean air. They marched the last two miles in the gloomy dark, no rain actively falling, just a sea mist clinging to their clothing, their faces. Charlie took a flashlight from his pack but there's no shining a light through fog.

'You think of everything,' said Graham, which Charlie likes to believe true. Come the evening they shared a twin room—they were to live out of their packs until Sunday—no return to the car until the walking was over.

They showered in the guest house and then set out to test the hospitality of the town, of Sidmouth. In the dim light across a modestly peopled sea-front bar, Charlie saw a couple of ladies who looked of similar age to he and Graham. One a fair bit older than the other that is. Both had shortish skirts on, and those can catch any man's eye.

'Shall we see if they want to share a table with us?' said Charlie.

During the course of their ten-mile walk, he had shared with Graham that he'd not had sex since assessment day, even shared who the recipient of his last go had been. Graham had answered no when asked if he currently has a girlfriend, offered him no wider explanation for the negative state of affairs.

'Younger one looks nice. Yours.'

'You could try if you want Charlie, just take your pick.' Then he cocked his head to one side, smiling. 'I'm gay, mate,' he said.

Charlie took it in his stride—very surprised, finds life does this to him now and then—it also made one or two odd comments of the year past fall into place. 'Jesus, Graham. Sorry if I've been insensitive, sounded like a randy hetero. Good for you.' Silly phrase to have said, he realised on saying it. Charlie has no idea what you're meant to say, the correct social etiquette for this announcement. Timing it just as Charlie was lining up a couple of ladies for the evening was funny. Why he hadn't spotted it before would gnaw at him, Charlie could already see that. Everything seems obvious looking back.

The pair chose to dine alone. Charlie ordered a steak; fish and chips for Graham. Before the food came, when they were still nursing their first pints of the evening, the older of the two ladies came across to their table. 'Are you two gents sitting alone? Do you mind if Sharon and I join you?'

A Pint of Beer

Extraordinary, thought Charlie, truly extraordinary. He looked across at Graham, unsure if it was an unwelcome turn, although to be gay is not to be lady-phobic.

'Feel free,' said the younger man, a broad grin on his face, one that Charlie thought ironic. He guessed the lady might be misinterpreting it, thinking it meant something other.

When the two women were sitting down, Charlie could see that Sharon was very young. Face made up, powder and paint, perhaps to hide acne scars. She didn't look a quarter as pretty close to as she had across the length of the bar. Might be eighteen and she might not; definitely closer than any girl he's looked at seriously since he first dated Mandy, and he had designated her to Graham before his friend took his breath away. He decided it was politic for him to talk mostly to the older woman, the one who introduced herself as Fran. She turned out to be Sharon's mother.

'You're not local then,' Fran commented when the men told the ladies of their drive down, their walk from Seaton.

Charlie thought his northern accent would have given that away earlier but then reappraised his view. These were the Devon girls of lore: not too bright, not too pretty, just the way the Devon men like them. 'Are you eating this evening?' he asked, intending to warn them of the impending food's arrival, offer them a chance to leave the table unless they wished to watch two hungry men stuff their faces.

'If you're buying?' Sharon tipped into the conversation.

Before Charlie could fashion an answer to the impertinent question, Graham began to question her. 'Where's your father?'

'Up in Exeter and he can stay there,' said Fran over the top of her daughter. Sharon mouthed a 'Yeah,' but it was clearly her mother's answer.

'Did Charlie say that we're both social workers?' Graham was up to something, Charlie uncertain quite what.

Fran whispered something to her daughter, then turned to Charlie. 'If you're eating, we'll leave you to your meal,' she stated. And then they left. Not just the table, the establishment too. Girl and mother walked right out the front door.

'Well played,' said Charlie.

'Social workers can't really cavort with prostitutes.'

That threw Charlie. Were they really? Pretty odd approaching strange men with her daughter in tow. He started to say they were just lonely, stopped himself before three words of the nonsense were out. He saw Graham in a more worldly light. Spot on about the social worker-tart thing. He hasn't touched one since leaving the army.

3.

'Can I see Graham,' Charlie asks the nurse.

'Lie still, please,' she says. 'The doctor is with him, doing all she can.'

'Is he awake?'

'The doctor is doing all she can.'

The lights in the hospital are far brighter than Charlie thinks necessary. It's not as if he is in theatre. They are neuralgically bright, he worries that they are flickering at a frequency that doesn't agree with him, makes him nauseous. Or something else is doing it if it isn't the lights.

'Is Graham in theatre?' he asks.

'I don't want to give you the wrong information. The doctor will be doing all she can.' The nurse wears a starched navy-blue uniform, he has registered that much, cannot picture her face although she was within his vision a moment ago. The voice is consistent; there may be other navy-blues on the corridor; only this one is attending him.

The light is playing with his vision. Or is it the worry?

A young chap breezes into the small cubicle, he wears the

A Pint of Beer

green of the paramedic, or possibly of a doctor, green pants, green top. Plasticky looking things; he has a white T-shirt poking out from beneath. The funny green jacket is short-sleeved, shorter than the T-shirt. The man's arms are thicker than Charlie's. Pumps iron by the look of him.

'I'm Dr Graham,' says the new arrival in the confined space. 'Let's check you over.'

'Thank God. How is he?'

'Sorry...'

'Graham.'

'Yes.'

The confusion takes a moment to clear.

'I've not seen your Graham, I'm afraid. Time to worry about him once we've got you back on your feet.'

'I'm terrified for him, doctor.'

Charlie finds himself welling up. He is lying on the aluminium-framed bed, on his back. He imagines that the tears are stuck, cannot emerge from behind his eyes so long as he retains this posture. But they are there, gathering. May drown him.

Dr Graham feels Charlie's limbs in quick succession. 'Nothing broken there.' Charlie knew that. And the nurse has checked him over already. Did it more thoughtfully than this pompous young ass. 'I'd like you to sit up.'

Charlie groans as he pulls himself into the position requested.

'Where was that?' asks the doctor. 'Did something hurt?'

'Inside my head. It's throbbing.'

'Can you tell me how many fingers you see?'

'One, only one.'

'I'm going to cover one eye and shine a light in the other. All right?'

The examination doesn't last long, but there is a moment in which Charlie panics, thinks the nurse has left him alone with the half-wit doctor. He looks around, has to twist his body to do so. 'You're there.' Charlie's voice finds a warmth for her that has been absent since the car flipped. The nurse is tying her shoelace, starts to rise back up. 'I'm sick,' he says suddenly, realising its imminence only as the second word has left his lips. The nurse steps into him, as if to check or assist; Charlie vomits on to the bed, his clothing. All over the nurse's clothing. She wears a thin throwaway apron; it won't have spared her completely.

'Dear oh dear,' says Dr Graham.

This doctor is fussing like an old lady. It annoys Charlie: he's been in a car that turned over, Graham's unconscious. Not a playground tumble. 'Sorry. Oh hell, I'm sorry.'

'Not to worry,' says the nurse.

For the first time, he sees her face, registers what she looks like. She has black hair tied back, her eyes and nose look like his colleague, like Yasmin's back in the office. It's nice to see but the voice isn't her. Nothing Yorkshire about it. 'I'm sorry,' he repeats. 'You'll need to wash them now.'

'Ushna,' says Dr Graham, it's a quiet aside to the nurse whom he beckons to step outside the cubicle. Charlie is holding tissues which she has given him, cleaning himself up. His clothes aren't too bad; she got the worst of it.

When the nurse steps back into the cubicle, she is alone. 'You've had a shock. The doctor doesn't think you need to be admitted, he does advise that you rest here for a short while.'

'Is your name Ushna?'

'It is. Did you hear my...'

'Can you take me to see Graham, please Ushna?'

'I haven't asked about your friend yet. I know you're very worried about him. The doctor will be doing all she can.'

4.

At breakfast in the guest house on Saturday morning, Graham was a different person. No longer the redundant rabbit who had stalked the council offices for the last fortnight of his brief public service career, nor even the shy young man who preceded him. Charlie enjoyed the transformation.

'Sniffer Quested, eh? Checking out the skirt in Sidmouth. Not your prettiest side, mate, but I suppose it's got to be done. Or rather, you suppose that while I, in stark contrast, lead a life of calm restraint. I don't carry a sniper's rifle to pick off the pretty girls or boys...'

'I chat, Graham. I don't use force. One should never carry munitions on a night out.'

'...and even the not-so-pretty ones might get sprayed if they come across your sightline.'

'Graham! I don't even know what that means.'

'You made me laugh, Charlie. So keen for us to be lads out on the pull, you forgot to check if I was a credible wingman, didn't you?'

The former soldier chuckled. 'You'll do. Saved the day probably.'

'Pulled the old man off the honeytrap, did I?'

'Marmite, Graham. Those girls were trying to spring the old marmite trap. I would have got myself out alive without you, but thanks.' Charlie looked levelly at his friend. 'Did you guess before you agreed they could join our table?'

'You were lining them up before they volunteered. Your ability to sniff out a chuck-herself-at-you girl from fifty paces is an astonishing bit of kit, Mr Quested. You should patent it, bottle it, sell it on.'

'Everyone wins the tombola once in a while. The snag is the prizes are generally that shit.'

Graham exploded with laughter when Charlie said that. 'I thought the same, and I haven't any qualifications in womanising. Don't really see what the fuss is over the best of them. Those two were no-hopers, weren't they?'

'I'll be honest,' Charlie told him, 'I thought having a

younger bloke with me when we came here would improve my chances in the evening light, so your sudden switch to gay was a negative...' He looked Graham in the eye. '...for me, not for you. Obviously.'

Graham's laughter spluttered on. 'You've known me for a year, Charlie. Do I attract the ladies?'

He took his time answering. 'Yasmin always liked you.'

'Married Yasmin who steers away from most blokes.'

'And Yasmin knows you're gay?'

'Not really. I don't talk about it.'

'Not until yesterday evening you don't.'

'Charlie...' Graham had a broad grin on his face as he said this. '...I only came out to pull you back from the temptations of Devon's tartest. It nearly didn't work.'

'Yeah. I was a fool to suggest it; should have looked closer before...' Charlie lets his thought drift across the quiet of the dining room. 'Glad you delivered the verbal bullets, pulled the plug.'

'And me? Now, Mr Quested, in fair recompense for my act of mercy, you and I are going to pull some cock tonight.'

'God, Graham. I can't, I owe you but...'

Graham bent his head down to the dining table, a more uproarious laugh than Charlie has ever before heard from him. 'You think I don't know that?'

5.

'Are you all right?' asks the nurse. It's a different one, older, tiny. Filipino, Charlie thought when he first saw her. Now he thinks nothing, his head is swimming. The nurse takes hold of his hand. 'Clammy,' she says.

Charlie has slumped into a chair, he put himself there for his own safety when her words sunk in. He has found the room in which Graham is resting.

The nurse came out to speak to him. 'You may be able to

A Pint of Beer

help us,' she said.

Charlie replied, 'Of course,' and then she started talking about relatives, who to contact, and how. He said, 'I can look on his phone if you've got it.' He was thinking quite clearly but when the nurse said the bleed-on-the-brain phrase, he sank straight away. Found the chair by chance, felt like he was gulping for air. He was at the wheel of the car. The other guy was to blame: undertaking, that's no way to drive. Not at a hundred miles an hour. Charlie at the wheel with Graham shotgun, feels like his fault when it probably isn't.

'I'm sorry,' says the nurse, 'I didn't know you didn't know.'

Charlie is drawing deeper breaths now, gathering himself in. He's a soldier, dammit. 'The phone,' he says.

'Wait,' says the nurse, she signals for a colleague to come across.

'Yes, Carmel?' says the young nurse as she approaches.

'Stay with this gentleman, a few minutes please, Natasha?' Then she turns again to Charlie, 'Please could you tell Natasha your name.'

'Quested,' he says, 'Charles.'

The older nurse, Carmel, says something quietly to the younger, to Natasha, he doesn't hear what it is. Charlie feels foolish, nearly fainting on the battlefield. He can see Graham through the glass side of the room; there is a plastic curtain but the nurses have left it undrawn around his feet. From the angle Charlie looks in, he can see his head, see the whole bed. Graham must be sleeping. He lies on it, propped up at forty-five degrees, his face uncovered. That is a good sign—good in a rotten world—he is not dead. A bleed on the brain: Charlie can't remember what that really means, what the prognosis might be. It sounds awful, brains are important.

'Do you often get like this?' asks Natasha, once the older nurse has taken herself back into the small brightly lit room in which Graham lies.

Raspberry Jam

He shakes his head, looks at this young nurse, her blue uniform shines against the black of her skin. It sits in Charlie's mind that she should be tending someone who has something actually wrong with them. Charlie's okay, not as tough as he used to be, might sum it up. 'Do you know how he's going to be?' He gestures Graham through the glass.

'I've not been with him. Is he your friend?'

'Work colleague.' Charlie dips his head into his hands, both palms holding his face just a few inches above his knees. 'And a friend. He is my friend. Not even a work colleague anymore. What I'm saying is that he's just a friend. A good one.'

6.

After the full English, the two men set off on their hike. Went along a short stretch of B-road before they came to the footpath, the walk proper. Graham's mood remained buoyant, he told his former colleague about the induction week he has undertaken with Stretch Care, the company which has rescued his social work career.

'I'm not in next week,' he said, 'not until the police check comes back; did the induction because it was all classroom.'

'Did you learn anything?' asked Charlie, a sceptic about the private sector but no critic of Graham for keeping in work.

'They were good, Charlie, really well thought out. They've got a better psychological model than anything we used to use in City. Within the grasp of all the foster carers. Not just lip service.'

This surprised Charlie; Graham is no mug, his insight worth giving thought to. For half a mile or so he asked him questions about the course. Details. As they talked, they found their way onto the footpath. It quickly deteriorated to mud. The rain in recent days has been intense.

A Pint of Beer

'Your jeans are pretty splashed,' Graham told Charlie.

'I hope you've brought a second pair,' said the soldier.

They came to a kissing gate—rusty old iron, the narrow gate all flat bars, a semi-circular frame containing its swing—connecting two fields. Charlie held his ordinance survey map out before him, dry within its waterproof mapholder, and then the sky opened up. Rain came pouring down. The narrow gateway was already awash with soft mud, the heavy downpour brought the puddles to life, their surfaces a frenzy of activity. The foul conditions rendered each step a squelch, the weight of the sticky earth slowing them down. Trying to stop them altogether, it seemed.

'At what point do we turn back,' said Graham, spoken loudly to cut through the drumming rain.

'At the end of the line.' Charlie was determined to put Graham through his paces, give him the full outdoor experience. Staff Sergeant Quested shaping a new recruit.

They kept going, it was always the plan. The walk meandered inland, many ups and downs before it would return them to the coastal path near Budleigh Salterton. Graham queried the distance they intended to cover that day. 'Eighteen miles of mud,' he called it when told.

'The forecast is fine, Graham. This is a freak shower.'

As Charlie said this, taking a stile into a small copse at the far end of the field, Graham's muddy boot slipped off, stayed in the mud as he was walking on. He stumbled forward, falling but catching himself with both hands. He had to put one knee down before arising, turning to show Charlie his two brown hands, the splatter of mud on his knee.

'Camouflaging yourself, good thinking,' said Charlie, and the younger one laughed.

The heaviest of the downpour seemed to be behind them; their waterproofs were decent. Graham got his boot back where it belonged. 'Tie it tight,' his commanding officer instructed. 'Onwards.'

As they made their way onto higher ground, something Charlie promised would give them a great view, Graham asked a question about the assessment day, wanted Charlie's opinion. Before he had time to answer, Graham changed tack, said to him, 'How do you know the views are good? You told me you'd never been here before.'

'Maps, Graham-lad,' answered Charlie. 'Look at the contours, you can visualise the high ground sloping to the sea.'

They walked on in silence. 'Too misty to see much today,' observed Graham.

Charlie thought it might clear in time; there were a lot of dark clouds but the wind was stiff enough to shift them. 'What was the assessment thing, Graham?' he asked. 'You were just unlucky, you know?'

'I wondered if you guys have compared feedback, made any sense of it?'

'I think those that passed were just relieved. When I give feedback to students on placement, it's mostly just positive strokes. You give it more thought when you're failing someone.'

'They ripped into me about my presentation. Said I'd tried to justify my role in the approval of foster carers based on a simple checklist, that I never showed a feel for the job. No real insight.'

'Ouch. You were great at that stuff. We worked a couple of applications together.'

'My thinking was that if you try and say you've got this sixth sense, something that helps you spot who will and who won't come up to the mark, you simply sound full of yourself. Like you're going to jump to unjustified conclusions. The checklist stuff is being fair, comparing like with like.'

'Don't beat yourself up about it. Did the panel ask you questions after the presentation?'

'Only Tariq, a nice enough question I thought at the time.'

A Pint of Beer

The rain intensified once more. Charlie looked crossly up at the sky. He'd wanted better than this. 'Uh-huh?' he said. 'About what?'

'How will your plan improve our department's performance? That was about the size of it, the question Tariq asked.'

'The trouble might be that Tariq wrote all the current procedures. He probably thought you were being critical of where he'd got the department to.'

'You think if I'd said present practice couldn't be improved upon, I'd still be in a job?'

'Who knows? The place isn't the same without you around.'

After he said it, Charlie thought he heard a little snort from within Graham's cagoule. The least talkative team member at most meetings. Being the only man working in fostering and adoption doesn't suit Charlie; he would have him back in a flash. Quiet Graham, or the loud one from breakfast. A good bloke whichever mood takes him.

The rain was falling harder and harder. They were on the edge of open country, looking across to a farmhouse about four hundred yards further on, the odd copse of trees, and a proper woodland away in the distance. Charlie looked at the black clouds massing above them.

'We could go and stand in that barn,' he said. Graham looked at him, hadn't heard his words through the raging wind. Hailstones started to fall from the sky. Charlie shouted his idea again. Pointed. The barn attached to the farmhouse. They upped the pace to a trot. Charlie felt like a soldier again, running through the storm with a backpack weighing down on his broad shoulders. Graham kept up with the pace, fitter than Charlie feared he might be. Lightly panting, they ducked inside the barn. 'At least the roof is still on,' said Charlie, looking at the stacked hay bales. A few rusty farm implements hung on hooks on the walls.

'Hide until the war is won,' replied Graham. Graham Never-a-Soldier.

7.

Charlie is looking at Graham's smartphone. No lock on it, he got into the contacts with a swipe and a button press. He scrolls over the names; his own is in there, and Yasmin Chowdhury. Most mean nothing to him. Caroline Ford and Rachel Ford must be his mother and sister. He tries to recall which is which, while thinking about how formal the naming is on this phone. It doesn't simply say, Mum, as his phone does for Grace Bell's number. Graham has spelled out his mother's Christian and surname, whichever of the two she is.

He has the use of a side room; the nurse named Natasha ushered him into it. Just a couple of doors down from the one Graham has just vacated. Charlie doesn't know if they have taken the poor lad to ward or theatre. He should have asked. Graham is to be operated on sooner or later. 'Looked at,' was the term the doctor used. Not the casualty department doctor, one who has come down from elsewhere in the hospital, may have come from his home. Come specially into wherever in Gloucestershire this hospital sits from whatever town or village he makes his home in. It is a Sunday: Charlie doesn't know if brain surgeons spend the weekend waiting for accidents to happen. It seems unlikely, however necessary. He appreciates how readily available this one has made himself.

He elects to go for it, tries calling Rachel Ford, it sounds like the older name to him.

'Graham,' says the nasal voice which answers the call.

'Hello. Is that Mrs Ford? This isn't Graham speaking.'

'No, I can hear that. Why are you using his phone?'

'Mrs Ford, I'm a friend of Graham's. We're at

Gloucestershire Royal...' The silence from the other end of the telephone is a blank face to Charlie. He speaks the lines he'd thought to tell. The car accident; confirmed that he was driving it. The bleed on the brain; her son will be in surgery at some point this evening.

She hears him out, offers no opinion. It must be difficult to take it all in. 'Thank you. Thank you for informing me. Did you tell me your name?'

Charlie is unsure if he did or didn't, does so now. He tells the lady that he and Graham were both social workers together for the city council before Graham changed his employer. She listens but says nothing. He cannot fathom how close mother and son might be.

'Will you tell his sister, Caroline, or would you like me to?' asks Charlie.

'Oh, I'll tell her, Mr Quested, but would you call his father, please?'

Graham has been coming out of himself this weekend, and now this call is revealing how private a person he is. His parents separated, and he didn't mention it all year they have been colleagues. Charlie would have remembered that, would have felt sympathy. His similar circumstances and everything. 'I don't think I've got his number,' he replies.

'Have you a pen, young man?'

8.

'I'm soaking,' said Graham, rubbing the heels of his hands against a large round hay bale. 'Look at me.' The bedraggled young man spread out his hands, indicated his soaking wet jeans, a mud stain on his right knee, the fringe of his hair dripping with rainwater from the hood of his kagoule. He looked a bit of a state.

At least the crown of his head should be dry, thought Charlie. 'There might be a tap in here,' he said, ever practical.

Graham's attempt to clean up was not a success and, whether he knew it or not, there was a smudge of mud on his cheek. Inadvertently transferred there by hand, most probably. Charlie walked to the back of the barn. Found no water outlet but came across a door he hadn't initially noticed. A faded butcher's apron hanging from a clothes hook was covering the handle. He grasped it, pressed down and the handle gave, pushed it open and he stepped through. Charlie quickly withdrew, barely crossed the threshold. Came back into the barn and closed the door behind him. Looked at Graham. 'It's the kitchen,' he said. 'Pots and pans, a private kitchen. We can't be going in there.'

The thrumming of rain on the barn roof was rhythmic. Far away, thunder rumbled. Graham appeared to be laughing, not with any sound, just enjoying being inside a barn. Out of the reach of the elemental forces which were trying to disrupt their weekend.

Charlie saw movement out of the corner of his eye, guessed its cause quickly and correctly, clicked his fingers and a black and white cat emerged from behind the row of hay bales. The cat stopped ten feet from Charlie, not minded to approach a stranger any closer. Nor did it scurry away. The barn was the cat's domain, the men were the intruders.

Graham took off his kagoule, threw it on top of the hay bale the side of which he had rubbed with his muddied hands. He tugged at his sweater, trying to gauge how wet it really was.

'We'll move on when the rain eases,' said Charlie.

Graham shrugged; they had a long walk planned but only to return to the same guest house at day's end. A flash of lightning, then a thunderclap, brought another smile to his lips. Charlie's talk of the rain easing was premature.

As the sound of thunder faded and they adjusted their ears back to the simple pelting of rain on the barn roof, the door which Charlie had earlier peered through flew open.

A Pint of Beer

The twin barrels of a shotgun poked out of the doorway. 'Off my property! Off my property!' shouted a woman's voice.

Charlie signalled for Graham to duck down, 'I'm sorry, madam, we were only sheltering from the rain. Didn't intend to trespass.'

'Off my property. Robbers and burglars, I can shoot. I know I can.'

'Madam, we're walkers caught up in the rain.' As Charlie said this, a woman came through the door from which only the rifle's nose had previously protruded. Grey hair, not that she looked so very old. Prematurely grey. A light-blue housecoat with navy-blue slacks beneath. 'Madam, we're not burglars. We're very sorry to have disturbed you...'

'Keeping out of the rain,' said the woman. 'You'll be wanting a cup of tea then.'

Charlie glanced at Graham, who was behind the hay bale. 'Can you put the gun down, please? We're really sorry that we've disturbed you.'

'Oh, this isn't loaded, I was just trying to frighten you. Thought you were gypsies.' Graham came out from behind the hay bale, holding his hands in the air. 'Stick 'em up, Muddy Face!' said the woman, grinning as she said it.

'Is it okay to put the gun down now?' asked Charlie again.

'Come in the kitchen for a cup of tea, then,' said the woman, the gun quickly put over her shoulder as she turned to go back through the door.

'We can leave you in peace,' said Graham. Another streak of lightning, a further crack of thunder, as he said the words.

The woman turned back on her heels, swung the gun around, pointed it at the younger man. 'I said, a cup of tea.'

'We'd like that,' said Charlie, 'but please put the gun down.'

'I told you it's not loaded. It just feels good. I've got one and you haven't.'

'Madam,' Charlie made a hand gesture, flat palm facing

forward, wanting to hold her attention. 'We will walk away. We're not coming into your house at gun point. We never intended to enter your home; it was the shelter from the rain we wanted, that was the only reason we came into the barn. You're right. It's your private property. I'm sure we shouldn't have, so we'd best go.'

'Nonsense, everyone needs a cup of tea. Look!' The lady swung the gun ninety degrees to the left, pulled on the trigger, but nothing happened, no audible noise. 'Bang, bang,' she said.

'I'll be putting it away, just come through, will you?'

'Can I carry the gun? I'm ex-army.'

'Oh, you're an army boy, are you? Well, this gun won't help you, not unless you're going to hit me over the head with it. I've no bullets, not had any since Gordon left. Maybe not for a tidy time before that.'

Charlie held his hands out. 'Can I see it, please?' Graham was standing silently by the hay bale, far more apprehensive than his friend. 'Cup of tea, mate,' Charlie said to him.

The woman laughed, 'That's the spirit.' She handed over the double-barrelled shotgun. 'Take a look.'

'Thank you,' said Charlie, turning aside and he immediately broke open the weapon, thrust his nose to the opened chambers. 'Not been fired in anger in a long while,' he said loudly to no one. To Graham via that circuitous route.

'I told you. Gordon shot it last.'

'And he's no longer living here?'

'No. He won't stop you two scallywags from raping me and nor will that gun.'

Charlie noticed that the grey-haired woman's expression turned suddenly forlorn. He wondered if he was wrong to take control of the gun, then quickly thought better of it. Having it pointing at him had been no fun at all.

9.

'Mr Ford?' asks Charlie tentatively.

'Speaking.'

'I'm calling from Graham's phone.'

'Graham who?'

'Ford. Your son, Graham Ford.'

'Right. Got you now.'

Charlie takes a moment's thinking time; can't fathom the relationship between them at all. 'Your wife gave me this number.'

Mr Ford starts laughing. 'She did, did she. Ex-wife. And who might you be?'

'I'm Graham's friend. I'm sorry to tell you, he's in hospital.'

'Good heavens. I didn't realise. What happened?'

'There's been a car accident. I was driving...'

Charlie explains as best he can. Says the motorist undertaking him was doing a tonne. Mr Ford asks a question or two, seems to take in the bleed on the brain, gives it a respectful pause to contemplate. When Charlie tells him that his son is going into surgery, he says, 'They can sort it? Well, thank God for that.' Charlie doesn't want to cast doubt on his assertion but he has many. Thinks himself more worried than the father of the injured.

When the conversation seems to be drawing to a close, Mr Ford interjects, 'I'm Brian, by the way.' Charlie has confirmed his identity at the outset, does so again now. The guy probably didn't take it in, was still waiting to learn the purpose of the call.

'Are you Graham's special friend?' asks the father.

Charlie finds himself caught between amusement at the antiquity of the phrase, and recognition of the dilemma Brian Ford is in. How would he approach future partners of Mikey's if his own boy turns out to be gay? Paul isn't,

Charlie's certain about that. He's caught him looking at eighteen-plus web pages, porn of the heterosexual variety. Similar to those he's chanced upon himself.

'I'm not. I'm just a friend.'

'...and I don't know what he's told you about me. I'm really not half bad. His way of life is just new to me, not something I can give a lot of time to thinking about.'

Charlie could tell Brian Ford that Graham never even told him his parents have separated, divorced, whatever it is that they have done, but that might imply that he is ashamed of them. Graham's feelings on the matter are completely unknown to him. Charlie has no wish to heap further agony on Mr Ford. His son is fighting for his life.

'...and please don't get me wrong: if you make each other happy, then I'm actually pleased for you. For my Graham in particular.'

'You've misunderstood, Mr Ford...'

'It's Brian. I will tell him how I feel, once he's through this operation.'

Charlie finds himself recalling the dumb homophobes in the First Armoured Division. He is unsure if Mr Ford is better, worse, the same. Maybe he—Charlie Quested— would have remained as unenlightened if he hadn't chanced upon a social work career. A liberal profession.

'Graham's my friend,' he tells the lad's father. 'I'm praying this op goes okay, really praying.'

'Yes,' says Brian Ford. 'Hospitals are marvellous; they won't let him down.'

10.

The lady told them her name. 'Just Irene. Not Renee or any of that.' Charlie and Graham tried to communicate with each other using facial expressions which they took care to hide from her. Charlie was trying to warn his friend that she

A Pint of Beer

is mentally volatile, a difficult statement to make with eyes alone. Graham's expressions suggested he thought her batty as a fruitcake. Irene sang a pop song while boiling a kettle, filling a teapot. Not a song that he knows. She said it was always on the radio but Charlie's never heard it.

Take up this song
So many years have gone
Take up this song

Could have been making it up as she went along for all he knew. She held a tune tolerably well.

'Cat got your tongue?' queried Irene once she was sitting at the table with the two men. She insisted they must drink their tea, said again that the gun was only to scare away gypsies. Her conversation was odd, she sounded alternately vulnerable and carefree. Neither featured in Charlie's expectations of a Devon farmer's wife.

'Do you farm the land? I saw the hay bales.'

'Of course I farm the land. You've not come to take that off me as well, have you? It's what it is: a farm. I live on a farm.'

'And you farm it on your own?'

'Gordon comes in and bales for me, does the tractor work. Cleans out the money from what I can tell. And him with his floozy and all.'

Graham came to life at this point, seemed to finally trust that the gun was gone for good. 'Gordon still farms? Even though you've separated.'

'I don't care for him; wish he'd never been my husband. I can tell you that for nothing. He can still do the jobs I set him. That seems only right and proper. You see, young man...' Irene stretched herself upright in her seat, held her mug of tea out before her like she was proposing a toast. '...it was always my farm, inherited from my father before me. Gordon never had any right to it save what I let him have. Now, will you be having some ginger cake.'

'Look, Irene,' said Graham. 'The whole gun-thing scared the bejesus out of me. Is it really so dangerous up here?'

She laughed. 'If I had a few cartridges, you wouldn't be sitting here.'

'No, honestly. Have you had break-ins? We're city people, live up north, and I used to be London. Know nothing of rural Devon.'

'No, you don't,' she said, a sharp swing to her head as she glanced between her two coerced guests. 'Oh, you probably have muggers where you are, think we just tend little lambs down here. You don't have the gypsy problem though, do you? The dirty so-and-sos hankering down in your fields. All over your property.'

'Accommodating different ways of life is difficult...'

'Don't defend the bastards,' she shouted. 'It was their lot who got Gordon chasing the floozies. Thinking he could do what he liked with who he liked. That's just the way they live.' She shouted this at a high volume.

Charlie made a hand gesture to Graham. Dial it all down; don't ask too much of this frumpily dressed fire-cracker. 'We can go, Irene, if our presence is upsetting you. It's your house.'

'Be quiet, Charles. You've not eaten your ginger cake...' Again, Irene made the quick darting eye movement, looking hurriedly between the boys. '...maybe he should go.' She eyed Graham as if he was a tarantula at large. 'I never wanted you here first time around.'

Graham looked at Charlie, a quick swivel of the neck, and back to the strange lady. A look of surprise on his face, widened eyes. She had no objection to him before this abrupt turn.

'You marry me, you take up with your floozies, you bugger off, and then back you come like nothing matters a jot. And it's Graham that you're calling yourself now, is it? That isn't going to fool anyone.'

'I'm sorry,' said the younger man, 'have I misunderstood something?'

'No, you're getting it now. I could have given it to you with both barrels if I'd only had a bit of shot. Ha-ha.'

'Irene...' With a deliberate exhalation, Charlie began using the calming tone Graham will have heard a few times back when they shared cases, the voice with which he introduces himself to a new foster child, explains to a prospective foster carer the reasons they are being turned down. '...this is Graham Ford. I really don't think you've met him before.'

'He can call himself anything he chooses, can't he? I could tell you that I'm Princess Marry Me from the Back of Beyond and you'd have to believe that I was, wouldn't you? Have to unless you'd met her already, married her already. Had yourself the chance to know better.'

'But I know you're Irene, and this is my friend, Graham.'

'Graham, Gordon, whatever he's calling himself now.'

Graham looked across at Charlie, eyes discreetly frowning. Charlie couldn't make head or tail of the crazy talk. Her ex-husband was unlikely to look a thing like Graham, must be twenty or thirty years older. The young man sat across from her with worry written all over his face.

11.

Charlie hands the telephone to Natasha at the central workstation. 'See that it's kept with his belongings, please?' He has written down numbers and addresses, names. He helps Natasha fill out next of kin information.

As she is tapping the keys of the computer, electronically logging all the information she can about the new patient, the nurse pauses, scrutinises Charles Quested. 'Sir,' she says, 'you don't look well.'

Charlie looks into her face. It's true that one of his eyes is flickering involuntarily, the eyelid moving repeatedly and he cannot control it. As he starts to speak, he has to suck in saliva. He thinks he is okay: a psychological wound is not a real one. But the events of the day—the motorway and here in hospital, learning of the brain injury Graham has suffered—have brought him to a dark place. Unlike any feelings he's had since the day Mandy threw him out. He coped then—sort of coped—hand-to-mouth for the first week or two. He drank as well, drank a hell of a lot on at least a dozen occasions. Something on those lines is troubling him now. Gnawing away. At the scene of the accident there were police who could have breathalysed him but didn't. He thinks that was because the paramedics told them he needed to be examined, had to get to the hospital quickly. Men in differing uniforms exchanged words; he didn't hear what they said. He's had a few tests since arriving at the hospital, none requiring him to breathe into a plastic bag. He wonders if he should volunteer for one. Like he volunteered the information to Mandy about all that he and Roselyn had done together. The sex, he doesn't think she would have been much fussed about the squash. He and Graham both had a skinful on Saturday night, doing so is pretty much the point of a lads' weekend. That is Charlie's understanding, and he is not a man to break with tradition. They slept it off—he's sure he did—he woke late on Sunday, head surprisingly clear. They didn't have much breakfast, did the Sidmouth to Seaton trek back to the car in double quick time, got away early afternoon and then pulled off the motorway at Bridgwater for a meal. It was a chain pub—food okay—a single pint of pale ale for Charlie. Graham had said, 'Do you want a half? Don't forget you're driving.' The ex-soldier had foolishly stuck with his initial shout. The full pint. Under the limit, stuck with the one. Not the six or eight of the night before but what was the bloody point. It was Sunday lunch; the drinking was more than done by close of play Saturday night. Still had to have the pint, show himself

A Pint of Beer

to be the easy-going beer guzzler that Graham probably laughs at. Would laugh at if he wasn't lying on an adjustable bed, a bleed on the brain inhibiting conscious thought. Preventing him from laughing, crying, swearing at the driver who drank a pint of beer for no good reason. The guy doing the undertaking—speeding and undertaking, driving like a lunatic—he was the one in the wrong. One little pint of beer isn't much, Charlie would have passed a breathalyser. He is so confident about it that he wishes they'd tested him. Given him a chance to prove the point. He wasn't at fault. Even the drinking session of the night before was a modest one—very tame by his old army standards—Graham matched him until near closing and he's not a proper drinker. The lunchtime pint will not have helped, it's not an elixir for driving improvement. He got the lane wrong first off; should have stayed in the middle one. He quickly corrected it once he caught sight of the speeder in his passenger-side mirror.

Not quickly enough.

12.

'Let me tell you, you little shit! You were so ruddy charming at the racecourse when we met. That was always your thing; it was never mine. I was only there on account of my older sister, Janine. Don't look so ruddy blank. You know Janine.' Irene spewed this out at Graham, a boy twenty years or more her junior, who she was—for the time being—calling Gordon, and imagining to be her returned husband. Charlie hadn't the first idea where Graham was meant to have returned from.

The young man just shook his head. 'I've never met Janine,' he stated.

Irene looked intently at the clock; it came into Charlie's mind that she was imagining it to be a source of knowledge. There was an intensity in her gaze. 'Is my Janine one of your floozies, too? Is that it?' Graham continued to shake his head, and Irene laughed, a funny thought initially and then her expression changed into one of pain. 'Is she? Is that what it's come to?'

'The tea has been lovely,' said Charlie. 'I think it's best if we leave you alone now, Mrs...' He paused, could not complete the formal phrase he'd begun. '...Irene. It will be for the best.'

'What's he?' she said sharply, looking between the two. 'Your father was never a soldier. It isn't him, Gordon, so what have you brought this fella here for?'

Graham looked at Charlie. 'Can we just go?'

Both men rose from the table. 'You're confused, Irene,' Charlie told her. 'I think you may wish to call a doctor next week. Early next week.'

'Sit down!'

'No, Irene. We're leaving. You've been very hospitable but it's unpleasant being wrongly accused. You are confusing my friend with your ex-husband. You need help.'

'Oh, don't come in here saying I don't know my own husband. If you're trying to send me potty, it's a game that won't work on me.'

The lady picked up the saucer on the table in front of her and threw it at Graham, did it with some force. He saw it coming, arms across his head and face turning away; the saucer caught him on the armpit he had facing her way. Fell to the stone floor and broke into pieces.

'We're not staying to clear it up,' said Charlie. 'You broke that, Irene.'

The two men walked quickly towards the kitchen door, the one that led out into the barn, the route they knew. Another saucer and a teacup rained down on them but they were quickly into the barn. Charlie pulled the door behind them, held onto the knob. 'Grab your stuff!' They had coats and rucksacks strewn on the top of the hay bales. In no time they were walking straight out of the barn's open frontage into the pouring rain.

As they were leaving the farmyard they looked back to a house-coated figure in the entryway of the barn, Irene remaining under shelter. Charlie thought she was crying, it was a guess from a hundred paces. Graham shouted, 'Thanks for the tea,' before his former colleague shushed him, laughing while doing so. Unsure if this was the funny breakfast boy or simply his over-polite self.

13.

In the hospital corridor, Charlie has a word with the police officer. He is not sure where this man fits in. The police were present at the beginning of the incident, on the motorway. Why one is here now is unknown to him. He doesn't recall the face, nor much at the time of the crash except imploring the paramedics to help Graham. He thinks he might have shouted, they certainly asked him to stand back. He asks this policeman—a couple of hours calmer—if the others caught up in the accident are all right.

'Broken bones.'

It's an answer but it doesn't say much. He wonders if he should enquire more, has no idea who the others involved are. What cars hit what. It sounded worse than it looked. The sound of the second collision frightens him still. The one that rolled the car. Rolled two cars. He thought there might have been more—one car into another—the domino effect. When he stepped out of the vehicle, he was surprised to see only one other car affected, plus the red car, way up the road. He doesn't wish the speeder a bleed on the brain, nor would he lose sleep over it. He hopes the police know what really went on back there. Whose fault it was.

'We'd like you to come into the police station tomorrow. Voluntarily.'

Charlie agrees to this, then says, 'Here?' He thinks he is in Gloucester, assumes that is where the Gloucestershire Royal Hospital is situated.

'Your home station if you prefer. I'd need to brief them before you went in.'

'I'm not leaving Graham.'

The police officer appears confused by this exchange. Charlie explains to the police officer that he is staying, he was thinking aloud. He has no car to get home in today, a friend in hospital down here. He'll find a room for tonight, cancel work tomorrow.

The policeman is very helpful, names a couple of cheap hotels. He understands that it is Charlie's friend who has borne the brunt of this accident. 'If you wait here, I'll call in, get someone to take you. Take you to pick your stuff up from the car.' Charlie feels a little surprised, the police feting him. He doesn't deserve this. 'It's quiet out there on a Sunday evening,' the policeman tells him.

* * *

When the policeman has left, Charlie uncovers an utterly desolate feeling inside himself. A hunger to push back time, to undo what has happened. He is waiting for a car to take him to collect his belongings, the clobber in the boot, and then on to a hotel. He is leaving his friend, who he only recently learned to be gay. The poor lad lost his job barely a month ago, seemed to have landed on his feet with his new one. He was funny company this weekend, funny in unexpected ways. Leaving him in a coma feels treacherous. He would like to sleep on a chair by the hospital bed, he did as much for his daughter, Michelle, a couple of years back. That was a suspected seizure, an enormous worry at the time. She's never had another. He cannot imagine Graham's injury is going to play out so easily, and he worried about Shelley for weeks and weeks. This sits heavily in his mind as, at the hospital entrance, he waits for a policeman to come by.

14.

The thunder and lightning exhausted themselves. The pair walked up the hillside without that accompaniment, grateful for the respite. Still raining, the sky promising better. Clearing in the west.

'What was with her?' said Graham. 'You seemed pretty relaxed but she was one crazy woman.'

Charlie didn't answer for a few steps; he did not yet feel entirely relaxed, but he had spotted that they were two healthy young men in the home of a single, not especially resourceful, female. Gun aside, the odds were always with them. Irene might, justifiably, have been terrified. When he was far enough from the farm to be sure that she wasn't following them, taking a path that tractor nor Land Rover could navigate, Charlie swung his rucksack down from his back. 'I want my gloves,' he said.

The rain was still falling but its weight was light, it flicked across them with the sea wind, the ocean itself remaining out of sight in the grey of the day. 'She was something else,' Graham observed.

'I wonder if we should tell somebody. Mentally ill.'

'Yeah. We'd know who to call if we were on our own patch. One floor below, aren't they? Adult services. The mental health crowd are all right. Pretty can-do, in my experience.'

'I don't quite know what to think,' said Charlie. 'You'd expect Gordon knows all about whatever's up with her if he comes and farms—might get her some help—I found myself wondering if there even is such a fella. It was you she was fixated on.'

'Thanks.'

'No, but really...' Charlie started to find the rhythm of his thoughts. '...if we phone Devon Social Services and tell them there's a crazy woman with a gun living on an isolated farm...' He looked back down the valley; they had gone far enough so that no buildings remained in view. '...they'll stop us right there. Want us to narrow it down a lot better than that. Tell them something they don't already know.'

Graham laughed for the first time since the shotgun poked around the barn door with Irene—if that is her true name—holding the stock. Catching gypsies red-handed; bang-bang to anyone taking shelter where she rules the roost.

15.

A different policeman takes Charlie to his car. This one has a kindly manner and still they speak at cross purposes. It has been a hell of a day and Charlie misunderstands where they are going, imagines that it is back to the motorway, where he last saw his car. In fact, they go to a large warehouse on an industrial estate. The policeman explains what has happened, his car brought here where contractors perform tests on behalf of the police. Check the vehicle's roadworthiness. 'A major incident,' says the policeman. 'We must be thorough whenever there's a major incident.' The word death never comes up, Graham still on the right side of that divide. Charlie worries that it is only by a thread. The fate of the other motorists—from the car he spun into and whoever was in that speeding Honda—he has still to learn. The previous policeman implied there were no fatalities. Charlie couldn't stand it if there were. The feelings coursing through him are familiar: had them after each of the two skirmishes that engaged his company down in the Gulf, nineteen-ninety-one. Not knowing is usually better than knowing, that is the sense he had then and now. Not a comfort but an absence of greater discomfort. He can keep going on that; it will not exhaust him as quickly as grief.

A Pint of Beer

Guilt. That's the one he's caught.

The policeman advises Charlie that he should take his belongings, Graham's too, from the boot of the car.

'Will I get the car back?' asks Charlie.

'Talk to your insurer,' replies the policeman.

As they look upon it, the dented old tin it is now, Charlie says, 'It'll be written off. It's what they do.' The front looks awful, bonnet angled up like a tent. Passenger-side rear corner is a mess: not there, in fact. The seats, where he and Graham were strapped in look unaffected. But his friend hit his head on something. Perhaps his seat belt was no better than the airbags. Everything failed.

On the way out of the hangar, after staring for too long at the car he once felt rather proud of, Charlie unburdens himself. Says what has been preying on his mind. 'No one breathalysed me. They wanted to but the paramedics kind of took over.'

The policeman shrugs. 'Your blood's been taken.'

Charlie feels jolted by the off-hand comment. Its implication. Have the doctors and police played a trick on him? He has no wish to evade justice, never has had. Not since he was fifteen, not since his foster mother talked a bit of sense into him. Loved it into him, he has always thought. It was only a pint of beer which he wishes he hadn't had. If they had breathalysed him, he would have passed. He is sure of it. Didn't especially want to see confirmation of the one he had drunk, just that he was under the limit. The police don't bother if you are, and no one has said he wasn't. Perhaps he would have reacted quicker without it—the pint—made a better judgement. Stuck to the middle lane. Graham's brain might never have been breached if Charlie had glugged table water, no show-off pint of pale ale.

'Can I get a taxi back into town?' he asks the policeman who has brought him this far.

'I'll take you. You've been through a lot.'

Charlie studies the policeman. Sees that he is young, Graham's age or thereabouts. He has all the equipment they carry—several contraptions upon his person—his kit and clothes must weigh a military measure. He carries Graham's rucksack and a loose holdall, taken from the back of the car. Charlie presumes the holdall is also Graham's, it cannot be Mandy's. Nothing of hers has been in the Fiat for months.

'Do you have a hotel in mind?' asks the policeman.

Charlie glances at him. Hotels are for holidays, for good times. This is a vigil. 'Do you know which is the cheapest. Not a dive but cheap, please?'

'Quiet Night,' he says.

Charlie has heard of the chain, pretty reliable, inexpensive. The policeman says it's close to the hospital.

16.

By Saturday evening, they were back in Sidmouth, staying both nights in the same guest house. Showering before going out to eat. Nothing in the eighteen-mile trek came close to the drama of Irene's barn, Irene's kitchen. They talked about her, on and off. Did she need sectioning, subjecting to an enforced psychiatric admission? Was she normal for Devon? They looked at it from every angle. She was winding up the grockles, a pretend mad-woman having a laugh.

'She must have been a good actor in her day,' Graham mused. 'I reckon Irene's only her stage name.'

Charlie shook his head. 'I thought she was the real deal. I've never worked in psychiatry but I've visited a few kids there. Discharges into fostering. Bloody horrible. Not my area of expertise. Nutters aren't actors, and actors can't fake being a nutter. It's that hard.'

They each took a long shower—Graham followed by Charlie—cleaned away the cold of the south Devon coast,

A Pint of Beer

the November grime. Dressed themselves up for a Saturday night in Sidmouth with a lowered anticipation than the older man had felt the night before. As they got ready Graham asked about the Chope boy, the disturbed lad living with foster carers in Ashbourne.

Charlie let his professional façade slide—it barely covers him on a working day—told Graham how he felt as a care leaver, a guy who had once been a kid in the same system Russell Chope is now reliant upon. 'These foster carers, the Goodings, they give me the nearest I'll ever get to religious hope. Give me hope where I know there is none. A victim of serial abuse like poor Russell can't lead a normal life, not so long as he remains a bit twisted, volatile. The poor boy was tortured by his dad. Physically, sexually, all the really sickening stuff. And now I think he's going to make it. They are completely nurturing, so accepting, the couple who have taken him into their home. I sometimes think they are like my foster mum but, to be honest, I was a pussycat compared to that lad. I had bad friends, a useless mother, I didn't dream of cutting babies' dicks off. I was nothing compared to Russell Chope.' Charlie told Graham how, when he read all the suitability documents, the form F, the panel notes, he was pessimistic before making the placement. 'I pretended I wasn't to Fiona, because I wanted to give the foster carers a chance. Give Russell a better chance than a dead-end children's home. Fiona has since said she was the same, not very hopeful at all, although she made out like she saw a rosy future for Russ and the Goodings. We thought we were saving the department a bit of cash until it broke down and the poor lad went off to secure. Now we both think the Goodings will see him through. Years and years, he'll be there. He struggles from time to time but he loves them.'

Graham queries whether the carers might become worn down. They sound terrific—he agrees with Charlie about that—but it must be challenging. As they stroll out of the

Bed and Breakfast, dark outside, and still a freshness to the sea air, rain cleared, Charlie thinks how much he might miss this. Shooting the breeze with Graham. Talking shop because it is what they do. Care about their jobs, about the lives of those who need navigating through these times. Kids brought up in families twice as mad as that horror-film farmhouse.

17.

Charlie sits quietly in the motel room for over an hour, contemplating the day, his good fortune: car flipped, airbags failed, seatbelt held. Graham's contrary destiny. It feels harrowing. His phone charges on the bedside table.

When it passes fifty per cent, when he feels a little more composed, he scrolls through his contacts, and presses the one named 'Mum.' The name he only took to using when he'd reached adulthood. She is his most trusted confidant. Grace Bell and Mandy, and the latter seems to have lost interest. She's a mum with whom he shared a roof for only a short period of his life, daily in his thoughts ever since.

'Charlie, Charlie,' she says when she has gathered who is calling. He feels a small replenishing on hearing the warmth in her tone; she makes him feel like a favourite in her phrasing, although he has met others. Several foster children keep contact with Grace Bell.

He explains that he has been on a walking weekend, that the car he was driving was in a serious accident. She is concerned, wants to hear that he is unhurt.

'My friend is in a coma,' he says, thinks his voice breaks as he says it and he's no wish for his foster mother to hear him going to pieces. He had to say it though, bear witness to the truth. He talks a little about who Graham is, an ex-colleague. Mentions learning that he is gay. 'Oh, that doesn't matter,' says Grace Bell, and he thinks he agrees with her. It might matter to Graham, it's neither here nor there on the grand scheme of things. Charlie hopes she cannot sense or piece together clues which make her suspect tears are tracking down his face. She has not heard him cry in twenty-five years.

18.

The Sunday morning after Saturday's wet walk, the cuppa with mad Irene, and an evening skin-full, was a tame affair. The weather was not special, cold sea mist, they walked briskly and Graham seemed to be getting into his stride. Not put off although nothing of England's rural idyll found them this weekend. Prostitutes, thunder and an out-and-out crazy woman. It was Friday's walk, in reverse, always going to seem shorter doing the same terrain a second time. They got to Seaton, back to the car, in three hours, no breaks except to look at the view. They managed all that on a small breakfast. Charlie had the works, the full English, put in front of him, then only ate the bacon and mushrooms, wasn't quite in the mood for it. Drank three cups of coffee alongside. It isn't a hangover cure, just feels like it could be. Graham managed only a boiled egg and a cup of tea.

'So, we're not going to report the mad lady?' Graham asked over breakfast.

Charlie shrugged. 'We know where the farm is but I didn't take a name. The social workers would involve police at the first mention of a gun. Bloody complicated for no pay off in my book.'

Graham doesn't disagree, he queries again if she needs psychiatric help, might become more unwell, more dangerous even. They both see all the risks—their training lays those out on a plate—it would be a confusing phone call should either of them choose to make it. They had no business being there, provoking her to point a gun at them.

'I think Gordon's on to it,' said Charlie. This was a formulation he used in yesterday's conversation about her. Graham had suggested he might be under the floorboards, not doing as much tractor work as crazy-Irene gave him credit for.

'How's your egg, Graham?' asked Charlie, just to avoid going round and round the same subject once again.

'It started off okay but now it's just more of the same.'

Charlie gave him a puzzled look.

'No need to report her, you're right. She hasn't any ammo.'

This was the same conclusion which they drew when they pinged it back and forth the night before. In principle Devon social services should be told about Irene: so far off her head she believes Graham to be her adulterous husband back from floozyland. None of the facts—not even the existence of the much-maligned Gordon, never mind his peccadillos—were they able to verify. Couldn't give a report secure enough to ensure a follow-up visit, so may as well not bother. They achieved the walking goals, despite the atrocious weather conditions. Weren't unduly deflected by having a gun pointed at them. If they had known the rain was to be so incessant, they would have cancelled and yet both declared—sincerely, it felt to Charlie—that they were pleased to have done it. Graham joked that it was all preparing him for a stint in the army now social work had gone belly up. Charlie had as good as shown him how to tackle a shooter.

The night before also included a lot of drink; Charlie was thankful to find no cock involved and Graham kept ribbing him on it. 'I'm not promiscuous,' he repeated, even managing, 'I don't even sleep with the boss,' when they were a few drinks in.

Charlie felt stung by the comment. He tried not to make it obvious; this whole weekend was about commiseration with Graham for unfairly losing his position. At one point

A Pint of Beer

the younger man called it a celebration of their companionship, although the older has no idea what that is, has only ever felt truly connected to his foster mother, to Mandy and to his three children. Mandy seems to want off the list now, and his indiscretion with which Graham was then jibing him gave logic to it. Mandy has even started seeing a different man herself; it was depressing for Charlie to contemplate. Only the assessment centre has gone Charlie's way recently, not much else. And he feared his connection with little Mikey could become tenuous, stretched out of shape. His social work training, awareness of the importance of deep-rooted attachments, gave him this aching fear. 'I was a dick there,' he offered his drinking partner, hindsight's appraisal of his relationship with Roselyn Pickford. 'A real dick.' A touch of bitterness evident in the tone.

'Shouldn't have raised it.' Graham's personal antennae was not yet entirely disabled by booze, thought Charlie, forgiving him the brief foray into a taboo topic.

The talk strayed back to the assessment day, something Charlie has barely dwelt upon since Roselyn told him he would remain in the city's employ. He guesses it looms up in Graham's thoughts every time he pours himself a drink of worth. Charlie posited a new insight. 'We pay it lip service, the idea that clients, service users, should have a say in recruitment, that their opinion of who comes across as a good social worker and who doesn't should be weighed in. The dilemma is, we can't quite trust them; they're reluctant customers, always stuck in their personal catastrophes before they become a service user in the first place. I'm not judging, Graham, it could happen to any of us, but having a social worker isn't like booking a holiday or buying a car. The actor might have been the best thing, particularly if he was honest with himself, recognised who pressed the right buttons inside him and who pressed the wrong ones. He saw what we are like out there. On the estates.'

'But I was shit, Charlie.'

This detail was not on Charlie's mind when he started his ramble. 'No, it was all unfair. I've been in the game for years, developed a style, confidence. They shouldn't have put you and Yasmin through the same as us, not in my book. You're still finding your feet. Good at your jobs, don't get me wrong, but it's too early to be measuring it in that psychometric detail. It's an art not a science.' Charlie says it—science not art, art not science—others in the office have done the same. It means nothing either way, as far as he can tell. Social work is social work. He follows orders and he can fix a bike; he was in care himself, desperately wants it to go right for those still trapped there.

'I think I got too into it,' said Graham, glancing down at the beer in his hand. 'I didn't think of him as an actor, or an assessor. I just thought he was a crappy foster carer. One we needed to get rid of but you can't just tell them that, can you? Have to gather more information before you try to ease them out. Build a case that can't be argued with.'

Charlie thought about this for a moment. 'I think I did. It saved my bacon.'

'The problem with phoning social services...' Graham slips back into talking crazy-lady again. '...the stuff with the gun will get the police involved. They'll want statements, and you were kind of cool, Charlie, while I just panicked away. Saying nothing, doing nothing. It's probably a good thing that this one doesn't get written up but how do you do it?'

'What do you reckon?'

'Well, you were actually in the armed forces; served in a war, one that I don't really remember, we have so many of the damned things. A real one. People died. I'm so glad you didn't, Charlie, but I think the experience has made you fearless. You know you can come through anything?'

'Soldiers aren't fearless, Graham, they just act on orders

despite their fear. That's what the training tells you. Obey! It doesn't guarantee you long life; obeying orders is just the best chance you've got. Nothing looks very permanent on a battlefield.'

19.

In the soulless bedroom of the chain motel—TV, minibar, room service menu, all untouched—Charlie is staring once more at his mobile phone. He has contacted Fiona and Precious, struggled to be very coherent in the conversations. In the second call Precious said, 'You were driving and you're all right?' She probably meant nothing by it but he felt an accusation. He taps another contact, composes himself before pressing call. He's sure she didn't mean to imply it was unjust; probably just checking he really had come through unscathed.

'Yasmin, it's Charlie.' It is not her. He cannot bring her partner's name to mind. It is in his head, stuck in there, not coming to the door. 'Sorry, is she there?'

'I will fetch her for you, Charlie,' says Mr Chowdhury, when he has learned who is chasing down his young wife.

'Hi Yasmin, sorry to trouble...'

'Are you all right, Charlie?'

'Yeah, I'm all right. Well not...'

'What is it?'

'It's Graham. We've had an accident.'

'You went walking?'

'Yes, Yaz, just him and I...'

'How did it go?'

'Driving home, Yaz, there was a pile-up on the motorway. He's in the hospital.'

Yasmin's voice goes quieter. 'And you're all right?'

'I got lucky.' He regrets the term as soon as it is said, knows Graham didn't. 'But...' He was standing but sits on the bed, lets himself drop. The phone slips from his grasp, and he quickly picks it off the cover. '...Yaz, Yasmin...'

'Yes, Charlie.'

'...it's a brain injury. I'm terrified for him, Yaz. The doctor called it a bleed, a bleed on the brain.' He can hear his colleague crying on the other end of the phone; Precious did that too. 'I don't know what to...' Charlie doesn't finish this sentence, there is nothing he can do.

'I'm sorry,' says Yasmin. 'Me and Graham started together.' He hears more crying; her partner is saying something in the background. 'What's the name of the hospital, the ward?' she manages to ask.

Charlie gives what detail he can, promises to keep her informed. It is a most difficult evening.

* * *

'Tariq, hi, it's Charlie. I won't be in tomorrow. Not a sick day, I don't think. I'm stuck in Gloucestershire. Graham is in the hospital. I was in a car accident. We were. It turned over.'

He listens to his manager for a moment. Tariq is concerned.

'No, I'm all right. Graham is in a coma though. I think it's a coma. Hasn't come round. It's awful.'

'Is this the first time you've spent the weekend together?' Charlie doesn't know why Tariq has asked him this. An odd question in the circumstances.

'A walking weekend; we planned it before the assessments.' Charlie feels like he is confirming it was not a sexual liaison they undertook in the Sidmouth bed and breakfast. Absurd. Or maybe that wasn't what Tariq meant. Charlie isn't thinking too clearly; he may be misunderstanding everything his colleagues say to him. Late on a horrible day, and Tariq will know nothing about Graham's sexuality, it couldn't be the implication. Charlie is the first city employee the boy has told, and that only happened this weekend. He said he'd not 'come out' in the office because he's pretty shy. And that could be an understatement although he came out of himself a bit this weekend. Only his parents, sister and presumably one or two other gay guys out there, seem to know about it. What he is. Graham never told Charlie about any specific relationship he has had. He told him gay websites are dodgy, and for all Charlie knows the straight ones are no better.

Tariq is practically minded. 'Have Graham's family been informed?' he asks. He has no follow-up when Charlie states that he has phoned them. Tariq seems to be ticking off a checklist, not visualising the day Charlie has had, the trauma he has endured. At one point in the conversation Tariq even says, 'Of course, he doesn't work for the department anymore.' He may think it an event he need not concern himself with. He sounds fairly sympathetic, no crying but he's a bloke. The new manager is hard to read. Tariq never really knew Graham, never became his manager and Graham did no adoption work in his year with the city. Charlie has no idea why Tariq asked if it was their first weekend together.

* * *

For a split-second he thinks it is Paul but quickly realises the voice is too deep. 'Who is this?' he asks. 'Can Mandy come to the phone please?'

'I could ask the same but I'm going to guess that's Charlie. Barry here. I'm sure she's told you about me. Shall we chat...'

He cuts the man off, hasn't thought about him for a moment since the accident. 'Mandy, please. It's important.'

'All right. But you and I really must talk sometime,' says Barry. Charlie can think of nothing that the pair of them might talk about. Not unless Barry wants to tell him his leaving date. In those circumstances, Charlie would even throw him a fuck-off-back-to-wherever party.

When she comes to the phone Mandy sounds a little impatient. 'What?'

'Mandy, it's important. I've been in a terrible accident. Me and Graham.'

'What happened?' He senses that she has dropped the irritation, trouble is, it's hard to be sure of anyone's demeanour over the phone. Can't do it in his drained state.

Charlie explains where he is, the mess the car is in, the mess Graham is in. Mandy doesn't know him but she says she's sorry to hear that. Doesn't seem to harbour any suspicion that by saying Graham he might again mean Roselyn. Which he really doesn't.

'Will it cost?' she asks.

He realises that she means the car. He hasn't thought about it. 'Insurance. It was the other guy's fault. The lunatic.'

She seems satisfied with this; Charlie asks if she'll tell the kids, says he might still feel shaken up when they next meet up. They need to understand why.

'I will,' she replies, 'and I'm glad you're all right for their sakes.'

'Thanks...' He wants to say more, offer some rejoinder, fathom if she is glad at all for more selfish reasons. Does she maintain any positive feelings for him; what she has just said felt like a no, and he would like her to modify it.

'I must get back to Barry,' she says. 'Take care.'

* * *

He thinks long and hard before phoning Brenda. He has had no contact since her leaving do, the evening in Fiona's loft apartment. She needs to know.

On answering, she sounds pleased to hear from him. 'Charlie, I was just thinking about you.'

He cannot interrupt the exchange of pleasantries, even her dig that Roselyn must be hating it now—the demotion—it is fully a minute before he is able to tell her why he is ringing. 'It's about Graham.'

Brenda is shocked. Charlie had not thought the two to be close but she cries every bit as much as Precious and Yasmin.

The thought of Graham in a coma is distressing. To her and to him. Brenda murmurs, 'Poor lamb,' down the phone and then asks for details, even visiting hours, which Charlie cannot furnish her with. Hasn't thought to find out. Then she seems like her old social worker self, goes through the accident with him, not prying, just letting him get it off his chest. Keeps coming back to, 'And you are sure you're unhurt?' When she says it for the third time, Charlie assures himself that this was the concern of Precious also. Not to rub his nose in it for getting off scot-free despite driving, failing to avoid the speeding car. He starts to rest into the feeling that these colleagues and ex-colleagues are concerned about him—Graham of course—but him also. They don't blame him. He feels a bit of a shit for not mentioning the pint of beer.

'We all miss you, you know,' he tries to sign off with.

'We should all get together once Graham is out of the hospital,' she says. It's a lovely sentiment; he hopes it will come to pass.

20.

The pint of beer at lunchtime was all part of prolonging the weekend. They undertook the walk on Sunday at a pretty hurried pace; the weather was still unreliable, just not as nasty as on Saturday. A bit of rain about. They had no choice but to walk it, the car was down there in Seaton where they'd left it on Friday, where they had to walk back to before they could drive home. Graham was the more hungover of the pair. He is less hardened by his drinking than Charlie, who has been an occasional supper of ale for most of his post-army years. Drank for England when he was in uniform. Charlie's enforced separation from Mandy has increased his intake of the stuff. His saving grace is that he tends to stick to ale. Graham was mixing his drinks the evening before:

lager, Bacardi, a glass of red, then back on the lager. That can trouble head and stomach.

As they headed up the motorway, Devon turning to Somerset, Graham had suggested he was ready to eat more than a boiled egg. They found a carvery, just off the motorway near Bridgwater. Cheap; chicken or beef; smelt brilliant. Charlie said, 'Hair of the dog,' when he asked for a pint of IPA to accompany his food, his well-piled plate of meat and veg. Graham had fizzy mineral water, and after once suggesting Charlie have only a half, he never mentioned anything about the pint again. It was comfortably within the limit.

During the meal Graham asked a question that threw Charlie, simply because he had not contemplated the answer for a second. 'Will you be telling everyone in the office that I'm gay?'

'I think I should do whatever you want me to do, mate.' When Graham made no request either way, Charlie added, 'It is who you are.'

'It is, isn't it?' said the younger man, as if he too was unsure what he wanted and Charlie was assisting him to make up his mind. 'I'm worried they'll think it a sad story though, that I couldn't come out when I was working there, working with them.'

'People will think whatever they think, Graham. I don't know one who doesn't think you were a bloody good social worker.'

In silence, Charlie glugged down fully half of his beer. One long quaff. It felt good to rehydrate, he'd had a few the night before.

Chapter Three

Back On the Dancefloor

1.

'Fiona, Charles, the city council appreciates your dedication,' says Deepika. And then she glances away. Fiona smiles straight back at her. Deepika avoids eye contact. Charlie also tries to meet her eyes; their colleague seems occupied by the sight of her own shoes. He likes her, she has proven herself to be a true team player. At first, they used to laugh when she did this sort of thing—forget herself—imagine she is still the team manager of those short weeks ago. A position from which she has fallen. She often gives the game away by saying something like this. Invites everyone else to remember her fallen state. She must have been a verbose team manager before all the assessment centre bullshit. Sweetly so, it's always the complimentary stuff she lets slip.

This little plum of overly formal peer praise has been doled out because the pair are off to Derbyshire tomorrow. Saturday. Fiona and Charlie will pay a visit to Russell Chope and his foster carers. Working late is quite normal. Doing so at weekends, visiting, being out and about for the cause on a Saturday morning is a much rarer thing. Making a visit the morning after the department's Christmas party—the raucous and boozy affair all anticipate—is the dedication which must have inspired Deepika to offer such fulsome praise on behalf of the department. To deliver the kind of managerial acclamation that Tariq never thinks to do, nor Roselyn before him. Charlie reckons Deepika might have been the pick of the managers, back when she had the stripe. Right On Track knew only the alphabet, bugger all about who was any good at their job.

'Not me,' says Fiona, 'I'll be drinking a bath-full of gin tonight anyway. Charlie's driving, tonight and tomorrow. He's the hero.'

'I'm off the drink, that's all.'

Deepika finally looks back at them, 'Thanks for driving me tonight too,' she says.

'We've not been yet,' says Charlie.

* * *

'Look at you,' he says when she comes to the door. She has dressed in a sari, not clothing she ever wears to work.

'Proper night out, innit,' replies Deepika, faking a Mancunian accent for the saying of it. 'You be me date tonight,' the funny voice goes on.

Charlie thinks it dangerous talk. Deepika is married but she has moved out of her husband's home. Currently lives in a flat just a few streets from Charlie's. The fracturing of her marriage happened straight after the turmoil of her undeserved demotion. She has talked to Precious about it, no one really knows if her marriage is done for or not. Deepika is a most private person.

'Dressed like that, it's a yes from me,' he says.

They take the stairs down, and out of the rear door to the car park. Charlie opens the passenger door for her. His unlikely date slides into the seat with a respectful nod to his courtesy. He goes around the driver's door, climbs in, starts the engine and they are away.

Next, they stop to pick up Fiona. Charlie leaves Deepika in the passenger seat, walks round the side to her building's entrance. Presses the buzzer for flat number twelve. She comes straight down. No talking through the intercom, an appearance at the ground-floor door in under fifteen seconds. Unlike Fiona to be so prompt.

'Danny coming?' asks Charlie. It was part of the plan earlier this afternoon.

'Nuh. Tell you about it tomorrow.'

Charlie shrugs. He is driving her to Ashbourne in the morning. Out to see Russell Chope, a foster child, and the couple who care for him. He might have to listen to her marital strife for fifty miles. Not that Fiona and Danny have formally tied the knot. Hopefully this spat is not a terminal one. Smashed-up relationships have become a contagion.

As they head out of the city towards The Kirkaldy Hotel—which Ted Astaire used for their fateful assessments, and has given further custom to for this Christmas shindig—they take a short detour to Yasmin's house. Her three-storey terraced on Lord Street. She climbs into the car, and they laugh about her clothing.

'An Indian wedding,' says Fiona, for this girl has dressed as beautifully as Deepika in the passenger seat.

'Pakistani wedding,' replies Yasmin.

As they are driving away, Fiona says, 'Lucky Charlie. You get to drive three drunken ladies home tonight.'

'You'll be the only drunk,' he says.

'Not if I have any say in it, she won't.' Deepika's comical voice is back.

'Be careful,' Yasmin whispers to Deepika. Charlie wonders if she has got wind of their colleague's flighty mood.

'Nah, bollocks, tonight's for pullin' innit, sister?'

They all laugh but this isn't her. Not the Deepika they know from Children's Services. Their newest fostering team member is prim and proper, talks of attachment theory and child development, not the snaring of men. Charlie wonders if she is serious, Deepika out on the hunt; something or other has broken her marriage. Either she imagines herself unworthy of her doctor-husband, or the man is heartless, and has made such a judgement on the basis of her demotion. Charlie also wonders if Deepika has done the whole pre-drinks thing—behaved like teenagers never did when he was a kid—drank alone before he picked her up. He was not expecting this of her. Thought she might be sniffy about Fiona who always knocks back more than a normal girl can handle. He likes her—Deepika—she's more than a nice face. He thinks about Mandy, his own wife-in-abeyance. Charlie doesn't want Deepika pulling in his car, pulling him. Nothing personal. It's the opposite of his way back to Mandy. Another good reason to stay off the sauce.

* * *

'This bloody place again,' says Charlie as they walk across the car park.

'You know why, don't you?' Without waiting for an answer—not for guesswork, the speculation of her colleagues—Fiona continues, regales them with her theory. 'Ted booked it, decided to bring us all back to the horrible assessment place, because we're the winners. We got through. It's his way of putting the past behind us. He expects us to all feel good about being here: the scene of our success.'

'Pah!'

'Sorry, Deepika,' she adds. The exclamation of their demoted colleague is a layer Ted may not have factored in.

'Just as long as that actor doesn't show up,' says Yasmin.

'Oh, then I'm setting Charlie on him,' says Deepika. All may recollect the story of their driver calling the assessment-day jester out as a paedophile. In the car park, Deepika puts her right hand on Charlie's left bicep, squeezes it a little—he lifts weights—firm to the touch. 'Knock 'im out this time, big fella,' she says in the funny accent. The possibly funny accent she has only tonight brought out in public. Charlie thinks it makes her sound a bit like Yasmin, and the latter doesn't seem offended. Maybe it doesn't even sound like her; he worries that he cannot differentiate properly between people whose underlying accents were unheard by him in his formative years. He can't help himself from beaming back at Deepika who still holds his muscular arm, has placed him on a lofty pedestal. The slayer of actors.

* * *

The bassline is stirring the air, a seventies Christmas hit by Ronnie Prousch. Sentimental garbage but the sound system is terrific; music sitting companionably on every shoulder, it has the collective ear. No choice about it, so comprehensively does the swinging sound fill the air. Smartly dressed men and women are pouring into the hotel, streetside and carpark: Christmas at The Kirkaldy, something tacky for everyone. Council workers, local firms, a few small tables of friends—or they could be titchy-tiny companies, Charlie can't tell—are all partying side by side. Deepika points out Tariq and Precious sitting together at one of the long tables. The new arrivals cross the floor to join them.

Charlie sees that Brantly has accompanied Precious. He shakes her husband's hand. 'Welcome to the madhouse.'

Each table is resplendent with a central bouquet of flowers. The red and gold of Christmas crackers. A green serviette at every setting, folded into the approximation of a Christmas tree. There is a small basket abundant with party poppers next to the flowers. Charlie recalls Paul, his older son, sneering at the things; Michelle—his middle child—loves them. A bunch of social workers firing them off is just daft. A sign saying, 'Fostering and Adoption,' confirms that they are sticking to the master plan, their team table. Charlie picks up a white bread roll, assumes the women will want the brown ones. At each place an empty soup bowl waits expectantly.

'This is what you're pulling tonight,' he tells Deepika, handing her one of the stupid party poppers.

'This and you, Charlie,' she whispers back, making her version of come-to-bed eyes. Pop! The string lands across

Charlie's short hair. Deepika has pulled first tonight.

Tariq sits at the head of the table, as if he is to begin a team meeting. Eyes stocktake the presence of each team member. He wears a suit, every bit as plain as those seen at work; an eye-catching tartan tie lends it colour without kowtowing to Christmas.

'Did you think it was the assessment all over again,' says Fiona, pointing at the smart accruement.

'That talk is banned,' says Ruth Cooper, an adoption social worker who sits beside Tariq. Another member of their reconstituted team.

The newly arrived quibble over who will buy the first round, whether to set up a kitty. Bottles of wine or gins and tonics. They resolve it without fuss, those not partaking of alcohol chip in less than the rest. Fiona and Charlie go to the bar. A different cheerful Christmas song assaults their ears as they walk past the Care Proceedings team table.

'Hiya,' says Roselyn, rising from her seat and taking Charlie's arm.

'All right,' he says to his former lover. Still a secret, he believes, in present company. Graham—who knows—is not here for more reasons than Charlie wishes to dwell upon.

'Happy Christmas,' Roselyn plants the quickest of kisses onto Charlie's lips.

He glances straight at Fiona; she winks back at him. 'He's mine tonight,' she tells Roselyn, taking a hold of his right arm. 'Me and Deepika have bagged him.'

They step away from their former manager, arrive at the bar which is awash with drinkers waiting to be served. Fiona gestures and Charlie leans over, puts his ear to her mouth. Loud background chatter and the blare of Christmas music makes this the only way to conduct a private conversation. 'She won't stay with Care Proceedings,' says Fiona. 'Hates it.'

Charlie has already heard that Roselyn doesn't get along with her new team. 'They can be boring as hell.' Charlie scarcely thinks it, it's just the received wisdom in Fostering and Adoption.

'She's probably sleeping with some of them; her marriage has gone the same way mine is heading.'

Charlie starts to laugh; Fiona has a funny way of telling. Indifference to everything that others might think important.

'Fiona, you can make up with Danny, right?'

'You're not getting out of slow dancing with me, Charlie. Look, the lowdown on Roselyn is that she's livid with Fred Astaire. She thinks she passed the assessment and he fiddled the result to knock her off her perch.'

'Is she kidding? If he did that then he might have fiddled the lot of them. Bring back Brenda!'

'Yeah,' says Fiona, 'could be. But Ted was more interested in the outcomes of those he's slept with.'

'No,' says Charlie. 'There's been a rumour but no one really knows any of that. Roselyn and Ted? It's pure speculation.'

'Well,' says Fiona, 'Roselyn told Deepika that she turned him down, thinks that's why he's parked her in Care Proceedings. Demoted her.'

'She told you that?'

'She told Precious, I think. It was definitely Precious who told me.'

Another man has slapped Charlie across the shoulders, friendly, giving him a thumbs-up. Saying the usual happy Christmas blather. Charlie raises his head from stooping close to Fiona's mouth, from listening to her quietly spoken gossip. Sees that it is him—wearing loud yellow trousers—Ted Astaire walks amongst them.

Charlie draws himself upright, stands to attention, away from the shared confidences of Fiona. 'Happy Christmas, sir,' he says, no volume, just mouths it really. Saying sir feels like grovelling but Charlie has seldom spoken to the director. He hopes Ted didn't overhear what they were saying as he approached. For all Charlie knows, Ted is the most faithful husband a woman could wish for. Rumours mean bugger all. In the army, the talk was that every navy boy is a homo. He heard officers swear to it. It doesn't matter, he doesn't care. He has tempered his language, broadened his opinions. And, by his own reckoning, it was never much more than seventy or eighty per cent.

Precious arrives beside them; she wishes the Director a merry Christmas. A cheerier sentiment than she directed towards him at the time of the assessments.

Fiona gives the big boss a peck on the cheek. A platonic kiss. 'Happy Christmas, Mister President,' she says. People laugh, Ted smiles. Charlie wonders if she is hoping to attract a few rumours of her own. It's certainly not beyond her. Then Fiona says loudly, 'I'm with Charlie tonight, we're a pair.'

Ted looks unmoved, probably knows nothing of the wobbly marital states of a great swathe of his workforce. 'No, Deepika's my date,' says Charlie, thinking it a funny comeback, and then regretting the infantility of it. Poor judgement for a sober man standing in front of the head honcho.

'We're both with him,' says Fiona, 'Charlie can handle it.'

Ted doesn't contest it, smiles benignly and moves on. He will circulate now and leave early; that was the template he followed last year. Any female who leaves at a similar hour will be subject to the next rumour. Charlie recalls Roselyn's name cropping up on the Monday after last year's do. He never believed it. Nor knew anything concrete either way.

Fiona finally has the eye of the barmaid, starts to order the drinks. She tells Charlie they should double up the first round, two of everything, that way they won't need to come back to the bar for a while. Charlie says a single orange juice will last him the night. Driver, teetotaller, reformed ale supper. His last drink was at a Sunday lunchtime carvery outside Bridgwater. Precious helps them carry the drinks back to the table. Roselyn again gets up as they pass her table, this time to speak to Precious. Takes her arm and the pair slide onto seats at the Care Proceedings table. Roselyn is a better source of indiscreet rumour than Tariq will ever be.

Charlie gets to the fostering table and places down the tray. Tariq takes the pint glass of coca cola; others need to clarify which drink is theirs. Ruth and Deepika wander over to Precious, she has the white wine. Charlie looks across at their new boss. Tariq is a quiet man, and still he looks serenely satisfied. Sips on the coke his underlings have fetched. Always polite, always a thank you, still he is the inheritor. Deepika and Roselyn are spent forces, and they were the bright young team managers this time last year. As she returns, he sees that, in her shimmering traditional clothing, black hair hanging loose, Deepika has a beautiful face. Her clothing exposes a thin line of midriff, not a lot, subtle, she looks pale and portly there, a contrast from the intensity and vibrance of her face. Roselyn, in contrast, wears a short skirt, red over dark stockings—stockings or tights, Charlie has no intention of finding out which—it is the clothing, her movement which carries allure. Deepika outshines her, elegantly dressed and a warmer face. His eye still seeks out Roselyn. A star in the sky is not made of flesh.

When they take their seats to eat, Charlie finds himself sitting between Deepika and Yasmin, the two brightly dressed south Asians. He makes a point of chinking glasses with Yasmin; he, she and Tariq may be the only employees of Children's Services who remain sober tonight. Across the massive room, party hats are atop of heads, the string of party poppers draped across many. Beers and wines and gins slip down gullets. Sobriety is a minority pursuit at an office Christmas party. The difficult choice.

* * *

Waitresses walk around the room dispensing rich broccoli soup from large metal jugs. They wear Santa outfits of a cut St Nicholas would not so much as try on. Short red skirts which may offend the feminists, of whom the department has its quota. Charlie knows they have a point, the clothing is meant to titillate, however mildly. It objectifies the waitresses, and if he were drinking, he might just be enjoying the sight of it. Sober analysis can be quite dull. 'Is this a school dinner or Hugh Hefner's house?' he whispers to Deepika.

Hefner is unknown to her. She asks Charlie to explain the joke, the cynical comment. He tries his best. Bunny girls are in her ambit; she had not previously heard of the mansion from whence they came. 'You want me to wear the sexy skirt,' she says in her funny voice. He didn't mean to imply that; his intention was to side with the feminists. Must have made himself clear, he was doing it under the influence of orange juice. It is Deepika who is not hearing him correctly. 'C'mon, Fi-fi. Let's get Charlie on the dancefloor,' she says.

'Lucky man. You've got yourself two ladies,' says Fiona, rising up from her seat.

'My soup's just arrived,' he says. One of the waitresses is still going around the table pouring from a metal jug.

'One little dance,' says Deepika, fluttering her eyes at him. Her deep-brown kohl-stained eyes.

'It tastes like phlegm,' says Fiona, her soup poured, tasted and rejected.

'One dance,' says Charlie.

His female colleagues take an arm each. As they walk across the room, he puzzles over who is playing a joke on who. At the dancefloor, Fiona slips away and says a quick word to the disc jockey. Deepika starts to twist her fingers, Indian dancing; Charlie shrugs, would feel foolish trying it. At the sight of this gesture, she leans right into him, takes his hands and places them on her own body. An

Back On the Dancefloor

approximation of a waltz. They impersonate the fare of Saturday night television; however, he and she cannot glide around the floor, neither has a clue how to execute the moves. Charlie suspects the music is not a waltz at all.

As Fiona arrives back at their side, the backing track changes. The deep bass notes of Northern Line disturb the air, The Browns hit record all the way back to the end of the millennium. Fiona has requested something that won't humiliate him, uncoordinated as he is. As the tune registers, many other revellers leave their dining tables, come forward like Friday prayers, all to join in the quirky line dance. The moves have been on show at parties and weddings nationwide for the last fifteen years. A crocodile starts to form and in thirty seconds everyone on the dance floor is in on it. The two girls each take one side of Charlie, Fiona demonstrating the moves with certainty, Charlie tentatively. He glances this way and that, following those who know it better.

Deepika comically jumps up and down; Northern Line is not Hindi music, the famous dance not an activity she has any familiarity with. 'I'm pissed,' she tells Charlie, pulling him into a little hug.

It confirms his theory about the pre-drinks, Deepika's excitable state when he first picked her up. He expects he used to behave as daft as she does at this sort of event. Most dancers follow the simple choreography; Deepika has raised her sari above her knees and she sashays her bottom into his. He can fathom no reason why she might do this beyond her alcohol consumption. Fiona laughs quite wildly; he imagines their colleagues back at the tables are watching. The Fostering and Adoption team at least. Charlie finds himself glancing down at her legs, rarely seen things that they are. Her skin is pale, pure, legs that look younger than the forty or-so years he imagines her to be.

'Say no to Fi-fi,' says Deepika. 'You're mine.'

Charlie laughs. Deepika was, until very recently, the most conscientious of managers—it may even be why the care proceedings team are such a sober crew—tonight she is giggly, inappropriate, a stranger to those who know her best. Fiona will go home to a partner, however fraught that relationship is or isn't. Danny's a funny guy, so is his wife. Concubine, whatever they call their legal status. They are sure to get through a little blip, seemed fine at the leaving do in the loft. Deepika is the one who has moved out. Slipped off the shelf, career and family. Charlie must extract himself from her long before either goes to bed. His stupidity has a bottom line; his post-Roselyn stupidity at least. He wants Mandy back. Nothing must jeopardise his chances. Her current lover must be got rid of before that can happen. Bringing him to mind—Barry Brice, usurper of his place on Bramley Road, his side of the bed—is Charlie's most miserable thought of the night. He looks again at the cavorting Deepika: funny-funny.

* * *

In as little time as Charlie decently could, he has ushered both girls back to the dining table. Once more, Fiona sits across the table from him, a sari-wearer on either side.

'It's pretty foul,' Yasmin warns him, as Charlie begins to spoon cold broccoli soup into his mouth.

He nods concurrence, takes a couple more spoonsful. He has paid for this dross. When its temperature and bitterness duly bring him to push the soup aside, he picks up another white bread roll, looks around for butter. Deepika, to his right, picks up a different roll and pushes it against his, grinds her brown bread against his white. 'That's what we be doin' later,' she says, once more deploying the working-class accent she doesn't have.

Charlie smiles at her, wonders momentarily whether to have a few drinks and book a taxi. On a personal level Deepika is nicer than Roselyn, a warmer character, and he nailed his former boss for no reason that lives outside his trousers. The new sober Charlie pats Deepika gently on the back. The least erogenous of all possible places, he hopes. Since surviving the accident that still holds Graham's future by a thread, he has determined he will do nothing that takes him further from where he wants to be. Must do whatever it takes to change Mandy's mind, to resurrect his marriage. Pry his ex from her recent attachment to a twat called Barry Brice. The man Charlie has yet to meet, and who preys relentlessly on his mind. Mandy told Charlie too much about her new beau when he was dropping the children back last weekend. Once a tennis coach. Not a terrible profession but aren't they all a bit full of themselves? Unjustifiably so. Professional sportsmen who've never won a tournament. And now the man earns his crust as a life coach. No more backhands down the line. These days he coaches anyone who thinks his advice might be worth a damn. Telling them how to stay calm, ride out the tensions of this mortal coil. She met him in the early autumn when, on the recommendation of a friend, she paid for a couple of life coaching sessions. Paid money—a commodity that the Questeds are not flush with, running two households and what have you—for Barry to help Mandy get her life back on track. Helped through the medium of talking. What the hell is life coaching? The question must have sat conspicuously on Charlie's face all the while Mandy was telling him. And more particularly, what class of life coach offers his own person as the solution. Your loving relationship has broken down: why don't you try me? Mandy said that she only paid for two sessions because, when it became apparent that they had feelings for each other, Barry wouldn't take any more money. Well, isn't he the gentleman? Charlie cannot consider life coaching a proper job, a profession, not unless snake-oil salesmen make the cut too. It's taking money for telling people who think they've cocked their lives up that they've done exactly that. Perhaps Barry Brice should have been talking to him—to Charlie—he is the one who cocked up Mandy's life but, oh no, he just made a play for her instead. The big fraud is currently living in Charlie's family home. That fact alone may be a far bigger impediment to getting his marriage back on the rails than a one-nighter with Deepika would be. His brain tells him not to test it. To stop looking at the flesh of Deepika's midriff.

Precious is raising a glass of red, offering a toast to absent friends. She names them. Brenda, Tina and Graham. Charlie raises a glass, turns his face away at the mention of the boy in the hospital bed. His comatose friend. Deepika puts an arm around his shoulders, a gesture of comfort. 'I know,' she tells him, leans in as his face swivels back to hers. They make eye-contact.

He pulls her into a onehanded embrace, orange juice still raised to battling Graham. 'Thank-you,' he whispers in her ear.

2.

For the longest time, to Charlie's way of thinking about it, Mandy has been everything to him. He was in the army when they met. She has a brother named Simon, who was similarly serving the country. She didn't mention him the night they chanced upon each other, although brother and sister are close. Her father talked a little about him later the same evening. And if it sounds an old-fashioned wooing— meeting Mandy's father on the same night he first met her— that was chance, not part of any scheme of etiquette. Charlie has never had one of them. He fell for Mandy, didn't give two hoots about her father. Turns out he's a nice guy anyway. Chance was behind their meeting, maybe it always plays a part. Centre stage that night. He still thinks that it was highly romantic. Probably the most love-charged night of

Back On the Dancefloor

his whole life. He has gone over it in his mind many, many times. Apart from his wooing of the wife he has let down, Charlie really hasn't done romance. Deep down he doesn't get it, never watches those films.

Mandy would worry herself sick a few years later when Simon was out in Afghanistan, Helmand a war zone. She never had to do that for Charlie, his fighting days behind him by the time they met. He was already on the lookout for his next job. The army paying him for his final weeks, the demands of the military waning. Uniform in the cupboard.

He recalls that she ribbed him about it, made light of the army, she was just poking playful fun. Said driving a tank on Salisbury Plain sounded a rum job—war against Wiltshire—teased him because she is small and he so tall. She respected what he had done. There are plenty—and a fair few social workers figure in their number—who despise the army. Charlie finds it odd that people of his own profession might miss the point: the trajectory of a life can take it to places others would never venture, we are not all born to identical circumstances. Sympathise, empathise, get beside; don't judge. That is what social work training taught Charlie. He did a course—and this was more than two years after he first met Mandy—targeted at those who had little academic experience. Degree-level training for those who might never manage such a qualification without a paring away of all the long words. It was mostly a practical course, lots of time spent on placement, embedded within social work teams. Exams and assignments were a struggle but Charlie persevered. Cracked it, digested a couple of textbooks despite his neanderthal brain. He thinks the fancier social work courses may have a different emphasis than the more down-to-earth one he undertook. Might slag off the army more.

When he met Mandy, she was on a night out, something like this one he's on now. But it wasn't Christmas time. Nor

Easter, just much closer to it. She worked as a receptionist back then, at a tyre fitting firm, a specialist garage. Harry Gifford, her boss, the man who put the G in "D and G Tyres and Exhausts", had paid for a year-end do. Friday the first of April, nineteen-ninety-seven. He was a man for marking the end of the financial year. Never sang Auld Lang Syne. It was to celebrate their bonuses, of which his will have dwarfed all others. Charlie and Mandy have marked it ever since, the anniversary of their meeting. It's April Fools' Day too, although it's the evening not the morning which they raise a glass to. And the sentimental guy buys her red roses: their own personal Valentine's Day. This oftentimes unromantic man thinks it highly important. What he feels towards her— not that he could or did declare it on that first chance encounter—must be love. Feelings so strong, so positive. In life he has had some ups and downs. If he sets aside her throwing him out of the house last July, he attributes none of the downs to Mandy.

He has not missed buying her flowers on a single year; the forthcoming one is looking dicey. Maybe he can pull a rabbit from the sack, have his roses accepted if Barry Brice will just bugger off, and he can wedge his own foot back in the door before the spring. He never did anything behind Mandy's back until this fateful year, this inauspicious twenty-thirteen. Not anything of note, never the whole hog.

Back in nineteen-ninety-seven, the time of their chance meeting, Staff Sergeant Quested was on the verge of re-joining the normal world. Parking his hard-earned rank aside and becoming a civilian once more. A nothing and an everything; one who need not obey. He was here, in this city, on a few days' leave from his regiment, applying for jobs. Preparing his next steps. It seemed as good a place as any to try. He's a Yorkshire lad but has no attachment to it. He planned to work in sales, had yet to gain an inkling of how ill-suited his pervading honesty would make him for such a role. How inept a salesman he would turn out to be. He secured a job at Greenlight on his second day in town. In a few short weeks, he would be working in telesales, pending references, and the army were only ever going to say positive things about Charles Quested. He obeyed orders, it was all that they asked. Following his successful job search, he rewarded himself with a night out at a club in the same suburb as the cheap bed and breakfast he was staying in for those few job-hunting days.

The nightspot was unexceptional, not a big deal to Charlie. He'd been to many similar with army buddies. It felt both duller and edgier to be there alone. The club was a very partial choice for the tyre company's year-end bash, and Mandy one of only two females in her party. Tyre fitters mostly, Mandy worked in admin. Women were welcome in the venue; however, the nightclub was pitched at men. The serving staff comprised girls and women—but none far into their thirties—serving drinks and meals, all suggestively dressed in school uniforms. Short skirts covering, and occasionally uncovering thin black garters which held up old-fashioned stockings; most had their hair in juvenile bunches. Charlie had gone firstly because there was no entry fee. And he was still a young man, liked the sight of navy-blue tartan skirts riding up to white knickers. An inch or two of thigh. Even the rougher-looking waitresses had an enticement about them, although with no company, platoon or squadron to share the experience, the pleasure was oddly private. Charlie knew not a soul in this city. He ordered a burger which cost a fortune, as did the drinks. While waiting for the food he watched the beckoning dancefloor, wondered if there might be a girl who he could spend a little time with. It looked a longshot, groups of men danced together but never so close as to suggest intimacy. Macho dancing: a hint of aggression in their every move. The females in the club—barely ten per cent of the clientele—all appeared to have a protector. Girl diners there were prized; daring by coming along, and looking undeservedly prim. Whatever they wore, it was a dull contrast to the scantily clad serving girls.

Charlie first laid eyes on Mandy while she was dancing with a tyre fitter. She was young, would have suited the school uniforms better than many of the waitresses, and she was wearing jeans. The most casually dressed girl in School Daze. Jeans and a red blouse Easily noticed by Charlie's roving eye. The tyre fitter—not that he knew what the man's trade was at this point in the evening—was seeking to pull the young girl into an embrace or a waltz and she, Charlie Quested's wife-to-be, was trying to evade his octopus' arms. That much was obvious. Charlie left his seat and made a bee-line for her. Asked to cut in, did so as a chivalrous act and not one he can recall doing before or since. He had a couple of inches on the tyre fitter, it was the girl's rejection he feared not the man's protest. The young girl in jeans said, 'See you, Racer,' to her overly tactile dancing partner.

He—Racer—stood his ground, looked squarely into Charlie's eyes. The new man in town held Racer's objectionable gaze, breathed in to accentuate his height. Then he nodded at Racer, the only person in the club whose name he knew, without his face showing a trace of the smugness he felt inside, and resisting the temptation to use the man's odd appellation. No sarcasm, lower the temperature. Racer turned and headed back towards his communal table

Young, confident, pretty and as-yet-nameless Mandy, danced before him, mouthing the words, 'Thank you.' He liked the enormous grin on her face. He tried to move like her. She was good at dancing as he was not; he knew better than to try to hold her close, mustn't paw a girl who had been so clearly shunting the last guy back to a safe distance.

As they danced, Charlie dipped his head in momentarily

to ask if he could buy her a drink.

She looked at him very levelly. 'And then what?'

'We drink and chat, I suppose.'

The girl gave him another smile, he really liked seeing those. She had something about her, dancing with a six-foot-two-inch stranger on the floor of a knicker-themed club. Wry amusement writ upon her face.

They headed for the bar; a man crossed the floor towards them, he clearly knew her but it was not Racer this time. He spoke to Mandy, a quick exchange out of Charlie's hearing. Then he turned to stare at him, before saying, 'All right, mate,' before abruptly going back to whichever dark corner of the club he had come from.

'Why are my work colleagues such twats?'

He was taken aback by her directness. 'What's the work?'

She explained the nature of the company, of the outing. The liquoring-up of tyre fitters as a reward for the fat profits of a man who left almost an hour ago. One drink and no food inside him as far as Mandy could tell. Charlie was impressed by her force of will. Some young girls may have elected to stay home and others may have tolerated the squeezing and groping which, she told him, epitomised the behaviour of the workforce at D and G Tyres and Exhausts. Mandy treated it like Charlie had those army assault courses. A bastard of a day, and definitely one to be mastered. 'I know who the twats are, you see. How to handle them. Can't not when I work with them five days of the week.'

The bar was exceptionally crowded, even Charlie's height seemed to glean him no advantage in catching the eye of the sexily dressed servers. Mandy tugged on his sleeve, 'It's noisy. Let's head outside.' He accompanied her to the tyre fitters table where she took a jacket off the back of her chair. The lads dipped their eyes, Charlie Quested had a certain presence. A broad-shouldered young man.

The club was on Saxon Street, may still be to this day.

Charlie assumes they will have updated the uniforms: put some men in shorts to accompany the girls, at the very least. On the street that night, Mandy and Charlie exchanged names, talked rapidly about why they were there. She was punctuating the boredom of living with her parents; he was charting the course of his post-army life. He enjoyed looking into her face. Dancing eyes, wild brown hair. Perhaps it started out neat and tidy, by this time of the evening it was heading a bit this way and a bit that. She looked terrific to the big fella.

'I'd have never guessed. I thought most army guys were bigger tits than tyre fitters.'

Charlie nodded at that. 'I'm not most.' He hoped it might become a truism of post-army Charlie.

She asked about the life he led, the drilling and parading. What living in barracks was like. Her questions weren't unintelligent but Charlie thought she might be trying to pigeonhole him. Understand him exclusively through the life he was about to step away from. When she told him, 'You're lucky that you've served between wars,' he was impressed by her unflinching certainty that there will be more. He needed to correct her error.

'Gulf war, Mandy. I'm a veteran of conflict.'

'Oh God, sorry. I was a kid then and I thought you were my age.'

He did not look to be her age, he was sure of it; Charlie found a charming sense of equality in her words. Mandy is tiny, her head goes only halfway up his chest. She has dark brown hair, wore it a little shorter then than now, and it has never been easily corralled; her skin was youthful, unblemished. That she saw herself on a par with the big veteran, was nice to hear. She seemed at ease with his interest in her. 'It was only six years ago. I was nineteen when I was in Iraq. Nineteen in a tank.'

Mandy turned quite solemn, seemed to give it more

gravity than most people his own age do. Than many in the army do unless they start talking casualties, allow in that other protocol. Mandy explained in answer to his questions that she was only working at D and G 'for the time being.' Told him that she might train to be a nurse or a nanny. 'Anything but the army. I'm no fighter.'

Charlie threw in an unconnected thought. 'I've paid for food back in that club. I don't like to miss it. Have you eaten?'

'I don't think I want to see the stupid guys from work. I'd rather they thought I'd scored. They'll be so jealous. Bloody pricks, all of them.'

The loose talk was exhilarating. 'I can fight them all off, you only need to look the other way as you're not into that stuff.'

'Nah. You haven't got your tank parked around the corner.'

'And that's a "No" to going back in?'

'Well, Mr Charlie...' Mandy once more pulled on his arm as she spoke. '...are we just stepping outside for air, or will you take me somewhere good?'

'Where would you like to go?'

'Anywhere the bar staff are not indecently dressed. I don't go out with men so that they can ogle other girls. It's a rule.'

'You win,' said Charlie.

3.

In The Kirkaldy, waiters and waitresses in their Christmas kitsch serve up turkey dinners. All the trimmings. It is a painful process. Upon a short row of large trestle tables, the component parts of the iconic meal go slowly cold as a never-ending line of revellers step up for the spooning. Sprouts, stuffing, cauliflower-cheese: all shovelled onto an expectant white plate. 'This is why Jesus came,' Fiona tells Charlie.

A man wearing an elf costume puts two slices of turkey on

Charlie's plate, the bedrock of the meal. He positions it off-centre, awaiting veg and whatnot. 'Pig in blanket?' asks the elf.

He nods. 'Me too,' says Deepika, beside him, plate held out for the simple delight. In her faux-Manchester accent she adds an aside to Charlie. 'It looks like Jesus's todger.'

Sober Charlie cracks up laughing, tells Deepika to shush a little. She seems quite drunk, and she was never cut out for stand-up. Fiona laughs, must have heard. She's catching up Deepika on the field of alcohol consumption front. Overtaken her, most likely, but handles it better. Down the line they get roasts and mash, red cabbage, bread sauce, cranberry, gravy. Nothing missing, not to Charlie's eye.

This gaggle of social workers—the hardcore of Fostering and Adoption—make it back to their table. Some begin to fill their mouths, while Deepika, confident from the success of her Jesus joke, tells Charlie that she wants to pull his cracker. They put down their knives and forks and everyone at the table links arms; a Christmas cracker in overlapped left and right hand, and they all pull. When the ritual is complete, Charlie finds no bounty in either hand. The short straw times two. Deepika has gambled and won, she passes one of her cracker bellies to him, putting a hand around his neck to do so, and giving the man a peck on the cheek. It's Christmas, he won't say anything. Charlie puts a green paper hat on his head, picks up his fork to eat the lukewarm food. Deepika reads out, 'Who delivers Christmas presents to our pet cats?' The table, those within earshot, contemplate the conundrum. 'Bloody stupid question,' she adds, 'I don't have a cat.'

'Santa Paws,' says Charlie, noticing a little cranberry sauce leave his lips for his white shirt front. Managing to stain his clothing while still on the orange juice.

'Clever-clogs Quested,' says Deepika, reading the back of the joke. 'Do you Christian boys have to swot up on these?

The answers are all in the bible, innit.'

'That's right,' he replies, 'it's a book of jokes. One laugh after another, even a crucifixion.'

Deepika picks up the little sausage—the pig no longer in its blanket—and puts it to her lips like a cigar. 'Good Jesus food,' she tells Charlie, bites off half and then quickly pushes the other half into his open mouth.

Charlie quarter-gags, then accepts it, goes with it. Deepika is crazy tonight. She is someone else. 'I can generally feed myself, Deepi,' he says between chews.

4.

Charlie and Mandy had barely walked fifty yards when she turned into him and pulled his head down to her lower level. Kissed him quickly on the lips. 'A proper date,' she said. Charlie was pleasantly staggered. He had known women but never known himself to be comfortable in their company. 'You've paid for food,' she added, 'you might as well eat it.'

Now he was quite nonplussed. 'You and I?' It was an open question, barely a question at all. The kiss indicated she was going nowhere without him. They were on a date.

'The D and G lads will be jealous as hell.' They had already turned around on the road; Mandy was the instigator, Charlie once more obeying orders. Heading back to School Daze, she linked her arm to his. They walked slowly. Outside the door of the club, Charlie hesitantly leaned in to give her another kiss. Mandy took his face in both her hands. Took her time, seemed to savour his lips upon hers. He let his hand rest in her hair, an ear gently caressed. He could have stayed on that street corner all night.

Inside the club, she clung to his arm as they walked past the table where her workplace party were sitting. Went straight by to the food counter at the rear of the large hall. When he showed his receipt, the waitress told him it was in the hotplate. They had assumed he was dancing. 'I'll bring it across,' she said. 'Which table are you at?'

Mandy pointed to a space on the end of a long table. 'We're there.'

It was an unusual pleasure to Charlie to have a girl so tactile with him. He had drunk three pints in quick succession before making any connection with Mandy. Cutting in, finding himself no longer alone. He didn't expect such a low level of alcohol to interfere with his decision-making but could not discount the possibility. Mandy was a new phenomenon to him.

A different waitress, ridiculously young—too much cleavage showing on a teen—brought his food across. Charlie made a point of gazing into Mandy's face, taking in the hazel colouring of her eyes, the small crescent shape that formed a moon to the right of her mouth as she smiled back at him. She met his eyes. He understood her earlier stipulation. Didn't look at the girl who placed burger and chips before him. 'Are you waiting too?' asked the waitress.

'I've eaten,' said Mandy. 'Just fattening this one up.'

The serving girl left, and Charlie again kissed his newly acquired girlfriend. It brought into his mind that he was a veteran of war not love. A few prostitutes and a couple of girls who didn't charge comprised his experience to date. He briefly dated a girl from his garrison town, North Yorkshire. So brief—three dates and given the elbow, his calls no longer returned—they barely made it as far as the level of physical intimacy he had already attained with Mandy. This was a dream, and perhaps that is what kept him grounded, aware. Already, at the age of twenty-five, dreams were not the places in which he usually felt at ease. 'Do you mind?' asked Charlie, gesturing at his burger, his need to consume alone.

'Just don't forget I'm here,' she said.

'Hey!' He had to protest. There could be no forgetting Mandy, never had a beguiling commanding officer before.

As he ate the burger, he fed the girl a chip or two. She raised a hand after that, needed no more. 'We had the works,' she told him. Then she seemed to look down, quickly glanced up. 'Racer's coming. Give me your face.'

Mandy again took his cheeks in her two hands, pressed their lips together. Her tongue quickly finding his. Charlie felt stirred by her, while calculating that the basic intent was to ward off the tyre fitter. He also recognised that Mandy's aversion to violence might require him to deal with Racer more intelligently than his army training had prepared him for.

'Come on, Mandy, you've had a few,' said Racer on arrival at their table.

'Leave her alone, please,' said Charlie, trying to take some control.

'Racer! I'm a grown woman, trot on back,' said Mandy, brushing him away with a hand gesture. Charlie found himself coughing to avoid laughing. A grown woman she is not. Over eighteen—he hoped—she was still just a playful kid.

'It's our do, your do,' said Racer, his eyes flitting between Mandy and the man she had draped herself around.

'I'm done. Just letting Charlie eat and then we're off.' Racer continued to stand over them. 'If Gifford can walk, so can I. Have a good night, Racer.' He narrowed his eyes and then turned away. Bitterness in the expression on his face, a grimace. Charlie guessed that his own presence was ruining Racer's night. Not that Mandy would have given him greater shrift if Charlie had not been there. 'Love you and leave you,' she said to his back, not at such a volume that he necessarily heard. Nothing in his gait told Charlie that he had.

'Mandy, you're something else.' Charlie patted a hand as nonchalantly as he could on the thigh of her jeans.

'I don't do this,' she said. 'I like you more than I know why.'

The young girl who had served Charlie the food was back.

'Is your meal all right?'

'Button up your blouse,' said Mandy before Charlie could compliment the overpriced fare. The girl turned back toward the kitchen. It was her job to dress that way.

5.

Faiza Pitafi, dressed in tight jeans, shimmering white blouse and an elegant gold headpiece—a necklace worn around her forehead in the South Asian style—leads the dancing. She is one of the Care Proceedings team of which Roselyn Pickford is a reluctant member. Faiza is the life and soul of the Kirkaldy, has most of the department up on their feet. Dancing social workers, and some of them surprisingly adept. Not Ted of course, he has long left. Never been seen to dance; even his smiles might be drawn from a supply of departmental issue facial expressions. A smile because his staff require it, not an involuntary expression. No mood but that American positivity that is so ill-fitting in a cash-strapped local authority in Northern England. Charlie hasn't seen Roselyn for a while; doubts if her absence is linked to Ted's. Coincidences happen. His table—the Fostering and Adoption crowd—are up with Faiza, moving to the music. Not Tariq, he stands at the side of the dancefloor. Adopting the position his daughter Michelle took at the swimming pool three years back. Wishing she could jump in while being frighteningly aware of her inability to swim. Charlie has no such certificate of exemption. He tries to follow the dance moves that Faiza does so effortlessly. Fiona and Deepika are relishing their chaperoning duties.

He knows Yasmin and Faiza are friends. They might be the most level-headed in here, alongside this sober version of Charlie Quested. The two girls have talked the DJ into playing something Asian; he thinks it's bhangra music but knows too little about the genre to be certain. The bass is

Back On the Dancefloor

fun: wobbly and expressive. Faiza has them all flickering their arms, twisty dancing. Bending at the knees while their feet stay stock still. Trees in the wind, swaying. Many revellers—joiners-in dancing to the bhangra beat—play no part in the city's children's services. Disparate groups: accountants and shipping clerks, a call centre, one or two extended families. Social workers have no monopoly on Christmas. The dancers follow Faiza's lead, whoever they are, wherever they hail from. No one has a better plan, and she is a good-humoured leader of drunks. Deepika knows how to dance this way. Moves she has seen before, no doubt, and it's quite a contrast from her hapless Northern Line. Both Fiona and Charlie are copying her, the latter half-heartedly. Fiona loves it. Having a ball, anyone can see. Precious comes across to Charlie, whispers in his ear. 'Roselyn wants to talk. She's outside.'

His smile sinks away. He thinks he has finally relaxed, more than he's managed since Mandy threw him out all those months ago. His ex-boss has no hold upon him. Ex-lover, his mistake. No claim to him, and he is no longer interested in her. Setting himself on a better course back to Mandy. 'I'll just be a moment,' he tells Deepika.

* * *

The outside from which Roselyn has summoned her former underling is not the true cold of outdoors. It is simply an alcove some distance along the broad corridor of the hotel. Away from dining hall and dancefloor. Precious pointed him the way, it quickly became familiar. Charlie waited here between the component parts of his assessment day in October. The girl with the pink streak in her hair had a desk out here. Right On Track—orchestrators of that arbitrary and portentous day—are long gone. Took Brenda and Tina down with them. Graham too, although he has sadly fallen furthest. Recalling it reminds Charlie of why he didn't really want to come to the stupid Christmas party. Many a soldier attends the regimental dinner only reluctantly. Mixed feelings. To follow orders is not to consider them wise; it is not to consider them at all. That's the way military discipline floats. Follow, follow, follow. Think twice and we're all buggered.

There is a small chaise longue where the desk once was. Roselyn lounges upon it and her red skirt has risen high up her legs. He meditated upon her allure earlier, the lighting here is less forgiving. The skin of her arms and face is newspaper white, the width of her thighs exaggerated in the posture of her small sprawled figure. He stands over her. 'Hi Ros, how can I help.' As he says it, he regrets abbreviating her name. He should off-load the familiarity he once had with this unpredictable Siren.

'Sit, Charlie.'

He does not.

'Oh,' she exhales, 'what are we fighting about?'

'I'm not fighting you, Roselyn. I'm not sure why I'm here.'

'Moved on to Deepika now, have we?'

It's an absurd thing to say, and Roselyn has tanked a few white wines by the sound of it. The ducks quack that came out of her mouth as she tried to say his newest team member's name. Once her managerial colleague. 'Ros, that's not fair.' He feels defensive towards Deepika; he likes her, assumed before tonight that she did not drink. Could even be her first time. If Deepika's tipsy-funny show this evening is making her flirtation obvious, it is what office Christmas parties are for. Roselyn is big enough to understand that. Not sober enough is all. And Charlie is not to blame for Deepika's mood this evening. Nor for Roselyn's sulk down the corridor. None of it is of his contrivance. They'd all just eat the food and go, if it was down to him.

'You shouldn't take advantage of her, you know. She's vulnerable, our Deepika, very vulnerable.'

'I'm doing nothing like that to her. Keeping her company.

It's what she wants.'

'Sit,' she says again. This time he relents. 'I'm vulnerable too, Charlie. I'm starting to think that those given the boot were the lucky ones. Demotion has been a daily piss-take. A reminder that we weren't quite up to the job we thought we were.'

'Yeah,' says Charlie. 'It's gotten to Deepika. I can see it. We like her, treat her as one of us. I don't know your team. Only Faiza.' She keeps staring at him as Charlie rambles. 'You were a decent manager, you know?'

'I know I was. Bloody Fred Astaire knows, and then he goes and schemes over how to make us all work harder, one way or another.'

Charlie is too sober to stay cross about Roselyn's maudlin talk. He can see it is within Deepika also, although drink has made her funny, blasphemous. The Christmas goblin.

'Are you still thick with him?' he asks.

'Thick? With Ted? He makes a lot of demands on me, Charlie. This project, that project. You wouldn't think I'd been demoted.'

'I heard you were getting a stipend for it, a bonus. Something like that.'

'Yes, I shamed him into it. Can you believe it? First, he pushes me into Care Proceedings, and then Ted asks me to lead projects on practitioner standards and an analysis of our most expensive legal cases too. Why do I do it, Charlie? I let him walk all over me.'

Charlie opens his mouth as if to comment, no worthwhile observation forming. A posse of girls walk past them—not social workers—mini-skirted, the make-up on their faces garish in the strip lighting. They are loud with alcohol. 'Toilets that way,' Roselyn tells them.

They laugh as they walk by. 'Thank you,' one of the girls calls out.

'Is Geoff back?'

'Charlie! You are not getting back in my bed that easily.'

'I wasn't. I was worried about your homelife. I think work has been fucking with all our marriages. You and Deepika particularly.'

'No, Charlie. You are the one fucking with our particular marriages. Have you heard that Carrie left Ted?'

This is from the top office. Not a rumour that has trickled down to him, or to any in his team, not as far as he is aware. Roselyn might have appraised Precious of the facts, if facts they are; they had a chinwag earlier this evening.

'No kidding?'

'She's gone home to America, to Philadelphia. I wonder if he's long for us. Might follow her back there, I can imagine. And he's put the wrecking ball through the department, wouldn't you say?'

As she is telling him this gossip, the snapping of a branch in the highest tree, the falling to Earth of the man whose name graces the social work journals on an almost weekly basis, Charlie's thoughts drift elsewhere. 'I think I did that to my family,' he says and hangs his head.

Roselyn looks sideways at him, may not wish to dwell upon her own participation in his misery. Might prefer credit for the fitful happiness that preceded it. 'Hey, hey.'

Charlie doesn't respond.

'I brought you out here to cheer me up, Mr Quested.'

He turns and takes her eye. 'We can't, can we?'

She looks at him blankly. 'I took Graham on a weekend walk, just to lift him out of these post-fuck-up doldrums. Look what happened there.' Now Charlie stands, not rudely, just taking his leave. He lets his hand rest briefly on her shoulder. 'We were fun, Roselyn, good, illicit, marriage-ruining fun. We should regret it but probably don't. We've neither of us got a shoulder for the other to cry on, have we?'

She turns her head, kisses the hand.

6.

'One dance before we go,' said Mandy. A ruse to upset a few tyre fitters. It must have been. Charlie walked her to the middle of the floor and then she danced quite hypnotically. Not that her moves were so special, she'd simply mesmerised him earlier in the evening. Under the spell, Charlie was a prop in her dance routine. Never the focal point. After a time, she took him in her arms, he quickly put his own hands upon her in a manner to make it appear that he might be leading. It was not the case. They smooched their way closer to the edge of the dancefloor. One or two underdressed waitresses were collecting glasses. Charlie scarcely noticed them, he was sinking into the presence of Mandy. A joyous immersion. She was the merest nineteen years of age on that unforgettable day in nineteen-ninety-seven. Today, at thirty-six, her face is infinitely more youthful than Roselyn's. If she cannot run down a squash ball as efficiently, it is only superficial fitness, not loss of shape. Time has made a fool of him in the intervening years, taken its time doing it. The man who could not form a relationship until young Mandy Blackburn nonchalantly ushered him into a fine one, has thrown it all away. Never understood it, how so simple an act managed to wreak that havoc. He had slipped into love more easily than he'd dreamed he ever might. He sometimes wondered what she saw in him; she said they were a couple who had found each other. She never disappointed him, he hoped she felt the same. It seemed so easy for so long. He thought it might be the way that marriages went. Affairs, forgiveness. Perhaps some do but he wonders now if he has even been paying attention. Mandy lived with her parents back then: the family home. Told him, on that first encounter, that she had date before but never seriously. Never had a boyfriend she felt minded to cling to, stay with.

Give herself to. She didn't say the words but he was astute enough to understand what she was telling him. Mandy remained a virgin. Charlie made no attempt to alter her sexual status on that first of April. He is not an especially sensitive man, and so he put a bit of effort into doing what Mandy wanted. Back then he did. He must have known he was dancing close up to a hedgerow bird. She only let him come close because she had the agility to flitter away. Rushing Mandy Blackburn into anything would never do.

The dance complete, they left School Daze hand in hand like the teenage romance it surely was. Heady compensation for how barren those years had been for Charlie first time around. From there they went to the cinema. He paid for the late film. It was a comedy, Mandy said she liked them. Neither watched it closely, not from the back row. Kissing, whispering, giggling on her part, took precedence over following a slapstick plot flung at them late on a rollercoaster of an evening.

When they emerged back into the streetlights, Charlie hailed a taxi and rode with it. Took Mandy to her house. He knew that he would need to walk back to his bed and breakfast, the taxi an expense he could justify only in his pursuit of the girl. Hoped he would be able to find his way, this city quite unfamiliar to him back then.

At her door, as she fumbled for a key, it opened up and a small red-faced man said, 'What time do you call this?'

Charlie stretched out a hand. 'Pleased to meet you, Mr Blackburn,' and with it, the man's tone changed at a stroke. He invited Charlie in. Offered him a whisky but Charlie declined, went about it politely. No wish to offend. He noted that Mandy wore an expression of bemusement on her face. Watched more than she spoke, as the unlikely courting of Charles Quested by her own father took place.

The three of them drank coffee in the kitchen, Mr Blackburn explaining that Mandy's mother was sleeping.

Charlie told of his forthcoming departure from HM services—he used exactly that term—Mr Blackburn looked worried, thought it meant he was on early release from prison. When Charlie corrected him, said he had served with a Yorkshire regiment, been out in the Gulf, Mr Blackburn tried again to get out the whisky bottle. 'Hats off to you.' What an odd way to speak.

'It's a good while ago now,' Charlie told him.

7.

Faiza still has a line of social workers and hangers on dancing in imitation of her entrancing Anglo-Pakistani moves. She is a Butlins red coat although her blouse is gold beneath jet-black hair. An elegance beyond her role tonight. Yasmin acts as cheerleader, and an enthusiastic, but very drunk, Deepika tries to do the same. Charlie watches them Bollywood dance to the Ronnie Prousch Christmas song. It is back on the turntable, once again making its festive stir. He would be joining in the fun if he weren't so sober. He drifts back to his table, notices that the Fostering-and-Adoption signage has fallen to the floor, lies beneath a chair.

There is no one else at the table, even Tariq finally dancing. A cold Christmas pudding sits dolefully in Charlie's place. He picks up the spoon, takes a small corner. It is rich, none the worse for being cold. There is an untouched pint of beer close to hand, not his. It could be anybody's. He puts his large fingers around the glass, it is very cold, only recently poured. He glances across to the dancefloor, releases his fingers. He is driving, never drinks when he is driving. Not a fucking drop. As he is half way through the pudding, eating it not from hunger but to appear occupied, Deepika slips into the seat beside him. 'You look like the only Hindu at the Christmas party?' she says. Absentmindedly he places a hand upon her back, feels the flesh between her shoulder blades, where her sari parts. 'Cold fingers,' she says. The hand which clasped the lager.

'I'm sorry, Deepi. I'm not really in the party mood.'

She doesn't argue, doesn't flirt. He likes that she is this sensitive, although even Roselyn saw fit not to argue when he became introspective. He never quite figured out what she wanted with him, not this evening in the corridor recess, not on the evening of the assessment outcomes. Not last summer either when the going was only a guilty conscience short of good. Absent-mindedly, he rubs Deepika's back, his thoughts flitting between his young children and Graham helplessly marooned in a hospital bed. They pass no words between them. Stare out at their colleagues on the dancefloor. Yasmin and Faiza continue to represent Pakistan in the dance Olympics. Fiona mimics them, not bad for a white girl. As they watch the revelry, Charlie and Deepika swivel their heads simultaneously as each feel a hand upon their shoulder. Roselyn is behind them. She leans in to Deepika, then, within Charlie's hearing she says, 'Watch him, you. He's a dark horse is our Charlie Quested. Don't let him touch you where you don't want him to.'

Charlie feels insulted by this. Ros must be drunk. Deepika is still new to the team. He coughs before putting her straight. Tries to think what he might say in his own defence.

'I'm his.' Deepika is back in funny voice. 'Office party, innit. I'm his.'

'Oh, do what you like, Deepika. He's no bloody good.'

Roselyn storms off. Charlie thinks that he must have let her down out in the corridor, wished for some kind of fellow feeling that he couldn't muster. He hopes that Mandy can understand this, that she can sense him edging back to her. He cannot see from here how the bloody hell she would. She has no more telepathic power than he does. Zero. Even sober, his late-night thoughts are a nonsense.

'She's a difficult woman,' says Deepika. 'She got like that

in managers meetings. And she's more frustrated now she hasn't any to attend. I think she's drunk too much tonight.'

'You too, Deepi, but it hasn't turned you bitter. You're always the better soul.' He rests his arm across her shoulders a second, then pulls it away. Mandy on his mind.

8.

Charlie and the sales job were a hopeless fit from day one. Vinegar shaken over trifle. The man is no quitter and Green Light gave him all the time he needed to figure his shortcomings out for himself. Repeated failure leaves an easy-to-decipher trail of clues. They were in no hurry to sack him, to reify what was long in the air around his unproductive desk. The company was as poor at performance management as their latest recruit was at telesales.

He spent nine months holed up there, trying to convert people with a passing interest in home insurance into becoming policyholders. Policies held with Green Light, if at all possible. It happened occasionally, in the way that a forcible wind might turn prostrate garden furniture back upright. The odd success between interminable barren spells. Despite this—and due to the good fortune of a decent basic salary—Charlie was able to acquire a mortgage. He had decent savings from his army days, a favourable interest rate through a scheme for ex-servicemen. The terraced house which he chose was about a mile from Mandy's parents' house. Where she continued to live. Charlie saw her every week. More than once a week if she allowed it.

He always had the feeling that Mandy picked him out on the first of April. He even worried that not being a tyre fitter was the stand-out quality which had attracted her, and he felt uncertain if it would be enough. He pleased and surprised himself, sustaining the relationship over time. It was a first for him, and—Mandy told him—a more lasting relationship than any she had previously enjoyed.

Mr and Mrs Blackburn were always nice to Charlie, and Mandy was their youngest child. Two older brothers had fled the nest, one serving in the army in Cyprus. They liked Charlie, loved their daughter still more.

When the house was in the pipeline—solicitors searching and conveyancing, running up a bill—Charlie kept Mandy informed. Could not quite bring himself to ask her to move in. The fear of rejection was complicated. And theirs was not yet a more physical relationship than had been so during their first hours together. Mandy was no prude but nor was she in a hurry. Charlie sensed the watching parents. Not that he and she didn't enjoy time alone. When he was still in rented, Mandy was happy to come up to his room. Mostly they just chatted, went a little further once or twice. Not too much further, Mandy's limits respected.

'When I do, you'll be the one, Charlie,' she told him once, during an hour in his digs, rain waylaying a planned weekend walk. 'Provided you don't go chasing anyone else behind my back like you're on a weekend away from the army.' Mandy had told him she and Simon—her brother who still served—were close. She probably heard a lot about the goings-on from him. Lads holed up in barracks tend to go a bit mental when they're let out. In the forging of this new and honest relationship, Charlie had told her obliquely of the couple of sexual conquests he'd managed without parting with cash. His past and infrequent patronage of prostitutes he felt no need to divulge. Nor was he tempted to repeat the experience. Charlie Quested was in love.

There was a memorable conversation, memorable for him although he has never sought Mandy's recollection of the same. Its importance might have all been from his perspective. 'Can I meet your mum?' she asked. Mandy was astute, more than aware of how heavily laden a question this was for him. She was holding his hand, holding his eye when she asked the question. Said it sensitively.

'Which one?' answered Charlie.

'Whichever one you think I should meet.' This was something that Charlie loved about her. She wanted to know him, not to mould him. Listened to what he had to say however tongue-tied or inarticulate his way of saying it. And Charlie certainly knew which mother he most wanted Mandy Blackburn to meet. Grace Bell and only Grace Bell, his foster mother: Mum.

Annie Corrigan, who was briefly Annie Quested, featured only fleetingly in his thoughts, and very low down in his estimation. She caused him more problems than she solved. A life-long condition. He kept contact with her, with his biological mother. Knew when she was and wasn't in prison. She told him she was proud of how he turned out. The army. But theirs was not a mutually respectful relationship. The telephone was all he could manage for months and even years at a time. Small doses of Annie Corrigan were tolerable, her absence an even better state. In the past he had done prison visits—felt a little trepidation when he told Mandy about these—worried that it might reflect negatively on how she saw him. His girlfriend was never judgemental, trusted him. Right up until the summer of the year twenty thirteen. This year. He needs to win back that trust.

Although Charlie felt that only one of his two mothers truly mattered to him, he decided that Mandy deserved to see him in full. He wanted her to understand him, God knows, she was more likely to figure him out than he ever was. They talked it over, planned a visit across the Pennines for the weekend. Bridlington first, biological mum, then Wakefield, the home he enjoyed with Mrs Bell. The parent he remained close to, phoned far more frequently than he ever did skinny Annie.

When they made plans, it struck Charlie as an odd thing,

that this should be their first weekend away together. He said he'd pay for a room each, but Mandy told him to leave the arrangements to her. She was working, happy to pay her way.

'I've booked us a twin room,' she said two days later. 'Loads cheaper than two singles.'

Charlie drove them and the meeting in Bridlington was pleasant enough, if stilted. His mother made an effort, wore a pair of unstained trousers, a blouse that looked properly washed, hair in decent order. Seldom were these things so.

'Oh Charlie, you've found yourself a beauty. Whatever does she see in you?' his mother tried to joke. He was able to confirm to her that Mandy was his first 'steady' girlfriend. 'Big strapping lad that he is, late starter, eh?' she chipped in. He worried over what his girlfriend made of this—Annie playing Mother Hen for the first time in her life—Mandy took it in her stride. And she made no discernible reaction when, towards the close of their ninety minutes together, Annie Corrigan said solemnly, 'I'm off the drugs now, Charlie. Off them for good.'

Charlie nodded sympathetically. He'd heard it all before, had zero confidence in it.

When they were driving back towards Wakefield, the bed and breakfast, Mandy didn't say anything for the longest time. 'Annie's a sorry soul, can't cope, should be pitied really. But for you, Charlie-love, that's no excuse. She let you down more times than any kid should have to cope with. Probably did all that before you started taking in what was going on.' Charlie kept driving, looking out the windscreen, nodded his head a little. He did not disagree. He felt choked up. It was not like him to get emotional about the woman he thinks of only sporadically, takes her telephone calls but never seeks them out. Has put the firmest lid on all he used to feel towards her. He thought it was his girlfriend's sympathy that was adhering to the inside of his throat.

Causing him to breathe more shallowly. Then Mandy asked him, 'Will you?' He knew that she was referring to his parting shot.

On the doorstep, Annie Corrigan had held a hand each of Charlie's and Mandy's and said, 'Invite me to your wedding, won't you?' Without dropping her gaze, but letting her hand slip and taking Mandy by the shoulder towards the car, Charlie had breezed a mean, 'Maybe,' over his shoulder and they were gone.

As he dwelt upon it on the drive to Wakefield, he suddenly saw that Mandy could have taken his maybe to mean that a marriage was not really on the cards. When he began to say this, to apologise if she had misunderstood, she interrupted. 'I get it. She never gave you a minute's certainty when you were a child. Payback time. I get it.'

A part of Charlie wished that he had never taken her, never shown that side of himself—he will never reciprocate Annie Corrigan's fey sentimentality—but deep down he thinks Mandy is the first person since Grace Bell to understand and accept him. She never sought to modify how he has assimilated a difficult past. What cannot be changed.

9.

The girls in their white-trimmed Santa coats and short red dresses clear away the Christmas debris. Plates strewn with uneaten food, paper hats and popper trails. The disco doesn't know any downtime; the beat goes on. People dance, draped around each other or on their own, plenty of each. Charlie allows Deepika to nestle on his shoulder, enjoys it, although he keeps thinking about Mandy. Thinking how he might eject Barry Brice from the household in which his children live. It will be Mandy's decision in the long run. That's been the way of things in his marriage. He wonders if he could nudge her in that direction, show her who is the better man. Dance this way with her, with Mandy in preference to Deepika.

Fiona and Faiza are dancing together, making a show of being shmaltzy. A slow waltz. Nothing too off-colour but funny. Deepika keeps an eye on them as if transfixed. Charlie lifts her head a little to enable him to twist around, see the two girls smooching. Deepika straightens herself up, detaches herself from him. 'I'm not like them.' Then in her mock northern voice, she adds, 'Too bloody serious me, innit?'

'Don't change,' and he wonders if he sounds too interested by saying it. She has been walking a thin line all night. The way of flirters who never flirt. An unlikely gravitas to the fluttering of eyes and the delivery of a double entendre.

She sinks back into him, rests the side of her cheek against his chest, rocks him gently. 'Can't be in my own place tonight, Charlie. Not another night alone.' He says nothing to this quiet assertion, he feels not even conflicted. Wants her friendship, not her body. Not a night together. He has no idea how to say it without sounding a brute, a soldier dispatching the enemy. He has no wish to appear that way to Deepika. Good and gentle Deepika. Whatever it is that has got into her tonight, he wants to help her through it. Do it properly, not exploit a situation. 'You heard me, Charlie,' she says. And he did hear her, even felt a little ache that belongs to his animal self, not to Mandy's husband. The father-of-three self that he clings to like a religion. He finds himself mouthing the words, 'I've drunk nothing.' He must have let a little air exhale from him as he did so. Deepika is crying in his arms. She gives him the smallest punch. 'What's Roselyn got that I haven't,' she hisses under her breath. 'She's a bitch and I'm not.'

Charlie puts a hand to her mouth, does so as gently as he is able. 'Shush. Sorry.' She pulls his head down with both her hands, brushing his hand aside and kissing him quickly on the lips. The DJ puts on some thumping Christmas music from the nineteen-seventies, glam-rockers wishing Christmas lasted a lifetime. Charlie breaks the hold, glad of the change of song. The upping of tempo. The singer's assertion, hankering for more of this, strikes Charlie as laughable. A never-ending office Christmas party? Purgatory, sheer ruddy purgatory.

10.

Charlie and Mandy prepared themselves for bed discreetly. The twin bedroom was inexpensive; these were times when guesthouses had a room or two without an en-suite. Mandy changed into her nightclothes in the bathroom across the landing, Charlie put on his pyjamas while she was in there. When she returned, she looked younger than her twenty years. The tartan of her thick flannel pyjamas brought his foster homes to mind. The foster home that he and she were to visit the next day. Grace Bell always had a full house, he understood it still to be the case; she and Norman still fostering long past their retirement age. Charlie was under the counterpane. He had not dimmed the light. Two beds on opposite walls, a dressing table that Mandy had earlier declared to be made from walnut, and Charlie never doubted her. He didn't know furniture, knew walnut to be used for the stock of the finest rifles, and it looked right. A lonely armchair kept vigil in the corner of the room. Mandy sat upon her bed and combed her hair silently for the longest time, and then, still wordless, she came across the room and turned on a wall lamp at the head of his bed. He tried to take her hand—to kiss it—but she evaded him. Then back to the door she went, turned out the main light. Left the room to the lower voltage of the bedside lamp. Her face looked more beautiful still to the smitten Charlie, the lightest of smiles on it as she trekked back, passed her own single bed and came straight to his. She lifted up the cover and snuck in beside him. He put a welcoming arm around his girlfriend, kissed her carefully. 'Hey, Charlie, it's my first time remember.' He felt flustered, even stammered when trying to seek quite what she was requesting. He did not wish to do anything that contradicted her wishes, so much did he treasure her. 'Pass me my handbag then,' she said when she understood his main area of consternation. He was in and out of the bed, turning his body to hide from her the disfigurement her promise brought to the outline of his pyjama bottoms. As she pushed a hand into her small brown shoulder bag, she retrieved a packet of what they needed. Mandy had planned the weekend very, very well.

11.

'B-ye, drive safe. Lovely evening, everyone.' Yasmin is effusive when he drops her off at the end of party night. She even comes around to the driver's door and, as he winds the window down wondering what she might request, ducks her head in and pecks him quickly on the cheek. 'Thank you. Thank you for driving us all back safely.' As he tries to smile back at her, he recalls how recently he failed the very same test.

Then she opens her front door, and he drives away. Fiona is telling Deepika something about Danny, it is quite negative, and Charlie even thinks she is suggesting that she and Faiza would make a better couple. It makes no sense, neither are that way inclined. Fiona is booze-befuddled. Or has he long missed some tell-tale signs. Graham flabbergasted him when he came out in Devon. He doesn't think he let it show, should be cool about that sort of thing but he isn't. It might be an insult to Faiza. Or it might be a compliment. Sexual politics are not Charlie's forte. When they arrive at Fiona's building, she insists both parties step out of the car for one last hug. Deepika is keen, Charlie less so. 'Look after her,' Fiona whispers while giving him the tightest squeeze of a tactile night. Kissing Charlie on the lips, quick but intended. He thinks it might be for a watching Danny, not that Charlie can see him from here. He wishes she hadn't. He wants Mandy back and kissing others is not on the roadmap. He imagines that this is a six-month window. If he remains in the doghouse any longer than that he will most likely throw himself at anyone and everyone. For how long can a man stay chaste?

When just the two of them remain, the car is silent. Charlie drives towards the flat where the evening started, where he first picked up Deepika. As he is turning into her road, she puts a hand upon his, lightly, not inhibiting his steering. 'Please Charlie. I need your company. I'll go mad in there on my own.'

He doesn't negotiate any ground rules, doesn't make clear what the sleeping arrangements may be, drives on. Parks a little later in a space reserved for occupants of the building in which he rents a small one-bed.

Together Charlie and Deepika climb the concrete staircase.

12.

'You shouldn't have gone to this trouble, Mrs Bell.' The lady insisted that she called her Grace but Mandy kept forgetting. Grace was the age of her nan.

'Like the old days,' said Charlie, forking shepherd's pie into his mouth. There were five sitting around the table. Mrs Bell had three foster children staying with her, one of whom had commandeered her husband, Norman, for the day, going on a pre-planned visit to the home of her birth family. Two were sharing the lunchtime meal she had prepared for

Charlie's visit. Charlie and Mandy.

'She's a beautiful girl, Charlie,' said Grace. Then she looked directly at his young friend. 'You have to know, when this lad first came to me—fine young man that he is now—he couldn't look at a girl without going the brightest red. Couldn't really speak in their company.'

Charlie laughed out loud. Nodded agreement that it was once so. Memories of everything with Grace Bell were good. She might still tease him with the truth, it was also a measure of the distance from there to here, what a good place he had arrived at. There had been no such joy, honesty or playful reminiscence the day before with Annie Corrigan. 'That was just the kid I was back then,' said Charlie, looking at Jennifer and Ahmed. Two thirteen-year-olds sitting at the dinner table, doing as he had many years earlier. 'I think I was angry and insecure. Moved from one home to another for about a year and missed a hell of a lot of school for years before that. I wasn't thick but I thought I was.' As he was speaking, Mandy placed her hand over the top of his. They had talked about his childhood many times; in this house, it was a more stirring recollection than any previous telling. 'You believed in me when I really didn't,' he told his foster mother. The two young ones looked surprised, Ahmed put his fork down, neither spoke. 'I'm sorry,' said Charlie, as if the seriousness of his tone were a breach of the social code in their home.

'Good for you, mate,' said Ahmed. The girl stared only at the food on her plate.

He noticed Mandy looking around. The room was clean, tidy enough, the wallpaper faded. In every cabinet and on every shelf, little artefacts cluttered the home. China teacups, rows of thimbles. A mantelpiece lined with matchbox cars, each one shiny as if diligently polished. He remembered Norman Bell talking to him about his car collection when he was upset. Not stupidly, a distraction.

Getting his mind off the mother he never wanted to see again. Charlie wasn't sure, just guessed that every piece of bric-a-brac he saw had been in a similar spot when he was a troubled foster child. Reliant on this kindly household. He glanced at his girlfriend's face, fearing she might see it in a poorer light—the house a throwback, an archaic place—Mandy was rapt. She opened her mouth, as if to ask a question, but no words came. Then Jennifer asked her, 'Are you in a children's home?' It must have been an odd question although Charlie knew that Mandy never really looked her years. Every landlord in every pub had to see her driving license before they would serve her a drink.

'No, I still live with my parents,' she said. Then she looked directly at the young girl. 'I'm a lucky one. I know I am.'

Charlie glanced at the two children, knowing it was a tricky area to talk about casually. He had no idea what kind of fractured home lives these two had come from. Knew better than to ask, to encroach.

'Her Mum has a little business, selling dancing clothes, dancing shoes. Ballet stuff mostly.' Charlie explained his girlfriend to the youngsters. 'Mine sold drugs a few times. So, you see, they're both business people, it's something in common. My mum got prison time for it. Mandy's mum is far and away the smarter.'

He saw Grace looking carefully at Jennifer, wondered if he'd overstepped the mark, but conversations in this house were always lively, honest. He remembered that quite distinctly, the content of one or two. It helped him, and made him think about his situation as he had never come close to before living here. It was how he learned to be proud of who he was in place of the shame he'd long felt for who his mother was.

'Did you go?' said the girl.

'Prison?'

She nodded.

'Sometimes, and other times I refused. Couldn't stand it.'

'Same for me but I think she's not my mum really. It's unbelievably shit.'

Charlie glances at Grace, she doesn't pull the girl up on the language. He guesses she's not been here long, stricter rules put in as the child can cope with them. 'It's an awful place to have to visit. And she's your mum, truly. But she isn't you, Jennifer. It's her in prison, not you. There for what she's done. You've done nothing. You'll feel all sorts towards her but she really isn't your responsibility.'

13.

'Deepi, I'm not thinking straight this evening.' He is pretty certain that she was sick in his bathroom. Now she's started to undress and he has tried to stop her.

'Just come to bed. We both think too much, Charlie.'

'Deepi, we're not really bedhopping people, are we? You have a husband...'

'A bloody useless husband, Charlie. Useless at this, and I'm hoping you're a bit better. Come to bed.'

'Sit down,' he tells her. Deepika Deshpande is on the edge of Charlie's double bed, her sari is across a chair and he struggles not to look at her thighs, her midriff. He senses that he must leave the room before she removes more clothing, reveals more than a weak-willed man can away from. Earlier this year he learned himself to be a less resolved than he once believed. Learned that the insecure boy who Grace Bell so successfully built up, never quite left him. He is capable of forgetting, of throwing away a lot for the excitement of the moment. He's not been a vandal or a truant for close to thirty years, sex turns out to be a more rewarding temptation. And the more punishing in the long run.

'I don't want to do this to Mandy. To my Mandy. It has

nothing to do with you, Deepika. I should have dropped you at your own place, I just saw how upset you were.'

She stands up in her half-dressed state. 'What's bloody Roselyn got!' she shouts, hitting him half-heartedly on the shoulder.

'I wish I'd never.' He knows this is only hindsight; knows not when Ros told Deepika about whatever he and she once had. He was all too willing that half year ago, never thought through the cause and effect when he did what he did. 'You need to sleep. I'll be sleeping on the couch. On my own.' He gestures the other side of the bedroom door. 'I'll be out there in the lounge if you want to talk.' As he is speaking, Deepika's hands are behind her back, unclasping her bra. 'Wear something if you want to talk,' he says, rising from the bed, moving to the other room in an unseemly hurry. 'I'm sorry,' he says as he closes the door.

14.

Charlie drove them back over the Pennines, their relationship more intimate than before in so many ways. 'You were as good as she was, Charlie,' said Mandy. He denied it. Said he knows only what Grace Bell taught him, Mandy talked over him, 'It was from the heart. I bet you're better than Jennifer's social worker. I didn't dare speak. My flipping perfect life and everything.'

The seed of an idea. And he had Mandy to thank for it. He failed at one more sales job before turning to social work. Finding his vocation. She spotted it for him in the course of a single mealtime, but Charlie can be stubborn. Reluctant to believe in anything new.

The house purchase was painful, stalled a couple of times for reasons that estate agents explained and Charlie barely believed. By the autumn he had a place of his own. He went to see Mr and Mrs Blackburn, Mandy laughed through most of the conversation—kept saying it was her choice whatever her parents said—it was all very good humoured. They were going to live together, and no one objected.

The pregnancy came before the marriage, and the marriage before baby. Charlie was true to Mandy. Never a carnal thought for another woman until the day Roselyn pulled him into a ladies' changing room after they had played a harmless game of squash together. That is what he tells himself, what he believes. And if he did think of straying, picture himself in the act of lovemaking with another, it was just a fabrication. Like reading a book of fiction or watching a made-up drama on the TV. Roselyn flipped him over, won him for adultery, used an old army trick in the doing of it. Pulled rank and he was helpless to do anything other than obey. A follower of orders.

Take responsibility, Quested, he tells himself, sticking to the couch as he said he would. Tempted by Deepika in the next room, and definitely not acquiescing. Not to the little soldiers' expectations of the big.

15.

Before he leaves to pick up Fiona with whom he has an appointment, work to do in Derbyshire, he knocks quite loudly on the bedroom door. He has not spoken to Deepika all night. He imagines she has slept, wonders how she did it. He barely got a moment.

When he hears her say, 'Charlie, forgive me, my friend,' he feels a certain relief. Thinks he may have got away with a poor decision. Letting her sleep in his flat has not been a total calamity.

'I've got to pick up Fiona, would you like me to bring her round before we go on the visit?'

'Heavens, no. I don't think you really want her to know I've been here. No reason that you need to tell her. I've been a bit of a vamp, haven't I?'

Charlie laughs through the door. It's crazy and apt. 'Are you decent; can I come in?'

'I'm under the covers, Charlie. I'll not ask you to join me, I promise.'

He pushes gingerly down on the door handle, opens the door so slowly it might be distrustful. Deepika has the bedside lamp on, the curtains are drawn. She is sitting up, knees making a tent of the duvet. She holds it up close to her person, properly raised above her bustline. 'How's your head?'

'I don't do this, I don't know what I'm supposed to be feeling.' She taps her forehead. 'I think there are some workmen bashing about in there. I hope they can straighten me out.'

'Deepika, I think I need to go soon; you're welcome to stay as long as you like...'

'Mandy won't be coming by?'

He feels a quickening as she raises this possibility but it is not on the cards. She's never yet put a foot inside this flat. He's fetched the children over here a few times. Collects them from the house on Bramley Road, the home he is still footing a mortgage on.

'She won't. You'd know what to say if she did.'

'I don't think I do but I'd try. You've been very kind to me, Charlie. I've been a bit mean to you. Very selfish, and I'm really not Roselyn Pickford.'

Charlie notices that tears are once more troubling Deepika's face. Only one, two, they track down from the corners of her eyes. He takes a step towards her, puts a gentle hand on her bare shoulder. 'I don't get it. You're a million times better than Pickford.'

'Just not more desirable,' she says.

Charlie will have none of it. 'I buggered up my marriage, I'm doing anything I can to get it back. Please don't think you're undesirable.'

She nods her head, gives him the hint of a smile. Not a happy smile, her innate civility.

'No more nights naked in the next room, I'll bloody crack,' he adds, and Deepika turns her face to his hand resting on her shoulder. She kisses it once and he quickly withdraws it.

'Go,' she says. 'Go, Charlie. Dreams were nicer in this flat than alone in my own. I have you to thank for that.'

* * *

The drive will take them the far side of an hour. Fiona seems barely the worse for wear, for all the gin and white wine she shifted. Lager too if Charlie's memory serves. When he asks her, 'How are things?' he hopes to hear a declaration that she and Danny are good. Their relationship restored to its feisty norm.

'Did you notice?'

Charlie sometimes thinks the world passes him by. Hasn't the first idea what it might be that he has failed to notice. He shrugs his shoulders as he clutches the steering wheel, passing through the outer suburbs of the city, his in-law's house just a parallel road away.

'I had the turkey, told him I would and then he wouldn't come to watch. Meat is murder: that's Danny's mantra. Mental: I can't be doing with his guilt-trip rubbish, and it actually tastes bloody good. The daft thing is, I don't mind the veggie stuff at all—it's all we eat in normal times—but I'm not paying the same as you guys just to eat nut roast.' Fiona pauses in her explanation, her revelation about the discord in her home. 'What? Why the grin?'

'Is this topic big in the divorce courts, Fi? Lapsing on the food fads.'

'It's not any kind of a fad, laddie. Danny is very concerned about the animal holocaust. And now he has me back in the murderers' corner. It should bother me. I don't even disagree with the various points he makes. It simply doesn't steam me up in the way it does him. Worse than child abuse to Danny. He says that abusers aren't so premeditated. They don't erect abattoirs. He's not wrong, but I don't think it adds up. We're all programmed to eat meat unless we condition ourselves to hate the stuff like Danny's managed.'

Charlie mulls over it as he drives. He can see where Danny's ire comes from but can't hold on to it. Enjoys steak too much.

'And he can't divorce me,' Fiona clarifies. 'We don't do paperwork. Him nor me. And I pay more of the mortgage than Danny ever could. He can make up or go. I've told him, no more meat for another twelve months. Can't believe he's still complaining.'

'You were married before, right?' asks Charlie.

'No. This is my third guy but I don't pretend they're permanent. I'm not stupid.'

'Maybe I am, Fi. Stupid in too many ways.'

'Don't get miserable on me, Charlie. Tell me how Deepika was. She got hammered last night. I think it might have been a first.'

'Well, I just took her home.' He pauses, what else is there to say. 'She managed the front door herself.' He lies for the sake of her reputation. His must already be shot through: thrown out by Mandy. And if he had slept with her, fulfilled her expectations and his reluctant fantasy, he isn't one to boast about it. Not to Fiona, she gossips too much. To Graham in the London hospital, perhaps. Lying closer to his family home than he has lived for several years. Since his school days. Graham—his one-time confidante—is no longer in the Gloucestershire Royal. Deepika is a classier lady than Roselyn. Truer, discerning. He cannot confess that she spent a drunken night on his bed while he slept where his eldest son has done when visiting. The truth would confuse Fiona, as it has him. Perhaps Graham would make head and tail of it. Charlie wants to go down to London, see him again. Knows that whatever he's thinking—if he thinks at all—the poor boy doesn't talk back. Not yet. Who knows when that miracle might come to pass.

Fiona accepts his fat lie. Probably has the same view of staid Deepika as he did until yesterday evening played out so strangely. 'She was well into you last night, Charlie. Your chance to take advantage of the separation.'

'Not really in my plans, Fiona. I miss her, my Mandy.'

'What's all that about then? Why has she given you the push?'

Charlie doesn't answer; looks intently at the road ahead.

'I hear she's got another fella, and that really won't do, you know?'

'It's complicated, Fi, and I'm a bit flummoxed by it all. Can't talk it over right now.'

'Sorry. Fill me in when you're ready.'

Fiona takes everything lightly, joked her way through the assessment. Laughs at her own ups and downs, was warm with Deepika and then wants to hear the low down. He cannot work out if she is more or less indifferent to the slaughter of the herd than he. She might be a kind soul. He should be able to confirm that, he has known her long enough. He can't say he's certain about anything concerning Fiona O'Shea. No pigeon-holing or pinning her down.

* * *

When they arrive at the Goodings' house—the foster home, their large three-storey terrace in Ashbourne—he pulls into the parking space. The hard standing that once comprised the front garden. Mary Gooding is standing on the step. Charlie wonders if she has been waiting for them, needing their visit more than he understood, or if her expectant presence is mere coincidence.

'Had to have the doctor out last night,' she says as they are walking towards her. 'Colin has had to go to the pharmacy for a prescription.'

That explains the space in front of the house. Charlie asks if he should move the car for Colin's return.

'No, no, luvvie. It's no bother. There are always spaces on the street.'

* * *

Inside the house, Mary tells them that Russell is still in bed. The late-night doctor sedated him. 'He was being psychopathic.'

Fiona looks both concerned and doubtful. 'Psychotic?'

'That's it,' Mary agrees.

They go over the events of the evening before. The social workers learn that Russell went out late at night, left home without permission. Mary says it was lucky Colin heard the front door being shut.

'How late?' asks Charlie.

'Midnight. Colin went after him. Found him a couple of roads away.'

'Well done,' murmurs Charlie. He has a lot of questions, wishes to hear Mary's account first. Chooses to give her the chance to say anything she feels the need to say. Will not let his questions inhibit her tale. Disturbed nights can wreck foster placements.

'He never undresses for bed, not until we're sure Russ has nodded off properly. I was asleep when Colin woke me, said he was going. I dressed and went after them in the car.'

'Has this happened before?'

'Yes, Charlie, but this time was definitely the worst. A very strange boy when Colin brought him back.' They talk quietly in the dining room, hoping to avoid disturbing the boy asleep in the room above. Charlie says that he will contact child psychiatry again, to which Mary gives him a concerned look. 'Does he really need it?'

'Certainly. He's a troubled boy. We take no chances, Mary. And it's not a reflection on you, you know? You stand by him fantastically well. It's not every foster carer who'll chase after kids at midnight.'

'We all do that for our own,' she says.

Fiona gives Charlie a quick look. It's a funny phrase, a true one, but he is unclear what meaning it has in Mary Gooding's telling. Russell Chope is not as truly her own as the phrase implies; it's a little bit wonderful that she thinks of him that way.

Colin comes back into the house clutching a white prescription bag, stapled at the top. Charlie and Fiona shake his hand, and Mary makes her husband a cup of tea. Offers the social workers a second. Charlie, after conferring with Colin, takes the tablets from the package, reads the label on the bottle of tablets. Writes down the dosage and the contraindications in the notebook he carries.

Fiona asks the foster carers if they feel Russell is becoming too difficult? Do they need a break? 'I even wonder if he needs to be an inpatient?' she muses.

'No one needs that,' says Mary. And Charlie—who has visited a child or two in those places, secure psychiatric units, the sterile environments which the over-medicated children must endure—is inclined to agree.

When they hear footsteps coming from the room above, Charlie notes that Mary is smiling, nodding, pleased to hear that Russell is coming round from whatever the doctor slugged him with last night.

'I wonder if he's remembered we were visiting?'

'He talked about you last night, Charlie, but it wasn't very nice at all,' says Colin.

'Well, I've had to make some decisions he might not have liked. Anything I need to know?'

'We don't need to bother you with it,' says Mary. 'Just rude words. I'm sure he won't be like that with you in person.' She makes her way to the stairs, to go to check on the boy.

'Tell him that I'll come up in five,' says Fiona.

* * *

Russell Chope sits in the lounge chair with two social workers in attendance on a Saturday lunchtime. A special boy, not for the best of reasons, but through no fault of his own. He is quite large now, putting weight on, the positive effects of a settled placement. Piling it on a bit. Several months back, he was sick after every meal. Not bulimic, not making himself sick, simply too anxious, churned up, for food to sit still within him. The Goodings have helped him to enjoy his mealtimes, who cares if he is getting a little jowly. Fiona whispered to Charlie, very quietly, that he's not psychotic. Or it is not obvious. The on-call doctor medicated him yesterday evening, it might have made the difference. She is not contradicting Mr and Mrs Gooding, just noting that the problem has subsided.

'It's nice that you come to see me, you don't really need to,' Russell tells them generously. 'Mary does everything for me. I know you mean well but she's the one who does it all.'

'Aye,' says Charlie. 'You might have a point. We've explained before how it works. We visit monthly, more often if we think we can be of help.'

'But Mary does everything.' There is a silence neither Charlie nor Fiona is in a hurry to fill. They are trying to get the measure of him, letting Russell do the talking. 'The Virgin Mary,' he says. 'I've got the Virgin Mary looking after me.' And he laughs to himself.

Fiona and Charlie exchange glances. Is that psychosis? The poor joke of a fourteen-year-old boy is the more likely explanation; Charlie logs it all in his mind. He'll pass it along to Doctor Tew on Monday morning. He knows how important it is to monitor this lad's mood swings, his state of mind. Russell Chope has had a tortured past, literally tortured by a swine of a father, a disturbed and disturbing parent not picked up by any professionals until far too late in the day. Removed from his family home about as damaged as a kid can be. The feelings buried inside this boy have still to smoulder out. A way to go by the sound of last night's episode. The less aroused they are the better. The Gooding's consistency has been brilliant, he and Fiona must ensure this hiccough doesn't knock it off course. Let the steam out slowly, then one day the boy might turn out normal.

Chapter Four

Squash is a Game of Cunning

1.

'You're a bit flippin' early,' says Mandy on the door step.

He cannot disagree, looks into her face to try to gauge the severity of his crime. She seems a little more flustered than he would expect on a day like this, hair a bit unkempt. It still looks nice but she usually makes more of an effort for a special occasion.

'Dad, Dad,' he hears his eldest shouting inside the house.

'What's up, Paul?' says Charlie, projecting his voice over his wife's shoulder. Ex-wife, wife, he doesn't know what he is supposed to call her. Still wishes she was his. Loves her eyes and the set of her face.

'Loads of Chinese left. Come and join us,' his son calls in reply.

'You're not joining our family meal,' she says. 'You're not family anymore.'

'Mandy, I'll not eat if I'm not welcome but those kids are so my family.' As he says it, he squeezes his eyes closely together, the pained look of a man wronged by words thoughtlessly spoken.

'Yeah, sorry,' his ex-wife replies. She must still think of him as family, the father of the three whom the pair love equally. She was just letting off steam. Can't deny her original point, he has turned up very early.

The patter of scurried feet sounds the arrival of Mikey. 'Charlie's here,' he squeals.

'Daddy,' he says. 'I'm Daddy.' A hand gently placed on the

head of his three-year-old.

'Come in then,' says Mandy.

Charlie walks past the kitchen-diner, where those already gathered sit. He may be early but he is still last to the party. 'Come to me when you're finished,' he says, taking himself into the lounge. It feels strange; the house was recently his, a family of five with no barriers between them. Nothing is different legally and his children arouse the same quickening within him—pride and concern—as they always did. They belong together, and yet it can no longer be.

As he sits alone in the lounge—television displaying ice skaters of no great skill, the sound muted—a wiry looking man comes through the door. 'All right, mate.' Barry Brice, the man who is screwing his wife. Charlie has no wish to be his mate.

'I guess I am,' says Charlie. 'It's Barry, isn't it?'

'Yeah. I just popped in for a word.'

Charlie waits. He can manage words while having none to say to this man. Thinks life would be simpler if he wasn't occupying Charlie's station in life.

'I don't want it to get awkward...not in front of Mandy's kids. They don't need to see us quarrel.'

'My kids. And we're not quarrelling, Barry. Nothing to see.'

'No, but Mandy said...' Barry looks long and hard at his own hands before continuing. '...you're finding it a struggle.'

Charlie lets the lounge—air scented by Christmas chocolate, even a whiff of this evening's Chinese fare layered across it—breathe by itself for a bit. He eyeballs Barry through the silence. 'How so?' he says when he thinks Barry has had sufficient time to reflect on his unhelpful icebreaker.

'She said you've stopped drinking.'

A smile comes over his face. 'You're not a social worker, are you?'

Barry shakes his head, talks quietly. 'You know I'm not. I'm a life coach which is more psychological really, very

Squash is a Game of Cunning

attuned to changes in people. The domino effect of it. We both help people. Your work and mine aren't so different.'

Charlie thinks that they are worlds apart. He is a practical man while Barry is away with the fairies. Or quite possibly a con artist. There can be no third option. He decides it is unwise to raise it, he is trying not to argue, as Mandy has asked. 'I'm good,' is as much as he offers.

'And Mandy has made her choice,' says Barry.

He coughs; doesn't deny it, will not confirm it. Mandy chose him first, even a pig-headed life coach should be able to figure that much out.

The door opens and Michelle and a friend of hers enter the room. 'We were watching this, Dad.'

'Are you going to introduce me?'

'You've seen Sophie before.'

'Oh, Sophie, hi,' he extends a hand for her to shake, not that it registers with the young girl. 'Are you both wearing make-up?'

'It's Mum's. She said we could.'

Charlie glances at Barry. This might be something else he mustn't argue about. He won't but he can't pretend he likes it. His daughter shouldn't wear rouge on her cheeks. Blusher, he thinks it is called. The two ten-year-olds take to the sofa, his little Michelle jumping upon it like a trampoline, then grabbing the remote from between two cushions and bringing back the volume so as to hear the pop music accompanying the celebrity skaters.

Charlie has no idea who the on-screen performers are.

'I do this,' says Sophie.

'You're a skater. Wow!'

She beams back at Charlie.

'How was the food?' He looks at Michelle as he asks this.

'It's Chinese. There's tonnes left.'

'I think I was meant to eat before I arrived.'

'Tonnes left,' she repeats. 'Tonnes and tonnes.'

Raspberry Jam

Barry is pointing at the door then quickly at his own mouth, indicating to him that he'd like a further word, away from the two girls. Not in their hearing. Charlie rises and the two men walk into the hallway. 'Don't do that,' Barry scolds Charlie.

'Don't do what? She's my daughter. We talk, always will.'

'But you're implying we won't feed you. It's just a boundary. You weren't invited to the family meal, only to the New Year's celebration. Mandy and I aren't being churlish, not trying to starve you. You simply need to respect the boundaries we've made. This is a reconstituted family.'

'It was Shelley offering me food, not me asking for it. She's confused, this type of arrangement confuses kids.'

'Which is why we have to keep to the boundaries,' says Barry.

'Is it important that Chinese food is thrown away?' Charlie feels wrongfooted when he knows he is right. 'Do you think children need life lessons in profligacy? The importance of denying a blood relative a forkful of fried rice because it wasn't in the plan a few hours back. I can't see the sense in that boundary, Barry.'

'Now you're just arguing for the sake of it.'

Charlie notices how much the man is perspiring; he probably knows that he—his girlfriend's real husband—is ex-military. Sat in a tank in the Iraqi desert twenty-plus years back; carried a sixty-pound backpack across the Canadian Rockies before and after that war. Up and down, camped in the contents. This guy has thwacked a few tennis balls, sounds to have given that up for life coaching. Whatever the fuck that is. 'I seem to be making a clear point and your objection is that I'm speaking, Barry. If we're going to get along, you'll have to do better than that.'

'Mands said if there are any problems, I'm to eject you from the party.'

Charlie laughs. 'Yeah, forced getting along is the best. I'm

Squash is a Game of Cunning

here to see my kids, mate. I don't need food. I might pop out for chips if I feel it rumbling.' He pats a hand on his stomach, clenching the muscles taut as he does it. Seen or not. The perspiring man nods his head, mouths something Charlie doesn't hear. A life coach's futile mantra probably. Please don't thump me or whatever words of comfort help a guy like this through his days of bluff and bluster.

'Dad!' Paul calls to his father. Charlie cocks his head, calculates that the shout came from upstairs. It seems his son went up to his room while Charlie was staring blankly at ice skating.

'Coming,' he calls. Pats Barry on the side of his upper arm with a smile. A bit of a sickly insincere smile. 'Coming,' he repeats as he mounts the stairs.

He knocks before entering Paul's bedroom. His son and a friend face a computer screen, a logo that Charlie doesn't recognise indicates the next game they will play. A repetitive heavy-metal riff seems to form a backing track, soundscape to the forthcoming game.

'Barry's a bit of a bell-end,' says Paul, and his friend snorts laughter at the comment. 'Look!'

'No need for language like that,' says Charlie at a barely audible volume. 'What's in the bag?'

Paul is holding aloft a paper bag; it smells of food. 'Prawn toast. No one had any and we're all stuffed.'

'Thanks, Paul. What's your mate's name?'

'It's Ryan, you remember him?'

He should have remembered Ryan; he has visited this house many times, done so when Charlie was still a fixture. He can even recall the lad's mum collecting him once or twice, a good-looking mum, it's all coming back to him. Ryan, Sophie: has living in a flat two miles away really atrophied his parental memory? 'Very considerate of you,' he says, taking the paper bag from Paul, drawing a piece of the slickened food out, biting into it. Sesame seeds fall to the floor, the offering is no longer even lukewarm. Charlie is hungry. 'Thanks, mate,' he says between chews. Tastes fine cold; gets one over on the bell-end.

2.

'I've joined a badminton club,' Graham told Charlie over coffee. This was much earlier in the year. April time. 'I need to get fitter.'

'I'm a squash player,' said Charlie. 'You?'

'No. Just badminton. I'm not great but I'm all right.'

'Do you go to the gym?'

Graham said a flat no to that one. Charlie started to pontificate about squash being the better workout. 'The court is a sweat-a-drome,' he told him. Graham made a bit of a who-needs-sweat face, might not have been as big a fan of the stuff as Charlie. A decent workout means a lot of sweat. Social work isn't as sweaty as the army, Charlie thinks it the downside.

Roselyn was listening in. Not an unusual thing, she often spent half her day in the team room. Networking, she called it. 'Squash eh, Mr Quested? I'm pretty good. I'll give you a game if our Graham won't.'

Charlie tried hard to keep any hint of a superior expression off his face. He considered himself a strong player, doubted that she could come close to matching him, knew better than to boast in advance of a ball being hit. 'I'm not short of opponents, Roselyn, if you think you can beat me, we can give it a go.' He cocked his head after saying it. Probably pitched it right, didn't want his time wasted lolloping soft shots to a girl with no fire power.

'It all depends how good you are, Quested,' she replied. 'If you let me put you through your paces, we'll find out, won't we?'

He liked her fighting talk, suggested they play at his

squash club. No charge for a guest, he assured her. She bested him: Roselyn said she was a member of The Harrington, a far more exclusive club. Private gym with squash, indoor tennis too. They chose to play at hers. She chose. Strange that tonight of all nights he should be thinking about that conversation, Roselyn butting in when he'd been angling for a game with Graham. How it all got going, the screw-up of a lifetime.

3.

It is still three hours away from the big twelve o'clock. Charlie has suggested that Mikey might want to go to bed. He's getting cranky. Both Mandy and Barry side with the little boy who says he wants to greet the New Year. Cottoned on to the big event, knows that midnight is special tonight.

'He's only three,' Charlie reminds them.

'And he's already missed the first two,' says clever Paul.

This gets a determined nod from little Mikey. 'Happy New Year,' he says. Premature but keen.

Charlie looks at Mandy once more and then he shrugs. He can do not arguing. Always thought he and Mandy agreed about the importance of structure for little ones. Doesn't think Michelle saw the New Year in when she was Mikey's present age.

The television is on a film channel, the two older boys wanted to watch it and both girls seemed to back them up. There is nothing festive about it, on a free channel dedicated to showing old movies. The plot is all bent lawyers and car bombs, drug dealers up on charges they will only get out of through intimidation and disruption of the trial. An adaptation of a novel Charlie read a few years back, he's sure of it. Exciting but hard to follow—it doesn't do a thing for the party atmosphere—and he keeps daydreaming about what he shouldn't. He takes his youngest son in his arms, sits with him scrunched in the corner of the sofa. Mikey clutches his strange monkey; a Christmas present from Mandy. If Barry chose it, that explains the oddity. It's cuddly enough but the expression on the creature's face is more fear than anything cuter: bared teeth. Charlie tries to play with Mikey, makes his toy talk, and the older children shush him. They are trying to follow the film, work out who bombed the investigator's car, and exactly why. Charlie's not in the mood for it.

He looks at the TV only fleetingly, Mikey quiet by his side, holding the monkey as father holds his son. Then he glances across at wife and lover; they are ensconced within a single armchair. Both are narrow of hips, sit side by side like Siamese twins. Barry has drunk a few, Mandy too. His hands are around her, could be anywhere on her person, so closely are they enmeshed. It isn't what he wants to see at a New Year's party, would much prefer it if he were the one in the chair with her. Not like that. Properly on his lap. It's happened in the past, although they never really frolicked with the kids around. Charlie wonders if Paul and Ryan have managed to sneak a beer, has no idea whether he should mind or not. He isn't going to get in a row with the other two adults in the room tonight. Won't do it even if right would be on his side. He and Mikey are sober, sure as sugar is sweet. The two girls drink fizzy pop through straws.

4.

Jesus, she was good at squash. He knew that he'd lost a little speed around the court since his army days; he expected to make up for it in shot selection. Roselyn played in white shorts and T-shirt, short sports socks. Not a feminine look, no skirt, no colour to catch the eye, but she was a sight to him. To red blood. She hit the ball so damned cleanly. It went fast and true into whichever corner she chose to make

Squash is a Game of Cunning

him bolt. She was the manager of the squash court; he was the dogsbody. Points went to both players, but the more he ran the fewer he got. She was holding court, directing traffic. Charlie picking off the odd error while Roselyn ruled the roost.

The very first time they played, the first of May, twenty-thirteen—eight months ago minus one day—there was a moment of comedy, of drama. Of another life in Charlie's mind. One he would like to forget or loves to remember, depending wholly on the mood he has caught. He dropped a short ball, barely bounced at all off the front wall, but she read it—of course she read it—pinged a reply high over his head. A floater that would come down at the back of the court, barely bounce out of it. Squash balls are sluggish like that. Charlie began to run backwards, dithering whether to turn left or right shoulder. Running backwards must be the daftest way to move across a squash court, no acceleration in reverse gear. It brought him tumbling down on his arse, that part of him moving faster than his feet could keep up. He flopped onto the floor, its knotted wood veneer stained with black smudges by the countless balls that have bounced, smashed against and been trodden into it. He became one with the rubbery, sweaty smell of the floor, as the back of his head gently knocked the surface. A little humiliation but no pain. Roselyn—still in complete control—pretended to trip on his flayed foot. She fell down in simulated slow motion, and rolled on top of him. Her thighs upon his, her white shorts intimate with his grey ones. 'How are you doing big fella?' she asked from that prone position, almost cheek to cheek. He never thought of it as intimate. It was a little feminist piss-take, the silk-and-steel girl squash player squeezing the last ounce of vanity out of the hapless man. 'Sorry, big fella. I tripped...'

'You've got the knack, Ros,' he said, abridging her name—not something ever done at work—for no reason but shortness of breath.

She put her hands on the floor either side of his torso. Press-upped herself away from him. 'You're my best social worker, Quested. Work on the squash.'

5.

Charlie has picked up a television guide lying on the coffee table. Flicking through it, he sees that this film will carry on until ten-twenty. He turns the magazine to Paul, pointing at a comedy show. 'Would that be better?'

'We're watching the film, Charlie,' says Mandy without changing her posture, still wrapped in a single armchair with Barry-who-doesn't-belong.

'It's all right,' Paul adds, agreeing with his mum. 'It's quite a good one.'

Charlie stares at the girls; they watch the action closely although he cannot imagine it is of much interest. Ten-year-old girls like hamsters, not car bombs. Little Mikey sits next to him—no interest whatsoever in the slow-moving crime film—intent only on staying up, avoiding the bed in which he really needs to be. Did he and Mandy really disagree about this stuff? What programmes to let their kids watch; bedtimes for tiny ones. Was Charlie a tyrant who Mandy couldn't stand up to without Barry round for backup? That's not how he recalls family life. They were good parents the pair of them; always on the same page. It was what he did away from home which knocked them off course, spoiled everything. No reason to change how they bring the kids up. He can't believe she really agrees with the life coach's approach. Laissez-faire is only a bus stop short of feral: bringing kids up like Annie Corrigan did him.

'Get us a couple of beers, Charlie,' says Barry, from his armchair tryst. 'Please?'

'The kitchen is off limits to me.'

6.

Nothing untoward took place on the squash court that day. If they'd made a film, kids could watch it. Roselyn momentarily lay on top of Charlie, a joke emphasising the superiority of her squash. He could not help falling, she was mimicking his sporting incompetence. And that is a relative measure derived from the quality of the opposition. He never played the ladies down at his own club. He saw them play for a few minutes now and again; knew it would be fairly one-sided if he took them on. Roselyn was something else.

Charlie made a few calculations, started to do so from that sorry spot on the floor. He can play a bit, never knew that Roselyn did until she laid down the challenge. She must be a tournament winner, could play for county, so comprehensive was her victory. His brain was thinking which parts of his game needed attention, how he could shrink the gap. Catch up with her; it would take some doing. Charlie positively gushed over how well she played. 'You wiped me out, Ros. Six points my best haul. You've kept your talent hidden.' Inside he felt only competitive, the thrill of seeing the bar set high. He earned his stripe in the army by working harder than the other squaddies, knows he did. His combative temperament is of little use in a social work team. That's why he plays squash. His defeat felt like a flood in his brain. How to come back? Action, action, action. He had long learnt that only this can put aside frustration, chase those feelings from his proud chest.

That evening, at home with Mandy, he said—for reasons he barely analysed at the time—'Graham beat me fair and square. Turns out he's a great player; funny he never said.'

It was not guilt which made him hide the name and gender of his actual opponent from his wife. Not yet. He had laid down the foundation for this deception in the morning, telling Mandy that this was who he would be with this evening, at a swankier squash club than his own. She had said, 'Fancy Graham being a member of The Harrington.' It did sound unlikely but that is what he let her believe. He didn't want her picturing him playing squash with a woman she'd met once, and knew that he met on a daily basis, weekends aside. Is that so unusual? A husband dodging an unnecessary interrogation.

And that one meeting—the only time Mandy ever met Roselyn—was a funny thing. It had happened the autumn before.

His manager picked him up from home because they were making a joint visit, Charlie's car at the garage for servicing. She arrived early, and he invited her inside, introduced them. Mandy made her a coffee. Charlie recalls how Roselyn asked her if she was a social worker. He was surprised she didn't already know the answer to that. He had let it be known that Mandy was on a career break, Mikey still pre-school. Perhaps he never said what the break was from; Mandy is smart but not a professional anything. When his wife told his boss that she was busy with children, Roselyn said, 'You were a social worker, right? That's how you two met, as I remember.' A million miles off. Everyone knows that Charlie's ex-army; Paul was born before he qualified. Roselyn hasn't the imagination to think time backwards, to believe people were ever anything other than how they appear now. She married a social worker; all her friends are social workers. Never had kids. Lives in a bubble, can't believe there's a world outside.

7.

Little Sophie passes Charlie the bag of crisps. She cannot be expected to understand the complicated protocol, the deeper meanings behind a quasi-involuntary act. The crisps were doing the rounds.

Barry has fetched bottles of beer for himself and Mandy from the kitchen, another for Paul to share with Ryan. His son carefully pours it into their respective glasses. Charlie sat up when he passed it over, said, 'What the...' but never completed the phrase. He is sticking to his not-arguing plan. Not with Barry or Mandy, nor even Paul and Ryan. Not tonight.

Mandy heard him anyway, came back at him although he'd really not expressed a cogent thought. 'It's a New Year's party, Charlie. You know the boys would be doing much worse if they'd gone to one without any parents present. Who knows what they might have got up to?'

Paul nudged Ryan, mimed smoking something; marijuana Charlie guessed. Paul is sharp, knows what might be funny, might be scary. It doesn't mean he's tried it. Charlie worries just the same. Annie Corrigan died in prison two years ago, her heart went crazy on her zillionth drug trip. Of course it worries him.

'What did we get up to at that age, eh Charlie?' said Barry.

The idiot has drunk too many. It's stupid boasting about breaking the rules in the presence of teenagers. Fucking stupid, no less. 'Life coaching,' he muttered, under his breath. Mandy ignored it, might have thought the same as Charlie. Barry probably didn't hear it, not with the film and the beer. His teenage reminiscence floating around in his head.

The two girls and Mikey all had a top-up of orangeade that Mandy brought for them while Barry was fetching the beers. Charlie warned Mikey he wouldn't sleep for all the sugar. It prompted Mandy to repeat her New Year's party excuse. Apparently, anything goes. 'For one night only, Mikey,' said Charlie. 'We are not big on sugar in the Quested household.'

'Quested-Brice household,' Mandy fired back.

That ugly phrase hung in the air only a moment before

Barry twisted it around. 'Brice-Quested: alphabetical.' A smug smile on his narrow-featured face.

'Quested-Brice; majority rules,' said Paul. Charlie liked that—loves his quick-thinking son—but it hasn't taken the edge off the agitation he feels. Sober agitation. In his army days, they called it combat-ready.

'What about my cup of tea?' Charlie asked the man who now sleeps in his bed. He requested a herbal when Barry went to the kitchen.

'Really, Charlie. Don't get pissy about the Chinese. You can use the kitchen.'

Charlie chose to stay seated; he has no need to fix himself anything. Instead, he dips his big hand into one of the two large packets of fancily named crisps which traverse the room—the one which Sophie Jones has unwittingly offered to him—not a party to the cold-shoulder which the adults in the room are showing him.

'Thanks, Soph, I'm starving,' he says, pulling a large handful of crisps from the bag and placing them on his left palm.

'Leave some for us,' says Barry.

'Life coach,' he mutters once more.

Sophie goes red in the face, looks hurriedly from one adult to another and then back at Michelle, with whom she is sitting thigh to thigh. The two girls are the only ones wearing party dresses, done up to the nines. This night-in is like a night out for them. New Year's Eve, midnight on the horizon. It is a landmark in a young life. Misunderstanding the significance of crisp sharing, or the correct way to perform its ceremonies, might detract from the good luck which twenty-fourteen promises. The little girl looks flushed, hot. She might be sensing the feelings Charlie harbours towards Barry, although he has done nothing more than mutter the man's job title once or twice. His stupid fucking job title.

'It's all right,' says Michelle, 'my dad can eat loads of crisps.'

Charlie watches Barry at this point, notices how he fixes his stare on the television, not wishing to contradict the ten-year-old. He is in the room, feet not so far under the table. He has won over Mandy for now, but she is a girl with her own mind. The children he has no hold over whatsoever. It crosses Charlie's mind that he could punch Barry Brice out of the living room, the house, the entire suburb. He won't, while imagining it would feel good if he did; he won't because it's not the action that might put his family back together. He knows he is the one who cast a dark spell on the Questeds. Prising out Barry-the-dickhead would be a good first step in the breaking of it. Very wise to have a goal; he has still to figure the method, the strategy. What endgame will leave him with pieces on the board, and Barry none.

8.

In the office the following day, Precious came over to Charlie and said—quite loudly, several others within hearing—'So Roselyn gave you a hiding on the squash court, Quested.' She was smiling from cheek to cheek, always calls him Charlie in real life. He understood that she just liked the one-upmanship of it, the wonder-woman-ness of the boss's victory. The army boy getting humiliated by a girl of a little over half his weight. The public announcement actually hardened his resolve: he was in the gym at five that evening. Weights, big heavy weights to get the most from his big strong arms.

That after-work work-out was a revelation for Charlie. It was as if he had forgotten how much he once enjoyed the feel of lifting. Calf, thigh, abdomen, bicep. He stirred them back to life. As a social worker there is no great call for it: nothing to carry, no one to punch. In the army there was a lot of the former, occasional forays into the latter. Twats in the barracks mostly. Charlie could handle himself. He might have been stronger than anyone else in the children's services department; thought it when he joined ten years earlier and nothing has revised his opinion except a lack of attention to what didn't seem to matter. He knew how conceited his self-congratulatory assertion sounded, said it only inside his head. And not frequently. He could count the number of challengers he had to that title on a single hand. Roselyn Pickford he never thought in the frame, and then there she was, giving him what for on the squash court. Her light frame is far tauter, more muscular, than he ever noticed it to be in her working clothes. When she played the game, little beads of sweat quickly gathered around her forehead, her hairline glistening with earned perspiration. She put in a shift on that squash court, and made his own impossible while doing it. Now he was raising the bar in the gym, giving himself a talking to each time he went up a level. Targets to achieve, strength to harness. He was once a very strong man, and that can be an edge on a squash court. Not sufficient on their own, but power and stamina have currency.

Squat thrusts, he hadn't practised them in years. They were an army thing, a putting through the paces in preparation for serious ground covering. The power in his thighs, the potential to push into a sprint that bit quicker, that's an important arrow in the quiver. A skill which the top players deploy every time they venture onto a squash court. Charlie decided to have a bit of that.

On all the working days that followed, Roselyn asked him if he wanted another game; she usually did it when Precious was close by, listening in. Their mutual joke. Charlie considered offering to play her—Precious—his over-pleased colleague, rather than his manager, while knowing it would be beside the point. Not worth troubling each other with. Charlie just smiled back at Roselyn, said something along the lines of maybe. It was two weeks later when they fixed a time, closer to three when they played. Roselyn asked, 'Can Precious watch?' but Charlie was well-prepared, ensured that the date chosen clashed with the Christian house group she and Brantly hosted every week. He feared another humbling, the gulf had been wide. It would be only the pair of them: Charlie and Roselyn. The office could come and watch when he was confident of winning, although Roselyn would surely prohibit that. Send them on statutory visits. And with these thoughts, Charlie knew he was getting ahead of himself.

Mandy—the girl now sitting across the lounge from him, entwined in the arms of a man his astute son has designated a bell-end—back in late May of this almost complete year, still believed that he was to be playing Graham. Not that she knew his male colleague, not directly. Graham was just a name to her, the other man in the office. Charlie doesn't think that Mandy is really the jealous type. Didn't used to. Mandy was secure in her trust of Charlie back then. Why not? He said he loved her, proved it in many small ways; their activities in the bedroom of this house for one. Keeping secrets: he really didn't know what he was playing at. In his army days, he never told his fellow soldiers that he was once a kid in care. Only training, qualifying as a social worker, gave him any sense that his background might possibly be something to draw pride from. In the department, he became known as the former kid in care, a role model for others, utilising the pocket of his life in which residual shame had once taken root. And then, May to July of this year he lied; by the second time, he could tell himself that it was to avoid letting Mandy know he was beaten at squash by a woman. And that never explained the first, no good reason why he ever set the ball rolling. Roselyn was a rival to Charlie on the court, an adversary in fact. He never thought her a rival to Mandy, not a challenger in any other domain. She lay upon him as a joke during their first game, rubbed in her superiority with it. He thought about that a few times before the second match, didn't trouble Mandy with the image, of course. 'I'll get the better of Graham sooner or later,' is as much as he told her. So little, it was less than nothing.

The second time he entered The Harrington, got down and physical on the squash court with Roselyn, was not significantly better than the first. Not in Charlie's book. No breasts on chests or any of that unlikely horseplay took place by or with the boss, still he was well beaten.

'You got yourself a few more points this time, Quested,' Roselyn noted. A raised eyebrow suggesting she knew there was a concerted effort involved. 'Will you play me again?'

'Of course I will. I'm the one with nothing to lose.' Those were the words he used towards the end of May. Thinking about them in front of the television this evening, he sees that his comment was a million miles off the mark. So many long and lonely miles.

9.

He isn't watching the film; he wishes his children weren't. Paul could, he's old enough for this, it's only a crime caper, and a bit heavy going to Charlie's way of thinking. Not a party film, and the two girls look ever so slightly frightened. Charlie is thinking about sex, wishes that he wasn't. Not with his wife-in-name-only who's canoodling in front of him, wrapped up with a scared-of-life coach. The sex he is thinking about is that which he briefly enjoyed with Roselyn, his contemplation of it simply passing the time because the film is of no interest. It occupies the others but doesn't create any atmosphere. No connection between them. He would far rather engage with his children, that's why he came here, New Year's Eve. Not to watch a run-of-the-mill film. On the screen, a character—one Charlie had

Squash is a Game of Cunning

surmised to be a good cop but hasn't paid enough attention to be certain—is stuck in a belted hoist hung from a cable line, moving slowly towards a kind of fan, not a normal one, sharp knives where the blades would be spinning around. Nasty. The camera shows the grimace on his face—anticipation of what is to come—then a splatter of blood. They use a funny effect, a spray on the camera lens, like it's on the inside of the TV screen. The knives rip him to shreds; the terror on the face of whichever famous actor Charlie is watching was on the nail. There is a piercing scream. Deafening, piercing.

'Shit!' Charlie has a hold of Mikey, hugs him, but the boy screams on. 'They're just acting, Mikey.' He glances at the girls. Little Sophie looks more ashen-faced than his own daughter. Michelle has asked him about Iraq, and he's answered honestly. She must be the more battle-hardened. The battle of confronting horror in life and on television. 'It's only pretend,' he says to his crying son. A quick glance at the couple in the armchair. 'Raspberry jam, that's all you've seen. No one gets hurt making movies. The makeup girls caked him in raspberry jam for that shot.'

Mikey gasps and gulps. Tears flood down his cheeks. He clutches his father's hand—looks into his face—the explanation is an interesting one. He is a boy who likes jam. Mandy has come across and she hugs her youngest son. Nuzzling him properly, real comfort, her brown hair falling into his little face. Barry and the boys are still following the stupid film.

Charlie steps quickly into the kitchen, flings open a cupboard and comes straight back into the lounge. 'Look at me, Mikey, I'm a famous actor.' He has unscrewed the top on the jam jar, pulls his shirt up to show some abdomen muscles. 'They shot me, son,' he says, falling to his knees on the carpeted floor. Fingers in the pot, then he smears a great blob of jam on his tummy. 'Oh God, look at me, I've been

207

shot.' He lies on his back. 'Dead-dead,' he tells the room. Mikey finally gurgles out a bit of laughter, he loves it when his dad mucks about. Charlie makes a few jolting movements, in the throes of an actor's prolonged death. 'Dead-dead. Uugh! Being dead sucks.' He thinks Paul and Ryan are watching him too.

'Me,' says Mikey. 'Make me dead.'

Charlie sits up, lifts up his little son's shirt, points middle and index fingers of his right hand at the boy. 'Bang! Bang!'

Charlie flicks a little raspberry jam into place, Mikey falls to the floor. Cannot say dead-dead for laughing.

'Quiet,' says Barry, 'we're watching the film.'

Charlie exchanges a look with Mandy, she screws her face up at him, laughs along with Mikey. Charlie thinks his wife must know by now that she is shacking up with a bell-end. The man lays out the evidence at fifteen-minute intervals. And she must know it can only be temporary. Not only can she do better, she actually has a better offer on the table. If he can just stop thinking about sex with that lightning-good squash player then he might have atoned sufficiently. He hopes so. Mandy is the judge, and he's not telling her where his thoughts have strayed. Barry out, Charlie back. That's what he thinks should happen, and Charlie is completely sober. No misjudgements when he's sober. Very seldom.

'Dead-dead,' says Mikey, little fingers smearing raspberry jam on tummy and T-shirt alike.

10.

He trained at his own squash club, took it very seriously. Never told Mandy that he paid a small fortune for four lessons in two weeks from a visiting coach. Never told Roselyn, obviously: that is the art of war. He learned that one in The Gulf War, the heady value of surprise. The coach was very good, considered every area of his game. Technique.

Squash is a Game of Cunning

How to improve the way he hit through the ball, get more from his strong upper arm muscles. 'If you've got it, use it,' was the coach's favourite saying. A practical man, Charlie already on board with his philosophy. Sports coach, not a life coach, keener to put the enemy to the sword.

As Charlie is washing raspberry jam off his stomach, putting Mikey in a quick bath to do the same with his little one, it crosses his mind that Barry, downstairs, was once a tennis coach. That's what Mandy told him many weeks ago, eager to tell him more than he needed to know about Slimeball Brice. Before he was a life coach, he was a tennis coach. She implied it gave his life symmetry. Charlie was army, then sales, then social work. Incoherent. And she dressed it all up as if Barry Brice was a decent sort, helping others with his coaching and coaxing. Charlie inferred at the time that Barry is a weasel, felt disappointed that Mandy couldn't spot it. She met him when, on the advice of her friend Cindy—a friend Charlie knows and likes—she sought the help of a life coach to get her through the muddle she was in. The upset that ejecting Charlie from the household had caused her. He wonders how he managed to keep it together at all in that revealing conversation. His wife sought relationship counselling under the guise of life coaching so that she did not have to take him into the same room. Her plan was flawed from the get-go. Then the bloody life coach makes a pass at her. One way or another, that's what happened. Mandy didn't tell him how their relationship developed, just that Barry is a life coach who makes house calls. She told him the story with a straight face, told him to close his gawping mouth while she let it all out. And he wasn't really open-mouthed. It was the words, what the fuck, dancing on his tongue. He never said them, held it together by a hair's breadth. Next thing she said was that Barry has a nice body because he used to be a tennis coach. Charlie has no recall of his wife previously telling him the positive features of other men's bodies. His own remains pretty damned fit on any measurable scale. Whether it is concurrently attractive to look at, he cannot tell. His knowledge of beauty begins and ends with the opposite gender. 'Does he still play?' asked Charlie. He did not want to hear a number, how many out of ten she rated the life coach. She used to give him nine; everything but the film-star face. Mandy told him that Barry gave up tennis coaching when he saw how much more fulfilment he can give and get through life coaching. The man's past profession doesn't show: Barry is out of shape. Nor does he talk sports. Silent on the rugby when he and Paul and Ryan earlier speculated about the six nations, ruminated across England's prospects. For all Charlie knows the man has stopped playing tennis entirely, perhaps his heart was never in it. Barry is more Nancy than Jock, Charlie thinks, although neither are terms that he allows to cross his lips. When he was in a tank regiment, long before he became the social worker he is today, they were the terms. You were a sportsman or you were a wuss. There are words, whole concepts ingrained in Charlie's brain which belong to the man he was in the army, the child he was in care. Words and phrases virtually unknown to social workers, unused by them at the very least. Saying the more homophobic of them could be a disciplinary offence. Charlie doesn't disagree with the professional standard, but he has the same brain lodged in his head that was there through those other lives. Even this maudlin reflection brings Graham once more to his mind, the poor lad still comatose on a hospital bed, no Christmas or New Year entering his migratory consciousness. Nancy-Jock, he wonders if he has been on the wrong side of this watershed. He was always a jock, knows they're a shameless bunch.

Mikey wears goggles in the bath; they are not required and nor do they aid the process, he just loves to see himself in the low mirror by the bath side. Charlie tells him he looks like a deep-sea diver; Mikey calls it his TV face. 'There's no need to scream about television, Mikey,' says his dad. The boy is calm, listens. 'It's all make-believe, pretend, every last second of it. I know that it looks scary but inside the box and life outside are nothing like each other.' Mikey is looking in the mirror, his funny TV face. It's late in the evening for this little one. The scream is probably forgotten, washed away with the raspberry jam. Charlie loves being in this bathroom, sharing time with Mikey. It's exactly why he came.

11.

As the credits are rolling, spilled raspberry jam duly avenged, his delightful daughter, Michelle, says they should all play a game. The youngsters discuss which and what, how festive it must or needn't be. Finally, four of the five children agree that they will perform karaoke. Ryan, Paul's friend, says he can connect the internet to the television, provide backing and lyrics. Charlie finds that miraculous, tells him he's a clever lad. All adults must sing, that is the instruction, Michelle the one insisting. Charlie primes Mikey, says that they will duet. Mikey only knows the words to a couple of television themes, kids' programmes, and he can't read the prompter. Success is in the balance.

Sophie and Michelle start the proceedings, sing a sweet little song about young love. Charlie has heard it in the car. The chorus just goes, 'Bobby, Bobby, Bobby,' about a thousand times, Bobby being the object, the heart-throb sung about. He thought it was a shitty boyband when it was on the radio, this time round he enjoys it. Paul and Ryan laugh because the two girls don't keep time with each other properly, sound a bit useless. Michelle starts to cry, and her mother hugs her, says that she will probably sing worse when it's her go. Charlie thinks she has overdone the white wine. That was not the line to breathe hope into their daughter. 'You're a star, Shelley. I loved it. You too, Sophie. Brilliant.' His wife nods, she doesn't disagree, simply isn't sober enough to work it out alone.

The boys sing Crazy Darkness, a hippy song that predates Charlie's own teen years. They are pretty good but the melody is simple. Shake their heads as if they have long hair.

Barry—the man's a life coach so he ought to be able to do something or other—makes a reasonable fist of singing When He Smiles. He tries to fit some dance moves into the act. It's a Carrie Collins song from many years ago. They all applaud when he finishes, the best so far in some respects. Charlie smiles when Paul says, 'Bizarre choice.' He's quite right; Charlie won't be singing about another man's smile. Mikey's maybe, definitely no other.

Mandy sings an old heartbreak song that was in the charts when Charlie was in care. She can't hold the tune for the higher notes but sounds nice on the downward crescendo each time the title comes around.

I don't know what to do
My heart has broken into two

Charlie thinks about raspberry jam, has no wish to get sentimental while knowing he's the bastard who broke hers.

When she's done—and all applaud, finally seeing it encourages reciprocation—Charlie whispers to Ryan to bring the song which the girls sang back on the screen. Bobby, its unimaginative title. He encourages Mikey to join in, while just singing the word, botty, over and over in place of the original. This is hilarious in the world of three-year-olds, and after a huffy beginning the two girls join in with them. Everyone likes to see Mikey in hysterics.

Botty, botty, botty

They sing it endlessly.

Barry protests against the lyrical improvement, offers some over-intellectualised reasoning. 'Inappropriate attention on body parts might screw kids up for life.' Utter nonsense: all three-year-olds love botties. Always will. Mandy handles the objector into a small slow-motion jive, and he gives up the argument. The five children and Charlie praise the posterior in song.

Botty! Botty!

When it's over, the girls have a go at When He Smiles. It was written for a girl to sing after all. At the end, Charlie makes a point of saying, 'Every bit as good as Barry,' loves it when Mandy says, 'Better.' The silly drunken life coach looks miffed. Looks like a girl has pinched his crayons.

* * *

The lads find more old songs that they know, belt them out with gusto. Barry has wandered out of the lounge. The family leave him be. Charlie thinks he's hunting down more booze, a bit driven. It must be this life coach's panacea for awkwardness. If he really was the best singer that was not the point. A grown man should see that. Charlie hopes that Mandy is taking note, counting the bottles drunk. Michelle and Sophie play nicely with Mikey, keep the little boy's crankiness at bay. He follows his rival to the kitchen. To finally make that herbal tea.

Barry is doing his best to get the top off a bottle of beer; the only opener he can find is in the crook of a tin-opener's arm. The man is struggling, looking at the contraption like he has shelves to put up.

'Do you want a hand?' asks Charlie.

'No, I've got this.' Then he pauses, looks levelly at Charlie. 'Are you having one? New Year, let your hair down.'

Charlie pours water into the kettle. 'Not me. I'm loving this evening sober.' He waits a moment before adding, 'I suppose we're a tricky family to tag along to.'

'Tell me about it,' says Barry.

Charlie cannot fathom what is meant by this phrase. That his own family is funnier, perhaps? 'How about you?' Charlie asks. 'Do you have an ex? Kids?'

'I've never been married. Did she not tell you that?'

Charlie shrugs. He expects he would have remembered if she had. Not that this guy is high on his list of interests. 'That wasn't the whole question,' he says. Charlie smells the ginger of the teabag—it's pleasant—then he drops it in the mug with his name on. Pleased he found it at the back of the cupboard, something of himself residing in the bosom of the family. He gestures for Barry to continue speaking.

The top has still not come off the bottle, and Barry has slid himself down onto a chair at the kitchen table. He looks directly at Charlie, in the brightness of the strip lighting. To the social worker's thinking, he looks miserable as hell. 'Kids, kids, kids,' he says.

'All right, Barry?' asks Charlie. It is more puzzlement than concern. He hates Barry Brice one way or another. Concern is too valuable a commodity to waste on him.

'Your kids look to you, not me. And I'm the one who lives here.'

'And I'm their dad, Barry. Been there since they were born; won't be going away.'

'Yeah. I get that.'

Charlie pauses before speaking. His training tells him how to assure Barry. God knows, foster kids have no reason to attach themselves to their foster carers, yet more often than not they do. Kids don't want a loveless, frosty household. Nor is Charlie the one to teach this rum fucker how to get along with his own children. He won't use Paul, Michelle and Mikey to come between Mandy and Barry, but expecting him to make it easy, smooth the man's way in, is another matter entirely. And Paul knows his bell-ends. 'You still haven't answered my question.'

Squash is a Game of Cunning

Barry takes his hands off the recalcitrant bottle, sets it aside, unopened. 'I don't really get kids.' He looks up, meeting Charlie's eyes. 'Used to be one, mind.' He giggles at his daft observation. 'I didn't mind them back then. Can't say I mind them now, it's just...' He turns his head away to look longingly at the bottle that has defeated him. 'I like your children, Charlie. They're better than most. Loud sometimes, it's just...well, it's a bit constant.' Then his voice goes so quiet it is difficult for Charlie to be sure what he's hearing. 'I've two kids.'

'You've two children?' He sounds like the social worker he is, echoing back the facts, waiting for the client to attach his meaning to them. The man sounds to have no fondness for children generally, and the two he claims to have didn't come around tonight, aren't seeing the New Year in with their father. Never invited, to the best of Charlie's knowledge.

'Yeah, two.' The volume knob is stuck at number one. 'They are about a year younger than your Shelley,' he adds in a whisper.

Charlie gives him a military stare. Barry never served, doesn't respond to that approach. 'Twins, Barry? Is that it? You have twins?'

Brice giggles again. Charlie thinks it quite inappropriate. He would explain the sequence of his children—Paul, Michelle and Mikey—to anyone who wants to hear. Would and has. A story filled with pride even though only his daughter was really planned. All are loved equally. Equally by both parents. Brice only giggles. 'Both boys. Not twins at all. Legacy of my tennis coaching days.'

Charlie stares. No smile, no giggle.

'When you coach ladies, in the daytime, there are too many opportunities.'

Charlie watches him, a little snigger escaping while tears also form in the corner of Barry's eyes. Whether it's a funny story or there's a darker room behind the entrance, Charlie cannot tell. He doesn't read faces, not for detail.

'Opportunities to go back to their empty houses.' Barry says it and giggles more openly.

'About tennis coaching,' says Charlie—he feels slightly uncomfortable, it crosses his mind that Barry is trying to smoke out the story of him and Ros Pickford, Mandy must have told him some of it, probably did so before the underhand operator made his move—'You no longer play, I gather?'

'Oh, I can hit a few balls up, but I was always more of a coach than a competitor.' He looks at Charlie levelly now. Talking tennis is not as funny as talking about his mysteriously absent children, it seems.

'How does that work? Don't you need to be a winner to become a decent coach?'

'Technique. I taught holds, grips, addressing the ball, how the spins work. Top and slice, all that. Helped the ladies loosen up a little so that they could hit through the ball better.'

'Ladies? You just taught ladies?'

'Beginners, men in my evening and weekend sessions plenty of times. Most of the individual lessons I gave were to ladies. Some would pay year after year.'

'And you had a relationship with one of these ladies?'

He splutters with laughter. 'Two ladies,' says Barry. 'I was running two like you tried to do, Charlie. No twins. My kids were born four months apart.'

Charlie stares the man down. Barry's giggling finally stops. Whatever he got up to, it was nothing like his own affair. His mistake. Charlie has never laughed about what he did, always wished better for Mandy, even while he was letting her down.

Paul enters the kitchen, rifles through the bread bin, pulls the pot of raspberry jam from the fridge. Then he looks questioningly at his father. The two adults must look odd.

Squash is a Game of Cunning

Neither has spoken a word since Paul came into the room.

'Barry was just telling me how he used to impregnate lady tennis players,' says Charlie. He turns his head back to the subject of his comment, just had time to see how rapidly Paul dropped his smile. To his surprise, Barry cracks up laughing again.

When Paul sees that it is not too tense between his father and this unwanted stepfather, his smile returns. 'Jesus,' he says, flicking an accusative finger at the man once more clutching the unopened beer bottle, 'is that allowed?'

Barry just keeps on laughing. 'It's the lady's prerogative,' says Charlie, and Barry places the unopened bottle in the centre of the kitchen table. His hands are trembling as tears of laughter streak down his face. He is incapable of opening the damned thing. 'Tell me about your kids, Barry.' Paul doesn't wait to hear him tell, takes his food—a couple of jam sandwiches—back to the television, now counting down some twenty minutes to the special midnight. Leaving the room while Brice is still laughing at the revelation a better man might feel shamed by. Charlie asks, quietly, in a friendlier tone than reflects his true feelings, 'Where are they now, Barry?'

The man's laughter dries up in an instant. 'I'm sorry,' he says, waving a hand across the tears upon his face, 'you are very dry.' Charlie picks up the bottle and the opener, flips off the top and hands it back. Barry's face registers the surprise of a child with a newly opened Christmas present, then he gestures for Charlie to sit down beside him. 'I know you,' he says. 'I don't mean to pry or to know secrets about you. Things that you wouldn't tell the world. But I'm with your ex, aren't I? She needs to talk.'

Charlie is seated at the same kitchen table, he inches himself a little further away, elongating the distance between the two men.

'You should know about me,' continues Barry. 'Fair's fair.'

217

He squints, rubs his free left hand into both eyes, thumb to the left, forefinger to the right. 'I'm a good guy but I've not always got it right. That's a fact I'll admit to. I fell for Cheryl, she fell for me as hard...' As Barry is trying to spill the beans, give Charlie a sense of him as a father and a man, his words are becoming slightly slurred. Charlie recalls that he was drunk at this time on New Year's Eve last. Charlie never regretted his minor inebriation then, and only Paul, of his children, was up to witness it, hear his own wayward tongue fail to wrap itself around the simplest words. Tonight, it must be Barry's turn. '...she never left her husband. He knows the boy isn't his. He's brought it up as his own. Very good of him, all things considered. I've offered money but neither of them will take it. I've no relationship at all with that boy, that's the truth of the matter.' The laughter has gone, self-pity looks to have filled the void.

'That's a tough one,' says Charlie turning his face away. He is not Barry Brice's social worker. He wonders what the hell Mandy is doing with him. If she's pregnant, he can take the sprog with him when he goes.

Barry carries on talking, confessing that he has only infrequent contact with his other pre-teenage son. 'I know it isn't ideal but what can you do?'

'What's his name, Barry? This boy.'

'John. John-Paul actually, like the last pope, but we all just call him John.'

'And his mother? Do you still...'

'She took up with another fella. Not even a tennis player.'

Charlie looks at him, stares into his face as Barry draws another pull from the neck of his beer bottle. 'Were you with her for a time? Try to make a go...'

'That's not me, Charlie. I used to see John once a fortnight but he started making excuses...'

'You never lived together?'

'...honestly, Charlie, I've never been suited to monogamy

until I met Mandy.'

He jerks forward in his seat. Jesus H. Christ, he manages not to say. Does his wife really believe this crap? A few seconds of silence seems about right. Ripens the air. He sips on his ginger tea, listens to the glug of another tug from the man's bottle. 'What you know about me might be awkward, Barry, I'm not a saint. I don't have a tennis club of abandoned mothers to avoid either.'

Barry quickly resumes his laughter, a hand again brushing some tears from the corner of his eyes.

'It's not really funny. Two kids who might need you. Not funny at all by my reckoning.'

Now it's Barry's turn to draw himself straight. 'But I don't have post-traumatic stress disorder.' His words come out clearer than they have for thirty minutes.

Charlie rises from his seat, the chair scraping the vinyl floor. It enters his mind to punch the stupid life coach, instead he just says, 'Fuck off,' and goes to sit with his children. What the hell has Mandy been saying. He had none of that. The sessions with the psych were army protocol. Three sessions. He gets army dreams, combat dreams. He didn't even punch Barry Brice and he had a hell of a lot of reasons why he might have. He could have done it on behalf of at least two women. A just war, as the generals say. On behalf of three women once Mandy comes around.

12.

When he confessed all to Mandy one evening last July, it was an odd thing to have done. He couldn't explain why to himself. Not the thought process behind it, not even if it was a conscious choice. It simply happened and did so on a working day in which he'd earlier had a lunchtime sandwich with Graham, over in the beer garden of The Grapes. Neither ever drank at work but the food was cheap; a good place for a coke and a snack. During that lunchtime natter, with a man he trusted but seldom shared real intimacies, he had casually said, 'Don't tell anyone but Roselyn and I are sleeping together.' He had no need to do it—not a prompt in the cloudless summer sky—but say it he did. It was like the matinee performance he was to give again in the evening to a different audience. And Charlie can keep a secret, did so for weeks. Not a boaster, he said it like a historian, ensuring the facts of the matter would live on should he fall under a bus. He had not thought about it, it was none of Graham's business. He can't say why because he didn't know he was going to. He said it, and that was that. Graham was funny— not deliberately—he asked why, and it cracked Charlie up. 'Because she lets me,' his reply. For about a minute, Charlie tried to justify the normality of it. 'Do you not want to run your hand up the leg of the prettiest girl at badminton?' Then he realised he was talking like a sapper, not a social worker. Graham wasn't shaking his head, his facial expression would have suited it though. Charlie felt taken down a peg. 'I know, I've let Mandy down. God knows what's got into me. And I doubt if Roselyn usually sleeps with her staff if you're getting ideas.'

Graham ignored the final point, justifiably it turns out, talked back once he seemed over the surprise of the admission. 'I won't tell a soul, but you should think over who else you might need to tell.'

They were Graham's words in The Grapes, the suntrap corner in the beer garden that they occupied alone that lunchtime. Charlie didn't think it over as asked, he thought Graham was embarrassed by the adultery conversation, hadn't found a long-enough-term partner to fund a fleeting fantasy about cheating on her yet. He didn't dwell on what Graham said; nevertheless, his counsel must have seeped into Charlie's brain one way or another.

* * *

Squash is a Game of Cunning

In the evening Charlie came home at his usual time, or more accurately his previously unusual time. He can recall Mandy asking him, 'No squash tonight?' The squash and gym—getting himself into shape—had delayed his arrival back in his family home many times those summer weeks.

Like a reflex, Charlie had answered, 'Graham has badminton on a Wednesday.' It might have been a stupid thing to say because he and Ros had done Wednesday before. Done it all on a Wednesday: the squash, the sex, all that he was hiding behind an imaginary squash game, an imaginary pint with Graham Ford. Mandy didn't seem bothered by the change of routine; she asked him if he'd like to cook the evening meal. Charlie's good in the kitchen, enjoys it. Made a hot chilli but with a blander pot for Michelle and Mikey. Kids still to develop any taste for the spicy stuff.

In the evening, the mid-summer evening, when the eaters of plain food were already in bed—Paul out with his friend, and not expected back until ten, this being the beginning of the holidays, and Mrs Cooper promising to drop him off at the agreed time—the couple sat together in the lounge with the patio doors open. White wine for Mandy, Charlie with a can of beer. 'I think I need to tell you,' he said, sitting on the sofa sideways on. Wearing his long navy-blue shorts, a red T-shirt, one he sometimes wore for squash. 'I've been doing something I shouldn't have.'

Mandy smiled at that, probably at the implausibility of it. 'What have you been up to, Charlie?'

Her face was composed, relaxed. They had trust between them which Charlie took to be a good thing. He gave her his most serious look, there was no going back.

'I shouldn't have Mandy, I slept with someone else.' For a moment Mandy looked back at him with the same smile. Waiting for the punchline that never came. Then in the silence, she broke down in tears. He had still to explain a thing. How it had happened, whether he was truly to blame or if it was just one of those things. She hung her head forward, hair deliberately screening her flooded eyes from the man whose words had caused this pain. Words and deeds. He told her it was over, finished, not itself a crystal-clear truth. It seemed probable in his mind, in the telling to Mandy. Ros had still to hear it. 'I'm sorry, I let you down.'

Despite her upset, her flood of tears, Mandy looked at Charlie directly. Stared through her filmy eyes. 'What?' she said, quietly but firmly. 'What happened?'

Now it was Charlie who was flustered. 'Squash. It's not love. Just seeing someone, running, close...' He had no idea what to tell her, had thought about it no more than when he brought the subject up in the beer garden earlier in the day. '...I think it might be the smell of sweat, Mandy. I'm sorry.'

She looked at him with widening eyes. 'You've not been having sex with Graham, have you?'

Charlie felt cold, he was clearing the air, not coming out. 'I was playing Roselyn. I've been playing Roselyn.'

'Squash, sex. What have you really been up to, Charlie?' Her voice penetrated the air with incision, demanded explanations beyond any he'd thought to prepare.

'Squash. I played her at squash. She's very good. There was no sex at first.'

'At first!' Mandy leaned forward and inadvertently knocked her wine glass over, spilled it on the floor. The glass broke, shattered into pieces.

'I'll clean that up,' said Charlie.

'Any-one can clean that up. You're the ruddy problem. I can't live with you sleeping around, sleeping with a work colleague...'

'My manager.' He said it stupidly like there was a material difference. Her seniority making it a less heinous offence.

'I hate you,' said Mandy through tears. 'Will you leave.'

'No,' he said. 'I'm not leaving you. I told you in order to put

Squash is a Game of Cunning

it right.'

'It wasn't a question, Charlie. I can't have you in my house. Can't. Will you, please, please, leave.'

Charlie looked down at his own sorry knees. Carefully he stooped to pick up the broken glass. 'I'll do whatever you want but I think I can put this right.'

'What do you know about right?' She stood up took her leave from the lounge, and while passing the kneeling Charlie, she clenched a fist and thumped him on the back. He knew it was only a gesture; she could have punched him harder. He deserved it and more.

'I'm sorry, Mandy.' He was talking to a closing door.

* * *

Mrs Cooper pulled her car onto the drive as Charlie was putting a small suitcase into the boot of the Fiat. Mandy said she would keep the Escort. Charlie would not be getting the better of anything from here on. Tears abated, she was extracting her due.

Paul asked him what was happening when he saw the case going into the back of the car. Charlie made a hand signal for Paul to stand still, he thanked Mrs Cooper for dropping the boy off, stood back, tried to imply that he didn't wish to talk.

'Paul lit the barbecue,' she told him.

His son looked away, tried to ignore the praise she was extending for this simple task. Charlie understood that. Paul can light a fire, it's what boys do.

'Great,' said Charlie.

'Well, I'll be off.' She pulled the car door closed, started the engine; Charlie feared his disinterest made him appear downright rude.

As she drove away, he spoke to Paul. 'I'm going away for a few days.'

Paul looked back at him blankly.

'A falling out.'

Still no recognition of likely cause and effect registered on the boy's face.

'Mandy and I,' said Charlie, before quickly correcting himself. 'Your mum and I.'

'You can't leave,' Paul finally managed.

'I'm not leaving you.' His voice broke with the words; a feeling of sickness rising in him as he recognised how little he and Mandy had agreed about the way this separation would work. How long it might last. Nothing had been drawn up, he felt entirely at the mercy of an unknown future. 'I love you, Paul.' He pulled his boy into a rare hug, a tight squeeze, feeling his shoulder blades as he embraced his skinny son. A lifebuoy on the roughest sea.

13.

Two minutes to midnight, Charlie takes hold of Mikey's hand, waves Mandy and Michelle over to him, the former coming only slowly. He shows his youngest son how to link arms. Explains the song—Auld Lang Syne—it means they will always be together, in their thoughts if not in person. Maybe both. They link arms, the family connected.

Paul and Ryan come across. Paul taking his mother's hand, Ryan to his right. Charlie did not expect these two to join in; the beer has uncovered their sentimental aspect. He used to get that six- or seven-pints in. Sophie is like Michelle: captivated by the novelty of it. She wants to sing, link arms in the funny manner.

'Should I get Barry?' asks Mandy, but none of the children seem fussed, and Charlie says nothing. An acquaintance to forget. Little Mikey is looking at his mother when she asks the question and it makes him hold his daddy's hand tighter. It is he, Charlie Quested, who has drawn him into this meaningful circle, who told him it means they will always be together in one way or another. What would be the point, thinks Charlie, of Barry Brice joining a circle in which his own two sons play no part?

As they sing together, Mandy staying with her children, Charlie gives a fleeting thought to the imposter in the kitchen. Imagines that the man is drowning in beer. Then as they are saying happy New Year, giving each other hugs, Mandy pulls Charlie close to her. It is the first time in months. 'Paul told me he has children,' she whispers in his ear.

He wonders who the incredulity in her voice is for. Him, Paul or Barry the bell-end? The man has not even told her. She has shared that he—her ex who wishes for a second chance—has post-traumatic stress disorder. She may have done so to put a distance between them, imply he is flawed and fractured, not the man she thought. Or it could have been to excuse his cheating. A rationalisation. He wants no excuses for his bloody stupid infidelity, wants only to atone. She's probably told Barry about his teenage years. Children's homes and a drug-addled mother. The born-to-be-a-failure-at-life coach has not so much as told Mandy that he's fathered any children. That he shagged around when he should have been playing tennis.

14.

Was he clever? Was he stupid? Charlie never knew how this should work. He stayed away over forty-eight hours, until the Saturday morning. He sent Mandy a couple of text messages, advising that he loved her, loved the three children, was 'with them in mind and heart.' He was proud of that phrase, he's not good with the gushing stuff. Bang-bang and dead-dead come far more easily to Charlie. Describe the action, not the feelings that are only your own. No-one really knows if what they feel is normal, or something downright strange.

When he pulled onto the drive, he saw that the Escort was there. Mandy was home, that was something. He wore his smartest casuals, had thought about that. Wanted to appear worth keeping. Not that he was in charge of the appraisal; Charlie controlled nothing but the clothes he wore, and that taken from a limited selection. A single suitcase.

He advised Roselyn that he had told his wife of their affair the morning after the confession occurred, after his ejection from Bramley Road. He said it as explanation for why he was wearing trainers to work, not that she was the kind of boss to bother about that. He didn't say that he was finishing with her, stopping the affair in its tracks. It was on his mind to do so. Before he could get around to it, she made exactly that point as clear as day. He often wonders why it is that he could bark orders at squaddies all day long, and still be so indecisive around women. The issues at the heart of it are of a different order. Interpersonal relationships are not battlegrounds, the weaponry too subtle for a practical man. No one dies, every-one gets wounded.

'You're back,' squealed Michelle, running to hug her father as soon as he had stepped over the threshold, letting himself in, still a keyholder.

'He's here; he's not back,' said Mandy to the air in the hallway.

Charlie gave his daughter a squeeze, lifted her from the carpet. Mikey came out of the kitchen, jam on his face, and Charlie kissed it just to get some jam on his own. Solidarity with his three-year-old's table manners.

'We need to talk,' he told Mandy. 'Now or soon. And I need to see my kids, you know I do.'

She said he should use the lounge. It brought to Charlie's mind the tragedy of contact visits, the rules of engagement that too many parents must abide by simply to meet, play and join hearts with their own children. He's a prop in the system, a social worker who arranges these for others in the widest array of circumstances. Never imagined being on the receiving end.

Michelle wanted to tell her father everything that had happened over the last forty-eight hours: school stories, and she tried to raise the matter of Paul's defiance of bedtime, not something that was usually a difficulty.

'I'll talk to Mum,' Charlie told her. He dislikes hearing siblings dob each other in the dirt. Hoped Mandy had not told tales on him although she would have had to say something. An explanation for his absence.

After about fifteen minutes, Paul came into the lounge still wearing his pyjamas. 'What's going on?' he asked. Charlie was tickling Mikey as he said it, and it felt like Paul had caught him having more fun than the situation could justify.

'Sit down, Paul. What has your mother told you?'

'You tell me!' his teenage boy shouted at him. 'You tell me why she cried her fucking heart out when you went and fucking left us!'

'Please don't swear; not in front of Mikey.' The littlest boy looked on the verge of tears. Whether it was bringing to mind his mummy's crying, or simply from hearing the sound of shouting, Charlie couldn't tell. He wanted to hug Mandy as he had back when she cried about her brother, Simon, serving in Helmand. And he sensed from the exchange in the hallway that this would not be happening today. 'I know I've messed up; this is between me and Mum. Nothing has changed between us, Pauly.'

Nothing has changed: a phrase seldom honestly deployed.

15.

When the hugging and happy New Year-ing has ceased, twenty-thirteen gone for good, twenty-fourteen rolling through the lower gears, Charlie tells Mandy that he will put Mikey to bed. She says, 'Thanks, Chuck.' A welcome return for an occasional nickname. With a hand around the back of his head, she pecks her husband's cheek for the second time inside a minute. Not since the sun was hovering close to the northern tropic, has he received such intimacy from her; the midnight hour is a bewitching one. 'I need to speak to misery-face,' she whispers.

He kisses her cheek as she tries to turn away, careful not to assume too broad an intimacy. 'Yeah, do. Come on, Mikey.'

His son's room is the smallest in the house, a bed snuck against a radiator which they had to disconnect. The pipes were scalding hot against his bed sheets. A small convector heater does the trick in its stead, they will not have him burn or go cold. Mikey tells his daddy that raspberry jam is very funny stuff. He's going to scare Robbie with it, a friend at nursery. He wants to take pots of the stuff with him when next he goes. 'It's messy,' says Charlie. 'Film companies employ make-up girls, women—maybe some men too—armed with wet wipes to make sure nothing's left sticky after the scene's been shot, the pretence upheld. Pictures in the can.' Mikey follows very little of this. His older brother has given him to understand that 'in the can' means the same as down the toilet. As Charlie is tucking his boy into bed, trying to find soothing words to help Mikey discover the composure to close his beady eyes, sink into the weightless stupor his highly strung body needs, he tells him, 'They flush it all away. Everything in the can. Flushed away. Down the pipes and out into the ocean where it surfs across to a little island with a single coconut tree. One day we'll all end up there, sweet Mikey, when, finally, we all get flushed away.'

He has gone, slipped into the dreams in which Charlie hopes raspberry jam plays no part.

* * *

Charlie sits with Paul and Ryan, pop video on the television.

The two girls have taken themselves to bed: sleepover night. The parents of Sophie and Ryan are unlikely to be in a state to drive although Charlie doesn't know that for a fact. He could have driven her home, of course. Would have, but Mandy hasn't been factoring him into any arrangements for some months. His wife and her ill-thought-through lover talk together in the kitchen, talk quietly; Charlie can't hear the words spoken. He thinks it could be a very difficult conversation, one he must not intrude upon. He has always trusted Mandy's judgement and finds himself back in exactly that groove tonight. Took a while to reach it, and now here he is.

'Your place,' says Paul, speaking slowly, 'you're flat-thing...'

'Yes,' says Charlie, encouraging his son to spit out what is on his mind.

'...when you're done, when Mum lets you come back here, can me and Ryan have it?'

As he laughs, he wonders if he might have cried at the same comment if he had a few drinks inside him. 'This is your home, your family, young Pauly. This is where you live. You're a smart kid; do you think she'll have me back?'

'If you leave other women alone, she will, Dad.' Charlie glances at Ryan; his eyes are strictly on the television, the music video. Another underdressed woman, the music channel has an endless supply of them. It brings a squash court to Charlie's mind.

A certain squash player.

16.

It was during his fourth visit to her exclusive squash club that Charlie found his true rhythm, hit the peaks for which Roselyn had no defence. He was swinging through the ball with zero hesitation; the greater flight this gave allowed him trajectories he had never used before. A fierce slice into the back wall that flew up to the front and died before his opponent had guessed where she needed to run. She got points, of course she did; Roselyn was good at this, fast, clever. But Charlie had trained up every advantage he could muster. Even his reach—much longer than hers—he drew upon relentlessly. Height, muscle, the reawakening of a killer instinct: with these he defeated his manager.

'The seven P's,' she correctly told him as they panted together on the squash court. Finished, job done. 'You remembered your seven P's,' repeated Roselyn. This was a joke, a reminder of the throwaway line which Ted Astaire used in a video-linked briefing to all staff. His upbeat summer message declaring how the small number of staff on the ground could get through the hefty volume of work required, keep the ship afloat through the holiday season. Prior preparation and planning prevent a piss-poor performance. He said it to inspire those working while their colleagues hit the beaches, the Med. Preparation, Charlie had certainly done that. Weights and a few coaching sessions. Ted had smirked a little when he said it on video, recited the mnemonic. There is only so much you can do when half the staff are on holiday. Charlie might be the only one who took it seriously. Took those seven P's up to a new level, applied it better on the squash court than anyone did in social work city-wide.

When they were going up the corridor of her exclusive club towards the changing rooms—coming to the door with the lady motif upon it—she said, 'Wait,' and Charlie did as she asked. Roselyn pushed the door open, stepped over the threshold, and appeared to look the room up and down, the edge of the door in her hand the whole time. She stepped back, scrunched the centre of his sweaty T-shirt in her left hand and pulled him into her private changing area.

Her lips were upon his, her hands searched him out. He reciprocated. Charlie likes rewards and he had played exceptionally well. Trained hard for it. She allowed him to push down her white shorts, her own hands equally invasive of his clothing. She negotiated her way to the shower, entwined with the big man. Both shed their clothing as they moved those short yards. Under the nozzle the water was momentarily cold: it dampened nothing. Then it was hot, the shower was steamy. Roselyn got more for herself out of losing than most squash players would think to ask for.

17.

'What channel is this?' asks Charlie. Paul is nodding his head fiercely as if at the rock concert he has so frequently asked his father to take him to. Ryan shrugs in reply. On the screen are men dressed in Abraham Lincoln hats, and not very much else. A bit of underwear. The song sounds macho, while the video, and even the lyric, are gay as a man-bag. He realises that, without Graham to interpret for him, he cannot explain whether it is cool, rude, homophobic or egging children to the lifestyle that he knows better than to object to. Not that he ever tested Graham's knowledge of the micro-cultural signs in pop videos. He would like to do so in the future—would welcome any conversation with him at all—he truly would.

'Wild!' says Paul.

The doorbell rings, and three look at each other with surprise. Charlie jumps up. He remembers some nonsense about neighbours popping around with a piece of coal; it brings good luck for the year ahead apparently. He doesn't think it has gone on in his lifetime, certainly not at any New Year's party he has sat or drank his way through. He can't think why it should have restarted this year. As he is opening the door, Barry comes from the kitchen and says, 'It's for me.'

'Taxi,' says the man outside, his car is visible out front. A light shining through the opaque glazing.

'I'll collect my stuff,' Barry tells Mandy.

She stands in the kitchen doorway. Her face has become a little stonelike, rigid in a way Charlie seldom sees. Used it once or twice when Paul has presented an awkward side, those inevitable teenage turns. There is even a hint of a smile on her face. Not properly, just the sense that one may not be so far away. She stays there, close to the front door, quite impassively for fully three minutes before Barry, who disappeared up the stairs, eventually comes back down. Laden. She waves her hand as she might if it was a neighbour popping back home after a coffee. No hug, no more words. Barry carries a holdall, a half-full bin liner. They will be his company for the taxi ride. For the foreseeable future, perhaps.

Paul and Ryan stay in the lounge, Charlie pictures them listening to this departure. Paul listening. A click of an upstairs door tells him that Michelle, too, is letting herself understand the New Year's development. The happy New Year Charlie can scarcely believe has come around. Barry is out of the house; a taxi door shuts with just a little force, then Mandy shuts their home's front door gently. 'This changes nothing,' she tells him, knowing no one else can hear. 'You can sleep on the couch or back to your little pad. Nothing has changed.'

He touches her arm, gently, not an intrusive intervention. 'Want to talk, Mandy?'

She holds his gaze, a tiny waver of her head, a glance to the door she is facing. Indicates that he may join her in the kitchen.

18.

'Geoff's been doing worse to me,' said Roselyn as they lay together in the double bed. They were talking after doing, in a more comfortable setting, that which previously they had

Squash is a Game of Cunning

done only at the squash club changing room.

Worse than adultery? For Charlie this conjured an image of violence, beating, something that made their privately shared pleasures insignificant. The smallest compensation. Nor could he picture this assertive woman being subject to such humiliation. Not Roselyn. And he has met Geoff: a small, slight man; intelligent but without Ros's presence, her vitality. 'What's he done to you?'

On this Wednesday evening they played no squash. After Charlie's win, they had one more go, again Charlie was in control and Roselyn once more sneaked him into the ladies' changing room. Taking for herself what he could not resist giving her. Eight days later, he told Mandy that he and Graham were to play squash again, but went instead to a hotel bedroom in which the only games played were of a sexual nature. Nothing perilous but some pleasures that Mandy never permitted him to take from her.

This was an achievement given Charlie's guilt-ridden arrival. Roselyn was already in the room; he told her that he had to leave by ten. Said it before he had so much as taken off his shoes. Roselyn was sitting on the edge of the bed in a short skirt. 'Are you sure? she queried as she stood, raised the hem sufficiently to show him the tops of her gartered suspenders. He didn't reply directly to her question. Mandy deserved better than his infidelity, he understood that much. The sight of Roselyn in clothing chosen to titillate— suspenders and nothing more beneath her short skirt— drove all thought of his wife from him. The blood that fuels his thinking brain had dropped halfway to the floor.

'I know what he's done, Charlie,' she said not quite answering his question. Talking around it. 'Geoff stays over in Huddersfield quite a bit. Says he has work to crack on with. He stays at Gordon's house, another manager in his department. Or so he tells me. He's even given me a phone number but I've never rung it. Gordon's in on it. He has another woman there; that's what he's cracking on with. He's always so pleased when he's packing a bag, saying he needs to work late. No one should be that pleased about working late.'

'Yeah, that's shit,' Charlie replied, knowing it was not worse. Similar at best and possibly an unfounded suspicion. Perhaps what he and Roselyn enjoyed behind the backs of their respective partners deserved nothing less. Tit for tat.

After sex, they talked in bed, mostly about work. Charlie went over a recent foster carer application, one which he thought they needed to refuse. It was odd, like a supervision session but he'd never before touched her naked breasts during one. He might have thought back on this one more than all the dull sessions endured in the glass box to the side of their open-plan office. Could be the way to make the message stick.

* * *

The following day, Brenda was leading the team meeting. Taking turns to chair their little gatherings was one of Roselyn's supposedly democratic innovations, not that it really shifted the balance of power. Charlie sat beside his manager at the long table. On sliding into the seat, it crossed his mind that they might look like a couple if he touched her or she him in a manner that was too familiar. That would not do. Perhaps he should have gone to the other side of the table but avoidance might have been as much of a giveaway. He had given no thought to the minutiae of office affairs. Ever. And he might just as easily have sat next to her before any of this. He is not a difficult man to manage. Tina and Fiona were always the stroppy ones. The Charlie Quested who stuck two fingers up at authority was tamed almost thirty years earlier, made army ready by Grace Bell. He even wonders if his affair was just to please a superior, a daft thought looking back on it. Mandy is the one in his life to whom he should have given the highest respect. Paul,

Squash is a Game of Cunning

Michelle, Mikey. Hindsight is a fat lot of use.

'I want to look at the history of child sexual exploitation,' Brenda told the team. 'Is it a short history or a long history?'

'Very, very long,' answered Tina, without looking up.

'Yes and no,' said Brenda, enjoying the hot seat, leading the talk. 'People like me, who've been in the game a long time, must all be feeling pretty ashamed of how we've handled this issue, the labels we've put upon it.'

The team members were all paying attention, the topic is a big deal, a worry across children's services up and down the country.

'Ashamed of what exactly?' asked Roselyn.

'Well look at this,' Brenda held up a tattered copy of an old legal Act. 'These are the two-thousand-and-two fostering regulations; one of the named reportable events is, and I quote, "Involvement or suspected involvement of a child placed with foster parents in prostitution." How did we dare to use that term, think that the problem was the child, not the predatory men who did what they did to them? Sorry Graham, Charlie, it's always men.'

'Point taken,' said Charlie, although Fiona chipped in, 'Nearly always,' and it set Precious off talking about a female nursery worker who had made the news five or six weeks before. A perverted woman, very unusual.

'Quite right,' Brenda continued, 'there can be exceptions, it's still almost always men. Then in twenty-eleven parliament laid down new fostering regulations…'

'And they finally had the sense to call it child sexual exploitation,' interrupted Yasmin. 'And about time too,' she added as the room waited quietly for Brenda to confirm she had stolen her thunder.

'Wrong, I'm afraid, Yaz. The twenty-eleven…' Brenda held aloft a copy of the Act, a thin pamphlet in much better shape than the two-thousand-and-two version, seldom thumbed by the look of it. '…also give the same reportable event.

"Involvement or suspected involvement of a child placed with foster parents in prostitution." We continued to blame the child for criminal acts which adults did to them. What do you think about that?'

Yasmin looked shocked. 'Who proofreads these things?'

'Ted, I expect,' slipped in Fiona.

'I don't think it was him.' Roselyn put on her straight face, defence of the department and all who sail in her. As she did so, Charlie felt her thigh brush against his. This was beneath the table, she was in black trousers today, it meant nothing, still he made a mental note never to sit so close to her again. And this child prostitution stuff was hardly sex talk; he always feels sickened by it. He knew that there were girls in care at the same time as him who were being exploited. They told all the other kids that they did drugs, had sex, could do each as often as they wanted. Teenagers like him, hardened but awkward, looked up to those more-worldly girls as if they were the adults amongst them. Nowadays he doubts if all of them made it into adulthood at all. He couldn't see it then but knows now—cannot be a social worker and not know—how very bleak their prospects were. He was lucky to find Grace Bell, lucky to be male most likely. He wouldn't have spotted the stupidity of the prostitution word in the regulations, not in his youth or even until very recently in his career. Possibly never. He's a social worker who does the right thing, whether he says it the right way or not. He'd punch the bloody pimps lights out if professional standards would allow it; the fine-tuning the precise meaning of words, not debasing children by the careless reliance on the language of our prejudiced past, is for those with fancier social work degrees than his.

'You all know,' Brenda continued, 'that the new care planning regulations, which came into effect on the first of this month, also amend the fostering regulations. That's the main amendment, rectify that stain. No longer will we ever think a child can be a prostitute. They are of an age when we grant them no agency to agree to sex, so they really cannot take money for it of their own volition. I feel a bit sick when I think that I've spent my whole career missing it.'

19.

'I've no one else to talk to, Charlie. I can't trust you a jot but I've no one else. Once I could...'

'I'm sorry, Mandy. You can, you know. I'm putting everything back to how it was, but I know it'll take time.'

'I can't. Not sure what I was...' Mandy lets the sentence slip away.

She has an empty wine glass in her hand which she turns and turns. Empty since midnight, Charlie thinks. She appeared to go into the kitchen for a refill, talked with the life coach instead. Barry Brice. His wife's lover. A lot to talk about for sure, and now he's gone. Fled from her better judgement. Or possibly just to sniff around a few more lady tennis players. His wife's ex-lover. 'Tell me. I'm a decent listener.'

'Yes, you've always been that. It was Paul who said something strange over an hour ago. Did I know Barry had a load of kids in a tennis club? It didn't make sense. He told me he was childless. At least, I think that was what he said in the never-married conversation that we had months ago. When I asked him tonight, he was sitting at this table, looking like the world was on his shoulders. He started up with this I-need-to-come-clean nonsense and that's when I knew he was worse than you. It took you twenty years to come off the rails; Barry had set off with a few wheels hanging over the side. Why didn't I see that, Charlie?'

Paul enters the kitchen where his father gestures, gently, kindly, and the son turns around, leaves his parents to talk.

'Will the old you ever come back, Charlie? I can't be doing

with being cheated on.' As she says this, Mandy rises and slaps a flat hand quite gently on his chest. Once, twice, three times. There is no intention to hurt, thinks Charlie, just to express what she feels. Towards him, towards Barry-fucking-Brice. Towards men. Charlie has a lot to answer for, he knows he does. He tries to wrap his arms around her, she pushes him away. 'Don't gloat. No ruddy gloating. I'm not cut out for having affairs or whatever the hell that was. I saw Barry to get over you, paid for life coaching...'

'Life coaching, tennis coaching, it's all screwing to that guy.'

'...shut up! Shut up, Charlie! You can't talk. You have no claim on me, not now. No claim whatsoever. You can go and have sex on a squash court any ruddy time you like.' She stops the flow of invective, looks at him, head in his hands, elbows on the kitchen table.

'None of it, Mandy. I'm doing none of it. So much has gone wrong because I've let you down. I even think Graham wouldn't be in the hospital but for that. The chain of events. And most of all, I know you deserved none of it. All my stupid fault, Mandy.' They let the stirred air return to its usual kitchen stillness. 'You know that I don't work with her, don't you? Tariq's my manager now. I hardly see her.'

'Chance, Charlie. Your manager changed, not because you quit your job, decided you had to keep as far from her as you could. It was chance, Charlie. I really don't know what to think about you anymore. I think I wasn't enough for you.'

'You're wrong on that one, Mandy. I just let my guard down, took what was offered without thinking it through. Now my brain's reconnected I can tell you—not a shadow of a doubt—you're everything. All I ever wanted. Everything to me, and if you don't believe me, I'll just keep saying it until you do.'

Chapter Five

Wide of Goodge Street

1.

'Where have you been all morning?' asks Tariq.

Charlie shrugs. 'A visit. Mrs Riley with the twins.' He often makes a call or two before coming to the office. They all do. He notices that Tariq is looking stressed. More stressed than usual and the man is a worrier. 'What's wrong?'

'We have to see Mr Astaire. You and I. Miss Makepeace has been calling since eight-thirty.'

'Oh. Okay. When can he see us?' Charlie is quite surprised. He has spoken to the director only occasionally and isn't quite sure who Miss Makepeace is. He thinks he's heard the name. Knows of no case of his which might be on the director's radar. Not currently.

'Now. Now, I expect. I'll call Miss Makepeace and tell her you're here.'

'Who is that?' asks Charlie.

'Miss Makepeace? His PA Charlie, surely you know her.'

He gets it now. Carly, he knows her as. Knows her by sight, doesn't recall speaking to her. And she's a pretty nice sight: a young blonde with a desk in the director's anteroom. 'Okay, Tariq. I can see him whenever he's free. What's it about?'

'Oh, my.' Tariq angles his head slightly to his left side. 'You don't know, do you?'

Both were standing as they spoke. Now he follows his manager into the small glass office, slides down onto a chair. Tariq sits too, describes the events in question, brings

Charlie up to speed. Russell Chope was at school yesterday—the boy attends a special school, hasn't the attention span to yet cope with mainstream—and during the day he had a run-in with another boy, Dayton Pearce. Charlie knows about Dayton already; he's discussed the situation with the teachers at the school once or twice. Dayton bullies Russell. Charlie confirms this for his manager. Advises that he has briefed the Goodings—Russell's foster carers—on the matter. They are all trying to keep on top of it. He reckons that school has handled it well. 'The other kid might be as messed up as Russell,' he says. Not excusing, it simply needs factoring in.

'That little boy's taxi never turned up,' says Tariq.

Charlie feels a tightening in his stomach at the use of the term, little boy. He's never met Dayton Pearce but had him down as a brute who beats Russell up if he thinks he can get away with it.

'Something happened outside the school gate, Charles. The police haven't sent us their written report yet but your boy seems to have tripped him or something. Then bashed him on the head with half a paving slab. Young Dayton is in the hospital, still to wake up. He has a fractured skull. We must all hope he wakes up.'

'God, that's awful,' says Charlie. 'Russell's never been violent before. Unpredictable, smashed plates and windows, never violent towards other kids.' Tariq says nothing for a moment, lets it all sink in. Charlie can see why this might be on Ted Astaire's radar. 'Is Russell in custody?'

'Of course. We have a place in secure psychiatric. It's the right place for him. He's terribly unwell. Most disturbed.' Charlie nods, takes it in. 'He is telling everyone there that he has killed Charlie Quested. That's what your Russell told the police when they first picked him up. Killed Charlie Quested. Maybe he had nothing against the Pearce boy. He must be out of his mind if he thinks he's murdered you outside a school gate in Derbyshire. You're here, Charlie. And you haven't been near him since before Christmas from what I can see on the database.'

* * *

'Charlie,' says Roselyn.

Just a quiet acknowledgement. She is his former manager and it tells the others in the room nothing more. He looks back at her and nods a puzzled head. No idea why she is in this meeting.

Fiona is here already, seated next to the Director. Tariq and Charlie take their places. Ted Astaire rises from his seat, leans across and shakes Charlie's hand over the table's shiny veneer. 'This can be awkward, I know, sir.'

Nothing in the phrase puts Charlie at ease. Quite the opposite. A dose of awkwardness is heading his way. Why else would the Director call him sir.

'Fiona, Charles, this is an informal meeting to mull over what has gone on. Prepare ourselves for how we will need to handle the matter in the coming days. It's a most serious incident. We should anticipate a professional review, regardless of whether the poor lad lives or dies.' He slows down the meter of his speech, it is how he makes a point. 'It has come so close that we will learn the lessons. Unpick what has gone wrong. We must. It is the very least that we can do. Is that clear?' Charlie and Fiona nod their heads. They seem to be on trial, not that either of them raised the paving slab. 'Ms Pickford is with us in her role as departmental lead for professional standards. I have asked her to commence reviewing this case with immediate effect. I'm interested to fathom—not now, I've no wish to spring it on you while you are digesting the news, but later—to understand your reasoning. Get a handle on your thinking about each and every decision made regarding Russell Chope. I need this in writing. Initially this will be for myself and Ms Pickford— she is conducting this internal review—but we may share your submission with external professionals at a later date. At an Independent Case Review; it might meet the threshold. The commentary you write now can sit alongside the records you've already made. Records which I have asked my assistant, Carly, to retrieve. She's doing it as we speak. Your reports must come to me first thing Monday morning—at the latest—please. You can email them to Ms Pickford, or pass them to her if you choose to write it out in longhand.'

As Charlie listens, glancing periodically at Fiona, he ponders the tone of the meeting. This doesn't feel like the supportive department Ted tells them it is every time he holds a motivational talk. He and Fiona are in the dock. He also notes the name Ted calls him by. Charles. He was Charlie at Christmas time. And Ms Pickford for his former boss. He's screwing her; Ted's wife is in Philadelphia. Ted screwing Roselyn makes a lot of sense, a win-win for both by the looks of things. Ted still gets his leg over while the wife is across the pond, there will be relief in that. And Roselyn was briefly just a social worker like him. Barely took a pause for breath. Now she's playing footsie under the top table. Seems to have assumed lead responsibility for investigating any shortcomings across Children's Services. Charlie never saw the role advertised.

* * *

As they arrive back in the team room, Tariq says, quite formally, 'Fiona, Charles, today is a normal day.' Then he leaves them for the security of his glass bubble.

Normal for Tariq. The singled-out pair click their respective screens to life. Begin to retrieve records. Simultaneously, they find that they cannot get into the Chope files. Access denied. The message tells them they don't have the correct level of authority, and they wrote every word on there. Charlie rolls his swivel chair out from his desk. Leaves it in the aisle as he marches to Tariq's office.

Fiona is virtually in step. 'This is ridiculous,' he tells his manager. 'If we are to write up what we did and why, we need to see what it was. We don't remember every second of our busy working lives. That's why we write case notes in the first place.'

'I had understood that they were being set to read-only,' says Tariq. 'I'll speak to Mr Astaire.'

Fiona is in the glass cube too; both stand over him while Tariq makes the call. He looks flustered.

'Miss Makepeace, may I...'

… … … … … … …

'I'm sorry, Carly, yes, I know it is Carly. May I speak to Mr Astaire...'

… … … … … … …

'He's speaking to the department, I see.'

… … … … … … …

'The case notes, case history, Russell Chope, have you blocked access?'

Charlie and Fiona exchange looks of frustration; why is Tariq being so polite with this jumped-up junior?

… … … … … … …

'You see, Miss Makepeace...'

… … … … … … …

Charlie wishes he could hear what Tariq hears. Tell the secretary she's got it wrong.

'...Carly. You see without having access it is very difficult for them. They wish to read their own notes so they may give a full account of their reasoning....'

Again, he stops speaking, listens obediently to the girl in the Director's office.

… … … … … … …

'It was Mr Astaire's instruction. Oh, I see.'

… … … … … … … … … … … … … … … … … … …

Charlie knows from the concentration on Tariq's face that

the girl is speaking at length. None of it is audible to him. Fiona makes gestures, angry ones. They may confuse Tariq or may give him a backbone. The point she is making is obvious.

'Miss Makepeace, my social workers only wish to remind themselves of the salient points in their recent visits to young Russell...'

... ...

'Okay. Ask Mr Astaire. I understand Miss Makepeace...'

... ...

'...Carly, yes. I am sorry to have troubled you. And Carly, whatever Mr Astaire says, of course we will abide by it.'

Before Tariq has a chance to explain anything to them, both Charlie and Fiona storm out of his little office. 'Whatever Fred Astaire says,' parrots Fiona. 'Three bags full, Miss Makepeace.'

* * *

It is only his fifth day back at the house, and this is the first time he has returned from work without feeling elated at being under the same roof as his wife and children. In his proper home. The Chope case is the cloud; Mandy and the kids might be the antidote. Family matters to him but thoughts of Russell and Dayton keep bubbling to the surface. He pulls onto the drive carefully, parking next to his wife's car, steps from his vehicle and opens the rear passenger door to retrieve the small holdall in which he carries his laptop. He takes the key from his pocket and opens the front door. In the lounge, he throws down the bag. It is not heavy: a notebook, a scarcely thumbed fostering textbook and a few pens accompany the laptop. That's it, the tools of the trade. It bounces once on the family sofa and down to the floor. Mandy is sitting slouched on the adjacent chair; she pulls herself upright. 'You've a flat to go to if you're in a bad mood.'

'Sorry...' His face is pained, contrite. '...it's a work thing.

Really bad.'

Mandy stands up and looks into his troubled eyes, strained and aged by the year past as war could not do to him. She lets him talk. He is living at the family home as the father of their children. They have talked amicably together since New Year. The flat has four-weeks' rent paid up but he prefers to sleep on the family sofa. Knows that it might be the only sleeping arrangement Mandy permits him for a long time. She said that she cares about him, and it was good to hear it. He has spoken the phrase, 'I love you,' more times in the last four or five days than he has managed since the first year of their relationship. His courtship of Mandy Blackburn. Those are words she has still to echo back. He wants to tell her that he never said such a thing to Roselyn, never thought anything of the sort. He didn't love her. He thinks saying it might be the wrong thing to do; bringing Roselyn's name into the room an indiscretion.

'I love you, Mandy,' he says again. It's the truest thing he knows. He is back on Bramley Road. Throwing down a work bag was petulant. How he feels about the way the department is handling this unfortunate occurrence. Nothing to do with his home life. His feelings toward Mandy are only good, so grateful to be back in her orbit.

'What's going on at work, Charlie?' She says it cautiously, leans forward to listen him out.

'There's a boy in hospital fighting for his life. That's what matters, and I really hope he pulls through. Hit on the head. Hit with a bit of concrete. On the back of that, the powers that be are questioning my competence. Mine and Fiona's. Implying that our planning—the perpetrator is a foster boy, one of ours—was part of the problem. Maybe they're right and we can't do our jobs. God knows, none of us have a crystal ball letting us know what's coming.'

This job means more to Charlie than he knows how to express. Earlier in his life the army trained him to kill people. Just in case. Then he put it into practice: the Gulf War. Nothing went wrong, not on his side. Just being there was a little bit of hell. Worry on stilts. These days, he can get a worthier buzz by helping others. Paid for putting people knocked sideways by life back on the trail. It's a job and a half. A true vocation he never guessed himself suited to. His treasured wife, Mandy, nudged him into the path of this better purpose.

She can be quite hard-headed—gently so—she touches his hand, his arm, with real sympathy for his plight. 'Do you think you got anything wrong? Missed a sign?'

'Me, Fiona, a psychiatrist, and two of the loveliest foster carers I've ever worked with: could be we all did. Not one of us saw it coming. Not one. We were helping a damaged kid, there's nothing more unpredictable. He was unwell, we knew that. The idea that he would smash a boy's head in, well...' Charlie stops talking, goes into himself a little, and Mandy waits. The children are shrieking upstairs but they sound good-humoured. Never been much need for intervention with the Quested kids. '...the thing I really don't get, the boy told the police he'd killed me. Broken my skull. I never thought we had a bad relationship. Nothing special—it's his foster mum who he loves—he always talked openly with me. Usually talked openly with me. Now he's in some secure kids' psychiatric unit telling anyone who will listen that he killed Charlie Quested. Proud of it too, apparently.'

* * *

Charlie thinks Mandy is listening at the lounge door while he is on the phone in the hallway. He doesn't mind at all: it feels like an intimacy. A throwback of a dozen years or more. The time when he first told his foster mother about his upcoming career change—social work training—trepidation, uncertainty, a lot of excitement too, back then.

'It's a work thing that's worrying me.'

Wide of Goodge Street

For Charlie, she's been a source of calm since puberty, says the right thing at the right time. Tells him he's a worrier when he thinks he isn't. Cares about him and that's the quality he seeks.

'One boy has put another boy in hospital. Serious stuff, Mum. A fractured skull.'

Grace Bell listens, murmurs, 'I see,' as Charlie tells the story.

'I don't know the little boy who's unconscious. The one who hurt him wasn't in his right mind, and it was my job to monitor his care, his placement.'

Charlie thinks he hears Mandy go from the lounge to the dining room, go through to the kitchen that way, not wanting to pass him in the hallway. He wouldn't have minded; a little physical contact right now would be a welcome thing. Perhaps it will come; he is back in the house. He hasn't explained his home situation to Grace Bell. Fears she would be as disappointed in him as Mandy.

* * *

The younger ones are upstairs while they watch the evening news, Paul sitting with his parents. Taking an interest. Midway through the local news, Charlie and Mandy stare rigidly at the screen. They weren't expecting it, perhaps they should have been.

> ***A fourteen-year-old boy is fighting for his life in a Derbyshire Hospital.***

The announcer is looking at his desk, reading it off a card or from a screen which is not in their view.

> ***This follows an unprovoked attack by another boy outside Peel's School in Ashbourne. A fourteen-year-old is in custody. He is believed to have carried out the assault. Neither child can be named for legal reasons.***

Raspberry Jam

'The world will never know,' says Charlie. He and Fiona, one or two social workers before them, have put a lot into finding the right placement, a bit of stability, for poor Russell Chope. The Goodings seemed like it, wonderful foster carers. Does anyone really know how to help a boy who lived an infancy of beatings and buggery at the whim of his father? A drug-addled fuck-up who was shut away in prison five years ago. Locked up for everything he did to Russell. Stopped so late in the day, it's terrifying. Russell's problems all started before he was old enough to lay down retrievable memories. And they continued for so long that the boy's nightmares must be a hundred times more harrowing than Charlie's army dreams.

'What? What is it? You know him?' asks Paul.

Charlie realises his boy is the same age as both the victim and the perpetrator. Thank God the trajectory of his life is so contrary to theirs. 'I'm sorry, Pauly. I really can't talk about it.' Charlie leans across the sofa to give his son a hug that the lad was not seeking.

'At least they got the one who did it,' says Paul.

* * *

'I don't think you should be phoning me, Fiona,' says Charlie.

Ted Astaire told them in the meeting earlier today not to talk together about this case. The department needs to examine their respective roles in the matter. A version they have cobbled together, mutually crafted for the favourable light it showers upon them, will not go down well.

'He isn't to know, is he?' says Fiona.

'I won't be telling him you called,' says Charlie, 'but if we put the same stuff in our statements then they'll know.'

Fiona talks on and on. It is not the first time she has phoned to vent a few work-related feelings. She needs this job, she tells him. Danny earns less than her. The academic pen-pusher, occasional eco-warrior, is only a part-time

Wide of Goodge Street

lecturer. His courses are of little value by Fiona's tallying. Intellectual gobshite pays less than social work. She says that their mutual security is down to her. 'And I'm good at it, Charlie. Just like you. Good at the stuff we do. The story is hitting the headlines and that means the council will want a scapegoat. It's what they do. Unfair on every count. Witch hunts always end with a burning. No witches, just burning some poor sod who looks as close to one as they can find.'

There is nothing in her rant that Charlie disagrees with. Nor does her unexpurgated vomit of fear make him feel any better.

The call came in around ten-thirty, everyone was in bed except Charlie. He was watching a comedy programme on the television. To distract; it had yet to make him laugh. Mandy must have heard his voice, the sound of him speaking, it has brought her downstairs wrapped in a thick purple dressing gown. A questioning look on her face.

'Sometimes, Fi, I think we just need to be honest. Trust the process to spot that we were making good calls in very difficult circumstances. Even Fred knows we can't see into the future. Nothing in the boy's past behaviour involved concrete slabs...'

Fiona interrupts him, Mandy is holding his gaze, and it is confusing for Charlie. He has no wish to ignore Fiona, but would prefer to talk it out with his wife. He suspects that she just wants him to come off the call, let her sleep. Her face expresses concern for him. There is still some love there, he is sure of it.

'I'd almost forgotten that,' says Charlie, Fiona having reminded him that Russell—before he ever lived with the Goodings—used to steal Barbie dolls from shops, decapitate them and smear some of his own blood on the severed limbs, the neck. An ominous hobby in a ten-year-old boy.

When the call is over, Mandy steps into Charlie and puts her arms around him. 'This is really troubling you, fella,' she says.

2.

Yasmin puts a hand on Charlie's shoulder. 'How are you bearing up?' she asks.

He turns to look into her headscarf-framed face. He never discussed the matter with colleagues yesterday, guesses that Fiona did. He knows the team to be supportive—always—that is how social workers sift through the unremitting misery of their clients' lives. They coax each other along, keep each other's spirits up. Charles Quested is a private man. Shares feelings, thoughts and past experiences only sporadically. The team has long accepted that he functions this way. 'In the Gulf—nineteen-ninety-one this was—I knew that we were facing a real shit-storm. I couldn't even be certain that I'd live through it. This is different. Kuwait had been invaded; Saddam needed repelling. We got it, understood what was going on however heavy it was. This? I don't know why it's happening, what brought it on. I can't believe Russell attacked that lad. He's not like that at all. Is it my fault, Yaz?'

'No Charlie, not even close to your fault. The problem is that the poor boy has suffered too much in his young life for any of us to blame him. You more than most, Charlie. Russell did a terrible thing but we're none of us cross with him. We're kind of sympathetic, want to work out what in his past caused it, how we can put that trauma right. If they can't lay a glove on the perpetrator, what do they do? Come looking for the next in line, Charlie, that's what. Not right, not right at all. It is simply what they do.'

* * *

The morning is not a productive one, not from Charlie's perspective. Around eleven, Tariq comes across and asks what he's working on. Charlie tells him that he has a case to go before the fostering panel the following week, a new foster carer application. 'It's complicated,' he says.

'What's the nub of it?'

'They're a good couple—same sex—sailed through Brenda's preparation for fostering course. Last one before she left. One of them has come a bit unstuck on the criminal records thing. Michael Sheldrake, his name. He has a GBH from years back. His take on the matter is that it was before he came out, long before. He hadn't confirmed for himself that he was gay, never mind admitting it to the rest of the world. He said his emotions could go all over the place back then. Nothing in twenty years. They're a lovely couple of guys.'

'Is it written up, Charlie?' asks Tariq.

He nods his head, indicates that it is.

'I'd best review it first. I'm sure you're right but this is a tricky time to be applying leniency in our assessments. We can't ignore serious offences.'

'I didn't ignore it at all, Tariq. You should know by now that in cases like this, I always start from a position of likely refusal...' Others across the open-plan are looking up from their desks; Charles Quested has raised his voice, it is the rarest thing. '...the guy has done eight years of youth work, through a church; I've interviewed the adults who work with him. He's dealt with tricky teenagers and all the rest of it. Dealt with them very well. The GBH was a different man, a long-gone time in his life. We can't change who we were, only who we are now.' He lets his voice come down a couple of notches. 'We've quite a few on our books like it.'

'Yes, Charlie. I take your point. I should still review it, make myself familiar with the detail. Just in case I have to present it to panel.'

Charlie turns away. 'Sure.' He knows that he has been unnecessarily loud, understands the implications of Tariq's final point too.

3.

Paul's friend Ryan is back around the house. Trustworthy boys. Charlie has always thought that, and Mandy too, it seems. She has agreed to come out with him, Saturday morning shopping. Mikey needs shoes and Michelle enjoys a trip out. Like old times, the four of them traipse around the shops, Charlie carries Mikey now and again. He can't stop thinking about the sofa he sleeps on, that using it shames him in front of his children. He doesn't think he deserves any better, but his children do. They deserve a better father. He is all they have, and his rehabilitation might help this family to relax again.

Inside the shop, Mikey has strayed from the stool and picked up a girl's shoe. He wants to try it on. Both he and Mandy are pretty set on getting him a pair from those designated for boys. His mother tells him, 'Girls' feet are a little different, Mikey. They aren't really made for you.'

He's not an argumentative boy. Mikey scuttles off the stool, brings back a red trainer that meets with both parents' approval. Charlie helps him put his foot into it. 'Now stand up, put weight on it,' he instructs his child.

Mikey limps across the shoe-shop, the mismatched footwear or his father's use of the word weight inducing an odd gait. Psychosomatic, funny to watch. Michelle follows him down the shop, dragging her right foot, an exaggerated copycat of her little brother. When Mikey looks around, they both laugh. Charlie touches Mandy's hand. 'I think it fits,' he says. Mandy gets the assistant to fetch the other of the pair. Charlie helps Mikey into this one too. Now he walks around the shop in his usual manner, then breaks into a trot only to trip head first over a pair of shoes left in the aisle. As he clatters down onto the polished floor, his hands make a loud slap, don't look to cushion him. Charlie steps quickly towards him, picks up his little boy.

'Good shoes,' says Mikey, and Charlie thinks it too. They are very good—he has fallen heavily without crying—remarkable shoes.

* * *

In the coffee shop Mandy has asked Michelle to help Mikey butter his toast. She has chosen to sit next to her husband, they share a croissant. The family occupied the only available table, so close to the front door that they feel the January chill each time someone enters or leaves. A blast of winter air. All wear their coats, Michelle and Mandy have scarves too. Mikey puts his gloves off and on according to his next move with the toast.

'This used to be the Youth Hostel Association shop,' Charlie tells his daughter. 'I thought of working here when I came out of the army. Only took the sales job because it paid better.'

'What's a youth hostel?' asks Michelle.

'They still have them. I expect you join online now. Youngsters can stay in hostels cheap. Mostly in the countryside. The shop sold rucksacks and stuff. Tents, hiking gear.'

'You like all that trekking out in the rain, don't you, Dad?'

'Not the rain particularly, you just have to be prepared for however it could turn out. Walking in the hills, that's great stuff. I could live outdoors.'

Mandy is quietly eating her share of the croissant. Listening. They did a few walks together years ago but it was never her thing. Charlie and an old army friend went walking in Scotland a couple of years after he'd left the forces. Ticking off the Munros, they called it. The only time he and Mandy holidayed separately since their first meeting. She in Spain with her mum and her brother's girlfriend, he in the highland rain.

Mikey has jam on his fingers. Charlie points and Michelle takes the branded brown tissue paper from beneath her plate, cleans her brother's hand, stops him from smearing it on his clothes. 'Would you take me?' she asks her dad.

Charlie glances at Mandy. She is looking back directly, even allows the corners of her mouth a gentle upturn. They always talked about not forcing their children to do anything. Finding out what they wanted, letting them take the lead. 'I'd love to,' he says, 'and so I will.'

Mikey makes a noise that seems to mean he'd like to come as well, although toast in his mouth is rendering the words incoherent.

'No hiking for you yet, little 'un. You need to grow a bit bigger first.'

The little lad nods solemnly. 'Get bigger,' he says. This might be something he can do.

* * *

Back in the house, while the children are playing upstairs, Charlie tells Mandy that he hopes to go and see Graham. Not now but before too long.

Mandy nods at this. Graham is in a hospital in South London. Dulwich. Moved to there from Gloucestershire; his family had to arrange a private ambulance, but he's still under the NHS. Charlie understands that Graham's parents visit, he's not sure how often. They seemed like a funny bunch. He doesn't really like his own thoughts when he talks to Mandy about this. He unwittingly used Graham as a stooge when he was playing squash, conducted the ill-judged affair with Roselyn. Graham Ford has still to learn that Charlie cited his name as the imaginary companion when—daft bastard that he is—he cheated on his wife. Now, Mandy seems to understand his need to see the boy again, talk to him. She asks if Graham's condition is improving. As they hold this conversation, Charlie again confirming for his wife that the poor boy remains comatose, he finds himself choking up. It was not the driving—he's a decent driver; the accident was the other guy's fault, even the insurer says that—it is how he has been living that is the problem. Living without due care and attention; it ruins lives.

4.

'She said the paper work checked out, no disciplinary,' whispers Fiona, as she comes out of Ted Astaire's office. Carly Makepeace coughs. It is as if they have broken the no-conferring rule, and they really haven't. Charlie is annoyed that this youngster has any role in the matter at all. Her job title is only personal assistant—she should book Ted's train tickets or type up his letters, not involve herself in weighing up the competence of his social workers—Fiona called her Ted's little rottweiler in their last phone call. That she looks good in the short skirt she wears, bothers him more than it should. Distracts from the true business of disliking her.

'Have I to go in now?' he asks, having given a quick thumbs up to Fiona as she left the Director's suite, spoke those encouraging words.

'Wait please, Mr Quested. He'll buzz me when they're ready for you.'

Mr Quested? This is a first names office. Ted but not Fred. 'Will do, Carly.' Breezy words but his true feelings are writ across his scowling face. He leans back in the uncomfortable easy chair, the low-slung armless nonsense that stops those called to see the Director from relaxing satisfactorily in advance of their meeting. He quickly hauls himself back up to his feet, disliking his head being below the girl's. 'I'll just get a cup of water, Carly.'

'There's a jug in there. He'll only be a moment, I'm sure.' She gestures that he should sit back down.

He does as the fair-haired green-eyed young thing has asked, wishes that there was more rebellion inside him than he is channelling. Irritation with the office junior is not a revolution. He picks up Better Lives, the social work magazine, from the table in front of him, holds it in his hands. Doesn't begin to read. Intermittently, he looks at Carly, she is facing a computer screen, paying him no mind. He fluctuates between thinking her face and gaze a stupid one, and suspecting she is very clever. The graduate who knows Ted's every move. She may even hate what's going on with him and Fiona: an investigation for the sake of it. Searching for a scapegoat. He turns to the back of the magazine, the job adverts. Charlie hasn't changed job in years. Transferred teams once but there was a reorganisation going on. It was a win-win: the fostering team was one short and Charlie dead keen. He scrutinises her hair. She has dyed it, must have. Charlie—suddenly a fashion guru—thinks that nobody looks that perfect without putting a hell of a lot of work into it. Why is he so bothered about Ted's PA? He takes a breath, tries to change lanes. He can't blame Carly for keeping him dangling on a thread; she is more of an underling than he is. Obeying orders nine to five. Or eight-thirty to five-thirty. Eight until six most probably. Everybody is desperate to prove their worth. Have been since the first hints of austerity. The bankers running the ship aground. He really should give Carly a break, she's just doing a job like every bugger else. Fiona is off the hook and she and he have been on the same page every step of the way with Russell Chope. The foster placement felt a bit of a long shot three years ago; it's been going far better than expected. A lad like that lasting so long in a single placement speaks for itself. Until the incident outside the school gate. Anyone can see how well it's gone; no one could've foreseen the sting in the tail.

* * *

Roselyn wears a rich brown waistcoat above matching trousers; her white blouse has puffed-out sleeves. Even tiny ruffs around the wrists. The romantic lead in a Shakespeare play, the male one. Charlie's only ever seen that stuff when he's channel hopping; it's what her get-up brings to mind. She never dresses like this. Never has before. He wonders what she and Ted get up to. Tries not to wonder because it might be nothing. His unruly imagination. He has to focus on the Chope case. His role in it, why he did what he did. Decisions that met Russell's needs for longer than many thought likely.

'Charles, thank you for coming to see us,' Ted begins. 'We appreciate it. You and Fiona both. Many staff would take themselves off in these circumstances, claim stress, maybe feel very, very stressed—God knows it's not easy—you two are both straightforward guys. We appreciate it.'

Charlie spreads his open palms out. 'Never taken a day off, sir.'

Roselyn turns to the Director of Children's Services, tells him that it is true. Confirms Charlie's assertion.

They sit around a small table in the Director's office. Ted Astaire has rolled his office chair across from his desk, although it elevates him above the optimum practical height for the furniture. Roselyn and Charlie sit on hard plastic chairs. The bum-hurting variety. Charlie picks up the water jug from the centre of the table, a paper cup. Ted gestures that he may pour himself some. Are there circumstances in which it is refused? 'Now, Charles, Ms Pickford is going to talk you through her file review, your case notes on the Chope boy. Then we will both chat with you about your submission earlier this morning. Hear your reflection upon it.

'Charlie,' she says, drawing herself upright in her chair, 'this case was interesting to go over with a fine comb, and we can see that you and Fiona both put a lot of time and effort into it. I think you were doing a good job for a long time. Finding the Goodings...' She turns her head briefly towards

Ted. '...the foster carers, you will recall...they seemed to be the best thing for Russell. He was tearing through placements before they came along.'

'You approved the placement,' says Charlie.

Ted raises a hand. 'Don't be defensive, son.'

Charlie lowers his eyes. Barely a decade between them, in no version of reality could Charlie ever be his son.

'Charlie, Charlie...' Roselyn is in her stride now, her Shakespearean costume giving melodrama to her oratory. '...what I'm telling you is that while you and Fiona worked it together, helped the boy and the Goodings, conferred, it went well. Russell Chope has been a worry to this department for a very long time, and that boy was finding some stability...'

Charlie interrupts her again, he wants Ted Astaire to understand the thinking behind his practice. 'Close on three years, Roselyn. Russ hadn't lasted three months in any placement before the Goodings. Not three months.' He turns to the director, the smiling Ted Astaire. 'Roselyn always said that stability is everything. Everything for kids who've never known it, feel insecure because the sun's up. Stability is everything.' The American just looks at him, no smile, no frown, and Charlie adds, 'She was a good team manager, took a close interest...' This is a dig at Ted, who demoted her, more than a resurgence of warmth for Roselyn Pickford. Why the hell she is investigating his professional practice, he doesn't know. She might muddle social work skill with sexual performance, and Charlie believes that unnecessary dalliance deserves his dismissal, banishment. Sackcloth and ashes. Deserves it for the havoc his actions have wreaked upon his family.

'Yes, Charlie...' She cuts him off, not needing the kind words. She is on the other side of the table. '...the problems only began to surface on your December visit, the one you made jointly at the weekend.'

'That was immediately after our night out,' says Charlie. 'The Christmas do.' He thinks it worth reminding Ted of this; going the extra mile with a Saturday visit when many in the department were nursing hangovers. Deepika for one.

'Yes,' says Ted. 'I'm sure you'd sobered up in the morning. Stopped chasing the ladies.' He says it with a wry smile on his face, both cheeks dimpling from the severity of his inane grin.

The comment makes Charlie recall meeting Ted at the Kirkaldy, with Fiona at his side. Or Deepi, he can no longer recall which it was. 'I was sober all night. Not a drop.'

'That's as may be,' says the director, waving a hand for Roselyn to continue.

'In December you learned that Russell was unwell. Mentally unwell.'

'We did,' confirms Charlie.

'I think you even learned that Russell had become fixated upon you, Charlie. Negatively fixated.'

'They mentioned it, Mary and Colin—the Goodings—they said he was rude about me...' Roselyn and Ted say nothing, keep their eyes fixed upon him without making actual eye contact. '...they were Mary's words. No, I think it was Colin who said it.'

Roselyn looks down, examines her hand-written notes. 'Charlie, did you read Fiona's write-up of the visit?'

'I couldn't. It was frozen. I was frozen out. You did it...' Charlie looks directly at his commanding officer. At Ted Astaire. '...denied us further access to the files.'

'Charlie,' says Ros, interrupting his moan, 'this was always a complex case. Did you read Fiona's notes in the days after the visit? Before Christmas?'

'No. I don't think I did...'

'You really should have done...'

'We talked it over in the car driving back. On the Monday after, I expect we both put something in the electronic log.'

Roselyn and Ted stare at him for a few seconds. 'But you didn't read it?' says Ted.

'It's been busy.' Charlie runs a hand over his face. 'Three staff down, Ted. The cuts. All the post-assessment-day redundancies.'

Roselyn stops his wider critique. Starts to drill into the heart of the case under review. 'Fiona thought Colin wanted to say more about Russell's antagonism towards you, her notes say that Mary cut him off, and you didn't go back to it. Professional curiosity, Charlie. We're always curious to learn more. And if a kid has bad things to say about us then the more so. Are we safe? Have we let them down? Don't stop because it might be a little awkward.'

'I see your point, Roselyn. I don't recall it being quite like that, I'm sure Fiona's notes will have been thorough.'

Ted reaches for the water, pours a little into a glass. Leaves the last comment to mature in the room.

'Hindsight's a wonderful thing,' says Charlie. He immediately wishes he hadn't; it feels like admitting a mistake.

The interrogation is neither arduous nor gruelling, it is politely unpleasant. He knows that he acted in this case as he has throughout his career. Sought the best for Russell, appreciated the foster carers who gave themselves lovingly to a most troubled lad. Roselyn noted that Fiona had queried if the boy needed hospitalising, wrote it in her notes. Charlie's notes of the same visit did not suggest this might be necessary at all. The word hospital didn't make the page.

'I don't decide that,' argues Charlie. 'I understood that the Goodings weren't pressing for it, they were coping, but it was always Dr Tew's call. First thing Monday morning I was on the phone to him. Well, to Dr Tew's secretary. Made an appointment for the following day.'

'Which Mary Gooding took the boy to,' Roselyn notes.

Charlie scrapes his chair back six inches, leans against the moulded plastic. 'I don't think you'd have signed off my mileage just to take him to out-patients when the foster carers have always done that stuff. Tariq certainly wouldn't have.'

'You didn't ask him, Charlie. You might have got a surprise.'

He puts a hand over his face. 'Might not have,' he murmurs.

'Charlie, am I right that you took the lead in monitoring the work of the independent fostering agency?'

This question throws him. The department mostly use their own foster carers. For a few of the most difficult children—those requiring specialist placements—they commission independent agencies. There is greater financial recompense for foster carers in that sector than through the council. It goes some way to explaining their willingness to stand by problem children, but Charlie recalls how this couple—the Goodings—impressed him from the start. They were more certain that they could help the boy than many with an easier child. 'I liaised right at the beginning. Read all the reports, held meetings with our contracts team. There's a manager of the fostering agency in Derby who I speak to quarterly. I'd call more if there were problems; the Goodings have always been keen as mustard.'

'Did you check their training records?'

'It's on the annual return. I can't recall what it says. They were bang up to date when they first took him, took Russell, into their home. I'm sure of it.'

'We're waiting confirmation from Derby; however, we don't think they've ever done adolescent mental health.'

Charlie looks directly at Roselyn, finds his nose turning up although there is no discernible smell to her Shakespearean look. 'It's a module in the basic training. They'll have done it. Keen as mustard, like I said.'

'Charlie, I know there's a mental health module in the basic training, but this couple took on one of the most disturbed young boys on our books. On anybody's books. You know that. There's also advanced level mental health which neither the independent agency nor you, as liaison case worker, seem to have considered.'

'That's more geared up to carers who act as a place of safety in crisis. Carers who provide a home which the out-of-hours teams can use in an emergency.'

'I think the Goodings offered a place of safety for Russell Chope. The better their training, the safer he—and those he came into contact with—might have been.'

As Charlie listens, occasionally stops listening altogether, to these two droning on, trying to find culpability in the fact that it didn't turn out right, he recalls quitting Greenlight, the sales company who were his first employer in this city. The reason he lived here before Mandy became the reason. Greenlight were not a company for staff appraisals, he would not have lasted so long on a sales team if they had been. After putting up with him for long enough, they called him into the head honcho's office, asked him to explain his poor performance figures. 'Statistically lower than chance,' was a phrase thrown at him. For a few minutes, Charlie argued the toss, told them he was close to getting a few more customers on the books. And he knew full well that hoping-for and close-to are utter strangers. Have never met. In the end, he walked out, stopped saying anything in his own defence. Collected his jacket from the back of his office chair and went. His manager—Christine, she was called, an older lady who talked about her dogs more than she ever did about selling insurance—tried to tell him that this wasn't what they intended. They weren't going to sack him. He found that he agreed with their general appraisal—he was useless—and just happened to have a more decisive temperament than any manager at Greenlight. Today, the

Wide of Goodge Street

impulse to walk is equally strong but he won't be doing it. He disagrees profoundly with the way Roselyn and Ted have singled him out. He cannot understand why Russell Chope hit a boy's head with a paving slab. The lad lost every fight he had ever been in up until that point in his young life. Nor can Charlie guess why the boy told the arresting officer that he'd killed someone bearing his own name. Killed Charlie Quested. None of that means his negligence, his poor social work practice brought it about. Above all he thinks that it wasn't him who tortured the boy, abused the boy, when he was one-year old, two-years old, three-, four-, five-, six- and seven-years old. That must have more to do with it; the trail of culpability points that way. His bastard of a father. But cause and effect are bloody difficult molecules to fuse into an element of their own. It cannot be located on the periodic table. This is social science, not the real deal, and in this city, it's Ted Astaire who gets to make up the answers, say what it all means. His call, whether there's truth or blarney at the core of his telling.

* * *

Before he leaves the office, Charlie goes down into a basement room. He checks that his phone has a signal down there—the room houses old paper files, records of yore—and then calls the local branch of the union. He wishes to set up a meeting for the next day. He is a member; they will support him. When he tells the girl taking the call that he has been suspended, she goes up a gear. Has a plan.

'Don't see us until the afternoon. We'll get the papers from Teflon Teddy, make sure we know what nonsense they're trying to pin on you.'

Charlie feels flattered by the lengths she is prepared to go to. He initially thought he was speaking to a young receptionist. Quickly revises this conjecture. He asks the lady for her name although he is sure she said it at the outset, when he was too full of his own importance—the social

Raspberry Jam

worker wronged—to take it in.

'I'm Karen. I'll assign myself to your case. We want to take that guy down a peg or two.'

When the call is over, he takes himself up the single flight of stairs and carries his bag to the car park on the next street, opens up his vehicle ready to drive home. He hears his personal mobile buzzing, chooses to let it ring out. He said goodbye to no one. Not Tariq, not Fiona. Not Precious who may be shedding the tears he will not. He has a plan of action now. Take Teflon Ted—and Roselyn who has turned out to be a cow after all—down a peg or two. Charlie and his buddy of the day, Karen Leicester, can achieve this. Prior preparation and planning. He did it on the squash court. As he shall at the disciplinary hearing. Ted Astaire's kangaroo court.

* * *

Arriving home, he feels disoriented. Quickly puts two and two together. He has been in this situation before, it's simply the first time in an age that he has arrived home from work before Mandy. He recognises the car on the drive. When Mandy is working, Mikey spends much of the time at Mr and Mrs Blackburn's house. Mid-afternoon Mrs Blackburn brings him here, awaits the arrival of Michelle from her school. And Paul from his. She's always been a great help, and Mandy will be back by five.

'Are you all right, Charlie?' asks Mrs Blackburn as she pops her head out of the lounge. Watches him put the holdall down in the hallway, take off his stiff black shoes.

'Not really,' he says, then tries to raise a smile for her. He is unsure what level of detail Mandy has shared with her parents about their marital disharmony. He saw them alone for forty minutes before Christmas. Dropped in for a sherry. They couldn't have been more civil. And he had to explain he was actually consuming no alcohol at all over Christmas and beyond. Not until he shares one with Graham whose plight they had not learned of before that visit. He explained it: colleague, ex-colleague, a friend in a hospital in Dulwich, London. He gathered then—not from words but from the tones of their voices—they were not impressed with Barry Brice. He hopes they don't blame Mandy for the whole thing. She should have disabused them of that improbability. She might have told them he started it. Mr and Mrs Blackburn are discreet. Didn't talk about it, don't seem to hold it against him.

'But you're early?'

'I'm just going to do a little work on the kitchen table, if that's okay.'

'Of course, Charlie. It's your house. Mikey's got his TV programme on now.'

He picks his laptop out of the holdall and steps into the kitchen, his mother-in-law returning to her grandchild. He unfolds it and presses the power on. The set-up is secure, the IT boys at County Hall have it fenced with a series of differing passwords. Gates to open. He punches in the first one and the screen resolves itself, the second, it shows the council logo, then it brings up an access denied message. 'Shit,' he mutters. Shut out of the whole damned show. How is he to prepare his defence if he can't access his diary, report on his many actions. Demonstrate that he followed the policies of the council. He switches it off and on again, goes through the same steps. Access denied. He even mutters the same expletive.

* * *

Mandy comes home and straight up the stairs to the bedroom. This room has been pretty much off limits to him since the day he told her of his infidelity. His return to the fold is a work in progress, not a done deal.

'Are you not well?'

He is still in his work clothes—shoes excepted—lying flat on his back in the centre of the bed last jointly occupied by the twat Barry Brice and his wife who must deserve better than either of them. 'Suspended,' he tells her.

She sits on the side of the bed. 'Charlie, what does it mean? It's the without-prejudice thingy, isn't it? They just want to be seen to be doing something.'

'I don't really know. They've got to blame someone. I look like the photofit. The social worker who should have stopped it from happening.'

'What'll you do, love?' She sits on the bottom end of the bed, puts a hand on his shin bone.

'Fight. Union meeting tomorrow. I've got one of them working on my behalf.'

'Charlie, it sounds scary.'

'It is. There's a little boy in the hospital down in Derby. He could die. That's big stuff. Awful stuff that I care about. And now I'm finding it hard to think over any of it without feeling like I'm being framed. Thinking it's not fair on me, and it is that lad who took the brunt of it. They're making out I caused exactly what I was trying to prevent. As if I've done what I never would. The Pearce boy bullied little Russell, probably not last week, but over the months. I'd have done more about it but, honestly, I never saw any of this coming. The boy has got a screw loose, my boy, Russell. None of us guessed he'd do like he did. They could sack the psychiatrist; he actually could have admitted him to hospital, but I wasn't recommending it and nor was anyone else. And if they sack a psychiatrist—those guys process about a hundred cases a week—we'd have none left after a year or two. No one to carry on the profession at all. Social workers are the more expendable.'

'Will you and Fiona both go?'

'I'm going nowhere, Mandy, I'm fighting to my last breath. Fiona predicted the whole thing apparently. Wrote that I forgot to put him in hospital or something. Got herself off scot-free.'

'Charlie! That's not fair.'

'I don't know what it is. I wish I'd read her notes. Wish I'd copied them into my own if that's all it would have taken to look good.' In the silence, he sits up, swivels his legs so that he is beside her, puts an arm around Mandy's shoulders. 'I love you. This is hard but you make it bearable.'

'It's still hard,' she says, smiling while pulling away from the kiss he fails to land.

* * *

Long after tea, when Mikey has gone down for the night and Michelle is taking a bath, Charlie talks to Paul. All that has gone on, his suspension from work.

'What did you do?' his son asks. He tries to explain it in simple terms and Paul connects it with the news item from five days before. When Paul has heard him out, he asks two questions. 'They don't expect you to tell the future, do they?'

Charlie answers him with a straight yes. Failure to do precisely that has been his error.

'Shouldn't the doctor have put the boy in hospital?'

This is an easy one for Charlie. He tells his son that Dr Tew can no more predict the future than anyone else.

Then the two of them talk about Nostradamus, the man who could. Paul seems a lot more relaxed when they settle on the new topic. Soothsayers of long ago.

* * *

There is a light tap on the lounge door. Charlie is standing in the centre of the room having just changed into his pyjamas, draped a duvet over the couch, prepared his bed for the night. Mandy enters. He thinks she is wearing a nightdress, a thin one, beneath her mulberry-coloured dressing gown. He might just be imagining what it covers.

'You're doing very well. I can see how stressful this is.'

He thanks her for the kind words, then looks into her face. It is so youthful. Mandy is only six years his junior but she's experienced neither war nor the care system. Her hair is straighter now than it ever used to be, not a change he knew to occur naturally. Hers must have chanced upon that journey. She wears it long, sometimes a ponytail but there is no such corralling of it tonight. The light brown of it is only a shade away from the hazel of her eyes. Her gentle shining eyes. He knows that the intensity of her gaze was briefly dulled—his actions did that, his infidelity—they have returned to magnitude. He wonders how that works. Do people's eyes really shine or do we see only our own reflection? He lost his shine. Mandy's nonsense with Barry Brice was forgiven before it began. She was paying him back. He could feel sorry that she didn't find a partner more her equal. Tries to push the strange thought from his mind. 'Have I told you who the investigating officer is?' Charlie drops eye contact as he says the words.

'Do you mean Karen. This union girl? I didn't think you'd met her yet.'

'Not her, the other side. The manager appointed by the department.' Mandy just stares at him. He fears his body language has given away the enormity of the forthcoming announcement. 'It's Roselyn bloody Pickford.'

Mandy seems to draw in breath, involuntarily as if she has picked her head up mid-swim. 'That's not right. Is she for you or against you? It's not right.'

'Investigating officer. I could tell HR the history, that shit. She'd have to step aside right away if I did that.'

Mandy pulls the cord on her dressing gown tighter, and after completing this action, she crosses her arms, raises them to breast height. 'Don't,' she says sharply. 'I couldn't stand it. I really couldn't stand it.'

'I'm sorry,' he says.

She turns her back and mutters something. 'It's all right.' That's what it sounded like. A reflex comment. It is not all right but nor is she cutting the thread by which he is hanging. The door closes and Charlie is alone in his bedroom, the family's lounge. Everything and everyone playing a role which is not quite familiar. He is grateful that he may sleep in this house tonight. Suspension upsets him but he did worse to Mandy. Charlie tries to sleep, head awash with all the thoughts that will prevent it coming to him.

5.

Charlie receives a telephone call from Karen at nine forty-five the next day. He likes how keenly she pursues his case, picks up from her tone of voice that something is wrong. 'Charlie, I've spent about ten minutes talking to this Miss Makepeace. Carly Makepeace. Quite frankly, she's being obstructive. I've come across her a couple of times and she's never straight. Slippery. We'll find a way around it, but she's not playing ball. Won't be sending the stuff—the case they have against you—across today. That's the short of it. They've suspended you and then the buggers won't so much as give me a category for your offence. It's ludicrous. Not much point in us meeting up until they do, I'm afraid.'

'Can't I just tell you what happened? My side of the story. Then we...'

'We could, and I'll only agree. I'm on your side, Charlie. All the way. That's my job. For this to work, I need to think like their barrister will if it all tumbles into a ruddy tribunal. I've got to know the worst things they can throw at you. Work out your defence from there, you and I together. You know the story, I know how employment law applies to it, what is reasonable. It usually rests on that, a definition of reasonably competent or satisfactory professional practice.'

'Can I call in anyway? Make a start.' Idleness has never suited Charlie, not since Grace Bell gave him a bit of oomph. He wants to act, follow a plan. Cut through the crap and get back to the job he knows. To be of some use in this world.

Raspberry Jam

Karen agrees to this. Does so a little reluctantly, he thinks, but it will be a start. 'Just to get the feel of the case,' she says. She books him in for fifteen minutes. 'We'll have a proper session just as soon as I've got the stuff from Ted, and this insufferable Roselyn Pickford. Have you come across her before?'

'Yes.' Charlie doesn't elaborate.

* * *

After the call, he takes Mikey to the local park. While the boy is gently rocking in an enclosed swing, he telephones Mrs Blackburn on his mobile. He knows that Mandy filled her in last night, the trouble at his workplace. She's aware that he is on enforced leave. He tells her that he has a meeting in the afternoon. Has to be there, everything riding on it. He can drop the little one at nursery school but will she do the pick-up, please?

'Of course I'll pick him up, Charlie. Mikey is used to me doing that. And it's an odd place for a man, isn't it? Standing at the nursery gate with all the young mums.'

It really isn't. He's done it a few times. Dropped and picked up Michelle there six or seven years back. He recalls he was never the only male either, seriously in the minority, but not the only one. It was always blokes talking together, or mums talking together. Not a bridge easily crossed. It's a sorry state if even Mandy's mum cannot trust him around lone females. He pushes that thought away. It's for his wife, not his mother-in-law, to worry over that stuff. Mandy's is the trust he is trying to win back. 'He's my son,' says Charlie, 'my responsibility. And you know we both appreciate how much you do for us.'

* * *

At the park it starts to patter with rain. Charlie tells Mikey they'd best head for home. Not a long way, still it's a long walk for short legs. 'Hood up,' says Charlie, when it starts coming down more heavily, pulling it into place for him. Hoping the rain won't penetrate the garment, soak the little boy's hair. Then he hoists his son onto his broad shoulders, tells him he is going to win the Grand National. He hears Mikey questioning him, repeats the assertion while explaining that it's a horse race.

Charlie runs down the road, occasionally putting on the horse's gait. Lolloping strides. Fast running, slow cantering, Mikey squeals with delight. His granny can't do this; a nice woman but she's never going to be a horse. They canter off the main road and onto the estate. Driving rain; Charlie runs home with the little lad on his shoulders. Mikey never complains but when, at their front porch, Charlie lowers him from shoulders to ground, the little boy says, 'Car sick.'

As he is opening up the front door, Charlie erases jockey from the list of professions which his son may be destined for. Soldier was on Paul's list when he was three, scrubbed out long before Mikey's birth. Social work he has long thought a fine profession for any of his three children, and now he's revising its standing. Directors of Children's Services can be funny buggers. He doesn't know what to make of Fiona for that matter. Plenty of occupations left; he'd never really pictured his son working with horses anyway. They are so big and Mikey so small.

* * *

Charlie beams at Karen, shakes her hand slowly. He wonders why he'd pictured her young and white, when she is old and black. Voices on telephones give little away about a person's appearance, his mind not even playing games. Guesses are of little consequence, and this lady seems exactly right on meeting her. A warm handshake, she's only a couple of inches shorter than Charlie, and there is certainty in her eyes. Together they can get one over on Teflon Teddy.

'I'd heard about that.' Karen refers to the initial incident. The terrible fate that befell Dayton Pearce.

He tells the whole story. The foster carer took Russell to hospital outpatients in December, Charlie made the appointment. The doctor changed his medication, hospitalisation not considered. He confirms that he spoke to Dr Tew within half a day of the appointment.

Karen Leicester puts a hand on top of Charlie's. 'Can I stop you there?' He was in full flow but does as she asks. 'We can include the facts but we won't be trying to pin significant blame onto this Dr Tew, whether you think it was his fault or not. It never sticks. Their professional body trumps our union. Sorry to say it but it does. We should emphasise that you and he agreed. There was nothing in your boy's presentation to suggest hospitalisation. Sure, we now wish there had been—seeing the way it all worked out—there wasn't at the time. You and the doc made the right call on the presentation before you.'

He contemplates her face, brow furrowed beneath grey roots. There is dye in the hair but probably none massaged in there for months. Grey is the winner. She looks pretty good with it; wise and elegant.

'What about the foster carers?' she asks. 'Do you think they should have told you more about the state of the boy's mind. Did they keep a lot to themselves, ignore their training?'

'They loved that boy, Karen. I don't really know how they managed to do it. They just did. I'm not passing the buck to Mary and Colin. The point is they are just what troubled boys need. A really caring couple—brilliant—they always put him first. It didn't work out. That wasn't their fault. These kids with histories like Russell's are an accident waiting to happen. Mary and Colin were his best chance; it's a tragedy he didn't quite make the most of it. I doubt they'll foster again after this. They must be heartbroken by it. They were the best foster carers...' He sees that Karen has sunk into her chair. Weighing him up. '...I know what I'm talking about. I was a foster kid myself, my teenage self.'

She nods her head while holding his gaze, his eye. 'Got it loud and clear. We'll not be suggesting the Goodings were at fault. My job is to find your best defence, and if you don't own it, it's no defence at all.'

* * *

As the allotted time is coming to an end, Karen asks him, 'Has Miss Pickford—Mrs Pickford, whatever she calls herself—invited you to an investigatory meeting?'

'I think that was yesterday,' says Charlie.

Karen Leicester lurches forward in her chair. 'You've talked to her?'

'I think it was informal. Ted was there but no one from the HR team. Nothing like that.'

'Oh, Charlie, that's so wrong. What did she ask? What did you say?'

He thought that the meeting was part of the process, didn't guess his former lover was happy to subvert it. He doesn't know if he's been wasting Karen's time telling her a version of events that Roselyn may repudiate by misquoting his testimony of yesterday. Nobody took any notes, not as he can recall.

'We're pretty much out of time; I've got a lady from residential services due in any minute. They're unqualified—low paid—it is my mission to give the same standard of advice and defence to all, Charlie. We'll reschedule, yes?'

He leaves the union office feeling like a schoolboy. He likes his new teacher enormously, fears he may have let her down before he even met her. Talking to Ros and Ted without representation, keeping the affair under wraps. He will continue to do the latter. Mandy is more important to him than Karen, grateful as he is to have her on his side.

6.

Before she goes to work on Thursday morning, Mandy tells Charlie that the kids like having him back. He knows it, of course, it feels special hearing her confirm it. On the difficult march back, it is a landmark passed, his family drawing closer together once again. The house is cleaner too—and it's down to his elbow power, a willing helper in all things domestic—the evening meals have been decent, two in a row. Charlie is a good cook; burgers, spag bol. Mandy doesn't mention these additional benefits, the unlikely boon of his suspension. They both know he is a better man working. Less agitated, more contained. He cooks and cleans to ward off despair. Keeps it in pretty well, tries humming a few hits from a decade or more past but it can sound forced. Charlie has no idea how he would have coped with any of this if he was still in that depressing flat.

Mikey seems to be the big winner. Today they are playing Lego. It lives for months on end in a cupboard. Paul and Michelle have lost interest and Mikey's skills are rudimentary. Charlie tells him to separate out the colours and shapes—shows him what he means—does the bulk of the sorting himself but keeps praising his son. The little boy is on task, they have a joint sense of mission. Charlie has yet to plan the construction. He asks Mikey what he would like, and shakes his head at 'House' and 'Castle' which sound too predictable for this ambitious father. When Mikey says, 'A horse,' he grins back at him. It will be red and white and black and yellow, and it will be a horse. They have masses of pieces. Charlie thinks carefully before starting. The seven P's.

When they have four legs, an unattached body and, as yet, no head whatsoever, they break for elevenses. Charlie makes himself a coffee, full-fat milk for the little one. His mobile vibrates in his pocket before he's finished the drink, the horse still a pipe dream to anyone without his foresight. 'Karen, yes,' he answers.

His caseworker tells him that she has, just fifteen minutes earlier, received the electronic file about him, prepared by the city council's human services department and 'reeking of Miss Pickford'.

He cringes at the phrase. There was a short time last summer when her specific reek, her squash-induced perspiration, ranked above chips frying in his league table of odours enjoyed.

'But get this: they want the disciplinary hearing to be this afternoon at four. It's crazy but we can't call to reschedule. They'd sack you in your absence if we tried it.'

He slumps back on the sofa at this phrase. Karen has not used the term before. Charlie is already suspended; it is logical that they should make it permanent if he is not acquitted. They want to flush him down the toilet without letting him get a handhold on the rim. It is intolerable. In the army you knew that you may not win every battle but you would always have an opportunity to fire off your gun. Give an adversary something serious to remember you by. He wonders why he keeps thinking back to that more primal career.

Karen agrees to see him at two o clock; she will clear her diary for the afternoon. She does not sound fazed by the developments, puts him more at ease than he thought she could after the initial exchange. Ted Astaire has certainly borrowed his strategy from Schwarzkopf's playbook. Surprise: it was a highly prized quality back in the Gulf War. Stormin' Norman Schwarzkopf. Charlie will be ready. The Brits were a match for any of the American forces in that war, down in the Gulf. The Yanks had more kit, more high-tech, not better resolve. Ted has only the dwindling resources of the city council. Teflon Teddy, not even a decent nickname like good old Stormin'. 'Don't laugh at the enemy but don't fear them.' They were his own—British—general's words about Iraq. The army Saddam assembled and which they subsequently took to pieces. Charlie isn't laughing but he is getting out his steely resolve, will put on his fuck-you face, muster a little hate into his eyes. Direct them at Ted and Roselyn if that's what it's going to take.

* * *

Charlie mollifies Mikey, says he'll crack on with the horse in a few minutes, has to first phone the boy's grandma. Sort out the little lad's childcare for the afternoon. When he has done that, he phones Mandy. She picks up which surprises him. Her role is supervisory but she works in store, often in sight of supermarket customers.

'I'm on a tea break.'

He fills her in on the news, and for the first time he says the 'sack' word as Karen had earlier shelled him with.

'I thought that last night,' his wife answers quietly. 'Not that you deserve it, it was just seeing the creep on tele...' Charlie had been unmoved by the short news item, Ted Astaire talking to camera. Perhaps he should have considered it in greater depth than he allowed himself. '...I'm meant to be back out there, supporting tills, sorry to be so brief. Listen Charlie, good luck. I really mean, good luck. I'm with you, lover.'

It is an old term, one they each used with the other before Paul could talk. Used it only discreetly after that point. It has not been heard for half a year, not been true for half a year. The promise of it lifts Charlie's spirits. He will get through this. He and Mandy will get through.

* * *

On the news, yesterday evening, there was an update about Dayton Pearce. A sobering one. His family were said to be by his bedside. Charlie doubts if this phrase referred to his true parents, the biological ones. They are not his day-to-day carers; he is sure he heard—in Russell's review at Peel School—that Dayton is in care. It could be a pair of saintly foster carers who sit vigil. Might be every bit as distraught as the Goodings.

Doctors say there is no hope.

Then Ted Astaire appeared on the television screen. Entered the Questeds' living room uninvited. The Director expressed heartfelt sympathy for the victim. Made a well-worded point that the perpetrator of this horrific injury is not only a minor but was not in his right mind. Most probably as a result of the horrific abuse he suffered earlier in his young life. Charlie agreed with that. 'I have instructed my officers to review the safety of our practice, the skills of social workers who manage high-risk children with mental health issues. It is not my belief, at this point in time, that our procedures themselves are at issue. If we find that they are, we will revise and reform them. If not, we will weed out those unable to apply them diligently.'

The news segment replayed in Charlie's mind is enough to justify Mandy's point. Very clearly. She was too kind, he too stupid, to talk it over yesterday evening. This afternoon he is for the sack. Karen is cushioning the impact. Her presence will aid the maintenance of his dignity if not his paid employment. He hopes it will.

This is a shit-storm.

* * *

He arrives at the union office a quarter of an hour before his appointment. A man with a ponytail greets him in the small reception area. Charlie smiles, his accruement could be snipped, transferred to the rear of the incomplete Lego creature he and Mikey have cobbled together. He managed to fit the body, has still to attach the as-yet misshapen head. A pair of ears and this gentleman's excess hair will complete the sculpture.

Karen comes straight into reception. 'I should have booked you for my lunch hour too. I never eat before this type of afternoon.' She takes him into her office. They sit as before; she comments kindly on the smartness of his clothes. He even wears a waistcoat. He speculated while waiting that it is to match his adversary's. The waistcoat is beneath an off-the-peg jacket; his shirt regular non-iron, inexpensive. Pale blue. He has tried his best but he is not a power dresser, army uniform and associated guns and grenades aside. Deep down he's a foster kid, carries all the baggage that goes with it.

Karen says that Ted and his cronies are going for capability. Citing his failure to make a better fist of the disturbance in December as the root of the incident this month. 'It has caused the department significant and catastrophic reputational damage,' she reads out from her computer screen.

'I don't think the link is fair,' he says. 'And why don't they say it caused poor Dayton catastrophic damage. Who gives a fig about the council's reputation?'

Karen laughs, not with sound, but her shoulders move within the thick green trouser suit she wears. 'Who gives a fuck, Charlie; that's the phrase in this office. And you are spot on. Ted's reputation is already mud around here. Shit if you prefer the term. In the hearing, we probably leave the whole issue of reputation alone. And if you do stray onto it, stick to fig.'

He thinks she's enjoying this. The fight. He might do too if he was fighting for someone else. Not just his own sorry skin.

They discuss Roselyn's submission. Charlie points out a couple of factual flaws, repeatedly states how tenuous the links between his action and the subsequent assault really are.

Karen breathes a heavy sigh. 'The thing is Charlie, we can't really win today, because Teddy What's-His-Face is hardly going to contradict his darling investigator, or his HR stooges who have typed up this mumbo-jumbo. Our best bet is not really today; for us this is just hearing the what and how of the stitch-up. We hope to win it later, down the line. At an employment tribunal.'

He mirrors her body-language, releases air from his tense lungs and thinks about what she has just told him. 'I'll be sacked and then I may get reinstated at a follow up hearing?'

'Well...' She looks at him across her desk, seems to be weighing him up. '...you are going to appeal, aren't you? No appeal and sacked is sacked. The employment tribunal can rule that it's an unfair dismissal. If they do that, then the employer may elect to reemploy the staff member. However, without the corresponding resignations of Ted Astaire, his first executioner, Roselyn Pickford, and your manager, Tariq—who is either in Ted's pocket or he's a dormouse, horribly silent, won't even take my calls—why would you go back? And, of course, those three horrors won't be going anywhere. The department has treated you abominably. You'll get compensation if we win; from your employment record I am guessing it will be close to twelve months' pay. If we lose, you'll get nada, Charlie. That's the hard truth.'

He stops her. So much here he has not thought through. 'I want that job. I want to help Russell Chope whether he intended to kill me or not.'

'Sorry Charlie, not in the reading of these tarot cards. Do you want to know the respective probabilities?'

He does. He's not a gambler, not even a scratch-card buyer, but numbers can be reassuring.

'Their case is fairly squalid, I don't think they sack weather forecasters for missing thunderstorms, and predicting a young lad's behaviour is about a million times harder. Social workers should try and keep placements going unless there's a compelling reason to end them. There wasn't. You were doing the right thing. Good professional practice. Hindsight should have no place in a disciplinary hearing, but it will occupy at least fifty percent of our time today. And the same again at the tribunal. The panel—not today, today is just Ted—when we get to tribunal, comprises three people. In my experience, two of them are utter bastards, I think it's in the tribunal rules. Our strategy is to convince whichever one has a human heart of the truth in your defence. Then hope he or she has a nice lunch with one of the other two, wins them over to our side. We score some decent victories that way. Quite often they will rule that the department has been precipitous, that competence was in question but incompetence not proven. You might be saying that about me later, it's what everyone says when the results don't work out.'

'Karen, I've nothing but good to say about you. It's not your fault if the outlook is bleak. It's a shit world and I'm stuck in the U-bend.'

'Very philosophical. It's all because of the public profile. Ted just wants to bury the story. Knock it out of the news. After they've sacked you, listen out for the next bulletin. They will broadcast the story—a social worker gone—but no names. They are sacrificing you, it's only personal while you're fighting. You're collateral damage. Two-Faced Teddy might even sign your leaving card.'

They sit a little longer. She makes two teas. He tells her that, looking back on his life, this fostering role and a placement in a children's home—which he did while qualifying—are the only jobs he's ever liked. 'I didn't mind the army when I was in it but I've come to think killing people is the wrong approach.'

Fifteen minutes before four o'clock, they walk across the road together, down the street to the council offices. His date with destiny. It brings the Gulf War to Charlie's mind. He doesn't tell Karen this, keeps his unbidden thoughts hidden.

Going down fighting is his way.

* * *

Carly Makepeace walks past the pair of them at least once a minute. They are waiting in an alcove just outside the designated meeting room. Not the main chamber; not where Ted Astaire held forth all those months ago, declaiming his great plan to reduce the budget, alter the structure while retaining the core functioning of their department. It didn't really come off, that is Charlie's opinion. Shafted a lot of social workers; the rump limps on, seriously overworked. That wasn't how Ted envisioned it on the day.

For this disciplinary meeting they will use one of the council's committee rooms. Bigger than they need but not an auditorium. When Carly finally ushers them in, telling them that Mr Astaire and his team are on their way, they discover it is unheated. Cold. Charlie has attended training in this room, and the heating worked then. He's surprised when Carly also sits at the large oval table. She was not in the previous meeting.

'I'm to take notes,' she says by way of explanation.

'Miss Makepeace,' says Karen, 'I'll be doing likewise. Shall we email each other our respective records, see that they match up? I'll send mine first thing this evening if you do too, please.'

'I can't send mine until Mr Astaire has approved them.'

'Miss Makepeace, if you are taking verbatim notes and then letting them be vetted and amended before sharing them, it rather compromises the integrity of the process, don't you think?'

'It's how we work, Mrs Leicester.'

'Ms.'

* * *

The door opens and Ted Astaire pokes his head inside—

looks the room up and down—as if he is seeking a hideaway, a retreat from the world. Charlie enjoys his nervousness, thinks the director looks the more scared of the pair of them.

'Mr Astaire,' says Karen, 'we meet again.'

'Yes, yes, Mrs Leicester. Karen, isn't it?'

'Yes, and you know Charlie Quested, fostering social worker.'

A lady Charlie knows by sight but not by name follows the Director into the chamber. Behind her comes Roselyn. Today she wears a long skirt, mauve in colour, quite pleasant. The top above it is a shimmering white, has ornate golden buttons. An odd style. He thinks she looked better in her squash clothes. Pushes the thought away.

They all shake hands. Charlie says, 'And nothing but the truth,' as he is pumping the hand of his former manager. She looks across him at Karen. He thinks that she—his defender, not his former lover—is the more striking. Fierce of eye, darting smile, her hair unkempt but glorious. Utterly wayward, the black and the grey and the sheer messiness of it make Karen Leicester look even taller. The authority in the room. Simmering serenely when all others display discomfort.

'Charles,' begins the Director, 'I'm going to let Ms Thompson conduct the business of this meeting. She's the employment law lead in the council's HR team...' Then he turns to Karen Leicester. '...she's a pedant and a cross-checker. We would never wish to mistreat anyone in this delicate situation.'

Karen gives the Director of Children's Services a withering look, opens and closes her mouth once before speaking, and then it is to Ms Thompson. 'We have met. Please let us hear the case you would like us to answer, and Charles and I will respond. And then you may wish to close the case, allow Charles here to return to work in Mr Ali's team. That is where he is most needed. I am sure you all understand that.'

Ms Thompson advises all around the table that they may call her Louise. Charlie turns to Karen and her eyes flick away. That name is off-limits to them. For as long as she is in league with the devil, they'll not grant her an ounce of informality.

Louise Thompson is keen to see everyone has a glass of water. She holds up a briefing paper. Offers to hand copies around the table. It is identical to that which Carly emailed to Karen earlier in the day. She and Charlie have copies which they have scribbled their own notes upon. They have no need for her freshly printed lies. 'We all understand the challenges of social work,' Louise tells the meeting. 'Monitoring the wellbeing of children is a complex task. There are many factors that professionals must take into account when assessing the suitability of foster placements. We're concerned...' She looks hard at her notes, glasses off and on again as she does so. '...with Mr Quested's failure to make proper enquiry into Russell Chope's state of health. To understand if the boy's needs were testing the limits of his foster carers' skill set.'

'State of mind,' says Roselyn. 'State of mind rather than illness.' It's an unnecessary interruption; she looks down at the paper as soon as she has said it. Louise Thompson is reading from a script and Charlie thinks Roselyn is its author. And she hasn't a clue what he missed because she would have missed the very same in his shoes. Fiona did but she is not being hung out to dry. She wrote up the visit better, not that it has changed the state of the world.

'The boy ventured out at midnight in December...' Louise Thompson again adjusts her glasses as she once more scrutinises the paper before her. '...in a disturbed state of mind. This gave Mr Quested reason to re-evaluate the safety of the placement. Colin Gooding raised with Mr Quested that Russell felt negatively towards him. Mr Quested showed poor judgement in following this up with precisely no questions. We also note his negligence in allowing a foster carer, rather than himself as a professional practitioner, to accompany the boy on his appointment with Dr Tew, Child Psychiatrist. This all evidences a lack of capability to fulfil so specialist a role.' She looks directly at Charlie, no longer reading from the paper, as she concludes. 'I am sorry to say, Mr Quested, that these errors have led to the death of a fourteen-year-old boy.'

Charlie's heart skips a beat. He feels his mouth go dry. Wants to weep for Dayton Pearce who he has never met.

Then Roselyn has a hand on Louise's arm. 'May yet lead to his death but we all sincerely hope not,' she interjects.

As his heartbeat returns to normal, Charlie realises he doesn't know what to wish for. The situation for poor Dayton is hopeless; it was clear from the television reports. Karen says to Charlie, and loud enough for all to hear, 'I see Ms Thompson's cross-checking is hitting her usual standards.'

'Now, Karen,' says Ted, 'this is a serious matter. Finding its way into the evening news, like it has, is hurting the council's reputation just when we need it least.'

Karen rises and talks to the room from a standing position. She has no need of notes. 'Mr Astaire, everyone, we all understand what is at the centre of these difficult times. The union has opposed the entire austerity project, we could all see that the coalition government is both uncompromising and heartless. As a consequence of their policies, you have had to implement cuts that will make effective social work still more difficult to deliver. When there are fewer social workers on the ground it is unsurprising if some important information is missed. It would be foolhardy for managers to over-conclude about the competence of staff members simply from a single undesirable outcome. They do not control the actions of children in their care, wish it that you might. For this reason, you must be mindful of the facts in this case. Distinguish them from what might have been. Charles Quested visited Russell Chope and his foster carers, with an equally dedicated colleague, on a Saturday morning. The morning after the department's Christmas party. They conducted the visit professionally, met with foster carers and young Russell. In the light of the midnight incident, they agreed to bring forward the appointment with his psychiatrist. Charlie arranged this for the following Tuesday. That was very prompt, getting an appointment that quickly. Good stuff. He advised his manager, Tariq Ali, exactly what he had done, including who would accompany the boy to the doctor. Mr Ali never asked him to do more. No other professional saw a need for hospitalisation. Your assertion that Charlie didn't press when he should have, strikes me as wide of the mark. No, not just me. The psychiatrist and Charlie's manager, Mr Ali, neither of whom appear to be in the line for censure although they were of the same opinion as Charlie.'

Roselyn raises a hand. 'Fiona O'Shea put in her notes that she suggested hospital in front of the Goodings and they shot it down with Charlie's agreement.'

'Not quite,' says Charlie. 'Fiona suggested it more as a need for the Goodings. Were they exhausted from caring for the boy? The hospital thing was a throwaway line. They didn't want it. Completely dedicated to caring for Russell, that pair. Giving him a better home was their goal. And I agreed with Mary Gooding. If you've ever visited any of them—kids psychiatric wards—you'd know they are grim places for any child to pass the time, never mind spending a Christmas in there.' Silence greets Charlie's heartfelt assertion. When it has gone on long enough, he adds, 'So long as they can function outside, of course.'

'Charlie, Mrs Gooding is not a professional. It's great that she thinks about his happiness; however, welfare and happiness are not entirely contiguous. We expect you to see further than the foster carer. Sometimes you identify too closely with kids in care, don't you?'

Charlie holds Roselyn's stare a moment, not sure which way to go with this. 'If you're saying I empathise too much, it's a pretty strange accusation to level at a social worker.' He feels pleased with his retort, then notes that Karen, who is hand-writing her notes at his side, puts a big question mark in the margin as she writes it down.

* * *

Ted makes very little contribution to this meeting, shares his presence but not his current thinking. Louise Thompson drills down on what Charlie considers to be flimsy points. One after another. He thinks Karen's defence is both resolute and well thought out. He never doubted her. He and Roselyn both make small, sporadic contributions. The amateurs in the room. It could be the first disciplinary hearing either has attended.

'I was pleased with how Russell was doing; he'd never had such prolonged stability. I don't think anyone could foresee that this small setback would turn out so tragic.'

'We can't settle for, "I think it'll be all right;" we have to go the extra mile for these kids. And that means us. Not leaving it all to the foster carers.'

Inside his head, Charlie thinks they sound like lovers midtiff. He wants to attack Thompson, not Roselyn, show his disdain for the lot of them, not just her, but can never think of replies when she is speaking. His attention latches itself more firmly to his former manager, sharer of each other's flesh. His true mistake.

It is after six o'clock; Karen has highlighted Charlie's exemplary sickness record, his disciplinary record—'Nothing at all before this charade'—and his standing with colleagues. She quoted a line which he had given to her from a past team meeting, a time when Roselyn Pickford called him 'Mr Reliable.' His character is intact, whatever the outcome.

Ted Astaire finally speaks, drawls from a slumped position in his chair. Charlie thinks he says only remembered words, a prepared statement. Saying it without emotion, without enjoyment. Doing as Charlie has done when telling a youngster his placement must end, carers no longer able to cope.

'If this was more complex, I might adjourn to think it through overnight. It is late. And this is a straightforward case. The job is complex, yes, and much of Mr Quested's work has been of a standard that has pleased this department, I do not rule out referring to this in a future reference should he wish to continue practicing social work in some form. However, a boy is close to death through his negligent practice. I dislike using summary dismissals, they go against the grain. We like to learn from our experiences, including any mistakes our hard-working employees may chance across. However, in this instance, the boy's parents, the public—me, as a council-tax payer in this city—should expect nothing less. We cannot risk incompetent practice threatening more than a single life. That would be negligent of me as DCS. You have my sympathy, Charles, but I am not sorry to sack you. At this point in time, your presence is a blight on the department. It is exclusively for your incompetence and mishandling of this most delicate case, that I am dismissing you. As of today, you no longer work for the City Council, for the Children's Services. Louise, Roselyn, Carly, thank you. Miss Leicester, it's been good to see you again.'

He quickly stands and goes to the door. Charlie says, 'What the fuck?' but Karen was rising too and the scraping of her chair upon the floor may have masked his muttered expletive. He failed to turn up for the war. Pointed no gun, threw no punch. Charlie hangs his head; his shame is in his performance at this meeting. Karen's was great but he wasn't really in the ring. He doesn't feel ashamed of his working practice, it's for a fabrication of it that he has been fired.

Karen left the room as quickly as the Director. Charlie can hear that she and Ted Astaire are talking together just outside the door. Louise Thompson looks concerned, half-rises from her seat. Neither party outside is speaking loudly. They do not even sound to be in disagreement and Charlie cannot think why that should be. There was no seeing eye to eye in the preceding two hours.

The three who remained are all still in their places when Karen re-enters the room. She goes to Charlie and puts a steadying hand on his shoulder. 'I'll tell you outside,' she whispers. Then turning to Ms Thompson, she says, 'Well, that was all bollocks. You people are going to have an awful lot of explaining to do in the tribunal.' She has taken Charlie's upper arm and, under her gentle guidance, the two of them walk together from the room.

She's good, he thinks. And it really was exactly that: bollocks from start to finish, as Karen has told them.

* * *

Charlie and Karen go straight out of the building, stand together by the roadside. 'You can come back to my office, if you like, or I can tell you what Astaire said out here. Whichever you prefer?' Charlie indicates a yes to the latter. She tells him that she only went out to question his comment about the reference. Ted told her they would write a positive reference, with an explanation about the sacking and the need for mental health training. Ted has to make a referral to the social work council, their professional body; it's a given whenever a worker on the register is dismissed. The Director is willing to temper it, cite his otherwise exemplary conduct. Charles Quested should keep his social work registration with that little sweetener. All provided he agrees not to appeal.

Wide of Goodge Street

Charlie looks at her. It sounds better than stacking shelves at the superstore under the supervision of Mandy. 'You turned it down? he asks her.

'No. It's still there if you think it's the way to go. I think it stinks. They don't really want to refer you to professional standards because their case is way too flimsy. But they have to refer you if they sack you. It's all a big game of bluff, Charlie. If the boy had hit him with cardboard instead of a paving slab you would still be on course for a manager's job. You could sack social workers in your own right then. Lord it over everybody else like that cow Pickford does.'

* * *

'It's all right, Shelley,' Mandy tells her daughter. 'Really, it's all right.'

Paul is looking back and forth between his parents, as if seeking out a clue to unlock the puzzle. 'Can you call in the police?' he asks his father.

Unexpectedly, Charlie feels the corners of his mouth upturn. 'It's a civil matter. Unfair dismissal isn't for the police because it's not a criminal act. I can take it to an employment tribunal. Civil law.' Even Michelle—for whom her father's dismissal is an overwhelming downturn in the family's fortunes—shows an interest in this distinction. Criminal and civil misdemeanours. Charlie learned all this in university, on his social work degree. He explains it well.

The young girl asks an odd but insightful question. 'Then they can't say you're a murderer because of the boy that died?' She upsets herself by asking it. Starts crying again.

Charlie likes her sensitivity; that she has not become hardened for all the honesty of his many talks with her. The army. And her dad is not a murderer. The family have long agreed that the war was an entirely different matter. The tank shells he discharged may or may not have killed; the record is not so specific as to identify which tanks killed who. Mandy had assured Michelle in those conversations.

'I'm sure your dad's all missed the poor Iraqis.' Charlie could recall that his section as good as wiped out a couple of Saddam's infantry regiments before their remnants surrendered. Didn't mention any of that to Shelley. It was carnage in the Gulf, utter hell unless you were on the winning side. 'No one is suggesting I participated in, or foresaw the injury the boy suffered. He isn't actually dead but we're all very worried for him.' As he talks, Charlie feels good, still feels like a social worker despite the afternoon's reversal. 'Messing up in your job is not a criminal offence. Or seldom. Not a suggestion of it today. The question is, did I mess up, or are they unfairly blaming me?'

'It's obvious,' says Paul. 'They should sack the doctor. The bloke in charge of admitting kids into hospital.'

Michelle starts crying again. 'I don't like sacking.'

He looks at his wife. He'd told her the outcome and they've only raised the matter with the children because of how it might affect them all. A reduction in available money is on the cards. Ironically, it was Charlie's throwaway reassurance—'We'll not starve'—which first turned his daughter from attentive to tearful. Starvation she has seen on television. From halfway round the globe but it makes a serious impression.

'Your dad is a very capable man,' Mandy tells her. 'He'll get another job, be occupied, do something useful. That's just what he's like. We wanted you to know, to understand why the next few weeks might be a bit up and down.'

'But you won't work for the council again?'

'Not for the city, son. Can't see me going back to them.'

'We won't have to move house, will we?'

Charlie again glances at Mandy. They haven't discussed this, Charlie never thought to. This house is only a couple of miles from the terrace he and Mandy first shared. Where Paul spent his first years and Michelle her first months. Since then, the family have lived on Bramley Road, a five-minute drive from Mr and Mrs Blackburn. Charlie holds her eye while shaking his head. 'I've not figured what jobs I'll go for yet but I'll drive there. You stay in school—you and Shelley—it's important. Stability is important for children.'

* * *

When their children have gone up to bed and Mandy asks Charlie if he'd like a glass of wine, he refuses—keeps to his plan—but tells her that he appreciates her asking. The implicit invitation. In any earlier phase of his life, he would have accepted.

'I think I might go and see Graham in the next few days,' he tells her.

Mandy nods. She and he haven't argued since he has been living back. Mostly their talk has been of practical matters. Anything with emotions attached left in the understairs' cupboard. Except his job, the losing battle. The council has treated him shabbily, they are agreed about that. Charlie feels unsure if he may be letting his family down by absenting himself at this time. But Graham has lain alone for too long, it runs around his head night after night.

'There's a stupid deal on the table,' Charlie tells Mandy. 'Not much—crap really—but it might be better than nothing.' He explains to her that he can get a decent reference, remain on the register of social workers. 'Not struck off.' So long as he confirms he will not appeal. He would miss out on compensation but getting any is far from guaranteed. 'If the tribunal think I've been unfairly dismissed, I could get a year's pay. The worry is, they'll not be keen to reward anyone when a little boy is dead or nearly dead. I reckon they'll back the Ted Astaire line. Share the same fear of looking indifferent to tragedy. If I get a reference, I could be back working in March, barely a hit on the purse...' Mandy seems to have tears in her eyes, and Charlie is not sure why. '...I just thought we should consider it.'

'I hate fighting, Charlie. And I think you've gone off it.'

He couldn't agree more. 'I never want to fight with you, Mandy. Never ever.'

'It is a crappy deal but if you think it's best, I understand.' Charlie stands and indicates that his wife should do likewise. He gives her a hug and feels reciprocation in it. 'I'm sleeping on it; taking it makes a certain amount of sense.' He tries to kiss her upon the lips, Mandy hesitates, leans her head back to see his face properly. He must do something right, look properly penitent. She accedes to his wish. The kiss a prolonged one.

7.

Charlie sits restlessly inside the screeching metal snake as it pelts towards London. He has promised Mandy that he will stay only a single night. Keep expenses down.

As he was leaving, she said something that surprised him. Pleased him, and it was thoroughly unexpected. 'Sleep in my bed when you come back.'

When he took her eyes, examined the intent, the dimples in her cheeks were back. He felt loved. Told her he would do exactly that. It was more than he could ask for. Her hazel eyes shone back at him: first sign of spring.

In his week without work, he has been applying for jobs here and there. A particular one has his fancy. He reckons he will get it, that it is fated.

A few of his colleagues have been in touch. A card from Fiona was nicely written. She blames Roselyn for everything, even her own easy let off. Something in the words—about Roselyn investigating them—made him think that she knew of his affair. She didn't say it directly. He might be oversensitive about the topic. He binned the card anyway, didn't want Mandy pondering it as he had.

Brenda telephoned—just told him what a great social

Wide of Goodge Street

worker he is—signed off with a little vitriol for Roselyn. Charlie finds he agrees with that now. She seemed a good boss at the time but perspectives change.

Precious and Yasmin called together at the door on the Sunday evening. They came inside, sat with him and Mandy, accepted a cup of tea. They both told him they were cross Tariq hadn't done more. 'If one of my team was being sacked, I'd be in the meetin' fighting for whichever side I thought was right,' said Precious. 'I hate people sittin' on fences.'

Charlie worried it would all prove a bit much for him but on balance it was nothing. He left the office straight after the meeting at which Ted suspended him. Transferred all his allegiance to Karen Leicester, the only person he spoke to— the telephone call—before he took his leave. She never let him down. He feels he may have done the reverse. Charlie has never doubted the purpose of the union but he's always been a one-man band. Couldn't see a better option so he accepted the compromise. 'Taking the short odds,' Karen called it when he phoned her on Friday afternoon.

It was not a difficult phone call, she wasn't pushy. He even said, 'If Ted Astaire dies in suspicious circumstances, will you be my defence lawyer?'

'Only if you bump off Pickford while you're at it.'

Charlie thinks he may be the only one who ever had a moment's appreciation for Roselyn. And he's gone mainstream now.

It's a foul day outside the bubble of the train carriage. Midday and the sky black with pessimism. Rain lashes the windows, hammers away a different tune with every bend of the track. Fewer than half the seats are taken. One or two suited men tap on laptops. Pairs of women natter together. A small child is in the aisle, Mikey's age. Kids don't like sitting still for very long; the kid's mother keeps calling him back. Charlie finds himself listening in to the man one seat

Raspberry Jam

in front. A young bloke jabbering away on his mobile. Talking aimlessly to a girlfriend by the sound of it.

A uniformed lady brings her trolley down the aisle. Drinks and snacks. Charlie gets himself a polystyrene beaker of tea. Holds no heady expectations of it being more than a warming comfort. She places the drink on his fold-out tray, then as he tries to extract the thriller he carries from his holdall, Charlie nudges too firmly into the tray. Upturns the tea. He is going to see Graham, cannot let these trivialities ruin the pilgrimage. He steps up the carriage to buy a replacement.

The lady in the uniform sees the damp patch on his jeans. Makes no funny joke; pours him another tea. As Charlie pokes inside the little pocket on the side of his wallet—coins to pay—she shakes her head. 'Say I spilled it,' she murmurs, taking no money from him.

'Very kind of you,' says Charlie. Thinks it. Really big of her. Putting his day back on track. Back in his seat the thriller awaits. He isn't sure if it's a good one. Hasn't been able to concentrate on the lives of fictitious people in months.

* * *

When the train pulls in, Euston Station is in chaos. The public address system throws a little light on the situation. The underground is closed—the whole thing—no trains running anywhere. The capital beset by a serious incident. No buses, no movement across the city until the police say otherwise. That is the announcement: stick to the station concourse. Stay where you are. No venturing out into the world. Euston is filling up with the arrivals from the overground lines. Getting horribly crowded by Charlie's reckoning. He likes the great outdoors. Open moors. This feels more and more like being in a cowshed, thousands of travellers gathered together on the concourse.

Charlie has a small rucksack with him, tries to walk around, stretch his legs after the long train ride. It is almost

Wide of Goodge Street

shoulder to shoulder, not much chance. He sees a woman looking into the screen of a small iPad. 'Do you know what has happened?'

'Armed police at Goodge Street,' she tells him.

He doesn't know where that is, starts to tap on his own phone. Trying to find a map. Brings one up on his screen. Calculates the length of the walk to his hotel, far to the south of here. Must give Goodge Street a wide berth; it doesn't look so hard, keep east as he goes south. Nothing to it. Charlie looks at the masses standing bored and unoccupied in the station. They don't look like they are under attack. A terrorist is loose in their city, this is the most tepid pandemonium imaginable, the grinding to a halt of the normal ebb and flow. The police, the authorities, have put a saddle on them all, held the reins gamely. The world has become resigned to these ordeals, the situation managed not mastered. Him too, it seems. Charlie baulked at the prospect of a tribunal. Took a reference when he might have staged a showdown. He doesn't think his driving Iraq out of Kuwait—the first Gulf war—contributed to the rise in jihadi terrorism, not his contribution at least. He hopes it hasn't; maybe it has. Charlie was only obeying orders; he's sick of all that these days. What do our so-called masters know? They don't have a masterplan. Never did. Keeping wide of Goodge Street will be his maxim. Simple: if he sticks to it, he lives.

* * *

His walk across London is unimpeded, there are people on the streets but far fewer than usual despite the lack of better transport. One terrorist in Goodge Street clears the city. He has never walked this route before, feared being lost in the city where Ordinance Survey maps have no utility. Finds it could not be simpler, street diagrams crop up on easy-to-spot boards at every other corner. He walks steadily; a gale blows around him, there is rain in it but not as much as there was up north. It must be a shit day for terrorism. He hopes they've shot the bastard, then reorders his thoughts. Probably best to learn what has occurred, who it is, why it has happened. A misunderstanding would be the crummiest thing to die for. He walks; six and a half miles to go says his phone. Fine-looking buildings stand indifferent to the driving rain. He keeps walking. Soldiering on. As he is crossing the river at Blackfriars Bridge, the rain comes down more heavily. Once he is over it—south of the Thames— Charlie takes himself into a coffee shop. He gets a drink and a panini; not even halfway to his guest house. The walk is nothing but the weather is off-putting. There are schoolchildren in the coffee shop. Their presence reminds him how late in the afternoon it is. They look to be wearing the uniforms of private schools, rich colours, an Edwardian cut. He is occupying a large table; a gaggle of girls join him unasked. The blue and black of their long skirts, the matching Alice bands which two of them sport are pleasing on the eye. The girls all have long hair, the one sitting closest to Charlie is Chinese. Of Chinese origin. She is most likely British, he gets that. She is here, London, England.

Charlie hopes to visit Graham this evening. He has paid too much attention to the conversations of strangers today; these girls' high-pitched exchanges register outside his range of recognition. He realises that one is pointing at his mouth, grinning, laughing. Some melted Mozzarella didn't quite make it into the garage.

'My table manners are no worse than your discourtesy,' he tells her pompously, and the girl looks down. He drains his coffee, rises up with his rucksack.

The girls giggle together. He feels foolish; would have let his Michelle tease him about it. Laughed along. And he generally eats tidily. No reason to be taking it so personally. He thinks he is reacting to unemployment, trying to find pride where he needn't. It doesn't do much good, truth be told. Ted sacked him to uphold the reputation of his precious department, easier than explaining to the evening news reporter how bloody complicated social work is, what a fucked-up childhood does to a kid. Let them think it will never happen again but everything does. He hopes it isn't some screwed-up care kid kicking off at Goodge Street.

Outside it is still raining, he walks on. This is now a test. Buses are passing him and people are going up and down at tube entrances. His walk is the urban version of the wet weekend he shared with his now silent friend. It takes him an hour and twenty to get from Borough to his guest house. So close to the intensive care ward, it is reassuring. Graham is in there, supported, clinging to precarious life. Charlie needs to change clothes, to shower, to get a little warmer than he feels. He puts on the TV news, learns that no one has died, although a knife attack by a man of Libyan origin has hospitalised three. An off-duty policeman tackled and held the madman. The armed police presence and the freezing of movement across the city was initiated in order to catch accomplices. The newsreader now states there are none. That's hindsight for you. Messed up the transport for a couple of hours; no one should be sacked for it, Charlie is adamant. It's just one of those things.

Before dressing, he slides under the bedcovers, hears other news. It is inconsequential. Something about Ukraine; some London news, the fatality of a cyclist. Not a famous one, just a man on a bike in the capital. Charlie's brain processes this through the medium of sleep. The bed far more comfortable than a couch. The mattress is lovely. He dreams that Mandy is beside him.

* * *

On waking, Charlie is furious with himself. He may have missed the early evening visiting time. He always planned to go tomorrow, wants to visit twice. He cares about the poor lad. Feels responsible, rightly or wrongly. Even Mandy has not heard how much this man's condition is eating away at Charlie. Like a stone in the stomach. He pictures the young man in the hospital bed as he jerks in the middle of the night. Most nights. Consuming his thoughts when he should have been planning next steps for Russell Chope. He wishes he'd played badminton with Graham all those months ago. Graham offered it; said they should. Charlie is a squash player, was a squash player. Was a tit, is a tit. He has serious ideas about being a better person. The perfect husband. Dead serious. Mandy deserves nothing less. He puts on clean underclothes, a fresh T-shirt. In his haste he never put his jeans over a radiator or anywhere else to aid the drying process and they are still damp when he puts them back on. He's not hungry; paninis are pretty filling. The hospital is only two roads away. The jeans will have to do.

* * *

It is after eight o'clock when he enters the reception area. The building is old, brightly lit, and the signage—standard NHS white and blue—looks out of place on the panelled walls. Charlie walks across the floor glancing at the signs, looking for the ITU. He has a ward name, doesn't know the hospital layout. There are quite a few other people in here, most appear to be leaving, some who may be working, visiting if it's still permitted. A huddle of people around a vending machine: the night shift, he guesses. No one challenges him, and he finds a flight of wide stairs that take him up two floors. He thinks the ward he is after is up here. Sees a young man, jet black hair, a tell-tale stethoscope hugging his shoulders. 'Do you work on Rutherford?'

'I do...' Before the man can explain more, Charlie asks him if Graham Ford is still on the ward. The doctor gives a smile of recognition. 'He's in the side ward.' He points a finger; a door to the right, just inside the entrance of Rutherford Ward.

'Thank you.' Charlie goes towards the room indicated. As

Wide of Goodge Street

he opens the door, he finds that it is in the dark, the main light is off but the glow from a battery of machines—monitors, pumps, miracles we all hope never to need—give sufficient luminance to make out the figure on the bed. There is a mask over Graham's mouth which expands with a push of air, and then retracts. The attached apparatus supports the boy, keeps him truly here. Man and machine act as one. Charlie closes the door behind him. 'Watcha mate,' he says. Graham makes no response but there is regularity to his assisted breathing. They are both alive in the same room together. It's been a while. 'Oh, mate. I've such a lot I could tell you.'

He waits, it seems indulgent for him to prattle on. Impolite. The boy is lying in the darkened room, a few tiny lights behind and around him, all part of the hospital paraphernalia. They're doing something for him but Charlie hasn't much idea what.

'How have you been?' Again, Charlie waits, allows time for an answer although no such event can occur. 'Not good, I suppose,' he finally says on his friend's behalf. 'I think things are thawing between Mandy and I. I really do; it's one of only two miracles I'm looking for, Graham. Get yourself well, mate.' Charlie runs a hand through his own hair. 'I don't deserve it, you know that. I want you to have my luck, Graham.' He waits a moment, has no reason to hurry this talk. 'Brenda asks after you. Phones me quite a bit. Everyone's rooting for you.' Tariq's indifference comes into Charlie's mind. 'Deepika,' he says, louder than intended, 'she's in the team now—always asking how you are—she says some Hindu prayers or something. Brilliant really. I don't think you two ever worked together.' He lets this feedback—the hopes and prayers of former colleagues—rest in the room. 'You don't know that I've been sacked. Don't be down on my part though, I'm over it already. You've had the worse mishap by a country mile. Mine was just the department...' He doesn't finish this thought. It is difficult to summarise in a few words. '...There's another boy, called Dayton Pearce, who's very, very poorly. A coma. The lad, Russell—you'll remember him, Graham, we talked about him—he hit that poor lad with concrete. Broke his skull. None of us guessed he'd do a thing like that, but I should have done, apparently. That's why I'm out. The push.'

Charlie lets Graham think about that. Talking in the darkness about these uncertain matters feels right. Just the machine lights giving out a little illumination.

'The thing is, Graham, I've been scouring the job adverts, and Stretch Care are trying to replace you. Awful really but you were still on probation. It might not be a surprise, I don't know. The thing is, Graham, and hear me out on this, please, I'm going to apply. I should get it; I fit the bill. It's more than symmetry. The minute you...' Charlie looks at the figure on the bed, still but for a small rise of the white sheet across his chest, aided by the breathing machine. '...the minute your cold's better, the jobs yours. I'm not taking it off you, I'll be keeping your seat warm...'

He hears Graham laugh; his own chest tightens. 'Cold?' says Graham.

'Graham, Graham.' He can see no change in the patient, the oxygen mask covers his lips. Charlie heard what he heard.

Now laughter fills the still room. 'Don't panic. I'm sorry,' The words come between guffaws. Charlie sees a hand raised from behind Graham, behind the breathing machine. It is not Graham who has spoken at all. The man raises himself from his secluded chair, touches his head as if doffing a hat. 'You're Graham's friend. I am glad you've come. It takes courage to see the poor boy like this.'

Charlie feels the tension evaporate from him. He was oddly frightened that the comatose boy was speaking. He would like nothing more but the sound of it was

Wide of Goodge Street

disorienting. And it is not happening. Not yet. Graham's prolonged silence continues.

'I'm Brian, Brian Ford,' says the man who is silently visiting his son, who's careful placement of himself had eluded Charlie for his first three or four minutes in the room. 'I think you're Charlie Quantum. You telephoned me. I recognise your voice.'

Charlie is silent for a moment, mulling over all he has already said—privately said to Graham—unaware that this man was listening in.

'You're a good friend to my son, Mr Quantum. You've come a long way to see him, I know that. And I am sorry about your job. His mother told me that Graham felt cut up after losing his. I really can't blame you for picking up Graham's position. I don't think this is the type of cold anyone gets over sufficiently to return to their desk. You sound very decent about it all, you really do. And I know...' He is slowly sliding back into the chair behind the breathing apparatus. In the dim light these machines cast he is again invisible. Not so much as a shadow. The voice is heard but it seems again like a thought Graham might be voicing. '...before all this, Graham may have told you I was damned awkward, opposed my own son in some way. I'm not here to disagree or take issue with him. If he could shake the cold, I would certainly do a lot better in my own relationship with the poor lad. I missed my chance. I don't need to know about you and him. That he had a special relationship, someone who cared about him, that's what matters to me now. I'm grateful, Mr Quantum. What we do in this world isn't forgotten, we just lose touch, sometimes, with the people who will remember.'

Charlie listens. He has some thoughts in his head, prompted by the man's rambling, but mostly they are things he wants to share with Graham alone. He has no interest in the poor boy's conflicted father. To explain this to Brian Ford is hardly going to enlighten the man; and his mistaken belief is strangely touching. He never really had a special relationship with Graham, simply cannot bear the feeling that his driving brought this state upon him. Charlie lets Graham's father speak, he couldn't manage it when his unresponsive son was the lone audience, now he thinks he has the man's lover to speak to, he has relaxed. There was clearly a time when he would have thought differently of a man in love with his son. Laughable that none of it is quite how Graham's dad thinks it is, but if it isn't love it comes close: Charlie feels for Graham more than he does for most in this world. For anyone but Grace Bell and that little cohort with Quested for a surname. And he would like to tell Graham more about Mandy. Confirm that he is living back, that the right side of the bed is to be his once more. He has no wish to confuse old Brian Ford with this stuff. The man is suffering, keeping vigil at the bedside of a son he misunderstood through the best years they both had to offer each other. And Roselyn? Charlie wonders if Graham should hear about her Machiavellian role in his vocational upending, his ejection from employment with the city council. He thinks Graham would criticise him for allowing it, not declaring the shared past. Straight as a die, that's Graham, he thinks, and then has to apologise to Brian. He is laughing at his own thoughts while pretending to listen to the man. The man who has learned again to love his son. A good man, Brian Ford is a good man. If our pasts cannot be forgiven, we are all lost. Charlie has all night, another visit tomorrow morning. He'll have it out with Graham a little later. And is he a good man, he wonders? Graham is but what about him, Charles Quested? The army boy who lost his faith in the power of the gun; a fostering social worker who may not be up to the job. The angry foster kid in whom Grace Bell found the reset button. He's a survivor. He can do it again, find another path, a different way across the rainy

Wide of Goodge Street

moorland, the locked-down city. He won't let Mandy down this time. 'It would be a bloody sight easier if you were with me,' he says to Graham. Brian Ford stands up. 'Sorry.' Charlie is unsure if he is speaking to father or son.

'Do you want time alone with him?' asks Brian.

'I do.' As he is trying to think how to follow this up, make it clear he is not seeking to eject the man from his son's bedside, Brian has stepped away, opened the door. 'No,' says Charlie, but it may have gone unheard. Graham's father has slipped from the room.

Charlie looks intently at his former colleague, places a hand on the boy's arm. He laughs nervously. This is what he wanted, time alone with Graham. 'I've said most of it, mate. I mean it. The job will be yours again, just so long as I secure it in the coming weeks. And I've thought about the weekend—mud and hailstones, that woman with a shotgun—would you do it again? Another walking weekend, you and me. No dumb stunts on my part. With the ladies. I've stopped all that, I really have. Mandy or celibate, that's me. Country walk and a couple of pints, that'll be our next weekend.' Charlie ceases talking, his large hand still holding the patient's forearm. He listens to the movement of air that the contraption which cradles Graham produces. A contented rhythm. The boy may not be able to walk again, to talk again. It is the deepest worry. The truth is, we can none of us predict the future. Graham hasn't said no; Charlie thinks he heard a little intake of breath, irregular, it might have been surprise. No flowers from Charlie—he doesn't give them to fellas—just the promise of another military march. Probably a yes, that is what the older man thinks. A yes to the question of doing it all again. And Charlie would at the drop of a hat. 'That settles it, mate. Scotland next time. A tent, a bit of cooking on the primus.'

The light in this side ward, emitted from monitors and through the frosted glass of the door, gives little away. The breathing mask Graham wears obscures much of his face. His eyes are open, Charlie could swear he sees them move, direct themselves at him on the saying of the last phrase.

'No tent? Have it your way. I know a few decent guesthouses if you prefer. You're not getting out of the hike, Graham. And if you need a bit of cock in the evening, then fair play to you. I'll sit it out though, mate. Mandy and I will be getting back together properly. Better than ever. It's all I ever wanted: that and the pair of us taking another walk across the hills.'

Printed in Great Britain
by Amazon